SEDUCTIVE NIGHTS TRILOGY

Lauren Blakely

A box set of The New York Times and USA Today
Bestselling Seductive Nights Series including the books
First Night, Night After Night and After This Night

ABOUT

Seductive Nights
Intended for 18+ due to
sexual content and mature themes.

The Seductive Nights Trilogy Bundle is a box set of the New York Times and USA Today Bestselling books First Night, Night After Night and After This Night.

• **First Night**

When a sinfully handsome man walks into her bar in San Francisco, Julia Bell simply wants a break from the troubles that keep chasing her. That escape comes in the form of sexy, confident and commanding Clay Nichols, who captivates her mind AND turns her inside out with pleasure. They share one scorchingly hot night together, but discover a connection that runs deeper than mere chemistry....

• Night After Night

Their world was sex, love, and lies.

He intoxicated her. Commanded. Consumed.

With a dirty mind and a mouth to match, Clay Nichols is everything Julia never knew she wanted and exactly what she cannot have. He walked into her life one night and unlocked pleasure in her that she never knew was possible. Possessing her body, captivating her every thought. Which makes him way too dangerous for Julia to risk her heart, given that she has a price tag on her head. She ran after one mind-blowing week with him, but now he's back, and determined to make her his own.

No matter the cost.

She was a sexy drug to him. Fiery, unforgettable, and never enough, Julia is an enigma, and Clay isn't willing to let her go without a fight. But she's got dark secrets of her own that threaten to destroy any chance of happiness. She's a wanted woman - the stakes are high, her every move is watched, and yet the lure between them can't be denied. Can two people burned by love trust again when desire and passion are met by danger at every turn?

• After This Night

Their world was passion, pleasure and secrets.

Far too many secrets. But Clay Nichols can't get Julia Bell out of his mind. He's so drawn to her, and to the nights they shared, that he can't focus on work or business. Only her. And she's pissing him off with her hot and cold act. She has her reasons though-she's trying to stay one step ahead of the trouble that's been chasing her for months now, thanks to the criminal world her ex dragged her into. If only she can get out of this mess, then maybe she can invite the man who ignites her back in her life, so she can have him-heart, mind and body.

He won't take less than all of her, and the full truth too. When he runs into her again at her sister's wedding, they have a second chance but she'll have to let him all the way in. And they'll learn just how much more there is to the intense sexual chemistry they share, and whether love can carry them well past the danger of her past and into a new future, after this night...

ALSO BY LAUREN BLAKELY
Available at all fine e-tailers

ALSO BY LAUREN BLAKELY
Available at all fine e-tailers

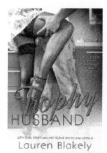

FIRST NIGHT
Book 0.5 in Seductive Nights

ABOUT FIRST NIGHT

It was only supposed to be one night...
When the sinfully handsome man walks into her bar in San Francisco, Julia Bell simply wants a break from the troubles that keep chasing her. That escape comes in the form of sexy, confident and commanding Clay Nichols, who captivates her mind AND turns her inside out with pleasure. The attraction is electric and they share one scorchingly hot night together, but they also discover there is more than just off-the-charts chemistry; the connection between them runs deep. Clay never thought he'd return to New York with this woman still on his mind. But he can't get her out of his system, and he needs more of her...He wants more than just the first night...

CHAPTER ONE

Eight inches.

Julia longed for eight inches.

Or really, eight inches and a brain.

Was that so much for a woman to want?

Some days it seemed like it. Julia had yet to meet a man who could hold his own on all accounts, and judging from the parade of guys who seemed to think getting into a bartender's pants was as easy as ordering a drink, she wasn't sure her luck was going to change anytime soon.

Like this guy. The one with his tongue practically falling out of his mouth as he ogled her while she mixed his third Purple Snow Globe.

"Here you go," she said as she slid the sugar-rimmed martini glass to the young hipster, decked out in too tight-pants, a plaid shirt and a goatee that needed to have been shaved off.

He wiggled both eyebrows and wobbled in his chair. "And how about a phone number too?"

She flashed him her best "not a chance in hell, sucker" smile. "I've got a phone number for a taxi cab and I'd be mighty happy to provide that for you soon."

Seriously? Did he think that line was going to work? She headed to the other end of the bar to tend to a pair of blondes in low-cut halter tops, hoping they'd be less likely to hit on her. It was San Francisco though, so you never knew. But then, she was used to it. Being propositioned simply came with the territory of tending bar, and Julia Bell let all the come-on lines she heard roll off her every night, like water off a duck's back. Most of the time she barely even noticed them – they became the white noise, along with sounds of beers being poured, glasses being washed, music being played overhead at the bar she was part owner of.

Some days though, she'd like to be propositioned by a man with a brain, a witty mouth and who had the kind of body she'd want to be tied up with all night long.

Or to tie up. She was pretty sure that with the right man, she might be into some equal opportunity bondage. But he'd need to be bringing eight inches. Anything less was a deal breaker. Though, truth be told, she had little room in her life now for either eight inches or for romance. Not after the pile of problems her ex had left behind for her. A heaping mass of problems, to be precise.

She popped into the back of the bar to restock swirly straws when her phone rang. She nearly bounced as McKenna's name flashed across the screen. Julia was expecting big news from her sister tonight. After all, she'd helped McKenna's boyfriend pick out the ring.

She crossed her fingers, but then she was damn sure McKenna would say nothing but a big fat yes.

"Tell me everything," she said into the phone.

"It was amazing! He proposed to me right before the play started that his sister is in."

Julia shrieked, and wished she could wrap her sister in a big happy hug right now. "And you said yes, I hope?"

McKenna laughed. "Of course I said yes! I said yes about twenty times."

"So how did he do it?"

"Right on the frigging stage, Julia. On a Broadway stage! He proposed to me on stage!"

"Before 2000 people?"

"No, dork. Before the play started. But oh my god, I'm so happy."

Julia was grinning in the supply closet, bursting with happiness from head to toe. Her sister had been through the wringer in the romance department, but when Chris landed in her life everything changed for the better. Sunshine and roses.

McKenna shared more of the details and Julia oohed and ahhed all throughout the tale. "You better make me your maid-of-honor," she said.

"As if I'd pick anyone else."

"Good. Now that we have that settled. Are you going to get married on the beach like a proper California girl?"

"I don't know. I haven't thought that far ahead. But listen, enough about me. Chris' sister is involved with the director, and the director's buddy Clay is coming to San Fran tomorrow night for business. I told him to go to Cubic Z and say hello. I told him you were gorgeous too."

She rolled her eyes. Her sister could never resist playing the matchmaker.

"Great. But no free drinks just cause he's a friend of a friend or whatever."

"Never. But Jules," McKenna said, lowering her voice to a whisper. "The guy? Clay? He's smoking hot."

Her ears pricked. "Yeah? How smoking?"

"Un-be-lievable."

* * *

Clay Nichol's redeye to San Francisco was slated to leave in two hours, but business was business, and this deal needed to be ironclad. If he had to push the flight back, he would. He loved nothing more than negotiating and closing a deal. Fine, there was one thing he loved more than deal making. A fiery woman, the kind who could dish it out as well as she could take it. But he hadn't met anyone in the last year who excited his mind as much as his body. So for now, business was his focus. It was opening night of a new Broadway play that his friend and client, Davis Milo, had directed, and that the audience had loved. Man, that made Clay one proud entertainment lawyer since he'd sewn up the deal for Davis to direct the show, and the next one his buddy was eyeing too – a production in London.

The two men were lounging in the empty seats at the St. James Theater, chatting with the London producers.

Davis shook hands with the producers then clapped Clay on the back. "He can handle the rest. I need to go."

His friend took off, and Clay wrapped up the final details of the contract, then left the empty theater and slid into a town car. As soon as the door was closed, he loosened his purple tie; it was his good luck tie, and he always wore it on nights like these. He unbuttoned a few buttons of his crisp white shirt, stretched his neck from side to side, and reached for his phone. He hadn't been to San Francisco in a while, but he found himself googling a certain bar on the way to the airport. Who knew if he'd make it to Cubic Z, but the woman who'd been proposed to before the show had told him that her sister worked there, then added, "She's gorgeous, and the best bartender in the world."

He shrugged to himself as the car sped to LaGuardia. He wasn't sure if he'd have the time to stop by a bar in San Francisco during this trip. But he found himself wondering about the gorgeous bartender, and whether she might be the fiery type.

* * *

That had been a bitch of a deal the next day. Too many attempts at nickeling-and-diming his client – a high-profile TV talk show host in the Bay Area. Pissed him off. Clay didn't take that kind of shit and he'd made damn sure the network knew that they'd walk. That's when the exec caved and finally started playing ball. That was the secret to negotiation. Always be the one willing to walk. In the end, Clay had landed nearly every point he'd wanted for his client. But he'd felt battered and bruised with their petty ways, so he tracked down the nearest boxing gym, worked off his frustration with a long, sweaty bout with a heavy bag, pounding and punishing until his muscles screamed, and even then a little more. After, he returned to his hotel for a hot shower.

It was damn near scalding temperature as the water beat down hard on him, and he leaned into the stream, washing off the day.

When he stepped out from the water and toweled off, he was nowhere near ready to crawl into bed and call it a night. Negotiations like that warranted a drink, and as soon as the thought of a drink touched down in his head, he remembered the name of the bar, and the name of the supposedly gorgeous bartender.

Julia.

Hmmm…

He had energy to burn, and the bar wasn't far from his hotel here in the SoMa district. He pulled on jeans and a button-down shirt, combed his hair, brushed his teeth, and headed out into the San Francisco night. He only wished he'd thought to bring along a pair of handcuffs, his favorite accessory. They looked mighty fine with black lingerie, thigh-high stockings, and heels on the right woman.

But that was putting the cart before the horse, wasn't it?

CHAPTER TWO

Not Again.

Honestly, how many times was the sloppy hipster going to make a play for her? He was staring at her chest tonight. Part of her couldn't fault him. She'd been blessed in the breasts department and filled out a C-cup quite nicely, thank you very much. But still. Tact was way sexier than ogling.

"What if I ordered drinks for everyone in the bar? How about that? Would you finally give me your number then?"

"No. Because my eyes are up here," she said, and pointed to her face.

He snapped his gaze up, caught red-handed. But he was relentless. "See? I can be trained. I'm a good boy."

"I'm happy to serve you. But the number is under wraps and always will be," she told him.

The dude was practically spilled across the bar, his chest draped on the sleek metal. "How about another Appletini then?"

"No problem," she said with a private smirk. Julia loved mixing drinks – she had a bit of mad scientist in her that thrilled at discovering new combinations of flavors. But while the bartender in her enjoyed concocting a cocktail, the woman in her wished that once, just once, a guy would be a guy and order a goddamn beer. Maybe it made her shallow, but she didn't care. She would never date a man who drank the sissy drinks she often served. She liked her men to be men. No man-scapers need apply.

As she mixed the hipster's drink – some vodka, some apple juice, a splash of apple brandy – a new customer sat down.

"What can I get for you?" she said before she even turned around.

"I'll take whatever's on tap."

She froze in her spot simply because the voice was rough and gravelly, and sent a charge through her with its masculine sexiness. But, the man behind that deep and husky voice was probably a dweeb, right? That'd be her luck. She plunked the Appletini down in front of her least favorite sloppy drinker, then turned to the man who wanted the beer, and holy heavenly fiesta of the eyes.

He was tall. He was broad. He had the perfect amount of stubble on his jawline, and those eyes were to-die for – deep brown and piercing. Then there was his hair – thick, brown, and ideal for sliding fingers through. She didn't want to take her eyes off him, but she knew better than to stare. She quickly straightened her spine, picked her gawking jaw up from the floor, and gave him a cool nod. "We have an India Pale Ale tonight. Will that do?"

"That'll do just fine," he said, his muscular forearms resting on the sleek bar. His shirt sleeves were rolled up and Julia couldn't help but notice how strong his arms were. She bet he worked out. A real man kind of workout. Something hard and heavy that made him sweat and grunt to mold that kind of physique. She poured the beer into the glass, and set it down in front of him. He reached for his wallet, peeled off some bills, and handed them to her.

"I take it you're Julia?"

Uh oh. How did he know her name. Was he an undercover cop? Had she accidentally served someone under twenty-one?

She was diligent and methodical in her ID checking and had never let an underage in. Or wait. Her spine stiffened. Was he onto her? Did he know what she did every Tuesday night at a dimly-lit apartment above a greasy restaurant in China Town that smelled of fried pork? That would be over soon though. It had to be. She'd done her time, and was ready to cash in. Soon, she kept telling herself.

"Yeah," she answered carefully, all her senses on alert. She wasn't really doing anything wrong those nights, was she? No, she was just taking care of business as she knew how.

"I hear you're the best bartender in San Francisco."

The tightness in her shoulders relaxed. At least he wasn't a boy in blue come to bust her. But forget his smoldering looks. He was like the rest of them, going for cheap lines, hitting on the woman behind the bar. "Yeah, where'd you hear that? Facebook?"

He smiled briefly and shook his head. Damn, he had a fabulous smile. Straight, white teeth and a knowing grin. But she knew better than to fall for a hot stranger simply because he was handsome. She'd done that before, and it had kicked her in the ass. That's why she was a No-Strings-Attached kind of woman these days. Not that she'd had any attachments of any sort lately – she had too much trouble to untangle herself from before she could even think about getting tangled up in love, let alone the sheets.

"No. Your sister told me. McKenna, I believe."

Oh.

Oh yes.

It all made sense now.

And far be it from Julia to ever doubt her big sister. Because McKenna's assessment was one hundred and fifty percent correct. He was smoking hot. Un-be-lievable. And he was no longer a stranger. He was sister-approved, he wasn't a cop, and he wasn't a heavy, so she shucked off her worries. "Clay Nichols," he said, offering a hand to shake. Nice firm grip. Before she knew it, she was thinking of other uses for those strong hands.

"Julia Bell."

"So how's your day working out for you, Julia Bell?"

She laughed once. Not because it was funny, but because it was such a simple and direct question. It wasn't a cheesy line. "It's not too shabby," she said. "And yours, Clay Nichols?"

He shook his head, let out a long stream of air. "Long, annoying, but ultimately victorious."

"What, are you a fighter?"

"Nah. Just a lawyer," he said then took a drink of the beer. He nodded to the glass in admiration. "Insert lawyer joke here."

"A lawyer walks into a bar," she said, then stopped to shoot him a playful stare. "Actually, that's not a joke. That's me giving a play by play."

He laughed. "You are an excellent commentator so far."

"Why thank you. I can keep it up all night," she said.

"All night? Is that so?" He raised an eyebrow, and his lips curved up in a wickedly sexy grin.

"It just might be. So, you were victorious. Does that mean you won your case?"

"Just won the right terms in the negotiations. My client is happy. That's what matters."

"What kind of law?" she asked, praying he wasn't going to say something seedy or sleazy – like personal injury law.

"Entertainment law," he said in that deep, rumbly voice that she was already digging.

"I'm a big fan of entertainment. Movies and me, we're like that," she said, twisting her middle and index finger together.

"Likewise. I wouldn't do it if I didn't enjoy the work. But I know what it is, and I know what it's not. I'm not saving the world. I'm not putting the bad guys behind bars. I'm just trying to help actors, directors, and TV show hosts get the best deals they can get. Put on a show, make some people happy. That's all I do."

Julia tapped the side of his beer glass. "And I believe I'm in the same field then. I'm not curing cancer. I'm not saving the whales. I'm just mixing a drink, or pouring a beer, and trying to make someone's night a little better. That's all I do."

A grin spread across Clay's face and Julia admired the view. He was a fine specimen of man, with a chiseled jawline, and hair that could be held onto hard when you needed to. But more than that, their simple conversation was just that – nice and easy. If someone asked her to define the meaning of life lately, then as far as she could see was to try to be happy as best you could. Right now, she was enjoying the way it was easy to talk to Clay Nichols.

Nothing more. Nothing less.

He wasn't pretentious. He wasn't pushy. He had a directness about himself and what he did for a living that was refreshing.

"To entertainment," she said, raising an empty glass in a toast.

"And to being entertained."

"Let's see if you can keep that up," she said, issuing a challenge, because she craved a distraction like this. The last few months of her life had been far too tightly wound. Too much pressure. Too much trouble. Too many things she shouldn't have to deal with, but was stuck with anyhow. Tonight, she wasn't going to think about all the things chasing her. Tonight was for fun and for admiring the fantastic view. Sometimes, a woman just needed to to flirt off her stress.

"I'm up for it, Julia. I'm definitely up for it."

* * *

That McKenna was right. Hell, she was more than right. Her sister was hot as sin with those curves, those breasts, and the perfect kind of hips that he'd like to get his hands on. Her hair was lush and reddish brown. Her lips were full and ripe for kissing. As well as other things. But more than that, she was feisty, with that smart mouth firing off innuendo with every word. She could dish it out, and she could take it. After the day he'd had, after the way his days went in general, he wanted a night like this.

So they chatted on and off as she served more customers. She asked him about the deal he'd worked on today, and he told her what he could tell. He asked her about the night she'd had, and she nodded to a skinny guy slouched over the corner of the bar, and there was something so easy – so completely lacking in the bullshit and abrasiveness of office hours — about talking to her.

As she mixed up a purple concoction with sugar on the rim, she crooked a finger toward him, signaling for him to lean closer across the bar. He obliged; he wasn't going to complain about being near to her.

"Do you want a Purple Snow Globe, Clay?"

He met her gaze straight on, her green eyes so inviting. "If it's that a drink, no. If Purple Snow Globe is a secret code word for something naughty, I'm game."

"Well played," she said, raising an eyebrow. She eyed the drink she'd just made with a proud sort of look. "It's my signature cocktail. Some day, I'm going to win an award for this bad boy."

He leaned back in the stool and took a slow measured drink from his beer glass, then set it down. "Will I regret not ordering then? For the chance to say I drank a Purple Snow Globe once at a bar in San Francisco?"

She flashed a sexy smile. "It's absolutely delish, so you might regret not tasting it. But I'm glad you didn't order it because it's nothing a man should ever ask for at a bar and expect a woman to want him," she whispered near his ear, her hair brushing his cheek, making him instantly hard. But that wasn't entirely true. He'd been borderline hard for most of the conversation. The feel of her silky strands along the with the words *want him* just ratcheted things up a notch or two.

She stepped away to deliver the drink to a customer and tend to more orders. As she returned to his end of the bar, he picked up where they'd left off. "What do you think a man should drink at a bar?"

"Scotch," she said, punctuating the word with a perfect O shape to her lips. "Or whiskey," she said, her voice a purr now. "Bourbon works too."

"I believe you just named all my favorite drinks."

"I had a feeling you might like those."

"Did you?"

"I always know how to match a drink to a man."

He tapped the side of his beer glass. "Then I'd like to know why I have a beer here in front of me. Tell me that, Julia."

She paused, tilted her head to side with a mischievous flare to her moves, then licked those luscious lips. Damn her; she was hotter than words, and she knew how to play. "When it comes right down to it, a man should drink what the bartender gives him," she said in a sultry voice that made him want to hear her say other things. Lots of other things. Like *Hold me down hard.* Or *Tease me with your tongue.* Yeah, those sorts of things. "That's the best match I can make."

"I don't want you making that match for anyone else then tonight," he said firmly, giving her a hard stare, reminding her that he could play too. Because he knew exactly what he wanted. *Her.* And he didn't want anyone else to have a shot. "Especially because I'm finding the bartender has excellent taste."

She raised an eyebrow. "She does. She has impeccable taste, and she's only making one match tonight," she said, layering her words thick and hot with innuendo.

He wasn't entirely sure where the evening was going next, only because he wasn't the kind of man to take a woman like Julia for granted. He wasn't going to make any sort of assumptions because assumptions got you into trouble in life. He knew that well from his line of work, and from the crap he'd dealt with from his ex, who'd brought heaps of heartache to him in their last few months together before it ended. It was also entirely possibly that Julia was a shameless flirt, angling for a big tip with her saucy little mouth. You couldn't rule anything out, and regardless of where the night ended up, he planned on tipping her well for her bartending work because the woman was doing a hell of a job.

There were other jobs he'd like from her though.

Soon the crowds thinned, and Julia finished up the last call, and then she leaned across the bar, her lips dangerously near his jaw. "You don't have to go when I lock up. In fact, you are more than welcome to stay."

Oh yeah. He was entirely sure where the evening was going now.

CHAPTER THREE

The sound of the lock snapping closed was wholly satisfying. It was the sound of one part of the night ending and another part beginning. A better part. A possibly delectable part.

Call it the no-strings-attached affair that she needed. This man, in town and then heading out of town, seemed like the absolute perfect fit for her.

She could act all prim and demure like she planned to just kiss Clay and send him on his way. But the thought of getting hot and bothered and then forbidding any south of the border activity had zero appeal to her. She was going for him, for all of him. She didn't care if that made her sex-hungry. She *was* hungry for sex. She was jonesing for the kind of roll in the hay that would demolish the tension in her shoulders, let her forget the things she wanted to forget. She had so much trouble in her life, thanks but no thanks to her ex, who'd left town and saddled her with all his problems. Life had been non-stop pressure and worry since then, and she needed a break from it for one night.

Yeah, she was ready to screw the stress right out of her system, and this man seemed the ideal candidate.

Clay was waiting at the bar, tall and hard and sexy as hell in his jeans and button-down shirt. Julia wasn't naive enough to think there was anything deeper going on than a chemical reaction. But what a reaction it was. Her body was drawn to him. His voice affected her, and his dark eyes were so mesmerizing they lured her in. But looks didn't always make for a good lover, did they? No. A good lover took care of a woman, made sure she came first, and then again and again. And Julia could go for an orgasm or two tonight. Maybe even three.

Could this man deliver the goods beyond the surface? Were his hands and his tongue as worthy as the rest of him?

When she returned to him, she didn't mince words. She didn't have time for bullshit, or dating. She was a woman who spoke her mind. "So here's the thing. I've got an idea of how I see the rest of the night playing out. What I'm wondering is if it aligns with yours?"

"Horizontally? That sort of alignment?"

She nodded several times. "I see we're in agreement. So does that mean you're going to put out for me tonight?" she asked with a wicked grin, teasing him with the teenage crudeness of her words.

He cracked up and so did she. Julia liked that he could appreciate her dry and dirty humor.

"Yeah. I think I'll put out for you tonight," he said, then stalked closer, his solid body nearing hers, erasing the space between them as he cupped her cheeks in his hands, and captured her mouth in a hot, wet kiss. It wasn't a slow kiss or a dreamy kiss. No, it was a hungry one that sent a rush of heat flooding her veins. He spun her around, lifted her up on the bar, then edged himself between her legs as he slid his tongue over hers, explored her lips and her mouth as he kissed her hard and furiously. Like she wanted to be kissed, his stubbled jaw rough against her face. He threaded his hands into her hair and he wasn't gentle with his touch, and she thanked her lucky stars for that. Softness was for kittens, pillows and pretty cashmere sweaters. Sex needed to be hard, hot and oh-so-rough around the edges.

She didn't want to be coddled or cuddled. She wanted to take and be taken.

He kissed her greedily and she was sure she'd still be able to feel this kiss tomorrow, in her bones, in her knees. It flared through her whole body like a comet, igniting her. She grabbed his firm ass, yanked him closer until she could feel the full length of his thick cock in her center.

Oh, he had it going on. He definitely more than met her requirements. She rubbed herself against him and he groaned, then broke the kiss, moving his mouth to her ear. "You like that?"

"I do like that."

"You like feeling how hard you made me?"

"I don't like it. I love it," she said.

"I've been rock hard for you all night, Julia. All night, I've been like this."

"That's a long time to be so hard, Clay. I bet you need me to do something about that."

He pulled back to look at her, arching an eyebrow. "Yeah? What do you think I'd like you to do?"

"It's not a matter of what you'd like me to do. It's a matter of what I'm going to do," she said, reaching for his hand that was looped through her hair, freeing it, then bringing his fingers to her face. She drew his index finger into her mouth, wrapping her lips tightly around it, and sucked hard. She watched as his brown eyes filled with heat. Then she pushed her hips against his, grinding against his hard cock, leaving no question as to where she wanted him next. She released his finger and hopped off the counter, missing the press of his body, but wanting to do this her way. She walked behind the bar, reached into her purse, and took out her favorite accessory, dangling her handcuffs for him to see.

She was a woman who knew what she needed, and she needed control.

His brown eyes widened with lust. "You keep handcuffs with you?"

"Never been used. Been waiting for the right man. And I have a feeling you'd like it if I cuffed you right now."

"I'm not going to deny you."

She walked to him and swiveled the stool around, so the wood slats on the back were easier to reach. She grabbed his wrists, pulled them behind him, and cuffed him to the wood. The sound of the metal locking into metal sent a thrill through her. He was hers for now. When so many other things slipped through her fingers like sand – money, hope, her future – *this* she could hold onto. This moment – his pleasure – was in her hands.

"Now, Clay. Tell me. How do you like it?"

"Deep," he growled. "Take me in deep."

"You want to fuck my mouth, you're saying?"

"I would love to fuck that pretty mouth of yours."

She slipped her fingers into the waistband of his jeans, sighing deeply as she felt the hard planes of his belly. She unzipped his jeans, pushed them down to his knees, and marveled at the thick bulge of his cock, the outline of his size deliciously visible though his briefs. Rock hard and all because of how much he wanted her. Heat tore through her as she pressed a hand against his length, palming him.

He hissed as she touched him, his broad chest rising and falling, a dark look of hunger in his eyes. There, that was it. That was what she wanted so badly it sent her body into overdrive – his reaction.

"Now, you're starting something, gorgeous," he said. "And you're going to need to finish it. When you take me in your mouth, you need to take me all the way in."

"Oh, I will. I most definitely will."

She pushed his briefs down, and hot sparks shot straight to her core, turning her molten as she looked at him for the first time. He had a beautiful, majestic cock. Long, thick, and perfectly shaped. She couldn't wait to taste him.

* * *

Clay rolled his head back in pleasure and breathed out hard. This woman was more than fiery. She was scorching and she was a giver, and he couldn't have scripted a better combination as she toyed with him. She gripped him hard in one hand, the way he liked it, squeezing the base, but then teasing the head with her talented tongue, swirling little lines around him that made him want to piston his hips into her lush mouth.

She licked him up and down, lapping him up like a lollipop, all while making the sexiest little murmurs as if she were enjoying it as much as he was. Was that even possible? Because his body was buzzing all over. Then he felt as if electricity had been shocked into his bones when she stopped licking and dived in, taking him all the way in.

"Oh, that's perfect, Julia. Yeah, I want to see those lips of yours nice and tight on me."

She glanced up at him, answered with the wicked look in her pretty green eyes that she intended to ride him hard with her warm mouth.

"You take me in deep, now, okay?"

He might be the one handcuffed, but he still wanted her to know that he liked to be in charge. He couldn't move his hands, and that was a shame because he wanted to pull her head closer to him.

With her lips gripping him, she stroked him with her tongue.

"Keep doing that," he rasped out. "But I want it harder and faster."

She didn't need his direction, but she took it, sucking him in as far as she could. He felt her throat relax as she drew him in, and he loved that she wanted all of him. That she inched her body closer, that she moaned as she tasted him.

"You've got all of me now. But I can't touch your hair with my hands like this, and it's killing me not to grab hard on all that luscious hair," he said as he began thrusting into her. The view of those red lips around his cock sent waves of pleasure through his body, hitting him deep in his bones with the intensity. "So I need you to know that when I take you soon, I'm going to have my hands all wrapped up in your hair and I'll pull harder to make up for what I'm missing right now having my hands cuffed."

She wiggled her eyebrows playfully, then swirled her tongue against his dick. She was the sexiest sight in the world, those gorgeous red lips opened wide and holding on tight. But as much as he wanted to keep watching her, he could barely focus anymore as his climax started to build, and he shuddered. He closed his eyes, rocked into her mouth, and told her what was coming next.

Him.

"I'm going to come any second. And I'm going to come in your mouth. That all right with you?"

She nodded and sucked harder, stroking him with her hand, all while keeping him far inside her delicious mouth. Then she grabbed his ass hard with her other hand, pulling him even closer as his orgasm tore through him, and she swallowed his release.

When he recovered the power of speech, he told her he needed a Purple Snow Globe.

Stat.

* * *

Julia had never been pinned with her own bra before. But here she was, spread out on one of the leather lounge chairs in the back of the bar, her hands above her head, the silky straps digging into her flesh. That man knew how to tie some serious knots. After buttoning his jeans, Clay had proceeded to take the reins. He undressed her quickly, stripping her down to nothing, his eyes raking her over as he tugged off her sweater, her jeans, her bra and then her panties, inhaling sharply when she stood naked in front of him, savoring the view before he laid her on the chair and quickly tied her own pink lace bra around her wrists.

"I liked that bra, you know," she said.

"It'll still work."

"Are you sure?"

"Do I look like the kind of man who would rip such a pretty pink bra?"

She shook her head. "I bet you are the kind of man who could take it off with his teeth."

"I might do just that next time."

"No cuffs for me?"

"Think of me like MacGyver. I use other tools," he said with a glint in his eyes.

"Fine. I'm all for equal opportunity bondage."

"And I'm all for equal opportunity oral." He kissed her mouth hard, silencing any more of her quips. But he quickly broke the contact. "Now where's that Purple Snow Globe you just made?"

She tipped her chin to the table next to them, eager to see what he had in mind for the drink he swore he'd never touch.

He reached for the glass, holding up the purple drink with raspberry juice, gin and her secret ingredient, then sugared on the rim. His lips quirked up in a grin. "Now I won't have any regrets about not ordering this, though I believe this is the only way I'd want to drink a Purple Snow Globe," he said, then carefully tipped the edge of the glass above Julia's breasts, letting some of the liquid spill between them. She shivered as the droplets slid down her belly. Clay bent his head between her breasts and licked up the dark liquid.

"Mmmm. That is an award-winning drink," he growled against her skin, and she writhed into him. He raised his head and poured more of the drink on her belly. Some of it spilled onto the lounge chair, but he quickly captured the rest with his tongue. A ripple of desire tore through her as he touched her. She wished her hands were free so she could push his head between her legs where she wanted him. Where she was dying for him. She desperately wanted to grab hard onto his hair, pull him into her, and let him plunder her with his tongue. She ached for his touch, and she was turned on beyond any and all reason.

But he had other plans, inching up to her breasts, cupping them in his big strong hands.

"Your breasts are gorgeous, and I bet you'd like it if I bite down just a little bit," he whispered roughly against her skin, and his sexy words made her even more fevered. He flicked his tongue against her nipple, drawing it deeper into his mouth until she cried out. Then he bit down. Not so hard it hurt, but hard enough that it hurt so good.

"That feels incredible," she moaned.

"Good." He licked a wet path between her breasts, squeezing them as he brought the other one into his mouth, sucking hard on her nipple til it was a diamond point in his mouth. Her hips shot up, her body nearly begging for relief. Every flicker, every touch of his tongue on her drove her wild, sending sparks through all her cells. He drew her nipple across his teeth, slowly, so torturously slowly that she cried out. "*Please.*"

"I can do so much more to you with my mouth."

"I want it," she panted. "I want to know all the things you can do with your mouth."

"Then I'll have to stop talking and start eating," he said, looking up at her holding her lustful gaze with his own dark, hooded one.

"You better," she said, and gasped as he settled between her legs, his strong shoulders against her thighs. He licked her once, swirling his tongue against her wetness. She arched her hips instantly, her body terribly desperate for his touch, for contact where she wanted him most. He pulled back to look at her.

"More, please," she said playfully.

"You like that?"

"Uh, yeah."

"I need you to spread your legs then, Julia. I can't go down on you the way I want until your legs are wide open."

Heat surged in her body as he dirty talked her.

"How far?"

She let her knees fall open, watching his reaction. His eyes grew darker, as he stared greedily at her center. She'd never wanted a man to go down on her more than she did in this instant. She was dying for his mouth. She wanted to feel his lips and let him work his magic tongue on her. She wanted to let go, to give in to the moment, to the night, to the tantalizing possibility of coming hard and good with him.

She needed it; the blinding wave of getting lost in release, the druggy bliss of pleasure and how it could drown out all your troubles, at least temporarily, and leave you awash in intoxication for a spell.

"I want you wide open for me. I want to see how far you can spread your legs," he said, pressing his hands on the inside of her thighs and pushing her legs apart.

She felt helpless with her wrists pinned over her head, as he opened her legs into a wide V. She was submitting to him, trusting him with her pleasure – naked, tied and spread on the leather chaise lounge.

"I need to make sure you keep your thighs wide open for me because that's how I like it. You think you can come from just my tongue? Because I'm not going to use my fingers," he said roughly, in a challenging tone, then flicked his tongue against her wetness to demonstrate what he could do with his tongue alone. The feeling of him was so astonishing she groaned loudly, wriggling her hips. "Yeah, I think I can come from your tongue."

"You sure? Because I want to save the inside of you for my cock. It's going to be hard for me to hold back, but I can do it. Can you?" he asked again as he pressed a hot wet kiss between her legs.

She moaned and rocked into him. "Yes. Your tongue is amazing."

"You have to do it my way, Julia." With a firm grip on her legs, he licked up the side of her thigh, causing her to shudder, then move her legs reflexively.

"Keep them open, gorgeous," he commanded. "If you close your legs, I'll stop."

"I'll keep my legs spread," she said in a raspy voice she barely recognized as her own. Hell, she barely recognized herself, she was so overcome with lust and the aching need for him. "I will."

"You listen to me, and I'll make you writhe and moan. If you don't listen, I will have to stop and wait until you can follow orders," he said sharply, staring hard at her, his brown eyes making it clear he was in charge. "Don't make me wait. I don't want to wait. I want to taste you so badly it's killing me."

"I'll listen because I can't wait either," she said, surprised how she'd shifted from the badass woman on her knees with his thick cock in her mouth, to the submissive, giving over her pleasure to this man she barely knew. But sometimes that was the point of being with someone you barely knew. Because you could give in to the purity of the physical. She was in that zone now; she wanted to stay there all night long. If that made her submissive, or bad, or sex-crazed, fine. She'd take any and all of those adjectives heaped on her. But right now, all she knew was *want*, and that was all she wanted to know.

To hell with her problems, her troubles, her past. To hell with her ex and to all she owed. To hell with everything else but *this*.

He pressed his tongue against her wetness, licking her, swirling delicious lines across her core. She angled her hips closer to his mouth, gasping in delirious pleasure as he kissed her hard and licked her. He explored her, sensually, deliberately, consuming her as if she were the best thing he'd ever tasted. That's how he made her feel with the sounds that rumbled low in his throat as he stroked his tongue across her.

He lavished attention on her clit and she screamed in pleasure, futilely trying to grasp at something, anything, with her tied-up hands – just to hold on – as he buried his tongue inside her.

She arched her hips as the sensations shot through her, hard and fast, like quicksilver tearing through her blood and veins. The feelings were so intense from his delicious mouth making love to her, and his hands holding her down hard, making her open and completely vulnerable. She had no choice but to let him go down on her however he wanted. He was masterful with his lips and his tongue, licking her clit while kissing her pussy senseless. Her pulse raced, her blood roared. Soon, she started to lose control, rocking into him recklessly. She wanted to pull him close, but her hands were pinned, and she liked it that way. No, she *reveled* in it – as the waves of ecstasy slammed into her, crashing into every corner, flooding her inside and out.

She shuddered and moaned, saying his name over and over. As the feelings ebbed, he tugged her close and kissed her cheek. Her forehead. Her neck. Even her nose.

Soft, sweet, fluttery kisses.

Her body felt like a noodle. She was warm and glowing, in that heady state after an epic orgasm. He seemed to sense that she needed a minute to bask in the aftereffects. Gently, he untied her hands as he buzzed his soft lips from her throat to her ear.

"Did you like it when my face was between your legs, Julia?"

His voice was low and soft, and there was a tender tone to it. So different from the rough way he'd talked to her when he issued his instructions. She pressed closer to him, savoring the momentary sweetness, loving that he had so many sides – hard and hungry, then gentle when he needed to be. He ran a hand down her side, across her waist, traveling to her hip. He bent his head to her belly, layering a soft kiss there, then over to her hipbone. She could get used to this kind of touch, to how he knew when to hit each note.

"I loved it," she murmured.

"Good. Because you taste fantastic on me," he said, then claimed her mouth in a quick, hot kiss. "And now you taste fantastic on you."

She looped her hands into his thick hair and wrapped her legs around his hips, letting him know what she wanted next. "Can you please sleep with me now?"

He raised an eyebrow. "You ready to feel me inside you?"

"God yes," she said. "But you need to get naked like I am." She quickly unbuttoned his shirt and pushed down his jeans.

He pulled her up from the chair, looked deep into her eyes, then raked her over from head to toe. "I am so glad I walked into your bar this evening, because this is the best night I've had in a long time, and you are quite possibly a perfect woman. So as far as I can see, the only thing that could possibly make it better is you bent over the chair with your ass in the air."

She hitched in a breath as a ribbon of desire was unleashed in her body. "I want it hard, Clay," she told him as she turned around and bent over, lifting her bottom for him. "I want it hard and deep and I want to feel your cock all the way inside me."

He fished in his wallet for a condom, rolled it on, and smacked her ass once.

"You will feel me for days, gorgeous."

* * *

That back.

So long and sexy and smooth. That hair. All silky and thick and perfect for tugging. But that ass. It was so inviting. Clay rubbed his palms against her smooth, soft skin, then placed a thumb on each cheek to spread her open. Her pussy was glistening and his cock twitched eagerly at the sight; the jumpy fucker was ready to be inside her, but he wanted to enjoy the view as he entered. She'd tasted delicious, so hot and sexy and willing, but maybe she tasted so good to him because she liked it the same way he did. She liked to dominate and to be dominated. She liked to talk dirty, and be talked dirty to. She was a scorching combination of everything he'd ever craved in the bedroom — never had he met a woman before that he'd clicked with in every way — and now he was was going to have her how he wanted. He teased her wet lips with the head of his cock. She whimpered, then raised her ass higher.

"You like how my cock feels against you? You want me inside you?"

"Yes, I don't want you to tease me. I want you to take me," she said in a firm tone, turning her head to shoot him a sharp stare.

"You telling me what to do, gorgeous?"

"Yes. I'm telling you what to do. And you better take me now because I don't want to be teased."

He rubbed himself against her, and her body responded instantly, shivering as he toyed with her. "But it seems you like teasing," he said playfully as she pushed back against him.

"Clay, please," she said, as if she desperately needed him to put her out of her pent-up misery.

"You gonna beg for it?"

"No," she said, reverting to her tough stance. "I don't want to beg for it. If you make me beg, I will go take care of myself."

He smacked her ass for that impudence. But he loved her feisty attitude; it shot sparks through his whole body. "I would love to watch you touch yourself," he said as he pushed the tip of his cock inside her.

"You think I'd let you watch?"

"Oh, gorgeous. You'd love it if I watched. You'd get even wetter with my eyes on you as you fingered yourself. Are you good at making yourself come, Julia?" he asked, sliding in another inch and rolling his eyes back in his head at the feel of her hot flesh surrounding him.

"So good at it. I will make myself come in seconds if you don't fuck me deep right now," she said, looking back at him, her green eyes fiery and demanding as she taunted. "Maybe I'll even torture you by letting you watch."

"I fully intend to take you up on that kind of torture sometime," he said. But not now. Because right now he wanted to be buried deep inside her more than he wanted to tease her, toy with her, control her. "But right now, you're getting what you want."

Screw teasing. Screw taking it slow. He sank into her and they groaned in unison. She felt extraordinary, so tight against him.

She braced herself with her hands on the back of the lounge chair. "You feel amazing," she murmured, and that made him even harder, hearing her unfettered reaction. No saucy talking back, no snappy mouth. Not that he didn't love those things. He did. A hell of a lot. But to hear those simple words escape her throat turned him on fire.

"*Clay,*" she groaned as he rocked into her, stroking in and out, hitting her far and deep, then pulling almost all the way out. Only to pound into her again.

"Is this what you wanted when you looked at me with those fuck-me eyes behind the bar?" he whispered roughly, holding her hips hard as he slammed back into her.

"Yes," she cried out.

"Did you picture bending over for me and letting me take you? Letting me own you with my cock so far inside you?"

He thrust into her again, and she wriggled her ass. Such a beautiful sight, that smooth creamy skin. He rubbed his palms against the soft perfect globes. He wanted to bite it, to sink his teeth into the sweet flesh and leave a mark on her, but there would be time for that later. For now, this woman needed a good hard fucking that would radiate through her beautiful body for days.

"I was just hoping you'd be eight inches," she said, and he could practically hear the smirk in her voice.

He thrust hard into her, making her cry out. Then he stopped his movements, remaining still and deep in her. He bent over her, his strong chest against her sexy back, and he gripped a fistful of her hair. Then he licked the shell of her ear. "More than eight inches, gorgeous. Don't ever doubt that."

She drew in a sharp breath. "Pull my hair," she said, and he did, tugging hard.

Then he drove into her again, each thrust reminding her of what more than eight inches felt like. Her cries grew louder and her breathing more erratic. He reached his other hand around to touch her clit. Fast, quick strokes while he buried himself deeper in her. His own climax started to build.

"I'm going to come soon, Julia. But you need to come first. I want you to come so badly. I've wanted it just as much as you wanted me inside you. Tell me how much you wanted me," he said, sliding his thumb across her as she trembled and bucked her hips against him.

"Yes, I wanted you so badly. And I wanted you to make me come, and now you are. You are making me come," she said in a broken, breathy voice. He let go of her hair, cupped her chin and turned her face to him so he could watch as he brought her to the other side, her eyes squeezing shut, her mouth forming a perfect O, that first silent moan. Then, she screamed out loudly, his name echoing around the bar, and he chased her orgasm with his own, groaning as the pleasure ripped through him, tearing through ever damn cell in his body, lighting him up with electricity. Then they collapsed onto the lounge, a sweaty tangled mess of limbs and flesh. He pulled her close, spooning her, and kissed her earlobe.

"Come back to my hotel. Spend the night with me," he said softly. "I want to curl up with you. I want to wake up with you. I want to make love to you before I leave."

She shivered and breathed out hard.

"Yes."

CHAPTER FOUR

Later that night, Julia lay in Clay's arms, blissed out and sleepily content from her third orgasm of the evening. The man had delivered on every promise. When he'd told her he planned to make love to her, he wasn't kidding. Back at the hotel, he'd worshipped her body, layering kisses all over her from head to toe – yes, he even sucked on a toe, and it felt exquisite – and then he'd entered her. It had been one of those lingering, unhurried and wickedly wonderful sessions. Her legs wrapped around his back, him taking his time with long, tantalizing thrusts, rolling his hips in and out, all the while kissing her neck, her face, her breasts. The man could fuck and the man could make love. He could give her orders, and he could take her direction. He could yank hard on her hair, and blaze a trail of sweet kisses against her damp skin.

Now, he snuggled with her, tucking her against his big, strong body. His toned arm was draped under her breasts, giving her a fantastic view of his tattoo, a tribal arm band around his left bicep with strong, curved strokes. She ran her fingers along the design, tracing it. "I like this. When did you have it done?"

"Thank you. Did it after law school to remind myself why I do what I do."

"How does this remind you?"

"It symbolizes passion. The thing I always want to bring to my job, to my life, to everything."

"I'd say you have passion in spades," she said, pressing her body closer to his so she could feel his smooth, flat belly against her back. The perfect position for apres-sex. "Mmm….this is nice," he said, brushing a soft, quick kiss on her shoulder. "I'm glad I met you."

"Me too," she murmured.

"Tell me something about you I don't know."

"Well, that would be almost everything, wouldn't it?"

He laughed. "I know plenty about you already. I just want to know more."

"Tell me what you know already."

"I know you're tough as nails, that you don't take shit from anyone, that you can size people up in a second."

"That's my job. Any good bartender worth her salt can do that."

"And you're excellent at it. I also know you take pride in your work. Even though you're not saving the world you like being good at what you do."

She shrugged against him. "I suppose that's true."

"So there. I know stuff about you already." He snuggled her closer, drawing lazy lines across her belly as they talked. "I also know you're daring, and not afraid to speak your mind, and that you have a healthy sexual appetite."

She smiled, and elbowed him playfully. "I do, but don't think I get around because I don't. You're the first man I've been with in a year."

"You've been with women in between then?" he asked, in a teasing tone.

"Ha ha. But not what I meant. Though I'm sure you wouldn't mind."

"I absolutely would not mind watching you eat pussy one bit. In fact, I'm going to add that to my bucket list. You, and all that gorgeous red hair spread out across a pair of sexy thighs as you lick and kiss and suck…"

She shook her head and laughed. "You are trouble. All I was saying is that I don't do this often. I don't hookup with men who come to my bar."

"I came in your bar too," he added, making Julia snicker once again. The moonlight shone through the window that overlooked the streets of San Francisco, and the white gauzy curtain blew gently in the night breeze. Outside the door, she was vaguely aware of a cart being rolled, which meant room service somewhere on the floor was being delivered. Maybe to another pair of new lovers who were famished after the best kind of workout. But even if there were other lovers nearby, she knew – beyond a shadow of a doubt – that no one else had this kind of mind-blowing chemistry. She and Clay were electric. "Anyway, I don't do this either. It's not a habit. You have to know you're irresistible, Julia. *Irresistible*," he repeated.

With that one word, her heart beat the tiniest bit faster; maybe it even started to leap. And a part of her wanted to bolt for having the single tiniest little feeling beyond the physical. But another part of her wanted to bask in that feeling a little more.

"So are you," she whispered.

He ran his strong fingers through her hair, touching her softly. "Now, let's go back to the start of this conversation. I want you tell me something about you. You're not getting out of this so easily."

She wriggled her rear against him. "I wasn't trying to. What do you want to know?"

"What do you like to read?"

She smiled in the dark. She liked that he'd asked first about books, rather than movies or TV, the world he trafficked in. "Books," she said dryly.

"What kind of books, Little Miss Sarcastic?"

"Adventure stories," she said, and she could practically feel him raise an eyebrow inquisitively. She shifted to her other side so she could face him as they talked. He shot her a quizzical look, as if the breaking of the physical contact perturbed him. He solved the problem quickly, reaching out to touch her, running his hand down her thigh.

"Can't keep your hands off me?"

"No, I can't. And I see no reason not to touch you. What kind of adventure stories?"

"Real adventures. Scary adventures. Like the ship captain who was held hostage by Somali pirates."

"A Captain's Duty," he said, and she was impressed he knew the title of the book, rather than simply the title for the film based on it. "Good book. Good movie too, Captain Phillips. What else?"

"Stories about SEALS."

"The fictional ones where they're back from their missions and they fall in love with the hot woman they're assigned to protect?"

"No," she said, laughing.

"Wait. The ones where they fall for the physical therapist who rehabs them after war?"

Another laugh. "My my, don't you know everything about romance tropes? But no, I mean the real ones about their real missions."

"That's it. You're going to have to stop talking now. Because if you say anything more it's going to become clear you are the most perfect woman ever made."

"And why is that? You a fan of SEAL stories too?"

"I'm a fan of you growing more fascinating with every detail I learn."

"I'm an onion. Keep peeling me."

"A sexy onion. Let me take off another layer," he said and bent his head to her shoulder, nibbling playfully.

"What about you?"

"What about me? What do I like to read?"

"No. I'm picking a different topic. What movies do you like? And don't name your clients' films."

"Of course, their works are all my favorites. But when I'm not watching their movies, I like heist flicks."

"Like Ocean's Eleven?"

He nodded. "Best heist movie ever."

"And The Italian Job?"

"Another excellent one."

"And Thomas Crowne Affair?"

"Brilliant plot."

"And Die Hard?"

"Seen it ten times. Maybe more," Clay said.

"I love them all too," she said.

"Okay, now you have to cease speaking."

"Because that makes me perfect?" she joked.

"Something like that," he muttered as he pulled her in close, and kissed her once more.

* * *

When she woke up the next morning, Clay ran a hand through his hair, then cleared his throat. "I can push back my flight until later tonight. Do you want to spend the day with me?"

She couldn't think of a better idea. "And we can talk more about movies, and TV shows, and books?"

"That. Or about the threesome we're going to have some day."

She arched an eyebrow. "I am not sharing you."

He smiled devilishly at her. "Good answer. And for the record, I would never ever share you."

"Good. Now for even suggesting that, I need two orgasms, stat."

He tipped his forehead to the bathroom. "Shower. You. Against the wall."

After he delivered on her request, they went out to lunch in Hayes Valley at one of her favorite restaurants that had 47 varieties of dipping sauce for French Fries. Clay agreed that it might be the best restaurant he'd ever been to and that fries were an unbeatable food choice.

But as the evening unspooled, Julia became aware of a ticking clock. Time seemed to speed up, to charge headfirst to the end of the night as the inevitable goodbye loomed closer. When his car arrived to take him to the airport, she said goodbye and planted a quick kiss on his cheek. There would be no poignant, postcard kind of kiss. They might have had fun, they might be insanely compatible in bed, they might even have the same taste in movies and books, but there was no *they*. She had too much baggage here in her hometown. Too much trouble that wasn't close to being wrapped up. And too many more Tuesday nights before she could call it even.

She needed to start erecting a wall. Clay would go down in her history as the best sex ever – a night of unbridled perfection in the bedroom. And, fine, he scored major points for being easy to talk to and fun to spend the day with. But he lived 3000 miles away.

"Nice meeting you," she said crisply and turned to leave.

He grabbed her wrist and pulled her to him, her body flush with his. Damn, she loved the feel of his strong chest against hers. She liked it too much.

"Julia," he said, and this time his voice was intense, serious. "I had an amazing time with you. I know this sounds crazy since we live on opposite coasts, but I need to see you again. I'm going to call you."

He kissed her deeply, a searing kiss that made her stand on her tip toes and thread her hands in his hair so she could hold on tight. When he broke the kiss, she felt wobbly and her lips missed his.

As he drove off, she realized maybe her heart missed him too. But she reminded herself that it was easy to say *I'm going to call you*. What was harder was doing that. What was Herculean was seeing someone on the other side of the country.

* * *

Clay pounded hard on the punching bag with a final hit. His breath came fast, his heart beating ferociously from the workout.

"Never seen you hit so hard, man," Davis said to him. "Who are you picturing now? That network bastard you had to deal with in San Francisco?"

Clay shook his head as he bent over the water fountain at the boxing gym for a cold drink of water. He hadn't been picturing the network exec at all. He'd been thinking of how much it sucked that Julia lived so damn far away. He'd been back in New York for one day. One stinking day, and he couldn't get that feisty woman out of his mind.

"No," he answered crisply.

"You should just call her," Davis said.

He snapped his head up, staring hard at his friend. "What?"

"The woman you spent the extra day with in San Francisco."

"How did you know?"

"You told me you were coming back in the morning and you missed our workout yesterday." He tapped the side of his head. "Remember? I know how to read people. It's my job."

"Anyway," Clay said, trying to brush him off.

"Are you going to?"

"Call her?"

"Yeah. Call her. Because you should."

Shrugging, he tried to act cool and casual. But the truth was he'd always been planning to call her. He hadn't been giving her a line when he left the other night. He wanted to see her again and discover if there was something more to them. He'd enjoyed talking to her as much as he'd enjoyed making her scream his name. She fascinated him, and he couldn't let her be just one night. He wanted more nights with her.

When he reached his apartment and shut the door behind him, he dialed her number. She answered on the second ring.

"Hello, person I never thought I'd hear from again."

He smiled, wishing he could tug her sweet little body against his, plant a kiss on her beautiful face, feel her melt into his touch.

"Hey, Julia. What would you say about coming to New York for the weekend? I have a new set of ropes I've been meaning to use, and a restaurant I want to try, and a big king-size bed you'd look spectacular tied up to. Oh, and there's also a new heist movie coming out this weekend that we could see."

She laughed once. "Let me get this straight. I'm being invited to the Big Apple for dinner, a movie and a little bondage?"

"Yes, that would be correct."

* * *

She didn't answer right away. She carefully considered his request.

She'd won big earlier that night. The kind of win that made the weight of her past start to lessen. Besides, he was only asking for two nights of her life. This wasn't a commitment. This wasn't a relationship, and she sure as hell wasn't going to get caught up in him.

"Then the answer is pick me up at the airport in a town car, handsome, because I'm going to be ready for all of that and then some as soon as I step off the plane," she said, as she sank down on her couch, kicked off her heels, and started counting down the hours til the weekend.

It was one weekend. Nothing more, she promised herself.

They stayed on the phone for an hour, talking about everything and nothing, and his voice lowered to that sexy growl as
he asked her what she was wearing. Then, he brought her there
again.

Just a weekend, she repeated the next day, and the next, and
the next, and all during the flight, and even as she walked
through the terminal and out the doors of LaGuardia.

But when she saw him in that hot-as-sin suit, with his tie already loosened, and sunglasses on, leaning against the town car,
she had a feeling she'd never want the weekend to end….

**For more of Clay and Julia read on in NIGHT AFTER
NIGHT….**

NIGHT AFTER NIGHT
Book 1 in Seductive Nights

"Clay Nichols is the perfect man. He treats his woman like a queen and would do anything for her, but he's totally up for f*&ing her like a porn star." —Jen at Sub Club

This book is dedicated to my good friends
Cara, Hetty and Kim. You are my naughty-planning
committee, and this book would quite simply
not exist without the three of you.

ABOUT
NIGHT AFTER NIGHT

"Let me control your pleasure."

Their world was sex, love, and lies.

He intoxicated her. Commanded. Consumed.

With a dirty mind and a mouth to match, Clay Nichols is everything Julia never knew she wanted and exactly what she cannot have. He walked into her life one night and unlocked pleasure in her that she never knew was possible. Possessing her body, captivating her every thought. Which makes him way too dangerous for Julia to risk her heart, given that she has a price tag on her head. She ran after one mind-blowing week with him, but now he's back, and determined to make her his own.

No matter the cost.

She was a sexy drug to him. Fiery, unforgettable, and never enough, Julia is an enigma, and Clay isn't willing to let her go without a fight. But she's got dark secrets of her own that threaten to destroy any chance of happiness. She's a wanted woman – the stakes are high, the danger lurks around every corner, and yet the lure between them can't be denied. Can two people burned by love trust again when desire and passion are met by danger at every turn?

CHAPTER ONE

The ace of diamonds was solo.

Such a shame, because it would look fantastic paired with, say, an ace of clubs, spades or hearts. But this was the hand she'd been dealt and it was ace high, nothing more. They were down to three still standing for this round: Julia, the Trust Fund Baby, and then New Guy. His name was Hunter; he was a beanpole and his hair was short, spiky and blond. He wore khaki pants and a plaid shirt, and had twitchy fingers. Probably because there was a no-cell-phone rule during the game, and he was missing out on emails from his *team,* Julia guessed.

She bet he was an Internet startup type, maybe a venture capitalist. He was used to risks; he liked to take them. That's why he'd been brought to this game, recruited specifically to play with her. But the trouble was—well, trouble for him—he laughed when he bluffed. Julia spotted it early, and then tracked it. He'd done it with a pair of fives a couple of rounds back that she'd easily beat with two jacks. He'd chuckled softly too with his king high a few hands ago.

Bless that newbie. He couldn't even hide his tell, and Julia could kiss him if he kept this up because it made her job so much easier.

"Five hundred," he said confidently, pushing another black chip into the pile as he cleared his throat. Julia was a panther poised for prey; muscles taut and frozen, lying in wait for the sign.

Then it came. It started in his nose, like a small, playful snort, then traveled to his belly, and finally turned into a quick, rumbly laugh.

Ah, brilliant. She could smell potential victory in the air. Of course, she could also smell the pork dumplings and pepper steak from Mr. Pong's downstairs. When she'd first started coming here, to this second-floor apartment parked atop a restaurant in China Town that smelled of takeout even when pizza had been ordered for the games, she was sure she'd never remove the stench from her clothes, much less her nostrils. Perma-scent. But she'd had no problems in the laundry department and as for her nose, well, now she was used to the smell that permeated every pore on Tuesday nights.

She never ate here, especially not with the bulldozer-sized heavy who stood guard over the game in the kitchen. She knew his name, but who cared what it was? To her he was simply Skunk; he had one streak of white in his dyed-black hair. His meaty fingers were jammed into the coldcut plate, pawing through the leftover slices of deli meat. Julia wanted to roll her eyes, crinkle her nose, or shoot him a hard stare.

She knew better, though, for many reasons, not the least of which was the square outline of the handle of the Glock poking at the hem of his pants. He'd never pulled it, but the gun was an omnipresent reminder that a bullet could be unleashed at a moment's notice. She shivered inside at the thought, but outside she showed no emotion, not toward Skunk, not toward Hunter the pawn, and certainly none for Trust Fund Baby when he shrugged, blew a long stream of air through his lips, and slammed his cards down. He held his hands out wide. "I'm out."

Then there were two.

She eyed the pot, her hand, and the newbie.

Her heart thumped, and a fleet of nerves ghosted through her, but only briefly.

Don't let on.

She had no tells. Her face was stone. She'd mastered the impassive look a long time ago. She could fake her way through anything. *A perfect liar,* the ninth-grade school guidance counselor had declared when Julia denied punching Amelia Cartwright in the nose after Amelia had called another girl a nasty name.

"Did you just hit Amelia Cartwright?"

"No," Julia had said. She didn't shuffle her feet. She didn't look away. She'd lied like it was the truth and that had served her well ever since then.

Perfect lie = perfect truth.

She plucked out a black chip from her stack, then another, rolling them back and forth between the pads of her thumb and index finger, her fire-engine red nails long and lacquered. The nails were part of the look—low-cut tops, tight jeans and four-inch black pumps for every game. The regulars knew her, but the new players never took a woman seriously, especially when she dressed like it was girls' night out.

That's why newbies were brought in. So she could hustle them. It was better that they underestimated her.

"I'll raise you $500," she said in an emotionless voice, sliding two chips into the pile.

This was the moment. Nerves like steel. Blood like ice.

Hunter sucked in a deep breath, like he was trying to inhale thick malt from a thin straw. He stared longingly at the pile of chips in the middle of the table, chewed on the corner of his lip, and glanced at his cards one last time.

"I'm out," he said, slapping the cards down on the scratched-up table that reeked of noodles, beer and regret. If tables could talk, this one could tell stories of all the wedding bands lost and sports cars gained here, all the highs and lows it witnessed.

"Then I'll take this," she said, not needing to reveal her ace high as she reached across the table and gathered up the pot.

She stood, walked straight to Skunk, and handed him the chips. "I'll cash out."

He stuffed a rolled-up slice of bologna between his thick lips, inhaled the meat, then licked off his stubby fingers before he counted out her money. Nearly five thousand, and she wanted to sing, to shout, to soar.

"You want me to give this to Charlie?"

She shook her head. "I will."

"I'll walk you downstairs."

As if she were going anyplace else but to deliver the dough.

Still, Skunk followed her, serving as her handcuffs, huffing as he waddled down the steps.

"You played good tonight," he said in between heavy breaths.

"Thanks," she said, wishing she'd liked playing so well. Like she once did. She used to love poker like there was no tomorrow, a true favorite past time. Now it was tainted.

"I'm proud of you," he said, patting her on the back.

Inside, she recoiled at his touch. On the outside, she acted like it was no big deal. Like none of this was a big deal.

A minute later, they weaved through the tables to the back of Mr. Pong's restaurant, mostly empty at this late hour. Tall and trim, Charlie was hunched over in a chair, swiping his finger across the screen of his iPad. He wore a sharp black suit, a white shirt and no tie. He smiled when he saw her, baring his teeth, yellowed from smoking.

The sight of him made her skin crawl.

His eyes traveled up and down her body hungrily. She pretended he wasn't undressing her in his mind as she turned over the cash. "Here."

"Ah, it's my favorite color. Green from Red," he said, stroking the cash.

She told him the number. "Count it."

"I trust you, Red." His accent was some sort of mix of Greek and Russian. Not Chinese, though, despite the headquarters in China Town. From the little bits and pieces she had cobbled together he both liked Chinese food, and had taken over this restaurant and the apartment above it. Probably from some poor schmuck who'd owed him, too. Someone who didn't make good on a debt.

"I don't trust you though," she said sharply.

"Funny," he said as he laughed, then counted the bills because there was no trust between either of them. "Very funny. Do you tell jokes that funny when you are working behind your bar? Or should I drop by sometime to check?"

Red clouds passed before her eyes. Julia clenched her fists, channeling her anger into her hands as she bit her tongue. She knew better than to incite him. Still, she hated it when Charlie mentioned her bar, hated it almost as much as his unplanned visits to Cubic Z. Drop-ins, he called them. Like a restaurant inspector, popping in whenever he wanted.

"You are welcome anytime at my bar," she said through gritted teeth.

"I know," he said pointedly. "And the next time I'm there, the pretty bartender will make me a pretty drink."

When he was done counting, he dropped his hand into the pocket of his pants, slowly rooted around, and withdrew a slender knife. Only a few inches long and more like a camping tool, it was hardly a weapon, but it didn't need to possess firepower to send the message—he could cut her to pieces if she failed to deliver. He brought the handle of the knife to his chin, scratched his jaw once, twice, like a dog with fleas, keeping his muddy-brown eyes on her the whole time in a sharp, taut line. He didn't blink. He shoved the knife back into his pocket, then raised his hand and snapped his fingers. Some kind of business goon scurried over, a leather-bound ledger tucked under his arm. "I knew you could take the VC," Charlie said to her, a nefarious glint in his eye. "That's why we brought

Hunter for you. You did a good job, separating the fool from his money." Julia's insides twisted with the way Charlie talked. Then he turned to his associate who'd opened the book. "Mark this down in the books. Red is a little bit closer."

The guy scribbled in a number.

"A lot closer," Julia corrected.

"A lot. A little. What's the difference? The only thing that matters—" Charlie stopped to raise a finger in the air, then come swooping down with it, like a pelican eyeing prey as he stabbed her name in the ledger "—is when this says zero. Until then, you are a lot, you are a little, you are mine. Now, you want some kung pao chicken? It's considered the best in San Francisco by all the critics."

She shook her head. "No thanks. I've had my fill tonight."

"I will see you next Tuesday, then. Shall I send one of my limos for you?"

"I'll walk."

She turned on her heels and left, walking home in the cool San Francisco night, leaving Charlie and his chicken behind her.

When she returned to her apartment, she tried to push the game out of her mind as she let the door slam. She washed her hands, poured herself a glass of whiskey, and was about to reach for the remote so she could lose herself in some mindless TV when her phone rang. A 917 number flashed across the screen. Her heart dared to flutter. Dumb organ. Then her belly flipped. Stupid stomach.

But it was two against three because only her common sense said *Don't answer*, and common sense wasn't winning. The brain rarely bested the body. The caller was Clay Nichols who she'd met a few days ago while she was tending bar. The tall, dark, gorgeous, filthy-mouthed lawyer from New York, who fucked like a champion and called her irresistible, and then asked her to tell him more about all the things she liked as they lay tangled up in hotel sheets, blissed out.

The man who lived three thousand miles away. The man she was sure was full of shit when he'd said he would call her again. The man she'd spent some of the best twenty-four hours of her life with.

She answered on the second ring. "Hello, person I never thought I'd hear from again."

"Hey, Julia. What would you say about coming to New York for the weekend?"

A smile started to form on her lips. "Tell me why I would want to go to New York for the weekend," she said, sinking down on her couch, crossing her ankles.

"For starters, I have a new set of ropes I've been meaning to use, and a restaurant I want to try, and a big king-size bed you'd look spectacular tied up to. Oh, and there's also a new heist movie coming out this weekend that we could see."

She laughed. "Let me get this straight. I'm being invited to the Big Apple for dinner, a movie, and a little bondage?"

"Yes, that would be correct."

She didn't answer right away. Her mind flashed back to her big win tonight. Regardless of the chains Charlie had on her, she *was* closer. And while she'd promised herself she wouldn't get involved with anyone till she was free, Clay wasn't asking for more than two nights of her life. Two nights were thoroughly finite, and therefore could be thoroughly enjoyed. She had off this weekend. Besides, the very thought of Clay had a way of erasing some of the evening, of blotting out those moments when she was so clearly under Charlie's thumb.

"Then the answer is, pick me up at the airport in a town car, handsome, because I'm going to be ready for all of that and then some as soon as I step off the plane," she said, as she kicked off her heels, and took a drink of her whiskey, enjoying the burn as the liquor slid down her throat.

They chatted for longer, and soon the tone shifted, and his voice lowered. "What are you wearing right now?"

"What do you want me to be wearing?"

"Thigh-high white stockings, lacy white panties, and a matching bra," he answered immediately.

"And what would you do if I were wearing that?"

"Drive you crazy through the lace with my tongue, then take your panties off with my teeth."

She didn't think it was the whiskey that was making her feel warm all over. "Funny thing, Clay. I believe that's what I'll be wearing on Friday afternoon."

The next day, she went lingerie shopping.

* * *

Carefully, so as not to run the nylon, Julia inched the stocking up her thigh. Her sister sat perched on a peach-colored armchair in the corner of the spacious dressing room of Hetty's Secret Closet on Union Street. McKenna absently kicked her ankle back and forth, a pleasantly distracting sight because her heels were sparkly peacock blue, matching her sapphire-colored skirt.

"What do you think?" Julia asked as she twirled around to give a full view of the bra, panty and stocking set.

A well-known fashion blogger and online video star, her sister has suggested this chic boutique for the shopping trip. Now, McKenna surveyed her up and down, pressing a finger to her lips as if she were studiously considering the undergarments in question. "It's a good thing you don't get cold easily. It's chilly in New York in April. I was just there."

Julia rolled her eyes. "It's not as if I'm going to strut around the Big Apple in this get-up only," she said, gesturing to her lingerie ensemble.

"I'm just checking," she said with a wink. "You'll pair it with what? A trench coat?"

"No. This thing called a skirt. Ever heard of it? Then a blouse, too. Then the trench coat."

"I am pleased to inform you," her sister began, flashing a bright smile, "you have the Fashion Hound seal of approval on your sexy outfit."

"Exactly why I keep you around." Julia began stripping off the stockings, the underwear and the bra.

"Wait. Don't I get a little sashay of the hips and all? A lap dance maybe?"

"I'm saving that all for Friday, Saturday and Sunday."

"You must really like this guy if he gets your whole weekend. You haven't given anyone three days in a long, long time."

"I haven't given anyone *any* days in a long, long time," Julia corrected, as she neatly folded the items, then pulled on her jeans.

"Not since Dillon."

"Yep, not since Dillon," she said, turning away because she didn't want McKenna to see how much it hurt to even hear that name breathed. Dillon was the reason she kept secrets from her sister, and from everyone. She shifted gears to her sister's upcoming wedding. "Hey, when are we going for your next dress fitting?"

"When you get back from New York, and we can pick your Maid of Honor dress too," McKenna said in a voice laced with true happiness. She'd found her match, and her happily ever after was in her hands. Julia wasn't jealous, not one bit. She was glad for her sister, even though the notion of a happy ending seemed about as far away to her as living on the moon.

* * *

Cubic Z was buzzing at happy hour. Thursday night was one of the busiest of the week, drawing in the one-more-day-till-the-weekend crowds of twenty-somethings as they spilled out of their nearby offices here in the SoMa district of San Francisco. Finance and tech guys and gals abounded, ordering up microbrews or fancy cocktails.

As Julia mixed a vodka tonic, she turned to her partner-in-crime, Kim. The petite brunette behind the bar was pouring a Raspberry Ale from the tap while absently running a palm across her round belly. She was due in a few months, the first baby for Kim and her husband.

"You're all set to run this place solo for the weekend?" Julia asked.

Kim rolled her eyes and shot her a look as if to say she were being ridiculous. "I run this place when you're not here. I know what to do. Besides, Craig is going to help me out," she said, as she handed the glass to a regular customer, a skinny guy who always stopped by after work. Kim and Julia were both part owners of Cubic Z; they'd bought an ownership stake a year ago, so they served drinks and made sure drinks served the bottom line. Kim's husband had just finished bartending school but hadn't nabbed a job yet and they didn't need an extra bartender at Cubic Z, so she was the sole source of support for the two of them.

"I know. I just wanted to make sure. What can I say? I'm looking out for you and the baby already," Julia said, as she slid the vodka concoction to a customer.

"Yeah, protect us from all the unsavory types," Kim joked, because Cubic Z was upscale, and might draw hipsters who hit on bartenders but didn't attract that sort of more dangerous clientele. "Like that guy," she said, lowering her voice to a whisper as she tipped her forehead to the door. A man stood with his back to them, talking to a friend, a shock of white in his dark hair. Tension knit itself tightly inside Julia, shooting cold through her bones. She didn't want Skunk anywhere near her bar. He'd been here once, and once had been enough. He'd parked himself in a bar stool, ordered a drink, and said one thing and one thing only as he nodded, surveying the joint, "Yeah, I like this place. I like it a lot. You give good pour."

But when the man swiveled around, he wasn't Skunk. He wasn't anyone Julia knew. And there wasn't a reason for her veins to feel like ice. She shrugged it off, the worry that tried to trip her up now and then, the fear that Charlie or Skunk would hurt her or someone she cared about. They hadn't yet. But they could in a heartbeat.

CHAPTER TWO

Clay finished off the rest of his scotch, then glanced at his watch.

"Got someplace to be?" Michele asked.

Damn. He was caught checking the time again, a bad habit he'd started since he invited Julia to join him in New York this weekend. It was nearing ten, and he should cut out of this bar and head home. She'd be arriving tomorrow, and tomorrow evening couldn't come fast enough.

"Yeah. Bed," he said dryly. Michele was his best friend Davis's sister, and his friend too. The three of them had known each other since college. She was one year younger, but had followed in her brother's footsteps, attending the same university.

"I remember when you used to be out till all hours," Michele teased, shooting him a knowing smile as she ran her fingers through her dark hair. She was a pretty woman, always had been, but there was nothing between them. Not since they'd shared a kiss one night at a drunken college party. A kiss that had never been repeated, and he'd chalked it up to her being sad that night over the anniversary of her parents' death and needing some kind of connection. Understandable. Completely understandable.

"Hardly," he said, because he wasn't the party-boy type, but then he wasn't usually the first one to leave either. Tonight, however, needed to end early, because tomorrow was the evening he wanted to last all night long. He called for the check, fished some bills from his wallet, and paid for their drinks.

"Why are you leaving so soon?"

"Because the glass is empty. I'll get you a cab," he said, and walked out with her, the neon lights of the diner across the street flickering behind them. "Do you want to . . ." she said, but the rest of her words were swallowed by the sound of a siren a few blocks over.

"Want to what?" he asked when the noise faded.

She swallowed, and then spoke quickly, faster than usual. "Do something this weekend? Have dinner, maybe?"

He shot her a look like she wasn't making sense as he hailed the first taxi he saw. "Davis is out of town," he said. He and Michele didn't have dinner together. Drinks, definitely. But dinners were something the three of them did together, and Davis was off in London for a few months, directing a production of *Twelfth Night* that Clay had hooked him up with.

"Yeah. I know," she said. "That's sort of the point."

"Point of what?"

She shook her head. Rolled her eyes. "Nothing. It was nothing," she said, and something about her tone seemed clipped.

"You okay?"

She nodded quickly. Too quickly. "I'm great," she said, as he held open the cab door for her. "Anyway, you probably have big plans this weekend."

"I think it's safe to say I'll be tied up," he said, though as her cab sped off, he realized it was more likely the other way around. That Julia would be.

He hoped she would be, at least.

* * *

He'd woken up at four-thirty, worked out at five, and hit the office by six-thirty. He'd skipped lunch, ordered in a sandwich, and reviewed a contract for a new sci-fi flick a movie director he repped was working on. He sent in notes to the producers, a list of points and items that needed to be changed. If they weren't, his client wouldn't be happy, and Clay was all about having a hefty stable full of happy clients.

His junior partner at the firm, Flynn, poked his head in around mid-afternoon. "Hey. I got a lead that the Pinkertons are looking for new representation," Flynn said, his blue eyes wide and grinning. A pair of British brothers, the Pinkertons had been bankrolling some of the most successful films in the last few years, including *Escorted Lives*, based on the bestselling books.

"We need to lock that up," he said, and he was sure the glint in his eyes matched Flynn's. Three years younger and eager as hell to grow his role at the firm, Clay had hired him fresh out of law school. Flynn had become invaluable, pulling more than his weight in helping to land top clients and sweet deals for them. They'd seen eye to eye on just about everything, with the exception of one minor rough patch a year ago over a client that Flynn had reeled in all on his own—a big-time action film director.

A client they'd lost.

"No kidding," Flynn said, tapping the side of the door twice for good luck. Flynn was like that, always crossing his fingers, and knocking on wood. "I'll get some more details and aim to set up a meeting with them next week."

"Perfect. The Pinkertons are huge golfers, so if you have to schedule a tee time, you should," he said, and it wasn't so much a suggestion as it was an order, and one he knew Flynn, a former college golfer, would jump at.

Flynn mimed swinging a club. "Shame I hate golf so much."

"All right, get out of here. I need to finish up so I can take the weekend off."

"I'll email you when I hear more."

"I'm not answering email this weekend," Clay said, making it clear in his tone that this was a do-not-disturb kind of weekend. "You can update me on Monday."

"Fair enough."

Flynn left, and he checked on Julia's flight, pleased to see it was landing on time. He brushed his teeth, ran his fingers through his hair, not bothering with a comb, because she was the kind of woman who'd have her fingers sliding through his hair in seconds, messing it up the way she wanted. He said goodbye to the receptionist, let her know she could shut down early too, and slid into the town car waiting outside his office. On the way to the airport, he worked his way through his west-coast calls, ending them just as the car pulled up to the terminal.

The sun was blaring high in the sky in April, so he put on a pair of sunglasses. He loosened his tie; he couldn't stand the way it constrained him. He glanced at his phone, hoping for a message from her. None was there, so he clicked on the app for his stocks, checking his portfolio, and looking up every few seconds to scan the crowds. He couldn't focus on the market right now.

He hardly wanted to admit it to himself, but there was something about this moment—the minutes before he saw her —that felt like first-date nerves. Like knocking on a woman's door, and waiting, hoping she'd be just as eager for the night to unfold. Weird, considering the way he and Julia had started. Free of pretense and bullshit, they went straight for each other, the physical chemistry overpowering anything else.

His phone buzzed. He clicked open the message and it sent a bolt of electricity through him. *White stockings coming your way . . .*

Stockings—one of those items of clothing that on the right woman could send a man to his knees. Especially the sight of the top of a pair of thigh-highs peeking out from a skirt, revealing an inch of skin, hinting at what lay beneath. On Julia, stockings were a playground for his eager hands.

The nerves in him disappeared and turned into something else—adrenaline, maybe. The sharp, hot charge of desire all through his blood and bones.

He spotted her before she saw him; that red hair was hard to miss, even in a sea of frenzied, frantic travelers jostling for a cab, a car, a bus. She wore a black trench coat, belted at the waist, black heels, and white stockings. A grin took over his face; she had done it. Of course she had done it. He was at attention in seconds and his fingers itched to touch her, to peel off those stockings inch by delicious inch, then lick his way down her legs to her ankles and back up, savoring her every single second.

Leaning against the town car, he kept his eyes on her the entire time she threaded her way through the crowds. She was a tall drink of woman, her red lipstick matching her red hair that was blowing in the late afternoon breeze. She brushed some strands away from her face. Soon, she noticed him, and smiled wickedly. He nodded, trying to act cool, even as his temperature rose. Then, she was in front of him, and before she said a word, her hands were on his shirt and she pulled him to her, pressing her lips to his.

She was lightning fast. A blur of movement, of teeth and lips, and that intoxicating taste of her lipstick that would be gone in seconds.

He responded instantly, kissing her hard like she deserved. Cupping the back of her neck, he jerked her close. He wanted her to remember that she might have made the first move, but he liked to lead. He nipped on her bottom lip then sucked on her tongue, drawing out a moan from her that pleased him deeply. He kissed more, sliding his tongue over hers as he lowered his hand to her thigh, skimming his fingers along the thin, barely-there fabric of her stockings.

When he broke the kiss, he raised an eyebrow. "They look good on you, and I bet they look good coming off too."

"Don't rush it. I want you to enjoy the view."

"I've been enjoying the view since the second I laid eyes on you, gorgeous."

He opened the door and gestured for her to enter the car, watching the whole time as she stepped inside and crossed her legs, giving him a very brief preview of where the stockings ended. He shook his head approvingly, and she shot him a look that said nothing short of *come and get it.* He took her suitcase as the driver emerged, scrambling to deposit the black carry-on into the trunk.

After he got in the car he hit the partition button, closing them off from the driver, with the tinted windows shutting them off from the whole wide world.

She looked at him, her pretty green eyes meeting him straight on. That beautiful face, that divine body, and that naughty, naughty mouth; it was hard to believe he'd only spent one night with her. She stared at him as if she was as famished as he was. As if she needed the same thing.

"You look like you need to be fucked right now."

"Do I?"

"You sure do," he said, raking his eyes over her, perched in the leather seat so properly, and so damn sexily at the same time. He ached to touch her but savored the tease, so he kept a distance between them, drawing out the tension as the car pulled into afternoon traffic.

"And I suppose you think you can solve that problem?"

"I don't think so. I know so. And I intend to. But not yet."

"You gonna toy with me?"

"Been thinking about it."

"Like a cat playing with a mouse," she said, her voice nearly a purr.

"You're hardly a mouse."

"I know," she said, and ran her index finger across her bottom lip then around to her top, so suggestively he nearly tossed his plans to wait out the window. He wanted her now. He wanted her bad, especially with the way her hot gaze was locked on him as she parted her lips, and ran her tongue along her teeth.

A challenge; one that he planned to meet. A low rumble worked its way free of his throat as he moved to her, his body next to her, just a trace of contact. Slowly, so as to torture her, he reached for the belt of her coat, taking his time untying it.

Her breath caught as he started to open her jacket, first one button, then the next, then another. As he worked his way up her chest, undoing the final button, she rolled her eyes in pleasure, closing them briefly as he slid a hand over her right breast, squeezing her.

She stifled a gasp, biting her lip.

"Don't pretend you're not turned on."

"I'm not pretending," she whispered.

"Then let me hear you moan. I want to hear everything." She opened her eyes, as he cupped her breasts over the fabric of her clingy sweater. "Are you wet?"

"Yes."

He glanced down at her short black skirt, already rising up to show more of her strong, shapely thighs. He desperately wanted to slide his hand under her skirt right-the-fuck now, but patience would be rewarded. "When did you start getting wet?"

"The exact moment?"

"Yes."

"On the plane."

"What were you thinking about at thirty thousand feet that was getting you wet?" he asked as his hand drifted down the front of her sweater, traveling over her flat belly.

"About all the things you might say to me."

"You like the way I talk to you?"

"Why don't you check and see how much I like it?"

"Why don't you wait for me to check," he fired back as he reached under her sweater, spreading his hand across the soft, sweet flesh of her stomach. She moaned as he touched her, and he wasn't sure he was going to be able to get enough of those sounds this weekend. He might have to spend the next forty-eight hours making her gasp and moan, groan and scream, because her noises were better than a cold drink on a hot day. The sounds she made fed him.

He ran his callused fingers along the waistband of her skirt, and she wiggled closer to his hand. "So your panties were damp all during the flight, Julia?"

"I wouldn't say the whole flight. I have control, you know," she said, shooting him that tough stare that turned him on even more.

"I know you do. You have excellent control. And I love breaking it down. I love watching you lose control," he said, dipping his hand inside her skirt. "So tell me what you thought about on the plane that aroused you."

"Your mouth," she said in a rough whisper.

"Nice answer." He trailed his fingers along the top of her panties, and her hips arched closer.

"Got any other questions for me?"

He nodded. "Did you get wetter when you saw me? Tell me the truth," he said, pulling his hand out of her skirt. She looked up at him, wide eyes full of need.

"What do you think?" She reached for his hand, locking fingers with him. She tried to tug his hand down to her legs, but he didn't budge.

"I think you're as hot between your legs as I am hard just from looking at you," he said and brought her hand to his erection, letting her press her palm against him. She grinned as she touched him, stroking him. He hissed in a breath, but then moved her hand away. "So tell me. Did I make you wetter when you saw me?"

"Yes. You leaning against the ear, with that tie all loosened and your jacket on, looking like a hot guy in a suit. Only I knew you weren't thinking of business deals—you were thinking of bedroom deals."

"I was watching you the whole time, getting harder as you walked toward me. Seeing you wore what I told you to wear," he said, teasing the top of her lacy stockings. He could feel her heat without even touching her. He bent his head to her neck, flicking his tongue against her collarbone, then up to her ear. "Tell me one word to describe how wet you are now."

"What is this? Mad Libs foreplay?" she said in as challenging a tone as she could likely muster. He was impressed with her fierceness. She didn't give it up easily, even as her body was melting under his touch. He traveled higher with his fingers, inching closer to the Promised Land.

"Yes it is. Now, I want one word," he said firmly, giving her a clear command. He stroked the soft skin of her inner thigh, causing her to quiver.

"Soaked," she said, breathing hard.

"No, your panties are soaked. I want to know about your pussy. One word about your beautiful pussy that I have been thinking about all week long."

"*Slippery*. Does that work for your little wordplay, Clay?"

"It does," he said. Did anyone else on the plane know you were so turned on?"

She shook her head.

"Good. Because I fucking love the image I have in my head now. You flying high above the country, your sexy legs crossed, trying to hold in how much you wanted me to touch you. Not being able to touch yourself, but wanting to so badly. Did you want to masturbate on the plane?"

"No. I wanted you to touch me. I was waiting for you to touch me."

"I'm not going to make you wait any longer."

She grabbed his arm, wrapping her hand around his bicep, sending him some kind of message with the sharp nails that dug into him, right where she remembered his tattoo to be. "You better not make me wait any longer."

He dragged one finger against the cotton panel of her panties, and a growl erupted from him: a long, slow, appreciative growl. Her breathing grew harder, nearing a pant as he stroked her.

"I was wrong," he said in a low voice.

"About what?"

"You are fucking soaked, and I can't let you sit like this. I can't let this delicious wetness go to waste," he said, reaching under her skirt with both hands, and tugging her panties down past her knees. He stopped at her ankles, and she arched an eyebrow in question.

"The panties stay here. I want to hold your ankles in place."

"You weren't kidding when you told me what was on the menu this weekend," she said, her lips curving up in a delicious grin.

"I take my restraints very seriously," he said, twisting her panties in his hand, tightening the hold on her feet.

Keeping the underwear in place, he ran his fingers across her sweet, slippery pussy, watching her mouth fall open, and her eyes drift closed. "It would be so wrong of me to just finger you," he mused playfully as he coated his fingers in her wetness.

"Are you going to fuck me then?" Her voice was so desperate, her body so in need of what he planned to give her.

"I'm going to fuck you with my tongue," he said, letting go of the scrap of fabric to grab her hips and slide her down onto the seat. He spread her open as he pushed his leg down hard on her panties to keep her high-heeled feet bound together. He was ready, *so* ready to taste his woman. "The last time I did this to you, I tied you up, Julia. But this time I want your hands free to grab my face, pull hard on my hair, do whatever you need to do. You can fuck my face hard. When I get out of this car, I want to look like a man who was eating pussy."

"Oh God," she gasped as her head fell back against the seat.

He buried his face between her legs, and she cried out. A loud, no-holds-barred yell that echoed off the windows of the car, it was the most beautiful sound in the world. She gripped his head with her strong thighs, an involuntary reaction to the first touch as he licked her. Then she let her knees fall open for him and he savored her, working her up and down with his tongue, his lips, his mouth. He lapped up all her juices, the taste of her intoxicating and making his cock even harder, if that were possible.

He drove his tongue inside her, setting off another shattering moan that was music to his ears. She was quite an instrument to play, so finely tuned, and if he touched her right, she made the most glorious sounds—raw, intense, absolutely delicious noises of pleasure as he plundered her with his tongue. She grabbed his hair, yanked and pulled him closer as he'd told her to do. She started rocking her hips against his face, her exquisite pussy rubbing all over his stubbled jaw. She moved faster, and harder, and she was fucking him furiously right now, taking charge of how she liked it, her breathing turning wildly erratic, her moans signaling how close she was to release. He thrust one finger inside her, crooking it and hitting her in the spot that turned her moans into one long, high-pitched orgasm. She shuddered against him, her legs quaking, and when he finally slowed to look up at her, he saw her hair was a wild tumble, and her face was glowing.

He watched her reactions, enjoying the way the aftershocks seemed to radiate through her body like waves. He moved to the seat, slid alongside her, and pulled her close, tucking her sexy body against his.

"Forgive my manners. I didn't even ask how your flight was."

"It was worth it, Clay. My flight was worth it."

CHAPTER THREE

They barely made it inside his apartment. Before the door even closed, he'd hiked up her skirt. Were they on the fourth floor? Or the fifth floor? Hell, if she knew. Hell if she cared.

She grappled with the zipper on his pants, tugging and pulling as he caged her in against the wall with his strong arms. She pushed his pants down, then his briefs, and she wrapped an eager hand around his cock, hot and throbbing in her palm. He drew a sharp breath at the first touch, and she loved this; the moment when a man was helpless to her touch. When the control all swung back to her.

They were so simple, men. When it came down to it, they were ruled by their erections. Even when she gave in to a man, she still knew who was always in charge. She was; the woman was. Especially as she watched the expression on his gorgeous face, his eyes rolling back in his head as she stroked him. He rocked into her fist, fucking her hand once, twice, three times.

She dipped her free hand into her sweater, then inside the cup of her bra, hunting out the condom she'd stowed there earlier. You never could be too safe or too ready, she'd reasoned.

She ripped open the foil, and the sound make his eyes snap open.

"You come prepared," he said.

"I prepare for coming," she replied, then rolled the condom on him, loving the way he watched her hands as they slid down his length..

"Now, fuck me against the wall, Clay. Fuck me hard and fast, and if you think I can't take it, fuck harder then," she said.

"You think you give the orders here? I'm going to make you pay for that later," he said, as he grabbed her ass, hitched her legs around his waist and sank into her.

Her mouth fell open into an *O* as he filled her, his long, thick cock buried deep inside her. He didn't move for a few seconds, giving her time to adjust to his size even though she didn't need to. She loved how he stretched her, how she could feel him deep and far inside.

He began thrusting, his strong hands gripping her flesh, his fingers digging into her cheeks. She was the helpless one now, immobile, pinned by the wall and his big, sturdy body, but she reveled in it. Her mind was blank, free of nothing but this moment, this pure, physical, hungry moment with this man.

"How are you going to make me pay for it?" she asked, her words coming out choppy with each hard thrust inside her.

"By teasing you later. By tying you up and bringing you close to the edge, and then stopping right before you come," he said, his voice a low dirty growl, his breath hot against her neck.

"No," she moaned. "That's not fair. I don't like teasing."

"I know you don't. And I don't like being told to fuck you hard," he said, slowing his moves to drive as deep as he possibly could in her, making her breath catch in her throat. "You think I'd do anything but fuck you hard when I have been waiting all week for this?"

"All week? You've been waiting all week?"

He dipped his head to the crook of her neck, planting a bruising kiss on her skin as he slammed into her once more, his cock rubbing her clit and filling her at the same delirious time. She moaned loudly, so loud she was sure the next street over heard her, and she didn't care one bit. He was fucking her worries away, and the harder he took her, the less she cared about the way she spent her Tuesday nights.

"Yes. All. Week. Long," he said, punctuating each word with a thrust. "I've been picturing your legs wrapped around me, your hot body against mine, and most of all, I've been thinking about making you come again. I want you to scream, Julia. I want to feel the way you grip my cock when you come on me," he said, in that rough, sexy voice that sent sparks tearing through her body.

"Me too, Clay. Me too," she whispered, letting go of the game, of the banter, of the way they teased each other because right now, she was starting to see stars, beautiful, silvery stars, as the world slipped away, and he filled her, taking charge of her body, sending her over the edge. Her belly tightened. "Oh God," she cried out.

"Yeah, just like that. Come for me now, come so fucking hard for me so I can feel you all over," he said, holding onto her as she shattered into the beautiful bliss of another orgasm, the pleasure riding through her, stretching and reaching into the far corners of her body and mind.

Then, as she was catching her breath, she felt her spine scrape the wall as he surged into her once more, the look on his face, the growl in his throat making it clear that he'd joined her, and that they'd come undone together.

* * *

She was willing to admit it. She had apartment envy, and she had it bad. He had not one, but two sets of *stairs*. Which meant he had three floors: the loft level up top, then a living room level in between, then the kitchen and dining-room floor.

She trailed her fingers along the granite counter in his kitchen, lined with dark oak stools. "And this is where you cook all your gourmet meals?" She eyed the gleaming stovetop that looked as if it had never been used.

"You think I don't cook?" Clay handed her a glass of Belvedere, then poured another for himself.

"Do *you* cook?"

"I *can* cook. I don't usually though."

"Why not?"

"Because if I cook, I want to cook for someone," he said. Pots and pans hung on hooks on the exposed brick walls of the kitchen.

"And there's no one to cook for?"

"Not lately," he said, and then gestured to the stairs. "Let me show you the balcony."

They left the kitchen area and he led her up six steps to the sliding glass doors in the living room that opened to a balcony; a gorgeous, drool-worthy balcony.

Her jaw threatened to drop but she knew better than to gawk outwardly. Inside, though, she was ogling the spaciousness. This wasn't one of those New York balconies you had to wedge yourself onto sideways and then lean over to catch a sliver of a view. No, the man had a balcony big enough for hosting a summer barbecue, for throwing a party, for strutting around and doing a dance.

"Yeah, it's not too shabby at all," she said dryly as she peered over the edge of the brick railing, looking down at the cars streaming through the West Village, their taillights streaking six stories below. She drank in the view—it seemed all of New York City was visible from her vantage point, and the city was prettier when you watched it from above, when the noises were muted, and the sidewalk smells weren't invading your nostrils. The distance was a protective layer from the soot and scents and madness. She could see clear across to Broadway as it sliced Manhattan diagonally, then down to Tribeca, and over to the Hudson River, glittering, like a sleek ribbon against the night.

She shivered once; the temperature had dipped some and while it wasn't chilly yet, she was only wearing Clay's white button-down shirt.

"You're cold," he said softly, wrapping his strong arms around her, pulling her close, her back to his naked chest. She glanced down at his bicep, and traced the lines of his ink. *Passion*, he'd told her. That's what his tribal tattoo stood for, and it suited what she knew of him so far.

"Not anymore." She smiled, and leaned her head back to look up at him. He brushed his lips against her forehead, and her heart fluttered. Actually fluttered, like a damn bird trying to escape. She was ready to swat it, but she decided to enjoy the moment instead. "I like your arms around me," she whispered, stripping away her usual sarcasm.

"The feeling is completely mutual," he said, reaching for her hand and sliding his fingers through hers.

"And I also like this view. It's amazing."

"It's not too bad," he said.

She elbowed him playfully. "Not too bad? This is magnificent, and I don't care if that makes me seem all wide-eyed. But it's true. Your apartment is gorgeous," she said. She was a sucker for all the exposed red brick, and the warmth it brought to his place. "It's funny, because I'd have pegged you as having some leather or chrome or steel furniture, all black and white and sleek."

"You are confusing me with someone who has issues with his masculinity," he said, holding her tighter, bending his head to her neck to plant a quick kiss.

"You're saying a man who has black leather and chrome in his apartment is compensating for his small size?"

He laughed, a deep rumbly chuckle. "Don't you think?"

She nodded. She liked that his home was warm and lived in. Yes, it was a man's home, but it wasn't the home of a man who was trying too hard. He even had a few plants on the balcony, and Julia didn't have a green thumb herself, but still, there was something nice about this New York lawyer taking the time to have plants. "I can't stand that whole *I'm a man, I need my place to scream mannish.* It's sort of like driving a red Corvette."

"You might notice I don't have a red Corvette. Nor do I need one."

"You definitely do not need one," she said, trailing her fingers down his chest, between his pecs, and across the ridges of his abs. "And your plants are adorable."

He raised an eyebrow. "Maybe if you behave all night I'll tell you their names."

"You do not name your plants," she said, giving him a serious look.

"You're right." He laced his fingers through hers, guiding her back through the sliding glass doors. "I don't name my plants."

They returned to the living room with its dark-brown sofa, and a sturdy coffee table that boasted a couple of books, some magazines, and a few framed photos. There was a picture of Clay in a tux standing next to another man, a handsome one too.

"Where was that taken?"

"Tony Awards a few ago. That's Davis. He's a friend and a client. That was taken the night he won his first Tony. Bastard has a lot of them. Three now," he said, shaking his head, but clearly proud of the accomplishment.

"And this?" She pointed to a shot of him next to a man who had similar features—square jaw, deep-brown eyes, broad, sturdy shoulders.

"Younger brother, Brent."

"Where's he?" Before he could answer she held up a hand. "Wait. Don't tell me more."

He furrowed his brows. "Why?"

"Because I'm famished."

"And that means you can't talk or listen?"

"It means I am saving that conversation so we can have it over food," she said playfully, as she started to unbutton his shirt.

"You're afraid we're going to run out of things to talk about so you want to make sure to hoard a topic for food?"

She wagged a finger at him. "No. I simply want to eat. Now, are you going to cook for me or take me out?"

"There's this thing called takeout. Want Chinese?"

She flinched inside at the mention. The last thing in the world she wanted was Chinese food. She hated that Charlie and his games had ruined that cuisine for her. Sometimes, she just wanted a carton of cold sesame noodles, but they re-minded her of all the bullshit she still had to deal with till she was even with Charlie. *If* she'd ever be even with that fucker. Some days, freedom felt a lifetime away. Charlie had her in chains, and even though she hadn't asked for his permission to go away for the weekend, he knew she was gone. She was keenly aware that this was only a temporary leave from the jail she was in back home.

The jail no one knew about. She refused to tell a soul—it was too shameful what had happened that made Charlie turn her into his property. But she also kept her mouth shut because she didn't want those men to sink their claws into the people she loved. She protected her sister, her friends, even her hair-dresser with her silence.

But she didn't want Charlie infecting her time away. She shoved all thoughts of debts and guns and knives back into a dark corner of her mind.

"Clay," she said, in a chiding tone. "I can get good Chinese like that—" She snapped her fingers "—in San Francisco. I want something that tastes like New York." The lie rolled off her tongue seamlessly, but he didn't need to know why she wasn't taking him up on his offer for Chinese. "I want to go out. To some place filled with brooding New Yorkers rather than San Francisco hipsters. Something that makes me feel like I'm in the West Village."

"My mistake. I assumed you getting naked meant you wanted to eat in," he said, eyeing her up and down as she unbuttoned the shirt.

"I'm not getting naked," she said. "I'm changing into my clothes."

He reached for her, gripping her wrist in his hand. "Don't."

"Don't change?"

He shook his head. "Wear my shirt."

"I don't even have a bra on," she pointed out, as if his idea was ludicrous.

"I know," he said, his lips curving up. "I like that."

"You like me all free-range?"

"You have beautiful breasts. I want to be tortured knowing they are just one layer away from me, and covered only by something I was wearing an hour ago," he said, trailing his fingers along the edge of the shirt, barely touching her exposed chest. A shiver ran down her spine.

"And what about my bottom half? You want me to strut around naked from the waist down?"

"I want you to put that skirt back on. Do not put on underwear. Just your heels, your skirt and my shirt," he said in a firm voice. He held her gaze, his eyes darker than usual, waiting for her answer.

"Are you giving me an order?" she asked, pushing her fingers through her hair that was still messy from sex. But she'd never minded sex hair. As far as she was concerned, it was a look that should be listed on the menu at all blowout salons. *Updo, blown straight, or sex hair? I'll take the sex hair, thank you very much.*

"I'm giving you a request. One that I very much want you to fulfill," he said, grabbing her hand and bringing her palm to his lips. He kissed her, his tongue soft and wet against her skin. She'd never expected being kissed on her palm would be so erotic, but it was, because everything about Clay was charged with his smoldering virility, like a trailing scent of lingering sexiness that surrounded him. She was familiar with the term "sex-on-a-stick," but that didn't even begin to describe this man. He was so much more than that. He was masterful, and he touched her in ways that felt unreal. As if it weren't possible to truly feel that good. But, this was no mere dream. It was an intoxicating sliver of reality.

"What if I want to wear underwear?" she said, challenging him because it was fun, because she could, and because he wasn't going to pull a knife on her if she did. Here, she could be herself without fear of retaliation with a weapon. What a relief that was.

"Then I will take it off at the table. So as far as I can see, you can leave your panties here, or I can remove them from you at the restaurant. That clear?"

She nodded. "Commando it is then. And I am going to make you so crazy with wanting me that you might regret telling me to go naked."

"Impossible. I'd never regret you naked."

On the way out, she grabbed her clutch purse—a sleek little number from Coach that she'd snagged second-hand—and her phone. The message light flashed.

"Damn," she muttered, when she saw the text from McKenna. *Are you alive??? Or are you otherwise occupied? I need to know if I should call the cops or congratulate you.*

Julia grinned at the note. Clay raised his eyebrows in question.

"My sister," she explained, tapping a quick reply. "I told her I'd text her when I landed. She worries about me."

"So much that it brings out that naughty grin on your face?" he asked, swiping his thumb across her lips, and it was both sexy, but also skeptical. As if he didn't quite believe her.

But this time she was telling the truth.

CHAPTER FOUR

The Red Line gave new meaning to the word *Lilliputian*. The restaurant was one long narrow hallway, as if it had been wedged in between the shops on each side. There was a long bar, and a few tables, and they sat at the far end near the restrooms. Clay had been here a few times; it was a popular neighborhood place on a cobblestoned street in the Village, and typified what he loved about this eclectic neighborhood— it was thoroughly New York, but it had an individual feel to it, from the black-and-white pictures of steam engines on the walls, to the dark-red counter, to the hip-hop playing faintly overhead, R. Kelly's "Ignition."

Julia had finished texting with her sister, and he was glad of that. He had nothing against cell phones, but the sight of one in a woman's hands while he was with her didn't sit well with him, and he had his ex, Sabrina, to thank for that. She'd kept her twitchy little fingers far too busy on the touch screen of her phone, then lied, lied and lied some more about what she'd been doing. She'd been involved in some bad shit, and had dragged him deep down into her troubles, too. It had taken him longer than he'd wanted to untangle himself from those tall tales Sabrina had spun, and the damage she'd done to him. Since then, he'd vowed to stay away from that kind of woman.

Julia's phone was tucked away in her purse again, where it belonged. They'd placed their order and she was nibbling on appetizers. She plucked an olive from a small plate, bit it away from the seed sexily, and then said, "Do you realize I don't even know where you're from?"

"Do you want to know where I'm from?"

"Obviously. I want to get to know you better. Much better," she said.

"And I want you to get to know me much better. Where do you think I'm from?" he asked, taking a drink of his scotch.

"Chicago."

He shook his head. "Try again."

"Ooh. Is this another game? You like games, don't you? First Mad Libs. Now I get to guess where you're from. What do I win if I'm right?"

He leaned in close to her, swept her hair from her ear, and spoke in a low rumble. "You can pick the next position. But I know you won't win."

"So you're saying you're setting me up to fail so you can choose how to take me?"

"You think I'd choose badly? You think I'd pick a position you wouldn't like?"

She shook her head. "No," she said softly, and she seemed to let down her guard for a second or two. "I like everything you do."

He couldn't resist her, especially not when she dropped the snark, though he loved that about her too. But when she revealed her vulnerable side, he found himself wanting to be even closer to her.

"I like doing everything to you," he said, looking her in the eyes then brushing his thumb gently over her cheek before he kissed her softly, drawing out the sexiest little whimper from her gorgeous lips.

She reached for his collar gently, holding on as she kissed back, and it was a kiss that held the promise of so much more.

So much of their contact was hard and rough, and they both liked it that way, but this was tender and sweet, and he wanted this side of her too. Judging from how she kissed him, she wanted it too.

Soon, she broke the kiss, and brushed one hand against the other in a most business-like gesture. "Now that that's settled, let the games begin." She studied his face curiously. "California?" She shook her head before he could answer. "No, you're not happy enough to be from California."

"I'm very happy," he said defensively.

"Sure, but California people smile all the time. There's this thing called sunshine that makes us all dopey and cheerful."

"Then how do we account for your sarcasm, Miss California?"

"I'm an outlier," she said, as a waiter brought them water glasses.

"Water for both of you. And the kitchen is working on your orders. They should be out in about five minutes."

"Thank you very much," Clay said, then returned his attention to the beautiful woman by his side who wore no underwear. "I'm not from California."

"Arizona? Nah. Somehow I don't think they make them so kinky in Arizona."

He couldn't help but smile. "You never know. Arizona could be an incredibly kinky state. There could be entire colonies of kink in Phoenix."

"If there are colonies, perhaps we should go exploring. But no, you're not from Arizona, and you're not from Oregon or Washington either. You'd be crunchy, or have more of a penchant for plaid if either were the case."

"I enjoy your process of elimination," he said, leaning casually back in his bar chair, crossing his arms. No one ever guessed where he was from, because it was the kind of place people weren't usually from.

She pressed her fingers to her lips, then pointed at him. "And you're not from Boston because you don't have an accent, and that's also why you're not from the south. Or Texas, even though you feel very Texas," she said, placing her palm against his shirt, spreading her fingers across his chest, tapping lightly with her fingertips. He was hard instantly from her touch. Damn this woman; everything she did was a direct line to his dick.

"So, is there a guess coming, Julia?"

She shrugged happily, held her hands out in an *I give up* admission. "Salt Lake City," she said with a smirk, and he laughed at her guess, so intentionally wrong.

"Vegas, baby."

Her features registered no reaction at first. She was simply silent. Then she laughed, maybe in disbelief. "No one is from Vegas. Vegas is where you go. Not where you're from."

"Born and raised there."

She held her hand as low to the ground as she could from where she sat. "Like, back when you were little?"

He nodded again. "All the way through high school too. Happy to show you my diploma if you need more verification. Lettered in Varsity Football at Desert Hills High on the outskirts of town. Lived there till I moved east for college."

"And how does one come to live in Vegas?"

"Generally speaking, one has parents from there."

"Clearly. And your parents? What do they do in Vegas?"

"My parents do exactly what you'd expect two people in Vegas to have done. They're retired now. Mom was a showgirl. Dad owns a small casino off the strip."

"Wow. That's just so . . ." she said, then let her voice trail off.

"So what?"

"Unusual. And surprising," she said.

"Why is it surprising?"

* * *

You have got to be kidding me.

Her heart had raced when he'd first said Vegas, but she'd reined it in, relying on her well-honed poker face. Because really, what were the chances that he'd hail from the gambling mecca?

Of all the places he could be from, she'd never have thought it would be the *one* place that had so much in common with her present, and the life of gambling she'd led. She'd been a card player long before her mandatory attendance at Charlie's Tuesday night games. She'd known her way around a deck of cards since she'd taught herself to play in high school, and then continued on during college at UCLA, finding late-night games in the dorms, winning handily most of the time, collecting extra money for her expenses, for textbooks, and meal plans. Back then, playing had been fun, something she enjoyed. She and her sister had taken many girls' trips to Vegas too in their early twenties. McKenna could never back down from a challenge, and even though board and video games were more of her sister's speed, she was the ideal cheerleader when they'd played the tables late at night at the Bellagio.

"Just because you hardly meet anyone from Vegas, that's all I mean," she said, making light of her comment. She wasn't going to tell him more. Not even McKenna knew how much Julia played these days, and how desperately she needed to win. Only her hairdresser had an inkling. It was better that way, safer that way for everyone. McKenna had had a rough go of things for a while with her douchebag of an ex-fiancé, but now that she'd met Chris she was happy beyond measure. Julia wasn't going to ruin her sister's happiness by letting her know about the crap she was dealing with. McKenna would only be worried, like a good big sister.

There was nothing McKenna could do about her debt, so there was no reason to let her know. She *had* to shield her sister from her troubles. If she kept McKenna in the dark, she could better protect her from Charlie's shadow, and any harm he might do. The same went for Charlie; the less he knew about her family, the better. Chris and McKenna both ran successful, high-profile video shows; she didn't want Charlie to get a piece of them. They were precisely the type of meal he enjoyed best —they were flush with green.

"You like Vegas?"

"I do. And I can hold my own at a blackjack table."

"Yeah?"

"Why? You think women can't gamble?"

"Why would I think that? Do I look like a sexist pig?"

"No," she said with a laugh, and held up her hands in surrender. "Do you play?"

He nodded. "I play poker a couple times a month. One of my lawyer buddies has a regular card-game going on. A few of my clients play."

"Do you let them win?"

He laughed, and shook his head. "Never. They'd know if I were letting them beat me. Besides, they're A-list actors and producers."

"Name dropper," she said, bumping her shoulder against his.

"Did I say their names?" he tossed back. "Anyway, they don't give a shit how much they win or lose."

"Nobody likes losing," she said, trying to keep the sharp edge from her voice. She despised losing because it kept her chained to that man, tied even longer to a debt that wasn't hers. Nobody could shrug off losing. But then, what did she know? She didn't have tons to gamble with, so she hated losing even more.

"True, but we all just play for fun. Nothing more, nothing less. Couple guys, smoking cigars, talking shit, and laying down some bets. My second-favorite pastime," he said, raising an eyebrow.

She flashed him a naughty grin, but inside, a sliver of envy wedged itself in her heart. She wanted to love the game, and part of her still did. But that part was crushed like an old cardboard box by the weight of all that she owed. Charlie had subverted both her skill and her love of poker into something dirty, making her his ringer to take down poker babies. Someday she'd like to play again for fun. Hell, maybe she could even tolerate losing if she didn't face the consequences of knives, guns, and threats to her livelihood.

"I know what your first favorite pastime is," she said, trailing her finger along his thigh.

"We could combine the two. You'd be nice to play strip poker with," he added.

"I'd beat you," she said instantly. She knew she would. Confidence coursed through her.

"I'd have to say in that game with you, I'm winning either way."

"You're an interesting man, Clay Nichols," she said, smiling at him. But smiling inside, too. She was enjoying herself so much, and so much more than she had in ages. There was something about him that simply worked extraordinarily well with her. They had chemistry in the bedroom in spades, but they could talk, too, and that was a magical thing. Rare, too. You didn't often come across someone who captivated your mind and your body. "I want to know more about you. So, you have a little brother. Where does he live?"

"Ah, the topic you were saving for dinner. Brent is in Vegas too."

"Wait. Let me guess." She flung her hand over her forehead, mimicking a fortuneteller. "He's a magician. He has an act with tigers and disappearing roses."

He shook his head. "Nope. But you're close in that he's on stage. He's a comedian."

She shook her head, bemused with his family story. "Your family does all the things you never really think anyone does."

"And we have Thanksgiving together every year, too. Mom makes a turkey, Dad carves it, and Brent bakes a pumpkin pie."

"Oh, stop. That's far too normal to be believed. Aren't you supposed to have issues? Like everyone these days? Hate your dad or mom? Or something," she said because her ex, Dillon, certainly was like that. Most of the men she'd known were prickly toward their families and, come to think of it, that might be yet another reason why they were exes. Shouldn't a man have a little respect for his mom and dad? There was no badge of honor given for hating your parents simply because that's what most modern men and women did.

"What can I say?" He held out his hands in mock surrender. "I aim to defy modern stereotypes. I might have grown up around gamblers, tits and ass, but there was no drama. No dysfunction. Why? Were you thinking I had some horrible childhood, and that's why I like to talk dirty to you?"

She pressed her finger against her lips, and peered at the ceiling as if in deep thought. "Actually, I kind of figured you were the same as me, and that you just liked it that way."

"Damn straight. I'm not playing out some childhood trauma in the way I like to have sex," he said in that smooth, confident voice she loved.

"Sometimes a cigar is just a cigar."

"You'd look sexy smoking a cigar. But then you'd look sexy in just about anything. Which is sort of my point. I like what I like, and I like it all with you."

A shiver raced through her blood at his words. She brushed her lips against his jaw. "I feel the same about you," she whispered, and he took her in his arms quickly, a warm, strong embrace. He didn't say anything, just breathed her in, and she did the same. The moment felt suspended almost, existing in its own blissful bubble of possibility. Her mind toyed with the potential of the two of them, of the ways this moment could turn into many more. She liked being with him so much, maybe too much.

"What's your story?" he asked after she slipped slowly from his hold. "Do you bake pumpkin pie at Thanksgiving?"

"I'm more of a pecan pie kind of gal. And yes, I have one of those—shockers—normal families too. Though not nearly as exciting as yours. Mom's in real estate, Dad's an orthodontist, and they live in Sherman Oaks, California, where I grew up. My best friend is my sister. Well, my other best friend is my hairstylist, Gayle, but then, who else does a woman tell all her secrets to but her hairdresser?" she said playfully.

"I hate secrets," Clay said in a harsh tone with narrowed eyes. His words jolted her, as if she'd been shocked by the unexpected ire in his statement. Julia's gaze drifted down; his fists were clenched.

"What do you mean?"

"Secrets eat away at people," he said, practically spitting out the words on the red counter.

She'd touched some kind of nerve.

CHAPTER FIVE

Okay, fine. She got it—secrets could suck. But she had a big one, and she didn't need or want to feel like she was doing something wrong by keeping it. She had no choice. She was boxed in by her awful ex and what he'd done to her, and now by what Charlie was doing to her as he made her pay for Dillon's crimes—crimes he blamed on her. Some days she felt like she'd never get out from under it all. Not from Charlie, and not from the need for secrets and lies.

She grabbed the steering wheel of the conversation and swerved out of the way of the topic. "I have a secret I can tell you. Mine is that I'm wearing no underwear."

That earned her a wicked grin. He laid a strong hand on her knee. "Hardly a secret. I knew that. Tell me things that are secret now, but won't be in a few seconds. Tell me what you love most in the world," he said.

"Cupcakes, my sister, and freedom," she said, and truer words were never spoken.

"And what do you hate most?"

That was easy. Too easy. "Being made a fool. Owing things," she said, and because she didn't want to discuss it more she turned the question back on him. "What do you love most in the world?"

"Scotch. Ties. Movies. Family."

"And what do you hate most?"

"Lies. I hate lies."

"But you're a lawyer," she said, furrowing her brow.

"So that means I can't dislike lies?"

"Don't you have to lie for a living?"

"No. I don't have to lie," he said, and his voice was strong and passionate. "I fight. I fight for what my clients want. There's a difference."

"What else do you fight for?"

"For the things I want."

"Do you want me?" she asked, turning the conversation down another street yet again.

"I want you so fucking much, Julia," he said, and he wasn't giving an order or a command this time. There was something almost naked in his voice, a vulnerability that he let show now and then. He pulled her close, buzzed his lips along her jaw, then up to her ear. "I meant it when I said I couldn't stop thinking about you all week. I wanted to fuck you, and I wanted to talk you. I want to spend more time with you. I want to get to know you more and more. You fascinate me," he said, kissing her neck, his sandpaper stubble rough against her skin, the feel of him melting her inside.

His words sent a shudder through her, filling her with that delicious feeling of falling in like with someone. Of flutters and wishes and the hope for more—more time, more moments. But saying she wanted more was hard for her. Letting someone in was even tougher, because she knew where it might lead to —to her being owned in yet another way she'd never see coming. So she shifted back to the pure truth of the physical.

"Now you're turning me on again," she whispered.

"It's a good thing you're not wearing any panties."

"Oh yeah? Why's that?"

He pulled away, glanced around the restaurant as if he were sweeping it for spies, then reached into his back pocket. There were a few other diners at nearby tables, as well as the bartender and the waiter. He took his hand from his pocket, his fingers curled around in a fist, like he was hiding something.

"Are you a good actress?" he asked.

"Sure. Why?"

"Because I'm going to test you right now." He slid his hand under her skirt; her legs were hidden under the edge of the counter. Then she felt it—a buzzing against her bare thigh.

"What is that?" She hitched in her breath.

"Something I got for you," he said. "Do you like coming?"

"Uh, yeah."

"Our dinner will be here any minute," he said, tipping his chin towards the waiter who scurried to the kitchen. "I want you to come before he arrives with the food."

"Clay," she said under her breath, but when he pressed his finger against her center, she bit her lip to silence her groan. The sensation was intense. He had some kind of mini-vibrator strapped to his index finger, and he wasn't messing around. He was hitting her right where she was hot for him, and the sudden friction against her clit turned her insides molten.

"Show me what a good actress you are."

"I'm a great actress," she said, through gritted teeth as he teased the vibrator in a dizzying circle around her flesh. Delicious sensations flooded her body, and she fought her impulse to hold onto the edge of the counter, as he rubbed her faster, sending sparks racing through her bloodstream.

A couple having dinner a few tables away pushed back their chairs, the legs scraping across the wood floor. The man held the woman's coat, and the woman looked in Julia's direction as she slid her arms into the sleeves. Julia plastered on a fake smile, pressing her lips firmly together, shutting inside her mouth all the moans and scream and cries she wanted to unleash.

"I'm looking forward to eating. I hope the food arrives soon," Clay mused, keeping one hand under her skirt as he reached for his scotch with his free hand. He tapped her clit with the vibrator, gently but insistently, sending an exquisite pulse between her legs that spread like ripples, reaching all the way to her fingertips.

Oh God. She wanted to roll her eyes in pleasure, to spread her legs wide.

"What about you, Julia? You hungry for your risotto?" He tilted his head to the side, giving her a deliberately curious stare.

"Sure." She sucked in a moan as a wave of intensity slammed down. She ached with a desperate desire to be touched, to be felt. *To come.* He moved his finger back and forth, the pad of the vibrator driving her into another world of pleasure. Involuntarily, her shoulders curled in.

"You okay?"

"I'm fine," she choked out.

"You sure?" He stroked her fast, then faster. "You don't seem like yourself?"

"Just hungry," she muttered as he pushed harder against her swollen clit, bathing her entire being with the thrilling sensations of vibration. She could barely take it anymore. She'd been reduced to nothing but feelings, the raw physical need for release from the flames lapping up her being. She wanted to throw back her head, run her hands through her hair, slide her palms down her own body to savor every second. But she knew how to bluff. She knew how to fake it.

"I think the food's on its way," he said, gesturing with his eyes to the kitchen door. The waiter appeared, holding it open with his elbow, balancing plates along his arm.

Julia swallowed hard, and wanted to pant, to moan, to scream. She wanted to climb up the walls, to rub herself against Clay's thigh, something, *anything* to relieve the build inside that was teetering on the edge of explosion.

"Looks like he'll be here any second. What about you? You ready?"

"I think I might be," she said in a choppy voice, trying so hard not to give an inch.

But he was hitting her where her body sang, turning her up, all the way on. And if she were alone with him, she'd have grabbed his shoulders and held on hard. Instead, she gripped the edge of the stool, her sharp nails digging into the wood, surely leaving scratch marks as she channeled there all her desires to writhe and moan and let herself bathe in the bliss of the orgasm that rocketed through her body. She was coming, and there was nothing she could do to stop it. The orgasm was on a high-speed chase, tearing around curves, racing through every cell. Julia Bell was coming at the bar, eyes wide open, lips sealed shut, body still as still could be. Every inch of her was lit up and ignited.

The waiter set down their plates as her entire body buzzed with the delicious tingles of an orgasm she hid fiercely.

"Your risotto, miss," he said, gesturing to the plate. Then he set down Clay's meal. "Do you need anything else?"

"I believe I have everything I could possibly want," Clay said, then flashed a quick smile, before turning to her. "What about you? Do you need anything more?"

"I'm good," she said, her eyes bugging out.

"Are you sure?"

"Yes," she said with a satisfied sigh, that one syllable strung out, the only hint of what had just gone down.

The waiter left, and she picked up her fork. "I am famished."

"You deserve some sort of award for that performance."

"My reward will be torturing you when you least expect it."

"I will count down the seconds until that kind of torture comes my way."

CHAPTER SIX

Her phone woke her up in the morning.

She'd turned the damn thing off last night, seeing as she was spent and exhausted from her time with Clay, but now it was buzzing. McKenna probably wanted more details on last night, since they always shared these kind of tidbits with each other—not the nitty-gritty sex details, but the *so you really like him* part. It had been a long time since Julia had actually *liked* someone. With Dillon, the *really like him* feelings had faded well before the relationship ended. Sure, she'd fallen for him in the start, for his self-deprecating humor, for his piercing blue eyes, for the sweet nothings he whispered to her that made her feel special.

She met him when he was one of her students at a weekend class she'd been teaching at a boutique bar in Noe Valley on the art of making cocktails. She'd taken on the class before she bought a stake in Cubic Z; the class helped supplement her bartending income. And Dillon had been her finest student, his keen eye for detail giving him a leg up as he mixed and matched the perfect amounts.

"You, sir, concocted a most excellent Margarita," she told him.

He'd tapped the side of the glass, and said, "Someday I'll be sipping this in Bora Bora or the Bahamas."

"Wouldn't that be nice? Sitting on a hammock in the sun with a nice cool drink."

"Blue skies and mixed drinks," he added. "A perfect getaway."

One time, after everyone else had left, he'd hung back, raised his hand as if in a classroom, and asked, "I have a question. I know student-teacher relationships are generally forbidden. Does that apply to bartending school, too?"

"Terribly forbidden. Violates all sorts of mixed-drink laws," she teased.

"Call me guilty then," he said, and then asked her out.

They'd gone to a Turkish restaurant in Russian Hill for the first date, then for a walk through that neighborhood. A photographer, he'd made a decent wage shooting interiors of homes in the city for realtors, so he showed her the outside of some of the homes he'd shot, including a rather tiny one that he'd made look palatial in a picture. He used to say that with the right-angled shot he could make any room look "spacious, open and well-lit."

Later, after they became a couple, he was the one who had encouraged her to expand her role at Cubic Z, and to invest in the bar. She didn't regret that decision, not one bit, though she sure as hell regretted him, and wished she'd gotten out sooner.

All his sweetness had leaked away by the end, and they were merely holding on, until he left. The unraveling of that relationship wasn't what hurt; it was the *way* it fell to pieces that stung like snake poison. The way *she* had to bear the brunt of the breakup and all he heaped on her, and she couldn't even tell McKenna the specifics. At times, Julia ached to pour out all the sordid details, especially because her sister understood heartache. But McKenna understood happiness, too. Newly engaged to a man who made her wildly happy, McKenna was in that haze of believing that every new relationship would turn out to be *the one*, so Julia fully expected a text from her sister asking when she'd be getting engaged too.

Ha. *As if* Julia were ever going to do that.

She fumbled for her phone, unlocking the screen. McKenna's name popped up and the first word she saw was *size.* She shook her head in amusement. She wasn't sure if her sister was talking about ring fingers or other measurements, but before she could open the note another text flashed.

Where is the pretty bartender? She wasn't at the bar last night. She should hope she's not skipping town. I wouldn't want to have to inquire with that other woman behind the bar. She seems like she might be preoccupied, and more so in a few months . . .

Her blood ran cold. He'd noticed Kim and her pregnant belly.

She wanted to punch the screen. That slimeball had gone to Cubic Z for one of his pop-ins. Those were the worst, when she had to serve him, and act like she didn't detest him as she poured his martinis. She hoped he hadn't bothered Kim, her hubby, Craig, or anyone else they worked with last night. She didn't want him near her co-workers. She could only imagine how that would go down, especially when Charlie took out his knife and nonchalantly scratched his chin. Those gestures were meant for her—reminders of what he was capable of.

And he was capable of a lot more than just itching a scratch. She'd gotten glimpses of Charlie's cold-blooded nature through Dillon. He'd hinted of things he'd seen while shooting pictures of the limos. Punches thrown, knees whacked, noses broken, eyes blackened . . . Charlie was a man who got what he wanted by any means possible.

Her skin crawled as she imagined him shaking down sweet Kim, the true definition of an innocent bystander.

That was the real rub, though. Everyone in her life was an innocent bystander, and she'd have to keep them innocent. The less anyone knew, the less they could get hurt. If they knew about her troubles they'd try to help her, and then they'd be in his debt somehow, and his crosshairs.

She swallowed back all her anger, and replied quickly. *Of course not. I have the weekend off. Don't worry—I'll be at the game Tuesday, and I plan on winning big again.*

Seconds later, he replied. *That confidence is so alluring.*

She sneered, then her heart beat faster at the next message, from Kim. *You'll be pleased to know there were no unsavory types here last night. Only the usual assortment of hipsters and VCs. So San Fran. Xoxo*

If only Kim knew that there was an unsavory type there last night, scoping them all out. But she planned to be back at the poker table on Tuesday night, working on winning more to line Charlie's pockets, playing hard, and taking down the marks to get out from under his yoke as soon as she possibly good.

She wrote back: *Glad to hear Cubic Z is representing the city so well. Love you madly. See you soon.*

She took a deep breath, reminding herself to push her troubles out of her mind for the weekend. She was far away from all her obligations, and she planned to enjoy her temporary break.

She shut off the phone as Clay stirred. Good—he hadn't seen her texting. He'd seemed perturbed last night when she was writing to McKenna, and she didn't want any weirdness between them. She wanted only good times with Clay, only dessert. This weekend together was the frosting on a scrumptious cupcake. It wasn't real, and that was A-OK. She sure as hell loved a cupcake, and right now she wanted another bite.

Now was as good a time as any to show this man what kind of wake-up call she could deliver, so she slinked down under the sheets and stroked him a few times, enjoying the low rumbles from his chest as he started to wake up.

She wrapped her lips around him, and instantly his hands were tangled in her hair and he held on tight as she licked and caressed him in her mouth. He groaned loudly, and she thrilled at the sound, at knowing she could do this to him, elicit this sort of reaction.

"Good morning to me," he murmured in a sleepy voice. His voice was rough, husky from the early hour, and the sound turned her on even more.

She let him fall from her lips momentarily. "It's going to be a very good morning in a few minutes."

"That's all it's gonna take?"

She arched an eyebrow. "You think I can't make you come quickly?"

"The verdict is out," he said with a lazy grin.

She narrowed her eyes. "For that attitude, Clay, you just bought yourself a wicked tease," she said and returned to his delicious cock, flicking the tip of her tongue up and down his length. He groaned lightly as she licked him, but she stopped short of taking him into her mouth.

"I'm going to take my sweet time now," she said with a purr.

"I can handle it," he said.

"I don't know if you can." She swirled her tongue around the head, then rubbed him against her lips, watching him as she administered her best torture. His chest rose up and down, and his eyes darkened as he stared at her. "It's getting harder, isn't it?"

"It sure is."

"You still want this? I'm not entirely convinced," she said, and blew a stream of air across his cock. He twitched against her lips and she quickly kissed the tip then released him.

He cursed under his breath.

"I didn't hear you. Are you sure you want me to do this?"

"I want you," he muttered, and she grinned, knowing how hard it was for him to have the tables turned.

Still, she wasn't ready to give in. She needed him to want her desperately, to need her terribly. "I think I might require you to ask real nice," she said, as she cupped his balls, lightly rolling them in her hand, then darting down to give a quick lick and kiss to that most sensitive set of parts. She gripped his shaft hard in her hand as she tasted him, and those twin actions set off a long, long moan from Clay.

"Please," he whispered, so low it was barely audible.

"I'm not sure I can hear you," she said, but started giving him his reward, taking him all the way in her mouth, surrounding his hot, hard length with her lips.

He panted hard, and nearly growled at the relief. But she stopped once again, peeking up at him, enjoying the view of his big, strong body stretched out on the sheets. "Do you want it? Ask nicely and I'll give it to you."

He shut his eyes briefly then opened them, holding her gaze. The look was both desperate and hungry. "Please suck me, Julia," he said, in a hoarse voice.

"Gladly," she said, and then gave him the full treatment. First hard, then slow, alternating between teasing him and taking him in.

"Maybe not too long now after all," he said as he gripped her head, sliding his fingers through her hair, tugging as she feasted on him. They kept at it for a bit, him rocking into her mouth, her savoring him all over. He was quieter than usual, though; he wasn't reeling off directions and telling her what to do. Maybe it was because she'd taken the reins. But then his dirty mouth woke up as he pushed her hair off her forehead, looking at her with dark eyes, "Use your teeth."

She slowed for a moment, dragging her teeth lightly against his shaft. "Like that?" she asked, glancing up at him.

The look on his face said it all as his features contorted with pleasure. "Yes. Like that," he rasped out.

"Damn, you like it rough, don't you?" she said, and returned to his cock, touching him exactly how he wanted, scraping gently with her teeth as she moved her lips up and down.

"I like it rough, but I also like pretty much anything you to do my cock," he said, and she took him in further. "Like that," he hissed out. Then she went deeper, drawing out a louder groan from his lips. "And that's fucking good too."

She swirled her tongue around the head as she gripped the base hard in a fist. He hitched in a breath. "That's perfect. Take me all the way in and use those gorgeous teeth, Julia."

Ah, there he was in full force, her dirty-talking, direction-giving man. She smiled, loving the way he used all his talents in the bedroom, his body, his tongue, his cock, and most of all, his *words*. She drew him in, nibbling and sucking and rolling his balls in her hands as he started to fuck her mouth harder, to drive deeper into her.

"You tell me now if I'm fucking you too hard, okay?" he said firmly, but they both knew she wasn't backing down. They both knew she liked it the same way he did. They were perfectly paired in the bedroom; he gave as good as he got, and she did, too. They were two tigers, tussling and tangling and taking each other, talking dirty, playing rough.

"I'm good," she said, even with her mouth full. She dragged her nails along the inside of his strong, muscular thighs, making him shiver, then grazed him right between his legs where his thighs met his cheeks, sending his hips shooting off the bed and deeper into her mouth.

"I love it when you use your hands like that. All over me. I want you all over me, your hands, your tongue. And your lips are so fucking beautiful wrapped around my dick," he said, his narration punctuated by grunts of pleasure. "Fuck, Julia, you're going to make me come so hard in your mouth right now."

She gripped the base with her palm, feeling him twitch hard against her as she sucked him off, his salty, musky taste sliding down her throat as his words started to falter, and his sentences broke into bits and pieces of truncated words. *Feels so fucking good, so good in your mouth,* and then her name, over and over, like a chant. Yes, that was her favorite dirty word that fell from his mouth, when he groaned out *Julia* with unbidden pleasure, and she couldn't help but be satisfied too to have gotten him off so thoroughly, so completely. He looked like a most contented man, a happy grin across his gorgeous face.

"Don't ever doubt me," she said playfully.

"Never." He pulled her up, drawing her next to him, and moved in to plant a kiss on her lips.

She shook her head.

"What? I can't kiss you after I come in your mouth? It doesn't bother me."

"No, that's not it. I just have to confess I hate morning breath, but I really want to kiss you, so how about we brush our teeth and then make out?"

He chuckled deeply, and smacked her ass with a strong hand. "Did I tell you yet how perfect you are? I don't like morning breath either, but then I'm not such an ass that I wouldn't kiss you if you had it." He tapped her nose with his finger. "But you don't."

"Thanks, but there's a toothbrush calling my name anyway."

After they returned to bed with minty-fresh breath, he ran a hand along her hip. "So, what else, besides morning breath? What are your other pet peeves?"

"You really want to know?"

"I really want to know. So I can avoid them," he said, holding her gaze with his own, his dark-brown eyes, so earnest and true, as if it were deeply important for him to know what irked her, so as not to do it.

"Washcloths," she said, and held out her hands as if it say, *what gives?* "I don't get it. I don't understand washcloths. Why use a washcloth to wash your face when you have hands? Put the soap on your hands and wash. Or worse, leaving a wet washcloth hanging up in the shower, because then it just becomes a damp, used, smelly washcloth."

He nodded several times as if taking detailed notes in his head. "You might have noticed I don't own washcloths. I don't need an intermediary between soap and my body."

She laughed. "Exactly. You're already ahead of the game." She looked around the room, as if searching for evidence. "Here's another pet peeve. I don't like seeing a man walking around only in his socks."

He mimed making a check mark. "Note to self: Remove socks first before taking off pants to fuck Julia."

"I don't like dirty sinks either. I see no reason for bathroom sinks to be anything but pristine."

"Did you notice how immaculate my bathroom is?"

"I did," she said with a wink. "Don't you just know the way to a woman's heart?"

"Evidently."

"I assume you were down on your hands and knees scrubbing every surface before I arrived?"

"Something like that. Or maybe I had it cleaned, knowing I was having company I wanted to impress."

She ran her hand along his strong arm over his tattoo. "You're getting the hang of it. You know what to do to stay on my good side."

"Am I on your good side?" he asked, propping himself up on his elbow.

She traced a line down his chest. "You are all good side, Mister. Nothing more."

"Good. How did you sleep?"

"Very well, thank you. You wore me out last night."

"I like wearing you out, Julia," he said, then brushed his lips against her forehead. "And I like having you in my bed."

"Your bed is pretty damn nice."

"You make it look good. I liked having you fall asleep in my arms," he said, then ran his fingers through her hair. He lowered his voice again, speaking softly, "I wouldn't mind seeing you in my bed more often."

There was something different about him in moments like this. Tenderness shined through his hard exterior; a sweetness, even. And it scared the hell out of her. Because it was easy to view him as a weekend fling. So incredibly easy. But when he was like this, she could feel the weight of one word pressing hard on her. *More.*

Like a temptress with a come-hither wave, inviting her in for *more.* More him, more moments, more getting to know each other. She wanted terribly to snuggle in close with him, lift her eyes to meet his, and say, *I want to be in your bed more often, and I want to be in your life, too.*

But she didn't have the luxury of *more.* So she made light of his comment, bringing it down to the sex level. "Oh, you just want to set some sort of record this weekend, don't you?"

"That's not what I meant," he said, and this time his voice was clear, and firm. He pulled her on top of him, threaded his hands slowly through her hair, keeping his eyes locked on her the whole time. "You know that's not what I meant."

"I know," she whispered, the words catching in her throat. She pressed her lips together so she wouldn't say too much, wouldn't admit how much she was starting to want from him.

"Kiss me," he said, giving her a command. She obeyed, exploring his lips with her tongue then crushing her mouth to his, trying to get closer, as close as she could be.

He let go of her hair, his hands drifting down to her backside. He reached for a condom and rolled it on. Then he cupped her cheeks, lifted her up, giving her full access to his erection, and she sank onto him. She inhaled sharply as he filled her, stopping momentarily to savor the sensations. He moved inside her, and it wasn't rough as she rode him. It was luxurious, and deliciously slow, and it felt disturbingly like making love, especially given the way he kissed her tenderly the whole time.

CHAPTER SEVEN

The thieves rode away in a convertible, the sunset streaking behind them, the jewels turned into money and the money tucked safely away in a bank account. The closing credits rolled, and Julia leaned in to whisper in his ear, her soft hair brushing his neck. "We need to stay for the credits."

His heart thumped a beat harder, and he couldn't deny that he was happy she'd insisted on proper movie etiquette herself. He didn't have to tell her he wanted to stay. She got it on her own.

"I always watch the credits, even when I don't have a client involved," he said, staying put in the red upholstered chair because he didn't want to miss seeing the name of the executive producer scroll up the big screen. He'd wait all the way through to the final shot, because that's what you did when you were in the biz. What happens before the credits brings butts to the seats, but what rolls on by after "The End" is why there's a movie in the first place. "But I do have a client in this film."

"Which one is yours?" she whispered as other patrons stood, and picked up emptied popcorn tubs and cartons of Junior Mints.

He pointed to the first credit. "That's my guy."

"And you took good care of him, I trust?"

He nodded. "Got him some very nice points on the back end."

She ran a finger down his arm, giving him an approving nod. "Impressive."

"I do what I can."

The names of the cast and crew, the key grip and the costumer streaked across the screen, and they watched them all. Soon, the movie reached its final frame, and silence filled the theater.

"What did you think of the movie? And don't tell me you liked it because I had a client work on it."

She rolled her eyes. "I have no need to suck up to you, Clay. You're already putting out for me. But I loved it. Especially because you're totally convinced at one point that there's no way they can walk out of the vault with all those jewels, but then it turns out there was a hidden wall," she said, her expression animated as she recounted the film.

He nodded enthusiastically. "That's exactly what I love about a good heist flick. The way the story makes you think one thing, and then all of a sudden," he said, twisting his hand to the side to demonstrate a U-turn, "you've gone the other direction."

"That's what a good story does, right? Surprises you. Challenges you."

The sweeping of a broom interrupted their conversation. Clay glanced behind him. A skinny usher was cleaning the floor of the theater. The thin theater employee dumped the contents of the dustpan into a trashcan and then left.

"I guess that's our cue to go." Clay stood up, holding Julia's hand and they exited their row. "All alone in the movie theater," he mused as they made their way up the aisle. "The things we could do."

"You never stop, do you?"

"Thinking of ways to seduce you?"

She nodded, tucking a strand of her sexy red hair behind her ear.

"Never."

"Your efforts are very much appreciated, but you do know you have this one in the bag?"

He reached his hand around her waist, tugging her in close as they left the theater, the bright lights of the lobby making him blink. "You are not the type of woman I would ever take for granted," he said, whispering low in her ear, because the words were just for her. She shivered lightly against him, and he wrapped his arm tighter around her.

"Why?"

"Why what?"

"Why am I the type of woman you wouldn't take for granted?"

He held open the door to the cinema, letting her walk onto the New York street first, admiring the view of her legs. It was a Saturday afternoon, but she was wearing black stockings and her trench coat. Heels, too. A young man in a slouchy sweatshirt stared at Julia as he walked by, nearly tripping over his Converse sneakers as he craned his neck to gawk. Clay wasn't bothered. In fact, he was a proud motherfucker to know the woman other men stared at was with him. "Because you wear stockings on a Saturday to the movies. Because you do it not just to turn me on, but because you are intrinsically sexy. Because you have this gorgeous internal confidence that has nothing to do with what men think of you. Because you stayed in the theater to watch the credits. Because you *get* why crime flicks are a damn good way to pass two hours. Because as much as I want to spend the entire weekend in bed, I also want to get to know you. Because I like talking to you as much as I like touching you. Is that enough?"

She stopped in the middle of the sidewalk, wrapped her arms around his neck, nodded her answer and planted a hard kiss on his lips. She tasted like kettle corn from the movies.

"Mmm," he growled, as a gray-haired couple sidestepped them. They were in New York City, kissing on the street, doing exactly what new lovers should do on the weekend together.

"Yes, that's enough." She grabbed his hand and laced her slender fingers through his. "And I think you are a fabulous way to pass the time," she said, and he suspected that was as much as she'd admit when it came to that most dangerous territory of *feelings*. But he'd take it; he'd happily take it.

They resumed walking, a crisp April breeze blowing past them that smelled remarkably like rain as they neared Christopher Street. The breeze billowed her coat momentarily, providing him with a full-on view of her long legs, and just the slightest peak of her panties as her skirt danced upwards too. "Because of that, too," he added.

"I arranged for that gust of wind. I ordered it to arrive at this instant."

He laughed, then gestured to a sushi restaurant at the corner. "You hungry?"

She looked at her watch. "It's four in the afternoon."

"I know. But we skipped lunch when I needed to eat you instead, and I figured once we return to my place you're definitely going to be tied up."

"See, here's the thing," she said, holding up her hands, as if offering them for shackling. "You've been promising me these ropes, Clay, and my wrists are still achingly empty."

He swatted her ass. "Get some food in you, woman, before I tie you up and tie you down."

* * *

Clay had been to this restaurant a few times, including once with his ex, Sabrina. She'd asked the sushi chef if she could lick the yellowtail. She wasn't drunk. Sabrina had never been a drinker. She'd been too in love with other substances instead, with little pills prescribed by doctors. "Little darlings for my headaches," she'd say when a migraine swooped down on her. But then the migraines, if she truly had them, became so crushing that she needed those pills more and more.

She needed them all the time. Up her nose. Every few hours.

But the worst part? The way she lied. The times she denied. How she hid what she was up to.

That was the problem. That's also why Clay didn't want any drama with Julia. He knew there were no guarantees in relationships, and certainly people had a way of making and breaking promises. Still, he was keen on this woman, he wanted to spend more time with her, and he wanted to be upfront about the past so they could have more of the present.

After they finished eating and left the restaurant, he cleared his throat. "So, what's your story, Julia? Got any deep dark secrets I should know about?"

She started coughing.

"You okay?"

She nodded, but kept hacking as they passed an art gallery. "Just a tickle in my throat," she choked out.

"Let me go back and get you some water."

She held up her hand to say no, and coughed once more. "I'm fine. But what kind of question is that?"

"An honest question. I'm just trying to get to know you," he said, his tone straightforward.

Then the sky broke, out of nowhere it seemed. The clouds heaved with heavy droplets of water, pelting them from above.

"Holy shit, that's some rain," Julia said, and grabbed at the collar of her coat, as if that would protect her from the water. A few feet away a man hailed a cab, racing to get inside the vehicle. A family down the block ducked into a coffee shop, and a car squealed to a stop at the light.

"We're only three blocks away, but do you want to go to the coffee shop?"

"No. I want to go to your place."

They picked up the pace, Julia's heels clicking loudly against the wet sidewalk. "You okay in those shoes?"

"Totally fine," she said.

"There's a little souvenir shop on the corner. Let me get an umbrella for you."

She grabbed his arm, wrapped her hand around it and pushed him against the brick wall of a shoe store. "Don't even think for a second that I can't handle a few drops of rain, Mister. I'm not some fragile flower."

He held up his hands in mock surrender. "Never said you were."

"I like the rain. And I've always wanted to kiss in the rain," she said, gripping his shirt collar, and running her fingers along it. "Now, give me one of those fabulous New York kisses in the rain that make all the girls swoon."

"Gladly," he said and cupped her cheeks in his hands, held her gaze, then moved in for a kiss, sweeping his lips softly against her, slowly kissing her in the rain, drawing out decadent little sighs and murmurs from her mouth. The sky unleashed a fire hose of water, and the rain became a goddamn downpour. Julia quickly broke the kiss, and pointed to her hair, now plastered against her head. "Okay, time to run because that was romantic for about ten seconds and now I'm just a drowned rat."

He laughed. "Somehow, you're still unbelievably sexy though," he said as he grabbed her hand.

They walked quickly, doing their best to dart and dodge passersby and sprayed-up puddles from cars. He kept his arm around her the whole way, and after another block, they were both soaked, but she couldn't deny that she liked being wet with him, even this kind of wet.

"My coat is useless," Julia shouted against the pounding rain. His jeans stuck to his legs, and her stockings looked waterlogged. Soon enough they reached his building and ran inside.

He took a deep breath once the world turned dry again thanks to four walls and a roof.

"That's a hell of an angry sky," he said as they stepped inside the elevator.

"And there's nothing romantic about getting caught in the rain."

He laughed. "Turns out that's all just a lie of the movies." He looked her up and down, her hair clinging messily to her neck, and her cheeks. Her mascara had started to run and a drop of water slipped down her face. "I know what we need."

CHAPTER EIGHT

Candlelight bathed the warm room in its soft glow. A D'Angelo album played faintly from an iPod in the bedroom, but here inside the spacious bathroom with its cream-colored tiles and marble tub, the world was warm again, and the water was the perfect temperature.

Hot.

Julia leaned back against him, her slim body aligning perfectly with his, the waterline bobbing near her breasts. He was sure he could stare at them for quite a while and not ever want to look away. They were gorgeous, full and round, with rosy nipples that he couldn't resist touching. He cupped one in each hand, kneading them.

"Hmm. Where did we leave off? Something about deep dark secrets and skeletons in the closet."

She leaned her head back against him, her hair fanning out in the water like a mermaid's. "Yes. I believe you were going to tell me about yours," she said.

"Ah, so many skeletons," he said, running his index finger across the soft skin of her belly. She sighed happily, snuggling in closer against him.

"I was once a dirty businessman and ran a Ponzi scheme like Bernie Madoff," he said with a straight face.

She turned to look at him. "Really?"

He'd said it so matter-of-factly that it had taken her a moment to realize he was teasing. "No. But the truth is, I ran a high-class call girl ring as a side business to my law practice," he said, in a deliberately confessional tone.

"Shut up." She laughed as she slinked deeper into the water.

"You got me. I never did that. A buddy of mine did, but he got out of that racket recently. Reformed."

"Good. I'm glad to hear that."

"He's the one who runs the poker games I was telling you about. He's also my go-to guy if I ever need to track down intel on someone I'm not so sure about."

"Like an investigator?"

"Sort of. He just knows stuff. He can find out anything about anybody, like that," he said, snapping his fingers. He shifted away from talk of his friend. "But those aren't my skeletons."

"What are yours, then?"

He reached for a bar of soap from the side of the tub, soaped up his hands, and began washing her legs, enjoying the feel of her sexy body sliding across his palms. "Actually, I don't think I have too many skeletons. You know about my family already. I've been a lawyer for ten years; I work hard for my clients, I like entertainment, and I hate lies," he said and she tensed instantly. He briefly wondered why she'd react that way. But then, he reasoned, nobody liked lies. She probably hated them as much as he did. He kept on going, moving from her calves to her thighs. Then he stopped because this was important, what he had to say. "They're a deal breaker for me. There's no need for lies. You agree?"

"Of course," she said quickly.

"I don't like being caught up in something that's a game, or a cheat. Been there, done that. I won't go there again," he said firmly, using his negotiation voice as memories flashed by of his ex. She was the reason he felt this way, and he needed Julia to know he didn't want and wouldn't tolerate a repeat. "I was involved with a woman named Sabrina for a few years. I thought I knew her well, but her whole life was a lie."

"How so?"

"She was addicted to painkillers, and denied it for the longest time. She started taking them for headaches, and she kept on popping more. And she became so wrapped up in it that her life was dictated by it. She missed work, she wrote fake prescriptions, and she started doctor shopping, then selling her stuff to pay for more pills: jewelry, her iPhone, Coach purses . . . anything that had value she sold off to buy more," he said, stopping to gently rinse off the soap from Julia's legs. "I tried to help her. Get her into rehab."

"How did she react to that?"

Clay shrugged heavily, the defeat of those days with Sabrina rising back to the surface. It had been a while since he'd ended things with her for good, and there certainly weren't any residual feelings or lingering love. Still, the memories had a way of wearing him down, because that last year with her had been rough. Her furtive phone calls, the late-night texts to slimy dealers and doctors who started providing for her, and the slide into all those lies. He could still recall the unabated shock he'd felt when he woke up in the middle of the night to find her rooting around in his wallet and pocketing some bills to buy more drugs.

It wasn't even about the money she took. He couldn't care less about the money. It was the lies, and the secrets, and how they both had wore away at him. That last year with her had been the worst twelve months for his firm. The only year his revenues were down from the one before. *Precipitously.* He couldn't concentrate on deals, couldn't focus on clients. The way she'd toyed with him had nearly cost him the business he'd worked so hard to build. Flynn had landed a big client for them—the action film director—and in the span of those last few months with Sabrina, Clay had gone and lost that client for them.

If he were a ballplayer, he wouldn't just have been benched. He'd have been called back down to the farm leagues for the way he'd messed up that negotiation.

"She was game for it on the surface. Did the whole contrite act. Said she had a problem and needed help. But she relapsed every time, and kept going back for more," he said, and while it had hurt like hell at the time, it didn't hurt anymore. She was the past, and he'd learned from it. He wasn't going to repeat those mistakes again.

Julia laid a gentle hand on his arm, resting it against the strong, curved strokes of his tattoo. "I'm sorry, Clay. That sucks."

"Yeah, it did," he said. "It's hard when someone you care about won't change and won't even try. I kept trying to help her and she kept promising to get help," he said, drawing a circle in the air with his index finger, "but it never happened. And so on you go."

"On you go indeed. And here you are," she said, twisting around to lay a sweet kiss on his chest. Then his shoulder. Then up to his jawline.

"Here I am."

"I'm glad you're here with me," she whispered, and it was so unlike her to let go of her hard edge, but he liked it when she did in moments like this. "I'm loving this weekend."

Here he was, falling faster than he expected to.

CHAPTER NINE

That's why he hated lies. Made sense. Made perfect sense. And, hell, she shouldn't worry because she didn't have a drug problem, like his ex had. Not even close. She had a money problem, and it wasn't her fault. But she also had a truth problem, because she couldn't tell a soul about all those dollars she owed Charlie. She certainly couldn't tell Clay. He did well for himself, and she didn't want Charlie to sink his teeth into her new man.

New man?

What the hell? It was one weekend. One moment. Nothing more, and she certainly couldn't think of him as her man, no matter how much she enjoyed every single second of these days with him, from the way he touched her to the way he made her feel in her heart.

Like it could open again.

Like she could let him in and not be burned because there was something about him that simply meshed with her. Maybe it was the way he held her, or it could be the way she felt when she was with him. *Free.*

It was a feeling she'd longed for, and it thrilled and scared her.

She buried her nerves in a kiss. Julia pressed her lips to his jawline, then tangled her fingers in his wet hair, the contact temporarily distracting her from what she knew was coming. The moment when she'd have to tell him something about her past.

"What about you?" he asked, and there it was. Her turn to share.

"You want to know my skeletons?" she said, slipping her hand down his chest, drawing a line across his fabulously firm body in an effort to rattle his focus. His breathing quickened, and his dick rose up in the water. But he reached for her hand before she could touch him.

"Don't distract me. We're talking," he said, in a tone that was playful but firm.

She pretended to pout. "But other things are more fun than talking."

"We'll get to other things, gorgeous. I promise you I have many things planned for you."

"But I have to 'fess up about the nudist colony I used to belong to first?"

"Yeah," he said with a grin, as he shifted her around so she lay against his body, her back to his front, his hard cock against her backside.

"And my days working in a high-class call ring with your lawyer friend?"

"Ha, that too."

"Fine," she said, ripping off the Band-Aid. "I have an ex named Donovan. We dated on and off for a few years. He was handsome and hung—"

"Hey, now."

"Well, not like you," she said, wriggling her rear against that evidence of how very well hung Clay Nichols was. So well. So unbelievably endowed in the length and width department. She thanked her lucky stars for that.

"Not like I'm even worried about that at all. I just don't want to hear about another man's prowess."

"Did I say he had prowess?"

"Julia," he said with a sigh. "Has anyone ever told you you're evasive?"

"Fine. How's this for non-evasive? Donovan and his schlong are history. But there was this other guy, Dillon. He was a photographer, and did some work shooting homes for realtors, making sure the rooms looked amazing and huge in all the pictures, and he also contracted with some companies in the city, taking product shots," she said, but didn't add the type of products he captured—like Charlie's limos. Nor did she add that while Charlie really did own and lease a fleet of limos, his limo company was pretty much his only legit operation. His other businesses were more of the racketeering variety, she suspected, and she had a hunch Charlie's Limos did some laundering too. Or so Dillon had told her. She operated on a "don't ask" policy when it came to Charlie. She didn't want to know about his business dealings; she already knew too much from the things Dillon had told her. It had all seemed playful at the time, when he'd come home from a photo shoot of a new stretch limo and flash a wad of greenbacks. "He paid me in cash again. I think Charlie's allergic to checks," he'd say.

"What a terrible affliction."

"They make him break out in hives."

"Receipts probably do too," she'd joked. Little had she known that Dillon was onto something, all right. He'd been dabbling with a most dangerous type of client.

"Anyway, we were together for a while," she said to Clay, pushing thoughts of exes far out of her mind. "But it was kind of fading out for the last several months. And well, truth be told, I honestly don't even know where he is."

"Really?"

"Yeah, really. It ended, and he's not even in San Francisco anymore," she said, and that was all true. Dillon had left. She had no clue where he'd gone. She had her suspicions. The Cayman Islands. Maybe Mexico. Someplace untraceable. Unfindable. Drinking Pina Coladas on the beach and having the last laugh. Yep. The laugh was on her. That was the other reason she kept her own secrets. She was ashamed, so terribly ashamed of how Dillon had tricked her. She'd been conned, and she didn't want anyone to know she'd been played for a fool.

"Why'd it end?"

"I told you. We drifted apart. Isn't that how it usually ends?"

"Usually."

"But Clay?"

"Yeah?"

"I don't want to talk about exes anymore. We've done that, and here I am in the bathtub with you, and candles are lit and music is playing, and you're hard because you're always hard, and it seems like now would be a good time for us to stop talking and start doing other things."

She stood up, reached for a towel, and dried off. Within a minute she was in his closet, selecting a white shirt and a cobalt blue tie to wear.

CHAPTER TEN

Lucky tie.

Knotted loosely at her neck, his power tie hung enticingly between her breasts, traveling down to her luscious belly button, then, like an arrow, pointing to the treasure that lay beneath her black lace panties.

She wore one of his shirts, freshly laundered and unbuttoned, and a pair of black stockings and heels.

Hottest. Outfit. Ever.

"Sit down, Mister," she instructed, pointing to the gray chair in the corner of his bedroom. The chair was usually home to whatever tie or shirt he'd tossed off at the end of the day. Now, he was parked in it, leaning back, getting ready for a show. He wore only a white towel, wrapped around his waist. His hair was wet from the bath.

She leaned forward, pressing play on her phone, giving him a delicious view of her breasts. Christina Aguilera's "Candyman" filled his bedroom, the pulsing beat deepening the already sexy mood. The lights were low, except for the one by the nightstand. He wasn't turning them off. He wanted to watch. He wanted to see everything.

As the opening notes sounded, she strutted over to him, and traced her fingernails along his neck, heating up his skin. "Welcome to the Girls in Ties club," she said with a purr.

"My favorite kind of club."

She ran her hand down his arm; her touch felt electric. "I have a feeling you will like our services."

"Does this club allow touching, ma'am? I don't want to break any rules."

"Only with certain patrons," she said, then swiveled around and walked in the other direction, giving him a fantastic look at her ass in her thong underwear. What he wouldn't do to tear that underwear off with his teeth right now. Bend her over, get on his knees, and pull hard till they ripped off, revealing her beautiful, wet pussy.

His imagination was already in overdrive. She turned, bent forward and shook out her gorgeous hair, and strands of sleek, wet red tumbled along her legs. When she flipped up her head, she swayed her hips back and forth.

Provocatively.

Oh so provocatively that his cock made a full tent of the towel.

She eyed his erection, her lips curving up in a wicked grin. "I see our club pleases you."

"It pleases me so very much," he said.

"Let's see if we can help you appreciate it here even more," she said, pressing her hands to her belly, then running them up her stomach.

She began to play with the buttons on his shirt, peekaboo, showing one breast, then hiding it under the fabric, then the other. She yanked the shirt closed, feigning innocence as she spun around, her hands on her knees now, shaking that delicious ass for him as the chorus of the song played loud.

A growl rose up in his chest, and his dick throbbed. He ached to take her, to touch her, to be inside her. He was a high-tension wire. Taut. But he waited patiently, his hands on his thighs, letting her play the part as she returned to him, her heels clicking against the hard wood floor.

When she reached him, she set her hands on his legs, slowly shimmying her hips as she danced. "The staff at Girls in Ties says you ordered a lap dance."

"Did I now?"

She trailed a hand along his thigh, teasing him with her nearness to his cock. "Did you want one?"

"I do when you take off that shirt."

She arched an eyebrow and opened one side of his shirt, then pressed her right breast against his chest. "Can I do this then?"

"Yes," he grunted, his entire body rigid as he refused to move, to give into his desire to touch her all over, and to be touched.

She opened the other side now, revealing her chest to him. "And this?" She moved in closer, as if she were a cat arching its back as she rubbed her breasts against him. He inhaled sharply through his nostrils. His fingers twitched with the desire to grab her hips, and slam her down on his painfully hard erection. But he kept his palms spread on his legs as she tugged off one sleeve, then another, dropping the white shirt onto the floor. She turned around, wearing only her thong, stockings, heels and his tie. She lowered herself onto his thighs, still covered in his towel.

"Oh my, it seems you like a lap dance, don't you?"

"Yes," he said in a strained voice, his hands itching to hold her.

She gyrated up and down, teasing him as she brought her delicious ass dangerously close to his erection, but not close enough. She wriggled lower, and once, just once, ground against him. He hissed out a harsh breath. He could feel her heat through his towel.

"You're soaked," he said.

She turned around, planting one high heeled foot on the arm of the chair, the other firmly on the ground as she rocked her hips towards him. "No, sir. I am slippery. I thought we established this already."

"Let me find out how wet you are."

"Only if I can find out how hard you are," she said, punctuating her retort with a thrust of her hips close to his face. He could smell her arousal, the delicious scent of her pussy so near to him. He wanted to inhale her, to be drenched in her juices. No longer able to restrain himself, he lifted a hand, and hooked his finger into the waistband of her panties, stretching the cotton panel against her.

"Oh," she said playfully, eyeing his hand. "Are these in your way?"

"Yes. They are obstructing my view. I want to see how you look right now," he said, then slid the panties down her legs. His breathing turned erratic as he watched her be revealed, the tiniest thread of her silky desire glistening from her lips to her underwear like a trail of evidence as he pulled off the scrap of fabric. He couldn't take it anymore. He needed to taste her, to drown his mouth in her scent, to feel her wetness all over his face.

But more than that, he wanted her screams of passion to fill his ears. He wanted to see reckless desire smashing through her body. He wanted to control her pleasure. As she began to open his towel, he grabbed her hand to stop her. "No."

"I can't touch you?"

"Not yet. Go get on my bed," he said, letting her know he was taking the reins now.

"The dance is over?"

"The dance is fucking over, and I'm going to show you what you did to me," he said as he stood, tearing off the towel, letting her know how much he wanted her. Her eyes darkened with lust as she stared at his cock. Her reaction made him hotter, harder.

"I'm being punished for turning you on?"

Another shake of his head. "No. You are being rewarded for turning me on. But we're doing it my way. You teased the fuck out of me, and now I want to watch you squirm. Crawl up on my bed and get on your hands and knees."

She held up her wrists, a sexy wink in her eyes. "I've been waiting for this."

"Go, woman. And leave your shoes and stockings on."

She strutted over to the bed. He followed, watching as she climbed up, and positioned herself on all fours in the middle of the white comforter on his king-size bed. His tie dangled down from her neck onto the covers. He joined her on the bed, bending over her, and reaching his hands around to her neck. "I'm going to untie this now, and use it for something else," he said, quickly unknotting it. The tie fell into his hands as she rocked back into him. He brought a hand down to her ass, spanking her hard.

"Did I say you should rock your ass against me?"

"No."

"Do you want to be spanked again?"

"Maybe I do," she said in that taunting voice, wriggling against him once more.

She was rewarded with another smack, and that drew out a long low moan as she arched her back.

"I'll check to see how much you like it," he said, dipping his hand between her legs to test her love of spanking. Oh yeah, there was the proof, so he slapped her once more, and she drew in a sharp quick breath.

Then he tugged her hands together, sending her falling forward onto her elbows. He wrapped his tie around her wrists, once, twice, then pulled it between them to tighten the hold. Finishing it off with a strong knot, he tied the loose end to the headboard. He grabbed a pillow, and stuffed it under her chest. "This is if you need to muffle your screams."

"Assuming you make me scream," she said.

"I will make you scream, Julia. I will make sure the neighbors know how good you're about to get it."

He moved to appraise his handiwork. She was on her knees and elbows, her hands bound together with his cobalt blue tie through the slats in the headboard, her gorgeous body stretched taut.

"Mmm," he murmured, stroking his chin. "Fucking perfect."

"So now what?"

"Now, I am going to tease the ever loving fuck out of you, gorgeous," he said, and ran his hands from her shoulders down her sexy back to her ass. Placing his thumbs on that most favorite spot where her legs met her ass, he spread her cheeks. "You have the most perfect ass I have ever seen. The things I could do with this ass," he mused.

"What sort of things?"

"Oh, you'll see," he said, teasing her with his thumbs, dragging them gently between her legs. "Did dancing for me get you hot? Don't sass me, or I will take my hands off of you," he said sliding one finger lightly across her entrance.

"Yes," she whispered.

"Could you feel your panties getting hotter with each move you made on me?" He rubbed his finger lightly against her swollen clit, and she moaned, lifting her rear higher. An invitation. A beautiful fucking invitation as she showed him with her body, with her moves, how much she wanted this.

"Yes. I could feel myself getting all hot and bothered, Clay."

"Tell me what it felt like."

"I felt like I was on fire between my legs. I was aching and practically gushing in my panties," she said, her words making him groan as he pushed his thumbs against her soft flesh.

"It made me so hard to see you strutting around my house, wearing my clothes, tying my tie, and teasing the fuck out of me," he told her. "You want to see how much?"

"Yes, please."

He let go of her ass, and dragged the head of his cock against her, coating himself with her glorious wetness. A low rumbling took hold in his chest at the feel of her, so wet, so ready.

She whimpered when he pulled away.

"But I'm not giving it to you just yet." He grabbed her ass hard, spreading her legs open wider, giving him the perfect view of her glistening pussy that was so damn tempting he could not resist burying his face between her legs. The second he made contact she groaned his name, a plaintive plea for more of his tongue. But he didn't plan to give her his tongue right now, so he flicked once against her clit, then stopped.

"That is for teasing me," he said sharply.

"*Clay,*" she cried.

"What do you want, gorgeous? Tell me what you want."

"I want more."

"No, you want to be fucked. I can see it as I stare at this beautiful sight," he said, returning his hand between her legs, and cupping her. "You're making my whole hand wet."

"Because I want you," she said, and he could hear the need in her voice turning into a ragged kind of desperation.

"I would be a cruel bastard to deny your pussy right now," he said, then plunged a finger inside her, and instantly, she screamed.

He thrust his finger in and out, bringing his other hand around to squeeze one of her breasts. He was bent over her, fucking her hard with a finger, and kneading her breasts, all while she could do nothing but rock into his hand.

She tightened around his finger.

"You needed more you said?" he asked.

"God, yes."

He thrust two fingers inside her, and felt her clench against him, her pussy drenching him with her arousal. "Now fuck my hand, Julia. Fuck my hand like you fuck your own fingers when you masturbate."

"You think I masturbate to you?"

"I know you do, gorgeous. I know you do. Now show me how or I'll stop," he said, pausing inside her, giving her the chance to feel what it was like to want to be fucked badly. Within seconds, she rocked into his fingers.

"That's how," she said, her breathing rushed, as she pumped herself onto his hand, thrusting up and down on his two fingers. "That's how I fucked my own fingers when I got off to you this week."

"I like it when you tell me the truth. Because when you do, I can reward you the way I like. Now, you keep riding my hand, and I want to feel you come all over me," he said, rubbing his thumb against her wet and throbbing clit as she rode him, and soon he felt her tighten all over his fingers.

She pushed back hard then screamed his name, her entire body writhing against his hand. Her noises echoed around his house, and soon, but not too soon, she slowed down. It was then that he nibbled on her bottom, and the next sound from Julia was one of surprise.

* * *

She gasped.

She was in another world right now, blissed out beyond any and all recognition. Barely aware anymore of what he was doing to her. Drugged out on his touch, her whole body felt boneless and beautiful at the same time. And he wasn't done with her. Not in the least. His hands were sliding all along her back, so firm and strong as he mapped her with his fingers, all while kissing the outline of her rear.

Her ass was in the air, and it was his for the playing. She had no clue how far he planned to go, or if she'd let him. Probably not *that* far, but she couldn't deny the way her insides melted as he ran his tongue along her ass, tracing the cheeks, then dipping down between her legs, darting against her molten center.

She could barely form words now. Could hardly talk after that orgasm. All she could manage was his name. "*Clay.*"

"I got this," he whispered. "I'll take care of you."

"I know," she murmured, sounding and feeling thoroughly intoxicated.

He returned to his kissing, this time beginning at the back of her knees, so he could lick his way up her thighs.

"Oh God," she whimpered, because his tongue was magic. He returned to her backside, flicking his tongue across her flesh, and then he kissed her between her legs. She wasn't sure if her pussy could handle it right now, being worked over by his epic mouth, but she was willing to see. But then, maybe that's not where he was headed.

Because . . . oh . . .

Was his tongue *there*? Was it supposed to feel that good? Her body answered for her, and she rocked back into him. A long needy moan escaped her throat as he flicked his tongue against her ass, spreading her cheeks wider with his thumbs. She felt so vulnerable, so open to him right now, and though some part of her was tempted to toss out a snarky comment, she was without words as he licked her, surprising her with how very much she enjoyed where his tongue was. Only him, only this man could get away with doing that. Tenderly, he pressed his thumbs against her cheeks, rubbing a finger along her pussy gently, all while licking her ass.

Sensations flooded her veins, pleasure pulsing through her body as he touched her in new ways, showing her what a masterful lover he was and how much he delighted in pleasing her. Because he did please. Oh, did he ever. Hot flames spread inside her, lighting up her skin as he worked his tongue against her rear with quick, hard flicks.

Soon, she felt her belly tighten, her sex clench, and she called out his name as another orgasm roared through her, chasing waves of pleasure all the way to her fingertips. Her vision blurred as she squeezed her eyes shut, giving in to the sensations, to the way he simply took her and led her down this path of absolute and pure pleasure. She sank down onto her elbows, her back bowing. She was damn near about to collapse, but she still wanted more of him.

"Keep that ass up in the air, gorgeous," he said, and she heard him tearing open a condom wrapper and rolling one on. He smoothed his hands along the backs of her thighs, causing her to quiver, as he lifted her ass higher, giving him the access he wanted to her pussy.

In one quick move, he was inside her, his hard length filling her so completely that she was sure this was the definition of intensity. She moaned and rasped out his name. "Clay. It feels so good to have you inside me."

"There's no place else I want to be right now," he said, wrapping his hands around her hips, holding her tight. "Look at you," he said, as he thrust into her, his cock stretching her so exquisitely that it was almost unfair to feel this good. "On your hands and knees, all tied up on my bed. Your perfect fucking body, here for me to take."

"You can take me anyway you want," she said, her voice more hot and bothered than it had ever been.

"I want to take you in every way possible," he said, driving deeper into her, his cock scraping across her swollen clit with each delirious thrust. "Watch you writhe in pleasure. Knowing I did that to you."

She wriggled against him, showing him how she moved for him. "Like this? You like when you make me writhe like this?"

"Yeah, it makes me harder," he said, his voice turning hoarse as he started to pump faster.

She could barely move with her hands tied to the headboard, but she didn't need to, because he was making sure she was in heaven again, taking her, sliding into her, gripping her hips the whole time. She rocked back into him, picking up the rhythm too, and soon they were in an achingly sinful synch.

"You're going to come again," he said roughly, bending over her back, his chest touching her as he braced himself with his hands on the bed. He covered her completely, and there was little she could do, but little she needed because this was all instinct, all natural, all intense pleasure that tore through her body. He gripped her tied-up wrists, holding them tight as he thrust deeper into her, taking her like he owned her.

Tonight he did. And though she hating being owned, in this moment she relished it. She savored it, thrilling at the feel of this strong man controlling every ounce of her pleasure and every square inch of her body. She was barely aware of how loud she was, of the sounds that escaped her lips, the animal-like cries as he filled her to the hilt.

But soon, she was heading for the cliff and he was riding her there, charging headfirst into another climax. "Bite down on the pillow when I make you come again," he said.

She muffled her screams as she raced to the other side, shattering into pure white-hot bliss.

"You make me come so fucking hard, Julia. So. Fucking. Hard," he said, driving into her, as he joined her.

CHAPTER ELEVEN

The moon glowed overhead, bathing the balcony in a shimmery light. Julia was snuggled in one of Clay's sweatshirts. It had the name of his alma mater across the front, and for some reason that made her like wearing it even more. Maybe because it was not only his, but it also said something about him. He was a man who knew his stuff. He was passionate about his work, dedicated, driven.

But then, Dillon had known his stuff too, hadn't he? He was a passionate photographer, until, well, until he took off. Hell, maybe he was shooting beach shots somewhere. She hadn't a clue.

She angled her chopsticks into the carton of pad thai, dug out some noodles and took a bite. Lounging across an outdoor bench, her legs rested on his thighs. He'd covered the bench with a blanket because the wood was damp from the earlier rain. Now, the night sky was quiet, and the faint hints of the earlier storm clung to the air.

He was clad in boxer briefs and a T-shirt that showed off his sexy, sculpted arms. She found herself enjoying the view immensely, even though she'd enjoyed plenty of views of him undressed already. He was ogle-able at all times—in a dress shirt, in a T-shirt, in his birthday suit.

"Mmm. This hits the spot."

He took a bite of the noodles too. "We worked up an appetite."

"I'll say," she said, then set the carton down on the table. He reached for her legs and began rubbing her calves, gently massaging them with his strong hands.

She stretched and wiggled closer, delighting in the relaxing feel of his firm hands sending a new kind of pleasure through her, one that made her muscles sing, and her veins flood with warmth. "You are too good to me," she murmured.

"Only way I want to be," he said and sighed happily, a contented sound as he rubbed her legs, then moved down to her feet, cupping her ankle in one hand as he massaged the arch of her foot with his thumbs. "I figure your feet can use this, with those crazy heels you wear."

"I like my crazy heels."

"I love your crazy heels, and I want to make sure you can keep wearing them."

"How do you like them best?" she said, playfully.

"With your legs wrapped around my neck."

She smiled at him, a woozy sort of contentment bathing the night. "What time is it? I feel like I lost all sense of the world around me tonight."

He bent down to kiss her shin. "Good. That's how it should be. And to answer your question, it's nearly midnight."

A brief hit of tension touched down in her body, like an alarm. Tomorrow night at this time, she'd be headed home. This weekend—perfect as it was—would be over. It would be a delicious memory, but only that. A slice of her life that was in the past.

There was a part of her that wanted to stop time, and live in this escape to New York for a while, forget her debts, forget her obligations, forget Kim and her hubby and the rest of the employees at Cubic Z. Ignore the whole wide world and live in this bubble of sex and chemistry and the delicious sort of getting-to-know you that fools a person into falling. Boy, was she falling for him, headfirst into a crazy kind of like, the kind that made her want to send him sweet texts and naughty texts, that made her want to talk to him about everything and nothing, that made her want to hear all about his day. Every day.

To be the first person he saw in the morning, and the last one he saw at night.

What a crazy notion. She must be high. Intoxicated on epic sex. She needed to clear her orgasm-clouded head.

"So, Miss Julia. How's this going to work out?"

She raised an eyebrow inquisitively. "What do you mean?"

He pointed from her to him, speaking in a clear, firm voice. "You and me. I don't want this to just be a one-time thing. I want to see you again."

She fixed him with a quizzical look. Surely, he wasn't the kind of man who wanted a long-distance relationship. But then, he said he'd been with Sabrina for a while, and she had no reason to believe he was a player, or a ladies man either. And while she wasn't sure what she wanted from him, she did know one thing for certain: she wanted to see him again. He'd rocked her world in more ways than one. With pleasure, and with laughs, and with the tender ways he had. That was the problem —he was so good for her, and she simply had no real estate in her life for this kind of potential. One of them or both of them would wind up hurt.

But she had enough problems, so she made a split-second choice—to be abundantly honest in this instant about how she felt. "I would like that," she said, without agenda, without teasing. "I live on the other side of the country though."

"I am aware of that, and I want to see you again and again. You're not seeing anyone else, are you?"

She rolled her eyes. "No, of course not. I wouldn't do that."

"And you like being with me presumably?"

"Obviously."

"So let's do this," he said in the most matter-of-fact tone. As if a relationship spanning three thousand miles were truly that easy.

"How? How are we supposed to pull this off?" As much as she liked him, long-distance love affairs had a gigantic built-in roadblock.

"There's this thing called an airplane," he said dryly. "It flies. You get on it. I get on it. We both get off on the other side."

"Oh ha ha, funny guy."

"Why thank you very much. I like to make sure all departments are fully functional, including the humor one."

"Well, it is. But I do work a ton, you know," she said, her natural instinct to erect walls rearing its head.

"As do I."

"So it might not be that often that we can see each other."

"If you are not interested in this continuing, you should just say so, rather than point out the obstacles," he said, his dark eyes fixed on hers, his gaze serious and intense.

She opened her mouth to speak, but it was as if she'd been injected with an overdose of nerves. One she needed to ignore. "I am interested in this continuing," she said, and it felt like an admission, as if she were confessing something hard but true. Because this was only supposed to be one weekend. This wasn't supposed to be more. But the idea of this—them—ending after one weekend felt like a stone in her chest.

"Good," he said, running his fingers across her calf. His touch was something she was already used to, and already going to miss desperately. "We will manage what we can then."

"Okay, but it might get expensive."

"I don't know how to break this to you gently, so I'm just going to be blunt. I do well for myself. I have frequent flyer miles and a credit card that works."

She heaved out a playful sigh, even though inside that was part of what worried her, and a big part of why she needed to keep him not just at an arm's length, but a football-field length from Charlie. He'd find a way to blackmail him, tie him up into all sorts of trouble. A prominent lawyer boasting a client list teeming with money? He'd have a field day with Clay.

"I want to see you, and I will buy you tickets and buy my own," he continued. "I also have clients in San Francisco, and Los Angeles, and I get to the west coast a lot."

"I am sure, but I don't want you paying for me. I don't like owing people," she said with firmness to her tone. She didn't want to be in anyone's debt ever again.

"I don't want to be paid back. I want to see you. I'm not buying you. I'm saying I want to date you, and some dates require a cab, and some require a town car, and some require an airline ticket. And if that's the cost of transportation—an airline ticket—if that's my fare from New York to San Fran, I don't see how that's any different than if you lived in Brooklyn and came to see me here in Manhattan over the weekend," he said, keeping his eyes locked on her the whole time as he spoke with such confidence.

"I guess, but I don't want to feel like I'm a kept woman," she said, even though she relished the idea of seeing him. He'd made a more-than-convincing argument that they should make a go of things.

He laughed hard. "No one ever in the whole wide world could keep you. I'm just going to be happy if I can spend a few hours with you."

"You like the sex that much?" she said, playfully pushing her toes against his hard abs.

"You know I like the sex. I think the part that's not getting through to you is how very much I like all the other parts. I like what's in here," he said, stretching across her to tap her forehead with his index finger, "And I like doing the things here," he said, sweeping his thumb across her lips, "that involve talking." He traveled down her chest, tracing a line between her breasts, and landing on her heart. "I also like the things I'm seeing in here."

Her heart beat in double time, and it was such a foreign feeling for her; it had been so long since she'd *felt* for someone. It scared her, but felt wonderful at the same time, too. But then, wasn't that what liking someone felt like? A little bit like stepping off the diving board, and taking the plunge? She grasped his hand, clutched it in hers, holding his against her chest. His eyes sparkled with happiness, a genuine sort of joy, as if she'd just said yes to him. Which, she supposed, she had.

"So you're gonna be my boyfriend?"

"Gorgeous, I'm not your boyfriend. I'm your lover. The only one."

"Obviously. You are my only lover. No woman could ever have you and want or need another man."

"Good. Now remember what I was saying about liking all the things we do?"

She nodded. "Yeah?"

He leaned across the bench, kissed her lips gently, then brushed them with his fingertips. The slightest kiss sent tingles through her. "I could do that and other things all night. But right now, I want you to use those lips to tell me more about you. You said your best friend is your sister. Besides your hair stylist, Gayle. Were you close to McKenna growing up, or did you become best friends later?"

Her eyes widened. She was impressed that he remembered all the details, down to her hairdresser's name. "We've always been close. We're one year apart. Irish twins, as they say. We fought like sisters do, but most of the time, we were like this," she said, twisting her index finger around her middle finger. "Read the same books, liked the same TV shows. We were both huge *My So-Called Life* junkies. The show was only on for one season, but we watched all the episodes over and over on cable, and recited the lines together, and we loved Jordan Catalano too from that show. So McKenna and I had this thing in high school when we started dating that we'd always check in on the other with a phone call."

"Ah, the old 'friend emergency call,'" he said, sketching air quotes.

"Yup," she said, nodding proudly. "But our deal was if one of us was having a bad time and needed to be saved, that person would say *I can't believe Jordan's arm is broken.* And if we were having a good time and really liked a guy we'd say, *You're watching My So-Called Life right now?*"

"Ring, ring. McKenna's calling. You better pick up."

Julia mimed answering a phone. "Hey McKenna, how's it going?" she said into her pretend phone. She paused as if listening. "Oh, I'm so glad Jordan's arm isn't broken." She locked eyes with Clay, and he grinned as she continued her phone call. "What did you say? You're watching *My So-Called Life* right now?" His smile widened, lighting up his whole gorgeous face. "That is the best show. Well, you have a good time, because I am having the best time."

She hung up her imaginary phone and ran her fingers across his stubbled jaw, rough with his more than five-o-clock shadow. "You, Mister, are better than *My So-Called Life*," she said, and was surprised by how easily the admission rolled off her tongue. This was precisely what she hadn't wanted to happen this weekend. *To feel.* To want. To have strings start to attach themselves that would extend well beyond a weekend.

But here she was, making plans, making commitments, telling him exactly how she felt.

What was she getting herself into? She needed to put on the brakes and deal with her debt first. But then Clay's mouth was on her, kissing her hard and hungry again, consuming her with his lips that made her bones vibrate and her blood sing, and all thoughts of brakes and debts and troubles turned to rubble in her brain, because desire had slammed hard into her body.

He picked her up in his arms, carried her inside, up the steps and into his bed. This time there were no ties, no binds, no hard, rough hands, though she had loved all of that.

Now, he simply laid her on his bed and kissed her from head to toe, his lips melting her from the inside out. She trembled, both from the way he touched her and from her heart thundering with hope for what they could be. They could be so good for each other. He entered her, taking his time, making slow, sweet, luxurious love to her as she wrapped her arms and her legs around him, reveling in all the ways they came together.

CHAPTER TWELVE

Brunch sounded nice. Julia envisioned one of those lazy New York mornings. They'd make love, then shower, then wander around the Village, stumble into some fantastic four-table restaurant that had fabulous French toast or decadent omelets. Wait, no. She had a better idea. They'd go to a diner, because diners in New York were the best ever, and diners in San Francisco could suck it. At the booth, his hands would be all over her, touching her back, her waist, her legs. They'd return to his place, unable to stop touching, then smash into each other in the elevator and fall into his apartment already in a state of undress. Fevered and frenzied, he'd take her one last time, the kind of urgent and desperate goodbye sex that would make them both miss each other terribly when she left for the airport an hour later, waving goodbye in her taxi, trying hard not to stare out the window the entire time as the cab drove away.

She stretched her arms over her head, enjoying that fantasy as morning sun streaked in the window, painting the bedroom in the early glow of dawn. Clay was a sound sleeper, and lay snoozing on his stomach, the covers hitting his hips. His gorgeous back, strong and muscled, was on display. She was tempted to reach out and touch him, trace lazy lines down his skin, but a light flashed on the nightstand.

Grabbing her phone, she headed into the bathroom and scrolled through her messages as she brushed her teeth.

First there was Kim saying they'd had a rocking Saturday night and raked in some serious money. Next, McKenna, saying Chris's TV show had hit an all-time high in ratings, and the network execs were talking to him about renewals. The note was followed by several exclamation points.

Then there was a message from Charlie.

Julia tensed as she opened it.

We have a big whale in town tonight. We're moving up the game. Need to see you there by nine. There is a chance for you to get a lot closer if you can take him down.

She wrote back quickly. *Can't. I won't be back till eleven.*

She set the phone down on the sink counter, finished brushing her teeth, and rinsed with a glass of water. Her phone buzzed again. *Perhaps you mistook that for a request. It was not. I will see you at nine.*

Anger slithered through her, hot, black anger at Charlie, at Dillon, at all the ways she was indebted to those two. She clicked on the message and dialed Charlie's number.

He answered on the second ring.

"I am not in town," she whispered through gritted teeth. "I can't be there."

"Red, I have seen the airline schedules. I even checked for you. And there will be a ticket waiting for you on the eleven a.m. flight back. It gets you into town at two-thirty, so you will have plenty of time to make yourself beautiful and show off those lovely breasts to help distract our high roller."

She squeezed her eyes shut, clenched her free hand, feeling like his prostitute. Like his dirty little trick to lure them in, because that's what she was. A woman used.

"Don't you get it?" she said in a low voice, not wanting Clay to hear, though the bathroom door was closed. "I can't."

"But you can. And you will. And if you don't, I will be happy to visit your bar more frequently. After all, it may very well be my bar someday soon. How do you think your pretty little friend with the baby in her belly would like working with me? Maybe we can even put her little one to work for me soon too," he said, and her insides churned with the thought. Images of sweet Kim and her family becoming part of Charlie's circle of indentured servitude made her want to vomit. Not to mention hang her head further in shame. "But I haven't decided if I will keep Cubic Z open, or if I will take great pleasure in driving it into the ground, and all that money you needed for your bar will be for naught. But you will have the reminder in front of your face to never try to take my money again," he said, and it was as if his foot were on her chest, digging in, keeping her pinned and prostrate under all his weight. "Unless you come back, and you play and you win."

If there was one thing Julia had learned in this lifetime, and in these few months being on Charlie's very short leash, it was that whoever had the leverage won. There was no bluffing when you owed money to someone who lived on his own side of the law, who operated by his rules. Call him a mobster, call him a gangster, she didn't care about the semantics. A real Tony Soprano but without the Italian heritage, Charlie was like Tony in the sense that he was the man, he was in charge, and you didn't fuck with him. There was no need for a poker face for Charlie because her cards were shit. He had a royal flush. He could take what he wanted from her. She knew of his ways, had heard of all the things he'd done, how he made sure money and debts were always paid to him, and for much more than the debtor bargained for.

The interest he charged damn near killed you.

When you owed him, he owned you and that meant everyone you cared about was in line if you couldn't pay the vig. Soon, he'd encroach further, plucking at her family, her friends, all her loved ones. She couldn't take the risk of pissing him off. He'd hurt someone to punish her for her impudence. She had no choice but to abide by his wishes.

"Fine. I will see you tonight."

She stabbed the end button on her screen, but it was thoroughly unsatisfying. She pushed both hands roughly through her hair, grabbing hard against her scalp, something, *anything* to unleash her agitation. She wanted to shake a fist at the sky, to slam her phone onto the floor. But in the end, she'd have to do what Charlie told her to do. Come home, slide into a tight black dress, and too-high heels, and sit down at the table ready to be ogled and to win. She was his secret weapon, a one-two punch with boobs and talent.

She looked at the time. The flight he wanted her on left in two hours.

The back of her eyes burned, the start of a thick sob threatening her. She inhaled sharply, drawing her hurt back inside, sucking it down. She was a fool for thinking she could manage any sort of relationship while she was still clawing her way out of the mess her last relationship had left for her. But that's what she was—a fool, a mark, a pawn. She'd been taken, Dillon had scammed her, and she had no clue it was happening until it was done. Damn him, leaving her saddled with this while he got off scot-free. Leaving her no choice but to walk away from a man she was starting to feel real things for.

But feeling more for Clay would only put him in the line of fire. She had to extricate herself before she made her problems his problems. No one wanted that kind of shit in their lives.

* * *

She was stuffing her clothes in her suitcase. Clay rubbed his eyes, and covered his mouth as he yawned. Maybe he was seeing things, but it sure looked like Julia was fixing to get the hell out of Dodge. Dressed in jeans and a sweater, she was tugging the zipper closed on her suitcase.

"I thought your flight wasn't till five," he said, scrubbing his hand across his jaw.

She shook her head. "I got it wrong. I transposed the times. It's 11:05, not 5:11."

"Let's just change it then."

"I tried. The later flight is booked," she said, and her voice was strained, as if she were speaking through a sieve.

"Really?" He arched an eyebrow.

"Yes, really," she said, but she didn't look at him. She kept tugging and yanking at her suitcase. He got out of bed to help, kneeling down on the floor next to her. His shoulder bumped hers, and she cringed as if he'd burned her.

"You okay?"

"Yeah, fine," she said, crisply as he closed the suitcase for her.

"You don't seem fine."

"I just need to go, that's all. I hate being late and missing flights. It totally stresses me out," she said, and there was a hitch in her voice, as if she were about to cry. Did she have some kind of bad childhood memory about missing a flight? Because she sure as hell seemed sadder than the moment warranted.

"Let me go with you then to the airport. We can at least spend more time together in the car."

She shook her head. "That's sweet. But I just have to go. The cab is already here." She stood up. "I need to get going. I'm going to have to work tonight, too."

He cocked his head to the side, saying nothing, just studying her. He was used to negotiations, to deal-making, to knowing when someone was lying, and his hackles were raised.

She didn't seem so stressed or sad anymore. She seemed full of shit.

"Which one is it, Julia?" His words came out more harshly than he'd thought. Or maybe they were exactly as harsh as he felt. "Are you working tonight or did you mix up your flights? Because I'd buy one, or maybe I'd buy the other, but two seems like you're piling on the excuses."

She huffed out through her nostrils, narrowed her eyes. "Do not even think about accusing me of lying."

"I did not accuse. I asked," he said. "But it's interesting to see where your brain went."

Her eyes widened, and they were filled with anger. "I have to go," she said, biting out the words. "I need to get out of here. I have shit to take care of at home, and that is that. I will call you later."

"I'm so sorry to hear Jordan's arm is broken," he said, not bothering to strip the anger from his voice.

She shot him a furious look, but kept her mouth shut as she grabbed her bag, headed down the steps to the front door and out of his building.

The door clanged shut, the sound of it echoing throughout his home, leaving him with cold, empty silence.

He could have gone after her. Followed her, gently grabbed her arm, and asked if she was okay, if he'd done something wrong. But there was no point. She didn't want to be stopped. She didn't need to be stopped. She was a woman who'd made up her mind, and he had enough self-pride and smarts to know he'd been played. Especially when he grabbed his computer and sank down on the couch in his living room to look up the email from Virgin Atlantic, since he'd been the one to buy the ticket for her.

His heart dropped. Hot shame spread in his chest. He had no clue what had gone wrong, but the time on the ticket told him that all this falling had been a one-way street.

She was still on the 5:11 flight.

He cursed more times than he could count as he slammed his laptop closed. He ran a hand through his hair, anger and frustration coursing through his bloodstream. The last thing he wanted to do was sit with this feeling. He pulled on workout clothes and went to the boxing gym to spend the morning punching the bag alone, letting all his anger pour out of him, and his hurt too. The stupid hurt he felt for having been left.

He'd only known her for a short time. Had only spent a few days with her. They had been perfect, fabulous wonderful days, but even so his heart shouldn't ache without her. Like a gaping hole in his chest.

It should feel like nothing.

Like nothing. He let those words echo in his head with each punishing jab until eventually his mind was blank, and his body was tired, and he hoped against hope he'd forget her fast.

CHAPTER THIRTEEN

Even-steven.

For a card player there were worse words. Like *lost it all*, or *lost big*.

But for now, the words *even-steven* stung.

That's where she'd netted out. With nothing to show for her race home to play Charlie's whale.

"You disappointed me tonight, Red. I expected more from you," he said, as he bent over a steaming bowl of noodles. He slurped up a spoonful, the noodles trailing wetly down his chin, the last one snaking into his mouth.

He pushed his index finger down hard on the ledger next to him. "This? This blank line for you tonight? This tells me you have something else on your mind. Do you?"

She shook her head, pressed her lips together as if she could hold in all the nasty things she wanted to say to him. Her fists were clenched at her sides. "No," she muttered.

He pushed back his chair, the sound of the legs scraping across the floor of the Chinese restaurant. He rose and reached for her chin, grabbing her roughly. His calloused fingers dug into her jaw so hard that he was practically pushing the inside of her cheek into her teeth. All her instincts told her to cry out, to yelp from the sharp, cruel pain. But he'd see that as a sign of weakness, and weakness had no place in his poker circuit. If she let on, he'd throw her out and find some other way to extort her. A worse way, surely.

He angled her chin, forcing her to look at him. "You lie to me, Red. You lie like you lie at the table with your poker face. You went away for the weekend to see a man, didn't you? And you can't stop thinking about him."

She rolled her eyes as if that notion were ludicrous. "I only wish I had done something so interesting. Told you I was seeing friends in New York. That's all."

"Your friends have distracted you then," he said, enunciating each word so crisply that a bead of spit flew out of his lips and landed on her skin. "Do I need to pay them a visit? Enlist them in my employ?"

"No," she shouted, as he poked at her deepest fears. "But maybe you shouldn't have called me back then. I barely got off my flight before I had to show up."

He sneered at her, his fingers drilling her face. "You had three hours in between. That is enough."

"Well, it wasn't enough tonight."

He yanked her closer to him, so close her eyes could no longer focus on his face. She stood her ground though, her high-heeled feet digging into the floor as his brutal fingers jammed her jaw. "I can't have my ringer bringing me nothing."

"Sometime you win, sometime you lose, sometimes it rains. That's the way it goes," she said in as flat a voice as she could muster.

He dropped his hold on her chin, then stared at her curiously, as if she were a science project. "I do not like baseball. Do not give me baseball analogies. Give me your best poker face and beat my whales. That is all I want from you."

"That's what you'll keep getting."

"But Red, I did not like your performance tonight. If it happens again, I will be adding on to your totals."

Her heart plunged and she wanted to shriek *no*. A loud, echoing cry that would carry through the night. "It's not even my fault. It's not even my money," she said, insistently, as if that might change his mind.

"It is your fault. It is your money. And you are mine until I say you're not," he said, rooting around in his pocket. He took out his knife, opened it, and stabbed it into the table. She cringed, and there was no hiding her emotions this time as the sound of metal parking itself into wood rattled in her ears. He didn't remove the blade; he left it standing there like some strange trophy. "Or do you want me to visit your pretty bartender friend?" he asked, making a circle over his stomach as a reminder that he knew Kim was pregnant.

Her heart twisted. "No."

"How about your sister? She's a lovely lady, and quite perky on that little fashion blog of hers," Charlie said in his cool even voice.

It was as if he'd sliced her open with his knife, her bleeding organs on display for all to see. Julia bit her lip hard, trying to stop her insides from quivering. Charlie had never gone near her family, or her friends. He'd never mentioned McKenna until now, and her heart raced at the pace of fear. She'd do anything to keep her sister away from him. "Please leave them out of this. This has nothing to do with them."

"That's right," he said with a firm nod, pointing from her to him. "It is our business, and we will continue to do business until it is all resolved, or else I might need to collect from them too. Is that clear?"

With his words, the floor felt out from under her. He'd done it. He'd done the thing she feared. Threatened her family. Fear coursed through her body, rooting itself in her belly in a twisted knot where it planned to set up camp for a long, long time. "Yes," she choked out.

"Now get out of here, and I will call you when I have a game you won't mess up."

She turned on her heels and left the restaurant, Skunk holding open the door. He lowered his voice to a whisper, as if he didn't want Charlie to hear him. "Want me to call you a cab?" he asked, and he sounded like a sweet, sympathetic bear. Like he legitimately wanted to do something nice after the way Charlie had spoken. He had some kind of soft spot for her. But she wasn't going to be fooled. She knew where his loyalties lay and it wasn't with the woman he wanted to help. It was with the man who owned him, just as Charlie owned nearly everyone he worked with.

Except her. She told herself Charlie only rented her, and eventually the lease would be up.

"No thank you. I don't need a cab," she said, and walked home, the fog crawling into the city, threatening to ensnare the night. She brushed her hand roughly against her cheek, wiping away a tear.

But another one fell, and then another, and that's how she walked home, wishing there were a way to unravel herself faster from Charlie's clutches. Wishing she'd never met Dillon, that he'd never made off with $100,000 from the mobster he worked for, and that he'd never claimed the money was for her.

When she reached her home and poured herself a glass of whiskey, her fingers itched to pick up the phone and call Clay. To tell him why she ran, that she missed him, and that this weekend was the best she'd ever had.

But she could still feel Charlie's hand on her chin, and she knew, she fucking knew she shouldn't be involved with anyone. Because when you get close to people, your debt becomes their debt, and theirs becomes yours, and you are left with nothing but an aching well of shame inside you as you try to claw your way out.

Clay could be just like Dillon—disappearing, and leaving her holding all his problems.

She put the phone in a kitchen drawer and shut it hard.

* * *

"Uncross your legs," Gayle said, pointing her sharp scissors at Julia.

"You have the weapon. I do as you say," Julia said, following orders. "But why is it that I see you every six weeks and I still can't remember to uncross my legs when you start trimming?"

"Maybe because you have too much else on your mind," Gayle said, patting Julia's shoulder then widening her stance so she could trim the ends of her hair.

The stylist dressed in black as she always did, and today's homage to the shade of midnight was a black tunic top and tight leggings, with black cowboy boots on her feet. Down her arm was her permanent mark—a tattoo in a swirling script that said *I want to be adored.* Julia loved the boldness in branding her own body with a wish for love. She longed for that sort of daring. The wish had come true; Gayle had worked in New York a few times a year, cutting celebrities' hair, and on a recent trip she'd met someone recently who she'd fallen hard and fast for, and he for her. There were no issues, no problems, no pasts in the way. He'd moved here to be with her.

Of course, you never knew what was coming. When someone would turn on you. She would never have predicted Dillon would be a world-class douche. A knot of anger was set loose in her body at the thought of her ex; like a marble in a Rube Goldberg machine, it rolled down the tracks, picking up speed. Her insides were twisted, and Dillon wasn't the sole cause. She'd been wracked with tension since she left Clay behind in a swirl of dust in New York. Every night she'd been tempted to text, to call, to chat. Every night she'd resisted.

Her chest felt like a pressure valve inside her. The valve was stuck, so the pressure kept building. She tapped her toe on the hardwood floor of the salon as Gayle cut.

"What's the story, Jules? You're jumpy today."

She sighed heavily, as if the weight of the last week were pouring out in that one breath. "Oh Gayle, it's getting harder," she said, because she couldn't take it anymore. Her stylist was the only person who had a clue about the troubles Dillon had dumped on her doorstep when he'd skipped town with Charlie's money, claiming Julia would be paying it off. Julia reckoned a stylist was akin to a shrink. Maybe even a priest. A stylist was the one person you could pour out all your secrets to. Gayle wasn't a part of her regular life—she was someone she saw every six weeks. Neat and cordoned off, safe from the harm that was circling her on the other side. "I still owe a crap ton of money, and the people I owe it to aren't making it any easier for me, and on top of that, I met someone I really like, but I can't let myself get close to him because of all this stuff going on. I want to trust him, but he might screw me over too, but I miss him like crazy, which makes no sense because it was only one weekend. Okay, it was two weekends, but still, they were both spectacular," she said, the words spilling out of her. Julia stopped talking for a second, stared in the mirror at her friend's reflection. "Wow. That was like a confessional or something."

Gayle squeezed Julia's shoulder, and then continued snipping. "I'm so glad you met someone you like. It's been so long since Dillon, and even then you weren't terribly fond of the douche. With good reason, of course," she quickly added, with a wry smile.

Julia narrowed her eyes. "He is such a douche. And I feel so stupid for ever trusting him, or even getting involved with him."

"That's the thing. Sometimes you just can't know how someone is going to turn out," Gayle said as she ran a comb through Julia's wet hair, appraising her work so far.

"Right? So I guess it's all for the best that things aren't happening with this other guy. He might turn out to be just like Dillon. I was an idiot for getting involved with him, and an even worse idiot for the way he scammed me."

"That's not what I meant. I mean, you can't beat yourself up for not knowing Dillon was going to con money out of his employer and pin the debt on you," she said, because that's the extent of what she knew. Not that Charlie was a gangster, but that Dillon had swindled money from him. "That man should have his balls chopped off."

"If I ever see him again, can I borrow those scissors?"

"I'll order a better pair. A ball-snipping pair. But let's talk about happier fates for balls. What's this other guy like?" Gayle said, stopping her cutting for a moment to bump her hip against Julia's shoulder, giving her a salacious wink in the mirror. "I want to hear all about him."

She couldn't help but grin at the memories that came racing back—images that warmed her heart, and sent her body soaring. Clay's strong hands holding her down. His tongue working her over. His mouth claiming hers. Okay, now she was doing more than grinning. She was tingling something fierce. A sharp bolt of lust shot straight to her core, and then a burst of warmth surrounded her heart as she flashed on all the sweet things he'd said to her. "He's the sexiest, dirtiest, smartest, and kindest man I have ever met."

Gayle's eyes widened. "More, more. Tell me more."

She told her about their weekend. Not every detail, but enough to make Gayle's jaw drop, and the tension to loosen momentarily in Julia. Just talking about him felt good. It was as close as she was going to come to being near him, because once she left this salon she was going back on lockdown. She'd tie her hands behind her back if that was what she had to do to resist him.

CHAPTER FOURTEEN

His junior partner's jaw dropped when he saw the gift. A new set of five-irons that Flynn had been eyeing for a few weeks. Talking about. Showing him pictures of on the Internet. It had damn near gotten to the point of golf porn. But Flynn had sealed the deal with the Pinkertons yesterday, and with the kind of dough the film producers were raking in, he was contributing quite nicely to the firm's bottom line. That kind of dedication and drive needed to be rewarded.

"Holy crap," he said as he reached for the set and removed one club, touching it as if it were some kind of rare treasure. He stroked it with his palm.

"Flynn, man. You can't start feeling up the golf clubs in my office. If you do I'm going to need to take them back," Clay joked.

"I can't help myself," he said, his eyes wide as he gazed at the club in his hand. "This is a thing of beauty. Almost better than a woman."

"You haven't met the right woman then," he said, and his mind latched onto Julia, and how she'd seemed like the perfect woman for him. Smart, sharp, witty, and with that vulnerable side underneath. His mind flooded with images of their weekend: her curled up on his bench on the balcony, him washing her legs in the tub, that kiss in the rain that she'd insisted on. Then, to all the things they'd shared, her stories of her sister, his tales about Thanksgiving, and the easy way they had together. Like two people who were meant to be matched. Until she walked out on a lie. His chest knotted up, and his shoulders tensed, both with anger and annoyance.

Damn.

This wouldn't do. He didn't have the real estate in his head or his heart to keep going back to her, and all the ways he'd wanted her. Good thing he was seeing Michele tonight. She had a way of keeping him focused on the present, not the past. "I'm out of here. Meeting a friend for drinks," he said to Flynn, then grabbed his suit jacket and took off, making some phone calls when he hit the streets of New York.

First, he rang his buddy, Cam, about their poker game this week, and to check in on some information he'd asked him to run down on another potential client—a TV producer who'd seemed a little shady when he came to him, claiming his studio had screwed him over.

"I looked into your guy, and I can see how he might seem like a crooked bastard with the way things ended with his last deal. But you know what? I checked him out six ways to Sunday and that fucker is squeaky clean as can be," Cam told him.

"Good to know," he said, relieved his gut had been wrong. It was rare when it happened, but that's why he liked to do his homework and research clients in advance.

"That's why you like me though. C'mon, admit it. You love me because you never know if someone is a slimeball, but I can *always* find out."

"That you can. And I guess I love you, in some pathetic needy way that makes me sick," he teased.

"Aww, you're so sweet when you shower me with compliments. So you gonna take this deal?"

"I probably will."

"Then cigars are on you this week. I want the finest Cubans you can get your grimy paws on, because I plan on winning all the money in your pocket," Cam said, and Clay couldn't help but laugh at his friend's brashness.

"We'll see about that," he said, and hung up to call Davis.

As it rang drops of rain began to fall. With his phone pressed to his ear, he navigated the rush hour crowds on Lexington Avenue. Women in skirts and heels and men in suits began to pop open umbrellas.

The rain wasn't hard enough or heavy enough for him to worry about getting wet though. "Are they taking care of you across the pond?" he said into the phone.

"Of course. You know the producers love me," Davis said.

"Modest as always."

"Just like you," he fired back.

"No troubles then? Anything I need to take care of?"

"You already got me that one-day-off-a-week clause so I could fly home and see Jill, so I'm doing just fine."

"Ah, I guess that's why I didn't see you when you were in New York last weekend," Clay joked, as he stopped at a red light.

"Amazing, isn't it, how I'd rather spend time with her than you?"

"Shocking," he said in a dry voice.

"What's the latest with you? What happened with the woman you were hung up on?"

Clay clenched his jaw at the mention, frustration eating away at him. He didn't feel like talking about Julia or how she'd taken off. It had been more than a week now without a word from her. He hadn't reached out to her, and he was doing his damnedest not to think about her, burying himself in work, in contracts, in doing whatever he could for his clients. That was his focus. Head down in business, and no place else. He could not tolerate a repeat of the Year of Sabrina, especially now that Flynn had reeled in the Pinkertons. He still felt guilty for losing Flynn's big action-film director client that year when his focus had been tangled up in Sabrina's troubles. Clay needed to train his associate right, and show him how to keep winning and closing deals. The Pinkertons were a prize, and he'd make sure they were treated right by his firm and given ample attention.

"She was a piece of work," he said vaguely as the light changed and he crossed, nearing the restaurant where he was meeting Michele. "I'm about to have a drink with your sister, though."

"Well, be sure to keep your damn hands off of her," Davis said in a light-hearted tone.

Clay shook his head and rolled his eyes. "Fuck off to you, too. I'll catch you later."

After hanging up, he pushed open the door, brushed off the drops of water on his suit jacket, and weaved his way to Michele, who was perched on a stool at the bar. She waved when she saw him, and as he reached her she wrapped him in a hug, and gave him a kiss on the cheek.

"You don't have an umbrella," she said, wagging her finger.

He loosened his dark-green tie, unknotting the damn thing. "I'm a man. Men don't carry umbrellas."

"I'm a woman. I carry a big umbrella," she said, tipping her forehead to the umbrella holder by the door. "Mine's the polka-dot one about four-feet high."

"Is that supposed to be a substitute for something, Michele?"

"Oh yes. You've figured me out. I have penis envy, so I carry a large stick." She patted the wooden stool next to her. "Sit. Have a drink."

"I need one," he said, taking off hia jacket and tossing it on the back of the stool. "Whiskey. Straight up," he told the bartender.

When the glass of amber liquid arrived, he downed it in one quick swallow then ordered another. That glass earned the same treatment. Michele arched an eyebrow. "Shit day?"

"Shit week," he muttered, running a hand roughly through his hair. He was sure his hair was standing up, unkempt. He'd been pushing his hands through it all week, as if that motion would someone ease the coiled frustration that had taken up residence in his bones and bloodstream, courtesy of one Julia Bell. It made no sense to him. He'd studied it from all angles, turned it inside and out and around. He didn't understand how they could have had the time together they did—a weekend that was unforgettable—and then descended into radio silence.

"Talk to me," Michele said, placing a gentle hand on his arm. He looked down at her hand. Everything about her was familiar and safe. He'd known her for years, and though he'd never put his hands on her again after that one drunken kiss in college, there was something comforting about her. Maybe because they were long-time friends; maybe because she was a shrink. She helped people for a living. Maybe she could help him make sense of that woman's exodus.

"Fine," he said, because the alcohol had already loosened him up. He wanted to jettison this tangle of anger and hurt from his chest. "You ready for this?"

"The doctor is in session," she said, sitting up straight and proper. "Only for an after-hours session, I insist on another one of these." She tapped his glass.

She ordered another round as he began talking.

"I met someone," he started, then told her the story. Not every detail. He wasn't about to confess that he'd had a raging hard-on for the last week and refused to do anything about it because he knew he'd think of Julia, and he wanted to stop thinking of his fiery redhead. He didn't tell her either that making love to that woman had been the most intense sexual encounter of his life. She was his perfect partner in every way —in the bedroom, and outside the bedroom. He'd never enjoyed a woman's company as much as hers, and he'd felt like they could do anything together. "We had a great time. A perfect weekend. And we were falling for each other. I was sure of it. Talked about seeing each other again, making a go of it," he said and Michele's features tightened; her lips pursed as he told her about the plans they made for a long-distance affair. "Everything seemed like it was clicking on all cylinders. Every single thing."

She drew in a sharp breath. "Every thing?" Her voice sounded strained as if the question were hard for her.

"Yeah," he said, trying to keep the desire out of his voice. His throat was parched just thinking of Julia. "We had a connection."

"Oh. I thought you meant . . ." Michele said, then let her voice trail off as she blushed.

He had meant *that*, but he didn't intend to share details of his sex life with Davis's sister. What a man did behind closed doors, or in a town car, or in a bar in the West Village—he shifted uncomfortably, recalling Julia's stoic orgasm at The Red Line as he worked her over under the bar—was between the man and the woman. Only the woman he wanted had run; she didn't want his business. "But the next morning, she was out of here like a bat out of hell. So tell me, Michele. Tell me, my wise little shrink. What am I missing? Is she secretly craving me and can't figure out how to tell me?" he asked, laying it on the line as he ached for an explanation. "'Cause I fucking miss her, and I want her in my life. Did I miss a cue from her? Fuck something up? Is there something I should be doing?"

Michele didn't answer right away. She reached for her glass and took a long drink. After she set it down, she looked straight at him, her dark-brown eyes both intense and caring. "I'm going to be blunt. I'm going to be direct, and talk to you like I would talk to one of my patients. And here's the thing, Clay," she said, reaching out to place her hand on his thigh. "That's not how a woman behaves when she likes a man."

His shoulders sank and he sighed heavily. "Yeah?"

She nodded. "She's history. I hate to say it, because clearly you have it bad for her, but she ran. Maybe there's something in her life that's tying her down. Maybe she has some deep, dark past. Maybe she's secretly married and really only could manage one weekend with you. But if she truly had a great time and truly was open to dating long-distance like she claimed, then she'd have called you when her flight landed. She'd have texted you. She'd be, I don't know," Michele said, forcing out a laugh, "sending you naughty pictures."

Clay winced, and his dick rose to attention at the thought of a naughty picture of Julia appearing on his home screen. Maybe a shot of her topless, of those full luscious breasts that he longed to lick and kiss and squeeze. Or that ass, so round and sexy, and calling out for a spanking. In his mind, he could hear the sound of his palm smacking her ass, the sharp slap, and the surprised *oh* that would fall from her lips, followed by a moan. She liked spankings. He was pissed that he hadn't had the chance to smack her ass more than once.

He wanted to slam his fist against the bar. "So the lack of naughty shots on my phone is the surest sign that this woman is history," he said through tight lips, barely wanting to acknowledge the cold hard truth Michele was laying out for him.

She flashed him a sympathetic smile. "Yes, Clay. She's history. When a woman wants to be with a man, she makes the effort to see him, to call him, to spend time with him, just as he does with her. She aspires to be honest and upfront. To share her heart. Besides, that's what you deserve," she said, and squeezed his arm.

For a second there it felt as if she lingered on his bicep. But maybe it was the booze making his mind fuzzy. Which reminded him—he needed another drink.

By the time he left, he was pretty damn sure he was buzzed. Walking to the subway stop two blocks away, he changed that assessment as the cabs and cars and lights around him grew fuzzier. He wasn't buzzed. He was drunk. So drunk, he saw no reason why he shouldn't text her as he headed down the steps to the platform, reaching for his phone from his pocket, missing it the first time. He nearly stumbled onto the subway car as his fingers flew across the screen.

I can't stop thinking about you.

He hit send, then cursed himself, wished he could take it back. He was going to get nothing in return from Julia, and that would only make her exit burn more.

When he emerged on Christopher Street, he hoped that maybe the gods of drunk-texting were looking out for him. That perhaps there'd been no signal underground, and he'd be saved from his own stupid desires for her.

But there it was, in his sent messages, mocking his traitorous heart.

CHAPTER FIFTEEN

Julia brushed some sugar crystals along the rim of a martini glass, and handed her signature cocktail to a woman in a standard, boring, black business suit who'd wandered in a few minutes ago rolling a large black case on wheels, the kind that was usually full of pharmaceuticals. Julia guessed she was a sales rep for one of the big drug companies and had been pitching docs all day with little success. Quite simply, the woman looked worn down.

She sighed heavily, resting her chin in her palm. Julia felt for her, without even knowing her woes. Life could be a cruel mistress. Sometimes the days wrung you dry. The nights did too, those lonely nights when all she wanted was a note, a moment, a sweet reminder that she wasn't one woman against the world, tackling everything solo.

"Enjoy," Julia said, sliding the Purple Snow Globe in front of the woman. "I hope it makes the day a little better."

The woman flashed a smile. "You have no idea how much I need this."

"This one is my specialty, but if it doesn't fit the bill, you let me know and I'll mix up something else for you instead."

The woman took her first sip, and her tired eyes lit up. Julia swore a switch had been flipped and they'd gone from muted to bright blue. "This is divine."

She smiled. "I'm glad you like it," she said, and for now, this was enough to make Julia's shit week a bit better. She might not have won her game, she might have lost her man, but at least she could do one thing right: mix a drink, and lift the spirits temporarily of the weary.

She moved to the tap, filling a Pale Ale for a regular customer, a skinny guy who always stopped by after work. She liked him; he'd never once tried to hit on her. He was only here for the drinks.

"The usual," she said, handing him the glass. He doffed an imaginary hat, and took his first swallow. She gathered up tips from other patrons and returned to the register, tucking some bills in the drawer.

"Can I pretty please have your most special, awesomest Diet Coke?"

Julia grinned widely, and turned around to see her favorite person ever: her sister McKenna, decked out in a vintage emerald-green dress with a white petticoat peeking out from the skirt's hem. On her shoulders she wore a faux white fur cape—one hundred percent pure-retro fashionista. Next to her was her fiancé, Chris, wearing a plaid button-down and jeans, dress-up attire for the most casual California surfer guy that he was. They were the happiest couple she knew, and yet another reason why Julia was never going to burst their bubble of bliss with her troubles. Seeing her sister in love was a singular joy, and she'd go to the ends of the earth to protect McKenna's heart from any more hurt.

"Always for you," Julia said, and leaned across the bar to give her big sister a hug. "And hello handsome," she said to Chris, giving him a peck on the cheek.

"Hey, Julia. How's business tonight?"

"Always good at Cubic Z," she said, beaming and glad for the chance to talk about the bar business. She was proud of her tiny little patch of land in SoMa; yet another reason why she desperately wanted to get out from under Charlie's thumb. She didn't want him to take over this place. The thought of him running his illegal operations from her bar, threatening other patsies with his knife that wasn't dangerous in and of itself, but symbolized all he could do, made her stomach restless. He could turn it to rubble too, leaving her, Kim, and Kim's family high and dry. She poured McKenna a Diet Coke, then asked Chris for his poison.

"Whatever's on tap," he said, and she winced inside at the words. Granted, she'd heard that phrase a few times a night, but it reminded her of Clay, of what he'd said the first night they met here. After she handed Chris his glass, she looked from McKenna to her man and back. "What's up with the fancy attire? You going to a ball or something?"

Chris smiled and shook his head. "Nope, but my network is having some shindig to celebrate our record-high ratings, so this is me dressing up," he said, fingering the collar of his shirt.

"You clean up mighty fine," she said, and once again her mind wandered back to Clay, to how delicious he looked in everything and nothing. She loved his sharp style, his power ties and crisp shirts, the cuffs and how he rolled them up revealing those forearms, so thick and strong.

A sharp pang of longing lodged in her chest. She wasn't only yearning for his arms; she was longing for the whole man, inside and out, from the way he held her to how he talked to her. He'd wanted to know more about her, and she felt one hundred percent the same about him. He fascinated her, with his mix of down and dirty, loving and tender. Though it seemed insane to miss someone she'd only spent a few nights with, she'd never met anyone like him, who captivated her mind and her body.

She shook her head, as if she could shake off thoughts of him. She reached for the tap to pour a beer for another customer.

"Speaking of record ratings," McKenna began in that voice that hinted she had something up her sleeve, "Chris is about to renegotiate his contract, and is looking for a new lawyer, so I was thinking about your guy . . ."

Julia's hand froze on the tap and the beer started to overflow the glass.

Your guy. Oh, how she wanted him to be *her guy*, and all that title allowed—the nights, the days, the moments, the tangling up in each other's arms.

"Oh crap," she said when she realized the liquid had frothed over. Grabbing a towel, she wiped down the side of the glass, cleaned it up and handed it to a customer.

"What do you think about that?" McKenna asked when she returned.

"He's pretty kickass at his job, right?" Chris said, chiming in. "I was talking to my sister the other day, and she said he's worked out all kinds of perks for Davis."

Julia straightened her spine. "I don't have any business dealings with him, but from what I've heard, his clients rave about him."

"Can you do an intro or something?"

"You're the one who introduced me to him," Julia pointed out.

"But that was more casual, something I mentioned to him in passing at the theater. I figured for this, a business intro would be better." Then something flashed in McKenna's eyes. Realization, maybe. Julia had been home from her trip for more than ten days and hadn't said much about it, other than a few texts that it went well, and she was home and busy, busy, busy. She hadn't told her sister that she'd bolted. McKenna leaned across the bar and narrowed her eyes. "Are you still into him?"

She was about to fashion an answer when she heard a customer call out. "Oh, excuse me!" The woman in the suit waggled her fingers.

Julia walked over to her. "How was it?"

The woman tapped the glass. "Never had anything like it. It's amazing."

"I'm so glad you liked it."

"Listen. I have a friend—his name is Glen Mills—whose magazine is running a search for the best cocktail ever," the woman continued. "I'm going to tell him about this."

"That'd be nice of you," she said, though she knew patrons said stuff like this all the time, so she didn't put any stock in it. No more, at least, than simple pride in a job well done.

"What's your name?"

"Julia," she told her, as the woman handed her a twenty.

"Keep the change, Julia."

Then she left, rolling her bag on the way out, only this time her pace was upbeat and energetic. Julia returned to her sister, eager to avoid any more talk of Clay. She didn't need to feel that empty ache for him all evening, especially since she was sure to feel it all night long alone in her bed. She looked at her watch. "Hey, it's about to get crowded here."

"So can you do an intro to Clay?" McKenna asked again, and clearly Julia wasn't going to be able to ignore this request.

She mulled over the question. She'd been trying to steer clear of temptation, locking her phone in a kitchen drawer in the evenings when she felt the desire to text him or call, going for a run in the mornings to try to clear her mind. But neither tactic kept him from occupying the prime corner lot in her brain. She'd been dreaming of him every night. The very mention of his name brought a flush to her skin, and heat between her legs. It had been a while; she hadn't even touched herself since she'd left. If she did, she'd only picture him, and that wouldn't help put him out of her mind.

Maybe, just maybe, a brief email for her sister would satiate this longing inside her, and quench her thirst for him. Sort of like a phased withdrawal. One tiny taste, and then she'd be done.

"I'll take care of it for you," she said, and something inside of her dared to spark. At least she had a reason to reach out to him, and she tried not to get too excited about the prospect of sending him a note, but she couldn't help it—she was excited. "Now, can we talk about something besides business please? Like your wedding? That's what I most want to chat about. I can barely wait another month to see my big sister walking down the aisle."

The two of them beamed, Chris and McKenna matching each other in sheer wattage of their smiles. He dropped a quick kiss on her cheek, and she threw her arms around his neck, and Julia was happy for the way her sister could be free with the man she cared for.

"So we're going to have karaoke, as you know," McKenna said and began rattling off all the details, and though Julia knew most of them already since she was Maid of Honor, she didn't mind hearing them again. Her sister's happiness brought a smile to her face, so she listened as McKenna updated her on all their wedding plans, and she too was counting down the days till the two of them got hitched.

* * *

Later that night, as the crowds wound down she reached for her phone to call when she saw Clay had texted her. Her eyes widened, lighting up with anticipation. With hopeful fingers, she slid open the message.

I can't stop thinking about you.

Her heart thrummed hard against her chest as she savored the words, each one like decadent chocolate. She clutched the phone to her chest, as if that simple act would bring him closer. She walked into the back room, needing a moment alone with his text. She closed the door behind her, leaned against it and stared like a love-struck idiot at the screen again, running her fingertip across his message.

She cycled through her options. She could pretend she never saw it. She could delete it. She could keep on ignoring him. But the very thought of that felt like thorns twisting in her gut. She'd been in a funk since she'd left New York. A real ball of piss. She'd slept badly, she'd been sullen when she went for her morning run, and she could barely focus on the book she'd been reading at bedtime. Her thoughts always careened back to him. A reply might unwind some of the tension knitting its way through her body.

Though she knew the risks, she became convinced with each passing second that answering his message wasn't dangerous. It was simply answering a message. Sometimes a cigar was just a cigar.

The very least she could do was write back.

Would love to know what you're thinking about . . .

Only later did she remember she'd forgotten all about McKenna's request for an introduction. So much the better. Another reason to be back in touch.

By the way, my sister's fiancé wants to talk to you about working together. I'll send you his info. Though I still want to know what you're thinking about.

She paused, her thumbs hovering over her smartphone. Then, she added, just so there'd be no misunderstanding, about her intent—*xoxo*.

CHAPTER SIXTEEN

from: cnichols@gmail.com
to: purplesnowglobe@gmail.com
date: April 16, 7:48 AM
subject: What I'm thinking about . . .

Everything. Your hair. Your ass. Your beautiful breasts. Your lips. You curled up in my bed. Your attitude. Most of all, why the fuck you left like that.

from: purplesnowglobe@gmail.com
to: cnichols@gmail.com
date: April 16, 11:08 AM
subject: The other thoughts please

Something came up. Can we go back to those other items instead?

from: cnichols@gmail.com
to: purplesnowglobe@gmail.com
date: April 16, 5:48 PM
subject: Not sure . . .

I don't know. Can we?

from: purplesnowglobe@gmail.com
to: cnichols@gmail.com
date: April 16, 11:48 PM
subject: Be sure . . .

You tell me.

from: cnichols@gmail.com
to: purplesnowglobe@gmail.com
date: April 17, 6:48 AM
subject: Ball. In. Your. Court.

You tell me what you're wearing. You tell me if you can't stop
thinking about me. You tell me why you're not here spread
across my lap, that beautiful ass calling out for my palm.

from: purplesnowglobe@gmail.com
to: cnichols@gmail.com
date: April 17, 9:48 AM
subject: Served

So you're saying you want to spank me?

from: cnichols@gmail.com
to: purplesnowglobe@gmail.com
date: April 17, 3:48 PM
subject: Hand is ready

You have no idea.

from: purplesnowglobe@gmail.com
to: cnichols@gmail.com
date: April 17, 3:49 PM
subject: Ass is too

Oh, I have an idea. I definitely have an idea. And I would like that very much. I also think you have a thing for my ass.

from: cnichols@gmail.com
to: purplesnowglobe@gmail.com
date: April 17, 11:48 PM
subject: More on that

It's perfection. I want to bite it. Lick it. Smack it. Grip it hard while I fuck you.

from: purplesnowglobe@gmail.com
to: cnichols@gmail.com
date: April 18, 1:01 AM
subject: Which means . . .

So you still want me, I take it?

from: cnichols@gmail.com
to: purplesnowglobe@gmail.com
date: April 18, 7:01 AM
subject: Yes

You know I do. That didn't change.

from: purplesnowglobe@gmail.com
to: cnichols@gmail.com
date: April 18, 11:34 AM
subject: Ditto . . .

I still want you . . .

Clay stared at the computer screen, his fingers hovering over the keys, considering a reply. But damn, those words were mocking him. *I still want you.* How could she say that with the way she'd left? It made no sense, and Michele had spelled it out for him in no uncertain terms that if Julia wanted to play ball, she'd be at the plate, not skipping and frolicking along the foul lines, darting in and out of sight. He pushed away from his keyboard, like an alcoholic trying to step away from the bar. Grabbing a pen and a contract from the pile of papers on his desk, he tossed his phone onto his desk, left his office, and locked the door.

If he stayed within typing distance of either device, he'd surely keep up this volley with her. Because she was as irresistible to him as she'd been that very first night. With his head down the whole way, he headed to a bench outside Central Park and settled onto it, trying his best to dive into the fine print on a licensing deal that the actor Liam Connor needed wrapped up before he opened a new restaurant in New York in a few weeks. Clay didn't usually do restaurant deals, but Liam was a long-time client and had asked him to look over the terms with the other co-owner. Clay shoved his hand through his hair as he studied the fine print, but soon the words he knew backwards and forwards, like *indemnify* and *liability,* were levitating off the page and he could barely put them in context. Reading this was a slow, cruel tease because he couldn't focus on a damn thing.

She weaved in front of him like a damn mirage, tantalizing and teasing him. Whenever he opened or closed his eyes, she was there. Beautiful and beckoning, she lured him in. He could picture her, he could feel the trace of her, touch the outline of her. She'd left her mark on him and he wanted her day after day, night after night.

He swore loudly and looked up. No one noticed his cursing. No one cared. It was New York, and the city spun on its own axis. So he sat and stared at the lunchtime crowds, at a harried doctor rushing by in her scrubs, at a guy in a suit, tugging at his tie while tapping out a message on his phone, at a pair of women in sharp jeans and sweaters, each balancing a cardboard tray of lattes in their hands. A bus trudged by on Fifth Avenue, pulling up to the stop and letting off several passengers who looked equally hurried as they raced to their destinations. Somehow, the chaos of the city soothed the tangled knots in his chest for the moment, and calmed his mind. He took a deep fueling breath, and returned once more to the contract.

A half-hour later, he'd found the one clause that concerned him most, so when he met Liam for lunch he told him about the points he wanted to iron out.

"That's why I keep you around, man," the actor said, flashing his trademark smile that made women swoon and patrons pay top dollar to see his face in lights. "You're going to come see me in *The Usual Suspects,* right?"

"As if I'd miss it," Clay said, and mentally marked the date on his calendar to see the stage adaptation of the hit film.

They spent the rest of the meal talking about Liam's upcoming work, the movies they'd both loved and loathed, and sports, always sports.

When lunch ended, Clay simply hoped he could keep harnessing that focus, and use it to stay on track in his business. He didn't need a repeat. When he returned to his office, refreshed—mostly—from the few hours away from electronic tethers, he clicked on his phone and found another message from the woman who was never far from his mind.

from: purplesnowglobe@gmail.com
to: cnichols@gmail.com
date: April 18, 2:23 PM
subject: On the subject of wanting . . .

So unbelievably much . . . in every single way.

All his control unraveled in a second as his skin heated up, and his heart beat faster, pounding against his chest with the aching want to have her in his arms again. Resistance was futile, so he banged out a reply, saved it in his drafts, and told himself he'd see if he still felt the same way that night. When the workday ended, he went to the gym to pound the punching bag until his shoulders were as sore as they'd ever been.

On the way home, he pulled out his phone, opened his drafts and made a decision.

CHAPTER SEVENTEEN

from: cnichols@gmail.com
to: purplesnowglobe@gmail.com
date: April 18, 5:23 PM
subject: Which brings us back to . . .

So why then? Why did you leave?

from: purplesnowglobe@gmail.com
to: cnichols@gmail.com
date: April 18, 8:48 PM
subject: Truth

I was afraid.

from: cnichols@gmail.com
to: purplesnowglobe@gmail.com
date: April 18, 11:24 PM
subject: Truth is good

Of what?

from: purplesnowglobe@gmail.com
to: cnichols@gmail.com
date: April 19, 2:03 AM
subject: It can be . . .

Of getting close.

from: cnichols@gmail.com
to: purplesnowglobe@gmail.com
date: April 19, 7:48 AM
subject: Re: It can be . . .

Don't be afraid.

from: purplesnowglobe@gmail.com
to: cnichols@gmail.com
date: April 19, 11:19 AM
subject: Re: Re: It can be . . .

But I am.

from: cnichols@gmail.com
to: purplesnowglobe@gmail.com
date: April 19, 5:59 PM
subject: Promise

I won't hurt you.

from: purplesnowglobe@gmail.com
to: cnichols@gmail.com
date: April 19, 10:03 PM
subject: Promises, promises

That's easy to promise. Hard to deliver.

from: cnichols@gmail.com
to: purplesnowglobe@gmail.com
date: April 19, 11:08 PM
subject: Question

Are you going to let the fear control you?

Good question.

Was she going to let Charlie control every aspect of her life? Right now, from his perch at the back table in Mr. Pong's, he stared at her like she was a gnat on the bottom of his shoe, and that was after she'd given him his money. The stack was flimsier than usual, but at least she'd won some.

"Get out of here," Charlie said to her in a cold, calculating voice. "You tire me because you take too long."

"I won for you tonight," she pointed out, but then, what was the point? Charlie was in a nasty mood, and maybe it had to do with her, or maybe it had to do with another one of his pawns underperforming.

"Hardly. This is hardly enough," he said, fanning out the thin stack in her face, smacking her on the nose with the bills. She flinched, surprised that money could wound that much.

As she left the Chinese restaurant, nearly bumping into a man with a well-lined face and sad eyes who stared longingly at the sign for Mr. Pong's, she pondered all the fear in her life. She was afraid of Charlie, of the veiled threats of him hurting her, hurting Kim, and taking more and more of her business until he was satisfied. Though men like him never had their fill, did they? She was scared for her sister, and wanted desperately to protect McKenna's hard-won happiness with Chris. Most of all she was terrified of screwing up. What if she couldn't win the rest of the money? Would she be in Charlie's clutches forever? Time was running out, and she pictured him snapping chains on her forever somehow, so she'd never ever escape from him.

She didn't know what would happen.

All she knew for sure was this fear sucked. This emptiness stung. And the only thing that had felt remotely good and real in her life was opening up to Clay. She'd been living in a cocoon of her own necessary lies for so many months, that the sliver of truths she could share with him was freeing.

from: purplesnowglobe@gmail.com
to: cnichols@gmail.com
date: April 20, 2:02 AM
subject: Good question

I don't know . . . I don't want to be controlled by fear . . . but I can't stop wanting you either.

from: cnichols@gmail.com
to: purplesnowglobe@gmail.com
date: April 20, 7:32 AM
subject: New side of you

Don't stop wanting me. This is the most open I think you've been.

from: purplesnowglobe@gmail.com
to: cnichols@gmail.com
date: April 20, 9:52 AM
subject: Blame it on email

Do you like it?

from: cnichols@gmail.com
to: purplesnowglobe@gmail.com
date: April 20, 3:22 PM
subject: Love it . . .

I like nearly everything about you, except when you run from me.

from: purplesnowglobe@gmail.com
to: cnichols@gmail.com
date: April 20, 11:08 PM
subject: Run the other way?

Would you rather I run to you?

from: cnichols@gmail.com
to: purplesnowglobe@gmail.com
date: April 21, 6:03 AM
subject: Yes I would

I would like you on your knees for that smartass comment.

from: purplesnowglobe@gmail.com
to: cnichols@gmail.com
date: April 21, 9:32 AM
subject: Love that position

I would get on my knees for you. You know that. I would get on my knees and take you in my mouth. Under your desk. While you were in a meeting. I love tasting you. So. Much.

from: cnichols@gmail.com
to: purplesnowglobe@gmail.com
date: April 21, 3:43 PM
subject: You're killing me.

I would be stone-faced and not let on.

from: purplesnowglobe@gmail.com
to: cnichols@gmail.com
date: April 21, 4:04 PM
subject: Relentless

I would do everything I could to break you.

from: cnichols@gmail.com
to: purplesnowglobe@gmail.com
date: April 21, 4:14 PM
subject: I know, believe me, I know

I bet you would. I have excellent control.

from: purplesnowglobe@gmail.com
to: cnichols@gmail.com
date: April 21, 7:17 PM
subject: Shifting gears . . .

That's why you're such a good lawyer. By the way, I hear you're Chris's attorney now. Thank you for taking care of him.

from: cnichols@gmail.com
to: purplesnowglobe@gmail.com
date: April 21, 7:43 PM
subject: From blow jobs to business . . .

Thank you for the introduction. I'm gonna make him an even richer mofo.

from: purplesnowglobe@gmail.com
to: cnichols@gmail.com
date: April 21, 11:23 PM
subject: Cocky, and I like it

I bet you are. I wish I had a reason to be in entertainment and have you be my lawyer.

from: cnichols@gmail.com
to: purplesnowglobe@gmail.com
date: April 22, 5:55 AM
subject: If I were

I'd fight for you, Julia. I'd get you everything you wanted. I'd give you everything you wanted.

from: purplesnowglobe@gmail.com
to: cnichols@gmail.com
date: April 22, 10:09 AM
subject: You would . . .

What about you? What do you want?

from: cnichols@gmail.com
to: purplesnowglobe@gmail.com
date: April 22, 5:12 PM
subject: One word

You.

from: purplesnowglobe@gmail.com
to: cnichols@gmail.com
date: April 22, 8:29 PM
subject: Re: One Word

The same. I want the same.

from: purplesnowglobe@gmail.com
to: cnichols@gmail.com
date: April 23, 11:10 AM
subject: You ok?

Still there?

SEDUCTIVE NIGHTS TRILOGY · 191

from: purplesnowglobe@gmail.com
to: cnichols@gmail.com
date: April 23, 3:53 PM
subject: Hi

Hey . . . you've been quiet . . . everything OK? Don't make
me call you :)

from: purplesnowglobe@gmail.com
to: cnichols@gmail.com
date: April 23, 9:01 PM
subject: Should I be worried?

Was it something I said?

from: cnichols@gmail.com
to: purplesnowglobe@gmail.com
date: April 23, 9:40 PM
subject: It was something you said . . .

What are you wearing?

from: purplesnowglobe@gmail.com
to: cnichols@gmail.com
date: April 23, 9:52 PM
subject: Not working tonight so the answer is . . .

Shirt. Stockings. Thong. Heels.

from: cnichols@gmail.com
to: purplesnowglobe@gmail.com
date: April 23, 10:04 PM
subject: Hard . . .

Truth?

from: purplesnowglobe@gmail.com
to: cnichols@gmail.com
date: April 23, 10:15 PM
subject: Full truth.

I swear.

from: cnichols@gmail.com
to: purplesnowglobe@gmail.com
date: April 23, 10:22 PM
subject: Better be

Are you sure?

from: purplesnowglobe@gmail.com
to: cnichols@gmail.com
date: April 23, 10:30 PM
subject: 100%

Yes.

from: cnichols@gmail.com
to: purplesnowglobe@gmail.com
date: April 23, 10:37 PM
subject: This is not a request

Take off the underwear.

from: purplesnowglobe@gmail.com
to: cnichols@gmail.com
date: April 23, 10:40 PM
subject: Your wish is my command

Done.

Julia startled when she heard a loud knock on her door. What the hell? It was eleven o'clock at night. Cold dread rushed through her veins. There could only be one person banging hard at this hour. Charlie, or his men. She took off her heels, padded quietly to the door, and peered through the key-hole.

CHAPTER EIGHTEEN

Her body reacted instantly. Viscerally. Her skin heated up, and she swore she was seeing things. To be sure, she slid the chain, unlocked the latch, and drank in the oh-so-welcome sight of Clay standing in the doorway, unknotting his tie then loosening the top button on his shirt.

She wanted to throw her arms around him. Kiss him hard. Tell him how damn happy she was to see him. She parted her lips to speak, but he was too fast. His hands were on her face, cupping her cheeks, his hot gaze raking over her body from head to toe. "You don't have heels on."

"I took them off when I came to the door."

"Put them on."

She slipped out of his grip, bent down and slid her feet into her four-inch red pumps. She grew taller as she stood and came face to face with the man she couldn't forget about. His whole body was ready to pounce, his muscles hard, the vein in his neck throbbing. His stare was dark and intense, and he radiated sexuality. His eyes roamed her body, prowling over her, turning her molten. His hands were clenched at his sides. He took a step closer and cupped her cheeks once more. Her knees nearly buckled; she and Clay were combustible. She wanted him so much, every solitary cell in her body cried out for him.

Her skin was ignited, and her heart beat in overtime. She watched him swallow, then brush a thumb over her lips. She panted from that single small touch, and nibbled on his thumb.

His eyes rolled back in his head as she bit gently into him. She thrilled at his reaction, at the way he breathed out hard.

When he opened his eyes, he stared at her momentarily then crushed her lips in a consuming kiss, one that told her he wanted to devour her. That he was hell-bent on it. When he broke the kiss, she went first, whispering her desperate need. "*Take me,*" she said.

"Turn around."

She bent over her kitchen table, her chest on the metal, her ass in the air where she knew he wanted it, offering herself to him to be claimed. She peered back, watching as he finished unknotting his tie and yanked it off, then unbuttoned his shirt.

Her chest rose and fell as she watched him, heat pooling between her legs with every move he made. He left his shirt open, and she marveled at his chest, at the hard planes and ridges. Her hand had a mind of its own, and she twisted her arm around to try to touch him. He swatted her hand away, and pushed her tight black shirt up her back, exposing more of her skin, then he ran his hands up and down her spine. He dipped his hand between her legs, sliding a finger across her swollen lips.

"Oh," she cried out, her eyes falling closed, and her mouth forming a perfect *O*.

"Have you been touching yourself?" he asked, sounding like a lawyer in a courtroom. She was a willing witness, eager to be cross-examined.

"No," she said, and he rubbed his fingers over her once more, drawing out a needy moan. She rocked her ass back against him. He raised his hand, and her breath caught, knowing what was coming. Her eyes widened as he brought his hand to her cheek, a sharp sting radiating across her rear.

He bent down to brush his soft lips against her flesh, and she whimpered as he soothed out the sting with his tongue. He slipped his hand between her legs again, sending sparks of heat throughout her body. "You haven't touched yourself once since I saw you?"

She shook her head. "No, I swear. I knew I'd only think of you if I did, and it would make me crazy not to have you." He thrust a finger inside her, and she saw stars as he flicked her clit with his thumb. "So you saved it all for me?"

"Yes." She panted.

"Good. Because I'm going to take it all. I want it all."

He took his hand away, raising it again and she quivered, knowing he was going to smack her once more. She craved the sharp sweet mix of pleasure and pain, and this time the smack was followed by his fingers gliding between her legs as he rubbed her where she wanted him most.

"I haven't touched myself either, Julia," he said as he began unzipping his pants. "You know what that means?"

"What does that mean?" she said as he pushed his briefs down, freeing his enormous erection. Her lips parted at the sight of his cock, thick, hard and throbbing. She wanted him so badly. Wanted all of him. He gripped his cock, stroking himself up and down. She watched, mesmerized, as a low moan escaped her.

"It means I've been rock hard since you left me. I've been walking around New York City at full fucking mast, thinking of you and not doing a damn thing about it for the same reason," he said, dragging the head of his cock against her wet pussy lips. Sweet agony sang in her body as she tried to rock back into him, to draw him into her body, awash with neverending lust. "I didn't want to think about you because you were all I was thinking about already," he said, as he reached into his pocket for a condom, tore open the wrapper, and rolled it on.

"It was the same for me." She could hear the desperation in her own voice. She needed this so much; not just the physical connection that burned hot between them, but she needed *him*. This man, the way he made her feel inside and out. He'd touched something so deep inside of her, a part she'd kept hidden and well protected. But he was there, working his way around the fortress of her hardened heart, and she wanted all of him. She could not be more grateful that he'd shown up tonight—the first clear evidence that maybe her luck was changing. "I kept thinking about you too. I want you so much."

"I want you too." He bent over her body, laying his chest over her as he rubbed his hard length against her entrance. "And I hated the way you left me."

"I hated it too," she said as she writhed against him, struggling to guide him into her. He gripped her wrists over her head, pinning her on the table.

"*Julia*," he rasped out, grazing his mouth along the column of her throat, eliciting a desperate groan from her. "I have to tell you something."

"Yes?" she asked, breathing hard, her back arching, her body molding to his.

He pulled back to look her in the eyes. His voice was ragged. "I'm crazy about you, but right now I'm going to fuck you like I hate you. I need to fuck you angrily but don't forget this: I'm crazy for you."

She bit her lip, desire coursing through her like a shooting star speeding across the sky. "I'm crazy for you," she murmured, but the last word was swallowed as he thrust into her, filling her in one quick move.

She moaned loudly and closed her eyes, savoring the feeling of his hard, hot length inside her. God, he felt amazing, stretching her. He began to pump, hard, fast, rough. Just like he'd promised. Her breasts were smashed against the kitchen table, and she didn't care that they hurt. She welcomed the hurt. The way every part of her body *felt* him. Her legs shook as he drove into her, her wrists twinged with his rough grip, and her cheek throbbed with how she was pressed hard against the unforgiving metal surface. But with each thrust, she took him in deeper, her heat rising. She grew wetter with every punishing stroke, needing terribly for him to fuck all the stress, all the problems, and all the troubles out of her life right now.

"Harder," she urged, and she was rewarded with a slam.

"Be careful what you wish for," he said roughly against her ear.

"I like it like this. I'm not regretting it."

"Don't ever regret me," he said, his stubbled jaw rubbing against her cheek.

"Never," she said in between pants. She raised her ass higher. "Touch me," she said, and she sounded like she was begging, but she knew he'd like that sound.

"You want me to touch your clit?" he asked as he pounded into her.

"Yes, please."

"Good. I like how you asked nicely for it," he said, letting go of her wrists. He stood behind her now, ramming hard as he held her hip with one hand, the other hand reaching between her legs to rub her clit. The second he made contact, she shrieked in pleasure.

"*Yes*."

It was all she could say. All she could manage. She shouted *yes* over and over as he pounded into her, taking her body, taking it back for him, claiming her with the hard, rough fucking she wanted. His finger raced across her swollen clit, hitting her at just the right pace, just the right friction until the world spun away, and everything blurred out but the unholy pleasure that rang through her body. Her climax rushed over as she tore past the brink. He was there with her, gripping her hips, plunging deeper, unleashing himself until he collapsed on her.

She breathed out hard, panting as if she'd just run a race. Then his lips were on her neck, kissing her softly, gently, as he mapped her with his mouth.

"I'm so crazy about you," he whispered, and though her body was hot from the coming together of their mouths, her heart flooded with warmth too from his words.

"I feel the same, Clay. Exactly the same," she murmured, turning her head so he could dust her mouth with his lips.

He pulled out, tossed the condom in the trashcan, and returned to her. He lifted her spent body from the table, where she was still splayed out, awash in the aftershocks, and glanced around, quickly finding the door to her one bedroom, then he carried her there. He laid her down on the bed, walked to the bathroom, grabbed some tissues and brought them to her. She cleaned up, and handed them to him to dispose of.

She wondered briefly how he'd found her apartment, but figured a quick Google search had likely revealed her address to him.

When he returned once more he scanned her bedroom, and she wasn't sure if he was going to stay the night here or not. Nerves raced through her, as she wondered what he would do next.

CHAPTER NINETEEN

So this is where she lay at night when she'd sent all those emails. Curled up on her king-size bed, on top of the wine-red covers, half-naked, wearing only her shirt .

At least, that's how he liked to imagine her, and how he liked to look at her.

He'd never been one to think much about a woman's home decor, but something seemed quite fitting about the deep reds, royal purples and gold colors in her bedroom—sexy shades for a woman who exuded sexiness in her style.

On her nightstand was an e-reader and he was willing to bet it was well stocked with the books she loved—adventure tales, she'd told him the night they met. Stories of naval rescues at sea, of daring treks up mountains, of beating the odds. She was an adventuresome woman, and what she read reflected that side of her. A purple scarf was draped over the lamp on the nightstand, and his mind flashed to other uses for that scarf. He checked out the framed photos on her bureau—pictures of her sister and her, and her sister and a dog, too.

"That's McKenna's dog. Ms. Pac-Man."

"Cute dog."

"She is cute and smart," Julia said, a note of pride in her voice, almost like an aunt beaming about a child. "She's also loyal and devoted."

"As a dog should be."

"And a person," she added.

"Yes," he said, agreeing emphatically. "Are you loyal and devoted?"

She nodded, her face serious, her green eyes holding his gaze. There was a fierceness in her look. A certainty. "I only want you. I only think of you," she said.

"I know the feeling well."

She patted her bed. "I like the way you look in my apartment."

"I like the way you look right now," he said, climbing up on her bed and joining her.

"Are you going to take off those pants and stay the night?" she asked, eyeing his half-dressed state.

"I am considering it," he said in a wry tone.

"What can I do to convince you?"

He was surprised to find her voice stripped bare of flirting as she posed the question. He was used to her seductive side, the way she'd trail her fingernails along his arm to get what she wanted. But this was a newer side of Julia, a vulnerable one, and it gave him hope that she was finally opening up to him.

He ran his index finger along her jawline. He swallowed, taking a beat. He was going to put it out there. Put himself out there. "Let me in," he said, as he moved his fingers to her heart, tracing it.

"How?" she asked in a wobbly voice.

"Tell me why you're scared. Tell me why you ran."

She sighed heavily, shifting from her side to her back. She closed her eyes; her face seemed pinched. He ran his hand along her bare arm. "Hey," he said softly. "You're here now. I'm here now. I want to know what I need to do so I don't scare you away."

She opened her eyes, turned back to face him. Her expression was softer now. "It's nothing you can or can't do. It's me."

"Right. It generally is. But tell me how I can help you be comfortable with you and me," he said. "Because for a while there I was damn sure you were history. My friend Michele even said so, in no uncertain terms."

Like she'd been burned, Julia jerked away from him, sitting up straight. "Michele? Who's Michele? Your ex?"

He laughed. "Michele is just a friend. Davis's sister. Known her for years. She also happens to be a shrink."

"You were talking to her about me?" Julia crossed her arms.

"Yes," he said, tugging on her hips, trying to pull her back to lie next to him. But she scooted further away into the jumble of pillows by her headboard. "Hey, I was talking to her about you because I like you, woman. Get that straight."

She narrowed her eyes, fixed him with a harsh stare, but said nothing.

"And I was trying to understand you, and I still don't entirely understand, so help a man out."

"Fine, but I don't want other women touching you," she said sharply as she glared at him.

Another laugh took hold of him, deep and rumbling through his chest. It warmed him up, knowing how possessive she was. "I believe I've made it patently clear that I am a one-woman kind of man, and you are my kind of woman. But this conversation isn't about me. I want to know what's going on with you," he said, succeeding this time in tugging her alongside him.

She took a breath, pursed her lips together, and then exhaled. She looked him square in the eyes; her pretty greens were tinged with sadness and a trace of fear. His heart lurched towards her, wanting to help her, reassure her. She licked her lips, and spoke in a wobbly voice that grew stronger as she pushed through. "I've got some trouble from my past chasing me. And I can't say anything more, because I don't want you or anyone I care about to get caught up in my problems."

He started to speak, to tell her he wasn't afraid of problems, and he certainly didn't expect anyone to come to a relationship baggage-free, but she held up her hand to silence him.

"Eventually, I'll be free of it, but right now there's just stuff I have to deal with, and that's why I left so quickly," she said, her voice raw and pained. "I'm sorry."

"Is somebody hurting you?" he asked, clenching his fists as he kept his voice on an even keel. He didn't want to scare her, but he sure as hell would hurt anyone who laid a hand on her.

"No," she said quickly, shaking her head. "Nor do I have a pill problem, or anything like your ex, I swear." She gripped his bicep, digging her fingers into his flesh to make her point. "I promise."

"That is excellent news. But what sort of trouble is it, then?"

"Clay," she said, soft, but insistent in her tone. "That's all I want to say. I have to keep the people I care about out of it. And I care about you. So deeply, and more than I ever thought I would," she said, reaching for his hand, and threading her soft fingers through his. "So much more," she added, squeezing his hand for emphasis, and her touch sent a shiver through him. She kissed his hand. By God, he could get used to this side of her. He would love to see this part of her every day. "It's my problem to deal with, and I'm dealing with it."

He wanted to help her, but he wasn't sure she'd let him so he tried another way to understand the scope of this *problem*. "Is it something I should be worried about?"

She shook her head. "No."

He raised an eyebrow, studying her face, trying to read her. He wasn't sure what was going on, but something in his gut said she was telling the truth. Or maybe he just wanted to believe her. Maybe he *could*. For now, at least. "Okay, I will try my best not to worry for now then," he said, though he knew that would be a tall order because already—deep in his gut—

he was concerned for her, for everything about her. He wanted to protect her, look out for her. That she was hardly the kind of woman who needed taking care of didn't factor into his thinking one bit. She was his, and he couldn't abide by anyone hurting her.

"Good," she said, and her face lit up again, her mischievous grin reappearing as she danced her fingers down his chest. "So, to what do I owe the pleasure of this surprise late-night visit?"

"In town for a meeting. I'm seeing Chris tomorrow about his renegotiations."

"McKenna didn't mention it to me."

He tapped her nose. "It was last-minute. Just scheduled it today, and caught an evening flight. I'm heading to L.A. early afternoon, so I'm squeezing the meeting in beforehand."

"I am glad you squeezed me in," she said, her hand darting to the waistband of his pants. "Now, have I successfully convinced you to take these off and spend the night with me? I'm not much of a cook, but I do know where I can take you tomorrow morning for some fantastic pancakes."

He pretended to think deeply about the food. "I do love pancakes."

"And spending the night with me. You better love that too," she said, playfully swatting him.

"I believe I could find it in me to enjoy another night with you."

"Wait. Where's your bag?"

"In the town car. Driver's waiting outside."

"So you could make a getaway?"

He shook his head. "Gorgeous, when is it going to get through to you that I'm not the one who's running? Nor am I a presumptuous asshole who's going to show up at your doorstep with an overnight bag unless you want me to."

"I want you to," she said in a sexy purr.

He dialed his driver, and a minute later, there was a knock on the door. Clay retrieved his bag, tipped the driver and said goodnight. He returned to Julia's room to find her leaning against the wall, her shirt shucked off and her stockings removed, wearing only her red pumps. Her hips jutted out seductively and his dick rose to full attention as he drank in the sight of her, the moonlight casting midnight blue shadows across her long and lean body, highlighting her curves.

"You didn't think I was going to bed, did you?"

"Not for a second."

"I want to show you one of my favorite positions."

"I have a feeling it's going to be one of my favorite positions too," he said as he kicked off his pants, and placed them on a chocolate-brown chair in the corner of her bedroom.

She pointed to the bed. "Take off the briefs, and sit down."

"At your service," he said, stripping off his final layer, and parking himself on the edge of her bed. She looked him over from head to toe, and he wasn't going to deny it—the hunger in her eyes was the biggest turn-on of his life. She stared at him like she'd never wanted anyone so much. As if she had never laid eyes on a man she wanted to feast on like this. Tremors rolled through him, and he ached with desire for her.

A low growl took hold in his chest as she strutted over to him. The sight of her gorgeous body was something he'd never get enough of. She stopped, placing her hands on his shoulders, leaning into him so her breasts brushed his face. A bolt of heat tore through him, and he reached for her, craving closeness, needing her beautiful body pressed against his. But she pulled back, wagging her finger, then walked away, heading for her nightstand. She grabbed the purple scarf and returned.

"What's good for the goose is good for the gander," she said in that sexy, smoky voice that could lead him to say yes to anything she wanted.

"You tying me up?"

"Just a little bit," she said, as she straddled him, sitting across his thighs. He felt the heat from her pussy even though she wasn't close to touching his cock. Still, being near his favorite place made his dick throb. She pressed against him once more, reaching her arms around him. She tugged at his hands on the mattress, adjusting them behind his back. She wrapped the scarf around his wrists, tying them together.

"Hey Julia, I got a question for you," he said as she tugged on the ends of the scarf.

"I grant you permission to ask."

He chuckled. "I haven't been with anyone in several months and I'm clean. How about you? Any chance you're on birth control?"

She leaned back, looked him in the eyes. "I am indeed. You saying you want to feel me coming on your cock in just a few minutes?"

He narrowed his eyes, and growled a hot *yes*.

"Then you can come and play without a glove," she said, gripping his cock in her fist. His hips nearly shot off the bed at her touch. Anything she did to him sent shocks of pleasure through his bones.

"I can not wait to feel your hot pussy surrounding me."

"You won't have to wait much longer, because I'm wet for you," she said, dropping her free hand between her legs and stroking herself.

His chest tightened and his dick throbbed in her hand. He watched her hungrily as she coated her fingers in her own wetness, then brought her finger to his lips.

"Rub yourself on me," he instructed her.

"As you wish." She traced his mouth and he licked his lips, drinking up the taste of her.

"More," he said, and his blood flowed thick and heavy as she slipped her fingers inside her pussy, drawing out more of her delicious juices. She dragged her fingers against him once more, and this time he sucked on her index finger, drawing it all the way into his mouth, lapping up every delicious ounce of her desire. "You taste fucking spectacular."

"Oh I do, do I?" she said seductively, brushing her breasts against his chest.

"You do, Julia. I love your taste, and your smell, and right now you smell like you want me inside you."

"I want to ride you so bad," she said, and swiveled around, straddling him again, only this time her back was to him.

"You are a cruel woman. You know I want to touch your breasts right now."

"And squeeze them too," she added, as she positioned herself over him, rubbing the head of his cock between her legs. Heat seared in his body, like flames licking across his skin. She leaned her head back, her gorgeous red hair fanning out across his chest and his shoulders, taunting him. He craved the chance to grip it hard, and tug, and she knew it. As she rubbed her wetness over him, she licked his neck up to his ear, driving him mad with desire. "Ask for it," she purred.

"Fuck me please," he said, his breath jagged as lust poured through every inch of his body.

She sank down on him, and he groaned loudly. The feel of her hot pussy gripping him tight was like a fevered dream. But it was real, everything real and raw and lingeringly primal in the way she rode him, taking her time, rising up and down on his cock, riding him like he was her plaything, and he wanted nothing more than to be just that in this moment.

His hands itched to touch her, to grab her hips, to hold on hard to her beautiful breasts. But he knew she was the kind of woman who let herself be dominated, but in return, sometimes she needed to take the reins. He let her have all the control, enjoying the view of her perfect body moving up and down on him as her moans grew louder, and more erratic until she was shouting his name, and the feel of her coming undone on his cock was all he needed to join her in climax.

* * *

The hot water beat down on his head and he soaped up Julia's breasts. For the twentieth time. Though it might have been the thirtieth, or fortieth. It was hard to count. They were too hard to resist.

"Hey, Mister. I'm pretty sure my breasts are scrub-a-dub clean. There's not an ounce of dirt on them," she said, poking his chest.

"Mmm . . . let me just make sure," he said, lathering them up once more. "You might be able to hypnotize me with these breasts."

"You will do my bidding," she said as she swayed her chest in a mesmerizing rhythm, then her hand quickly darted up and she snagged the soap from him. "Ha!" She held it up victoriously. "Now, I can finally get clean, because this gal wants to go to sleep."

He grabbed the soap back from her, tugged her sexy body against his. "Let me. I promise to wash the rest of you."

"Fine," she said, holding out her hands. "Have at me."

He kneeled down in the shower, the water pelting his back as he washed her legs, then gently between her legs, then back up to her belly and down her arms. He rubbed the soap once more against his palms, then dropped it in the soap dish and washed her neck. She leaned her head back, exposing the delicious column of her throat to him. Tenderly, he ran his hands over her, then positioned her under the water and rinsed her off. He wrapped his arms around her, her trim waist fitting perfectly in his embrace. "Mmm. I like holding you," he whispered, as he closed his eyes.

He could feel her smiling as she molded her body against his, taking what he was giving her. "I know," she said in a soft, sleepy voice. "I like being held by you, Clay. And I'm so glad you're here tonight."

It was the *so* that took hold in his heart, finding purchase, tethering him to her. He thought he could deny himself. He almost believed he could forget her. But he was too far gone to let her go. She was his, and there were simply no two ways about it. She had to be in his life. "Me too."

Soon, she broke the embrace, and took her turn washing him, working her nimble hands across his body, the mischievous look in her eyes telling him that she enjoyed touching him as much as he craved her touch. She stopped at his arm, running a finger along the lines of his tattooed bicep. "Passion," she said, in a reflective voice. "This is so you. It's perfect for you. You are the most passionate man I have ever known. You are passionate in your heart, and passionate in bed, and passionate in your beliefs, and in every single thing you do."

She *got* him. She knew him. She understood who he was, and what made him tick. It was heady being that connected to someone. "It's easy to be passionate with you, Julia."

"And thank you for letting me do that just now in the shower," she said, trailing her fingers across his shoulder.

"For washing me?" He arched an eyebrow in question.

She nodded. "And for letting me tie your hands."

"As I've said before, I've got no issues. No hang-ups. I'm pretty much game for anything and good to go."

"I like that."

"What about you? Anything you don't want me to do?" He asked as she turned the shower off and handed him one of her big fluffy towels, taking another one for herself. "Nice towel," he mentioned offhand.

She didn't answer immediately; instead she folded her towel in half, then in quarters, the long way. He watched her curiously. She raised the towel to her eyes. A knowing grin broke across his face for having gotten her charade.

"Got it. No blindfolding."

She returned to drying off. "I just like to be able to see, that's all. Blindfolding is the only thing that I'm not wild about. And it's not because I have some terrible past with trauma about blindfolding. But the thought of it makes me feel a bit too vul-

210 · LAUREN BLAKELY

nerable, and for a woman with trust issues, well, I'm not sure it's the best kind of kink for me."

She hung up her towel on a hook and he did the same.

"There are many other forms of kink that I'm happy to try with you, Julia," he said, then reached for her hand and led her back to her bedroom. Once they slipped under the covers, he wrapped his arms around her, then brushed her hair away from her ear. "I guess I'll just have to imagine then how you'd look with my tie over your eyes, wearing nothing but stockings, sitting in a chair and touching yourself while I watch."

She craned her neck to give him a curious stare. "Is that your fantasy?"

He nodded. "It is one of many."

"Maybe someday, handsome. Maybe someday."

"I have another fantasy," he murmured softly in her ear, tugging her closer as they spooned.

"What's that?" she asked.

"Falling asleep with you in my arms."

"I think that's about to become your reality."

"Lucky me."

CHAPTER TWENTY

The pancakes were as delicious as she'd promised. With breakfast finished, they walked past a block full of graffiti art and consignment shops in the Mission district. An up-and-coming neighborhood full of hipsters and Internet startup folks, the shops here bore the evidence of the clientele, but there was an element to these few blocks that bothered him. He didn't like the idea of her living in a neighborhood still plagued with crime and trouble, even if the numbers were improving. She was an independent woman though, and it wasn't his place to criticize where she lived.

"You like living here?" he asked, keeping the question casual.

"Sure," she said with a laidback shrug as they sidestepped a sleeping homeless man. "There's a kickass bakery a few blocks over, some fabulous coffee shops, and lots of boutiques that my sister loves, so I get to see her more often."

"Maybe we should all do something next time I'm in town," he suggested, and couldn't deny the touch of nerves in his chest. Last time he'd asked for something more, she'd gone running. But maybe dinner with her sister was something she could handle.

212 · LAUREN BLAKELY

"I would love that," she said, and his nerves departed with her simple answer. "And you're going to love Chris. He's the best."

"I'm looking forward to meeting him in person," he said, checking the time on his watch, "in about twenty minutes."

"Let's get your bag so you're not late," she said as they turned onto her block, passing a vintage clothing shop a few doors down. His driver waited in a town car by her building. Clay gave him a quick wave, then headed to her third-floor apartment. Her cell phone was still on the kitchen counter. She'd left it there all morning, and he'd been grateful to have her undivided attention, a luxury he'd rarely had with Sabrina. He grabbed his suitcase and tapped her metal table. "Good table. That's a keeper."

"I was planning on framing that table because I love what we did on it so much," she said, and then led him back down the stairs and out of her building.

She stopped in her tracks and cursed under her breath. "Fuck," she muttered, and ran a hand through her hair.

"What is it?" he asked, and his shoulders tightened with worry. He zeroed in on her eyes then followed her line of sight to a large man built like a slab of meat pacing a few feet away. The man had black hair, with a white streak down the side. He was scanning the street, and very quickly set his eyes on Julia.

Instantly, Clay reached for her, draping an arm protectively around her. He turned to look at her, holding her gaze tight with his own. "You okay?"

"Yeah," she said in a thin voice as the freight-train-sized man walked toward them.

"You know him?"

"Sort of," she said, as she pressed the tip of her tongue nervously along her teeth.

"Julia," the man barked as he reached them. "You don't answer your phone? Is everything okay?" He sounded strangely concerned, almost paternal, and that irked Clay.

"I was out to breakfast," she said through tight lips. Clay glanced from Julia to the man and back, wanting to know who the hell he was and why he was talking to her like he owned her.

"Charlie needs you tonight."

Julia didn't answer him.

"Julia," Clay asked carefully. "Who's this?"

The man held out a hand, flashed a toothy smile. "I'm Stevie. Who are you?"

Before he could answer, Julia squeezed his arm tightly, some kind of signal, it seemed, then started talking. "This is Carl. Carl and I met last night at the bar. He's just heading home now."

She shot Clay a pleading looking, asking with her eyes to go along with the lie.

"Nice to meet you, Carl," he said, and out of the corner of his eye, Clay noticed a bulge by the man's shins, as if a hard, square barrel of a gun were held safely in place with an ankle holster. Clay didn't have a clue who this man was or why he was packing, but blood rushed fast through his veins, adrenaline kicking in as he quickly cycled through escape routes for the two of them if he pulled it. Down the block, into the building, behind the car. Or better yet, Clay could move first if he needed to. He could take this man; Stevie was big and slow, and Clay had speed on his side. A quick, hard jab to the ribs would double him over, giving them time to get away.

"Likewise," Clay said, calling on his best acting ability. He had no idea why she needed him to lie, and he didn't like it one bit, but he wasn't going to make things worse for her in the moment. Papa bear attitude or not, the man had *thug* or *dealer* written all over him.

Dealer.

Once that notion touched down in his head, he couldn't unsee it or unhear it. It was déjà vu all over again. The sidewalk felt shaky, and the stores on the other side of the street seemed to fall in and out of focus. His chest tightened, and his heart turned cold as if she'd just shoved him into a walk-in freezer.

"When you don't answer," the man said, tilting his head, and explaining in a gentle voice that didn't match his size or his weaponry, "Charlie gets worried."

"I'll be there," she said, and her voice was strained, her body visibly wracked with fear

The man nodded, seeming satisfied with her answer. "I will tell him. See you later. And nice meeting you, Carl."

He walked away, his big frame fading down the block. Clay turned to her. "What was that about? Why did you tell him we met at the bar last night?"

Something dark and sad clouded her eyes. "I don't want him to know who you really are."

"What the hell, Julia?" he asked, his heart still thumping fast and furious. He took a deep fueling breath. "He. Had. A. Gun."

"I know," she said in a broken whisper, a guilty look in her eyes.

"What kind of mess are you in?" he said, holding his hands out wide.

"I can't tell you. You just have to trust me on this. I couldn't say anything about you or use your real name or anything."

"Because?" he asked, annoyed as hell now because she was giving him no reason to think this was acceptable. Lies were never acceptable.

"Just because."

"Who are these people, Julia? Why does Charlie need you tonight, and why does Stevie carry a concealed weapon?" He wished he were in a courtroom because he usually knew the answers to the questions he asked. Now he was swimming blind, without a clue as to his direction.

"There's something I have to help Charlie with," she said, and it was one of the most dissatisfying answers he'd ever heard, and it left an acrid taste in his mouth. He was ready, so damn ready to get the hell out of town. A knot of anger rolled through him, but then he swallowed it away, because there was that image burned in his brain—the outline of a gun. And if you weren't the one carrying the gun, you were usually the target. Julia was in danger, and he couldn't abide by that.

His feelings for her ran too deep to just walk away.

He needed to do everything he could to get her out of the line of fire. He softened, cupping her shoulders. "If you're in trouble, let me help you," he offered, doing his best to let go of his past with Sabrina and to trust the woman in front of him, especially after last night and how she'd seemed to finally open up. "If there's something going on, I want to help you. I know my way around."

"I can't. I have to do this on my own."

"Why?" he asked, the word strangled in his throat.

"You have to trust me on this."

"You're making it awfully hard to trust you," he said, tucking a strand of hair behind her ear.

Her lower lip quivered. "I know," she said, and her voice was starting to break.

"Tell me," he said, pleading now. "Tell me what is going on. Tell me what they want from you. What they have on you. I'm a goddamn lawyer, Julia."

"Clay," she said, softly, pushing back. "You negotiate deals for actors and directors."

He exhaled sharply, not liking the way she'd put that. "Yes, that's what I do, and I'm damn good at it. That means I know how to solve problems, and I also understand the fine nuances of how people interact, and when you— " He stopped talking to point at her "—lie to someone who's carrying a gun, that's a problem. And I want to help solve that problem, if you'll let me."

She worried away at her lower lip, and he wanted to gently kiss her fears away and tell her it would all be fine. But he had no way of knowing that, because she'd given him no reason to put faith in her words.

"I appreciate that. You have no idea how much. But I can't let you do it."

"Can you give me a reason why? Because every instinct inside of me is telling me to walk away and not look back. You told me last night not to worry, and now I am worried, because whatever trouble you're in is looking bigger and bigger. So why won't you let me help you?"

She squeezed her eyes shut, so tight and hard as if she were in pain. Then she opened them, and it was like looking in a mirror—her eyes were etched with the same kind of desperation he felt. The problem was, she held all the cards, and he didn't even know what game they were playing.

"I just need you to trust me. That's all. I need you to. I swear I need you to."

He ran his fingers gently through her hair, wanting, wishing to be able to do this with her. To go all in. But the moment was far too familiar, and it felt like a flashback to his worst times, especially when she grabbed his arm hard. "Please," she said.

He'd been here; he'd seen the same routine from Sabrina, begging him to believe her, pleading with him to see that she wasn't hopped up on pills. Claiming she was getting help, when she was really selling off her purses and jewelry to buy more drugs. He has no idea if Julia was buying drugs, or shaking off a past as a stripper, or hiding some other dark secret, because she wouldn't say. She wouldn't give him the courtesy of the truth. That left him with one cold, hard fact—she was lying. Whether directly or by omission didn't matter. She wasn't being honest.

And that both hurt and pissed him off.

His veins felt scrubbed raw with a scouring pad as he gently, but firmly, peeled her hand off his arm. He didn't need this in his life again. He had business to take care of for his clients, and he couldn't risk the chance of another fucked-up relationship with a trouble-laden woman distracting him from his job.

Julia was perfect and captivating, clever and sexy, and tattooed head-to-toe with the warning sign that read *trouble ahead*. Good thing he'd seen it now before he went in too deep.

"I can't do this Julia," he said, grabbing the handle of his suitcase. "I need to go."

He shut the car door hard behind him, locking it, as if that would keep thoughts of her at bay. He couldn't risk letting a deal slip through his fingers again, and certainly not over a woman messing with his head, and his heart. There was one choice for him now.

He'd have to find a way to forget her, hard and fast.

* * *

She dug her heels into the ground, imagining weights pinning her down, preventing her from doing what she desperately wanted to do.

Go after him.

She bit down hard on her bottom lip. Something, anything so she wouldn't shout his name, chase the car down the street, bang her fists on the metal, and beg him to roll down the window so she could tell him that she wasn't lying; she was protecting him.

But she couldn't live with the chance that he'd become a target too.

She wanted him in her life, wanted him with every ounce of her being. But seeing him hurt would be worse. She sank down on the cold concrete steps of her building, crumpled in a mess. Like her whole damn life, and her stupid heart too. A heart that ached for the man she'd fallen hard for, and had to let go.

Julia and Clay's story continues in After This Night...

AFTER THIS NIGHT
Book #2 in the Seductive Nights series

ABOUT
AFTER THIS NIGHT

"Let me control your pleasure."

Their world was passion, pleasure and secrets.

Far too many secrets. But Clay Nichols can't get Julia Bell out of his mind. He's so drawn to her, and to the nights they shared, that he can't focus on work or business. Only her. And she's pissing him off with her hot and cold act. She has her reasons though–she's trying to stay one step ahead of the trouble that's been chasing her for months now, thanks to the criminal world her ex dragged her into. If only she can get out of this mess, then maybe she can invite the man who ignites her back in her life, so she can have him–heart, mind and body.

He won't take less than all of her, and the full truth too. When he runs into her again at her sister's wedding, they have a second chance but she'll have to let him all the way in. And they'll learn just how much more there is to the intense sexual chemistry they share, and whether love can carry them well past the danger of her past and into a new future, after this night...

The sequel to the sensual, emotionally-charged erotic romance, Night After Night, from the New York Times and USA Today Bestselling author Lauren Blakely...

This book is dedicated to Gale, who listens to my stories, and helps shape them. You are indispensable to me, and I am so glad our paths crossed.

CHAPTER ONE

The dress was so perfect it brought a tear to her eye.

"He's going to have the breath knocked out of him when he sees you walking down the aisle," Julia managed to say while wiping her hand across her cheek.

Her sister, McKenna, twirled once in front of the three-way mirror at Cara's Bridal Boutique deep in the heart of Noe Valley, admiring the tea-length dress she'd picked for her wedding in a few weeks. The dress was pure McKenna, down to the flouncy taffeta petticoat underneath the satin skirt.

"It's so playful and pretty at the same time," Julia said.

"Speaking of pretty, do you like your dress still?"

"Of course," she said with a wide-eyed smile, gesturing to the sleek black maid-of-honor dress she wore that McKenna had picked for her.

"It's totally you. I wanted you to have a dress you could wear again. Maybe to a date? A fancy night out?"

The words fell on her ears with a hollow clang. Because she could no longer wish for a night out with the man she wanted terribly.

Clay had left her that morning on the streets of San Francisco, ending their brief love affair and driving away in his town car. She couldn't fault him for taking off. She couldn't give him what he wanted—an end to her secrecy. That's what Clay needed more than anything. More than her body, more than their chemistry, more even than their endless nights together. She couldn't tell him the truth about why she'd lied to the guy with the gun who'd been waiting on her doorstep that morning when they had returned after breakfast. What could she say? *He's the mob heavy who's been assigned to me to make sure I pay off a debt that isn't even mine?* If she told Clay, he'd be a target too, because that's how these men operated: they circled you, ensnaring you on all sides until the people you loved fell into their crosshairs, too.

That's why she'd claimed Clay was just some guy she'd met in a bar, rather than a high-profile entertainment lawyer with an even higher-profile list of clients. She wanted to protect his identity and keep him out of the line of fire.

"And I will wear it again. Again and again. I promise," she said, tugging McKenna in for a warm embrace, even though she had no idea when or where she'd wear this number.

After they stepped out of their dresses, McKenna paid the final deposit on both, plunking down her credit card on the counter without a second thought. Julia felt a sliver of envy for the ease with which her sister could navigate matters of money. Shrewd businesswoman that she was, McKenna had turned her fashion blog into a fashion empire. If she'd owed a big, fat debt, it could be paid off instantly from her flush savings account. If she asked, McKenna would pay Julia's debt too, handing over the dough in a heartbeat. But she wasn't going to attach her sister to this problem because that's how it became hers in the first place—when it was passed on to her, like a disease.

"Chris said the meeting with Clay went great today," McKenna remarked as they strolled out of the shop and onto the busy street, crowded with mid-afternoon foot traffic: moms pushing strollers into coffee shops and young hipsters heading back to work after lunch at cafes with all-organic menus.

"That's great about the meeting," Julia said, as casually as she could.

"Did he tell you about it?"

"Chris? Why would I be talking to him?"

McKenna shoved her playfully. "Um, no. The hot guy you went to New York for. The hot guy I know you're into. Are you going to see Clay while he's in town?"

She shrugged and looked away, and those twin gestures were enough for her sister to stop in her tracks and park her hands on her hips. "Whoa. What's going on?"

And with that, it was as if a tight knot started to unravel in her. She might not be able to tell her sister about her money troubles, but she could at least let her know about her man woes.

"I did see him last night. I don't think it's going to work out between us," she said, and she didn't bother to strip the frustration from her voice, or the residual sadness. A sob threatened to lodge in her throat and turn into a fit of dumb waterworks. But giving in to the tears was like kicking a brick wall. It didn't do any good, and you were left mostly with a stubbed toe.

"Oh no. Why do you say that?"

"He's too far away in New York. And I'm just busy here. And he's all about work."

"That stinks," McKenna said, and she stomped her foot on the sidewalk. The gesture was so child-like that Julia couldn't help but laugh. "But at least you weren't too far in?" she said, her eyes full of hopefulness. She wrapped an arm around her sister.

Julia was tempted to reassure her. To tell her it was nothing, just a night here, a weekend there. But it wasn't. He was more, so much more.

"Actually, I really liked him a lot, so it's a bit of a bummer."

"Then we need to go drown our sorrows in French fries and cake. Let me take you out," McKenna offered.

Julia said yes, and though the French fries were fantastic, they weren't enough, not even close, to forget about the man she couldn't have. The problem was she didn't have any room in her life for him, and if she let him linger any more in her heart, she'd surely lose the game tonight.

Tonight was for winning.

CHAPTER TWO

The venture capitalist with the laughing tell was back, and he spent most of the game staring at Julia. But Hunter must have gotten a tip to strike that laugh from his repertoire because the first time he chuckled Julia went all in, and lost a cool grand. He'd really had three kings. No bluffing.

He'd likely snagged himself a poker tutor, some former pro player who now trained eager wannabe card sharks in the ways of the game, or a grizzled old veteran needing to earn a dime or two after he'd retired. She'd seen it before among the hotshots. A pivot here, a change-up there—all signs that they were being coached on the side. And that they thought they were hot shit.

He wasn't. No one was.

"I'm in," he said, shoving a black chip into the pot, eyes on her the whole time. Like she was his prey.

So wrong.

She was the predator. They were all her enemies, every last one of them, and just because she'd lost a hand didn't mean she was going to lose the game. She rubbed her index finger against a black chip, checked out her cards again, then scanned Hunter's face. Pale skin, pock marks from acne probably garnered only a few years ago when he was in high school, and a nice, straight nose. His blue eyes were locked on her, and that was another clue he'd hired a tutor. He'd probably been told to stare her down, the tutor thinking that would knock her off her game.

Didn't work. Not in general, and certainly not tonight, when she had jetpacks of anger fueling her. She was pissed at Dillon, pissed at Stevie, pissed at Charlie, pissed at Hunter, and most of all, pissed at Clay for not believing her. If only he could see her now, he'd feel like a goddamn heel for casting all that doubt on her. He'd acted like she was a lying drug user, like his ex. Ha. Couldn't be farther from the truth. She wished she could record this game with a secret hidden camera and show him. *"There. See? I'm this scumbag's ringer 'til my debt is done. Happy now?"*

Screw him and his lack of faith. Screw Hunter and his lack of a tell. Screw his tutor. Screw them all. She was ballsier than Hunter, and she'd play to her strengths. *Guts.*

She had two tens, and she was betting on them.

"I'll see your $500 and I'll raise you $1000," she said, pressing her long red fingernail against one chip, sliding it in, then methodically doing the same with the next two chips.

He showed no response for a few seconds, as if he were trying to hold in his reaction. Then his eyebrow twitched, and she wanted to pump a fist. New tell, perhaps?

The rest of the crew had folded. The guy who owned a sporting goods shop leaned back in his chair, eyes flickering between Julia and Hunter. He was a regular, and a plant. He won some, lost some, and generally was in attendance to balance out a game. There was also a young guy with chiseled cheekbones and wavy hair who drove one of Charlie's limos. All here to pad the table.

Over in the kitchen, Stevie the Skunk sifted through a plate of fresh-baked cookies, scarfing down another one. She had no idea who'd baked cookies for a rigged card game, but maybe it was his mama or his wife. Or maybe it was his colleague. There was a new guy with him, a baby-faced fellow named Max with gray eyes and a barrel-like body. *Perhaps he was a trainee of Skunk's,* Julia had mused when she'd met him before the game. No gun on his ankle yet, though. Maybe he hid it elsewhere.

Hunter surprised her by grabbing two chips and dropping them in the pile. "Time to show the cards. Lucky sevens," he said with a lopsided grin, all confidence and bravado now. She wondered if his tutor would pat him on the back for that move, and say *good boy.* She wondered if she cared what his tutor thought. She decided she didn't. All she wanted was that money, so badly she was damn near salivating for it. All those black beauties in the pile would bring her a touch closer to freedom from Charlie's thumb, and his knife, and his goon who followed her around with a gun.

She laid down her hand, revealing her pair of tens. Hunter nodded once, all steely-eyed and cool at first. But when Julia pulled the chips over to her corner of the table, he pointed a finger at her. She raised her eyes, mildly curious.

Hunter didn't speak at first. She could see the cogs in his head turning, like he was adding, multiplying and dividing.

"You don't play like the rest of them," he said in an even voice.

"You don't say," she replied, emotionless.

"You play like a shark. I see it in your eyes. I know that look. I'm a venture capitalist. I have that look every day when I take a risk. You're the same."

"Just call me a VC then," she said as she stacked her chips, keeping her hands steady even though her heart was thumping.

"You're not just a player," he said, with narrowed eyes.

"Call me a player. Call me not a player. I don't care. Why don't you just deal the next hand?" she said, keeping her cool as best she could.

Skunk looked up from the cookies when he heard the chatter. This was more talking than usual for this kind of a game.

"No," he said, shaking his head as he rose. "I'm not gonna deal. You're a fucking ringer, aren't you?"

Stevie the Skunk took the reins. He ambled over to the table and pressed his big hands on the wood. "What's going on? We all playing nice?"

"No. She's a ringer and this game is rigged. I knew something was up the first time, and I know it for sure now," he said, pointing his finger accusingly at the big man. Max marched closer but kept his distance, watching the scene.

Julia's blood raced along the speedways in her body, panic galloping through her veins. She had a sinking feeling about what was coming next, and she was right. Skunk reached for his gun with a speed she'd never imagined the lumbering man possessed. "Get the fuck out," he said coolly to Hunter. "And you're not welcome at the restaurant, either."

"I was right," Hunter said, practically hopping in righteousness.

Julia clamped her lips shut so she wouldn't shout, "*What did you think it was? What the hell else could this game possibly be?*"

"Charlie told me it was an executive game, but it's not," he insisted and he must have been the ballsiest VC in the Valley because he wasn't leaving.

Stevie waved the gun. "Was there something unclear about what I said? Because it sounded clear to me. But if you're having trouble hearing, I'm happy to head on down to the local precinct tonight and make sure my friends on the force know that you put your fucking hands all over this woman here," he said, gripping Julia's shoulder with his free paw, in a gesture that felt both strangely protective and thoroughly invasive. "And I've got witnesses who'll vouch for me, right?"

The chiseled-cheekbone guy nodded along with the sporting goods fella.

The tiny hairs on the back of her neck stood on end, and she was oddly grateful for Skunk, and disgusted at the same time. He'd protected her, but he'd really protected Charlie's investment. And he'd done it in the same way Charlie had subverted her for his uses—by betting on her being a woman. By betting on men underestimating her at cards, and now by suggesting she was a helpless little lady who'd been manhandled.

Hunter grabbed his few remaining chips. "I'm cashing out."

"No you're not. You're getting out. That's your penalty for disrupting the game. Out," Skunk said in a low and powerful tone, pointing to the door.

Hunter held up his hands, huffed out through his nostrils. "You won't be seeing the last of me."

He left, the sound of his footsteps echoing as he clomped down the stairs.

* * *

Charlie glared at her. "What did you say to him?"

"I didn't say a thing."

"What did you say that made him figure it out?" Charlie pressed, dropping his chopsticks next to his plate of pork dumplings at the Chinese restaurant underneath the apartment where the game was held. The restaurant was empty. It had closed an hour ago.

"I told you. *Nothing.*"

"I don't need all of the VCs knowing our game is rigged. He and his friends come to my restaurant every Friday for lunch. Their employees eat here too," he said, stabbing the table with a finger. "I had some of his friends from Steiner Hawkins coming to the next game. They just sold a social media startup they backed for $50 million. They are flush with cash. You know what that means?"

Julia shook her head, fear rippling across her chest. "No."

Charlie pushed back from the table and rose. He stalked closer to Julia, forcing her to back up against the wall. He crowded her, caging her in with his hands on each side of her head.

"Let me explain what it means, Red," he said, spitting the words on her face. "It means they're not coming. They're not playing my game. It means I won't get their money. And that also means the next time you play, you take a fall."

"What?" She furrowed her brow in disbelief. "How does that help any of us?"

"It sends the word to the street that my games are fair. You take a fall. And you are in my debt, Red."

"I won tonight," she said, trying to insist. "I won $6,000. I'm close. I'm almost there."

"You didn't win $6,000," he said breathing on her. The scent of fried pork coming from his mouth curled her stomach. "You cost me $6,000."

She wanted to sink to the ground, to crouch down and hug her knees and curl up in a corner. She felt like she'd been smashed with an anvil. Every time she got closer, he moved the finish line.

"It's not even my debt," she said, her voice bordering on begging.

"It is your debt. I have seen your pretty little bar, with your pretty little bartenders, and my pretty little money that you put into it. And let me remind you of what happens if you ever think I will forget that you owe me."

He grabbed her by the hair and yanked. She stifled a scream, and her mind flashed to how different it felt when Clay pulled her hair or boxed her in against the wall. When he did those things it was fair and it was wanted, and it was part of the way they played with each other. There was no game with Charlie. He played to hurt, and he gripped her hair so tight she believed he had the strength to tug it right off her scalp.

He jerked her through the empty restaurant, out the door and into the foggy night, then down the block, stopping in front of a pub. He let go of her hair, and she wanted to cry with relief. "This bar? See this bar? Picture it as yours. It's Cubic Z, and if we're not clear by the end of the next month, it's mine."

"No!" she said, trembling from head to toe. She had employees; she had a co-owner. She was responsible for them all, for their livelihood, even for the little baby growing in Kim's belly.

"Yes," he said with an evil smile as he nodded vigorously. "Yes, it will be mine, and I have not decided if it will be Charlie Z or if I will simply take great pleasure in running it into the ground and then having my way with you." He stopped talking to coil a strand of her hair around his index finger. "I might be starting some new businesses with some very pretty women who can make money for me the old-fashioned way. Would you like that, Red? To be on your back?"

Every cell in her body screamed as fear plunged its way through her veins. "No," she said, her voice shaking.

"I didn't think so. Now get out of my sight."

He turned her around and shoved her hard on her spine. In her skyscraper heels, she stumbled and the sidewalk loomed ominously close, but she gripped the doorway of the bar in time, and walked away from him. When she reached her building, she stopped at the mailboxes in the lobby and grabbed bills, flyers and coupons. She quickly sorted the letters, tossing credit-card offers and carpet-cleaning deals in the trash. Then she spotted a letter that would make any citizen groan.

From the IRS.

She slid her finger under the flap as she trudged up the stairs, wondering what the government could want from her. She paid her taxes on time every year. She unfolded the letter and scanned it—a letter of inquiry. The IRS was asking if she knew where Dillon Whittaker was living these days since he hadn't filed his taxes for the year before.

She scoffed as she unlocked her door. If Charlie didn't know where Dillon was, the IRS sure as hell wasn't going to find him.

* * *

Later that night, the hot water from the shower rained down on her head and her mind returned to Dillon. When they'd met he seemed like the easygoing photographer, the funny guy with a quick wit, and a sweet word.

But he was so much more. He was insidious in ways she never imagined he could be, because he'd figured out how to leave town with $100,000 scot-free, and no strings attached. Tra la *fucking* la. She could still recall the moment when her world came crashing down. She and Dillon had already split, and she wasn't keeping tabs on him so she didn't know he'd fled the country. She'd been mixing a pitcher of margaritas for a bachelorette party when Charlie strolled into the bar, parking himself on a sleek, steel stool. He steepled his hands in front of him, and cocked his head to the side. "How is the expansion going?"

"What do you mean?" she asked curiously. She knew Charlie, had met him once before through Dillon, but they'd never broken bread or toasted together.

"I understand you needed some money for your bar. Dillon asked me for a loan on your behalf, and since he's been good and loyal to me, and was willing to pay 15 percent, I happily said yes. And seeing as Dillon has left the country, it seemed the right time for you and I to get acquainted."

The saying *you could hear a pin drop* took on new meaning as the sound in the bar was vacuumed up. She could hear everything, from the chatter of nearby patrons, to the waiters placing drinks on low tables, to the frantic beat of her heart and the blood roaring in her ears.

"What do you mean?" She carefully set down the pitcher she was holding. If she held it a second longer she'd drop it, and it would shatter and break. It would be her tell, and if there's one thing she knew from the mobster movies she'd seen, you don't let them smell your fear. When they do, they pounce.

He drummed his fingers against the counter. "What I mean is we need to talk, Red."

"About what?" she asked, feeling like an animal crouching in a corner.

"About what you can do to repay me."

Her eyes widened. "But the money wasn't for me. I didn't even know he got a loan from you," Julia had said, her voice rising in fear, her skin turning pale.

Charlie arched an eyebrow. "That's very funny."

"But it's true. This is the first I've heard of this, I swear. I never got that money. I never saw a dime. I had no idea," she said, trying so hard to prove her innocence, as her stomach twisted and her hands turned clammy.

This couldn't be happening.

Charlie cackled. "That's what they all say. *I had no idea*. But now it's time to have *an* idea about how you're going to pay me. I hear you like poker. Make me a gin and tonic and I will tell you how you will be playing for me. Because what this means, Red, is that you are mine."

She still was his, and she had no idea how much longer she would have to pay for that son-of-a-bitch's twisted act of deception.

* * *

Julia couldn't sleep, which bugged the crap out of her. She'd never suffered from insomnia, not even in the darkest days with Dillon. Not even in those early weeks of Charlie's indentured servitude when she was still dazed and shocked that this had become her life. But now she lay wide awake in her king-size bed, the window open, the late night sounds of San Francisco drifting in: the occasional car horn, the faint hum of the bus that ran on electricity, the crash of a garbage can, likely knocked over by a vagrant.

Clay had seemed a bit wary of her neighborhood, and while her section of The Mission wasn't bad per se, it hadn't yet come into its own. She didn't mind the seedier elements; she knew real danger didn't lie with the guy panhandling on the street corner. But she liked that Clay had a protective side, and a helpful side, too. He'd tried so hard to get her to open up the other day and tell him all her troubles. She'd been tempted. She could see herself laying them at his feet and serving them up for him to solve.

But then her problems would become his problems, and she couldn't abide by that. Dillon had sloughed off his garbage onto her, and she wasn't going to hot potato it on to someone else, especially someone she cared so deeply for. Because she did care for him. So much more than she'd planned to when she said yes to that one weekend in New York. She'd thought she could jet across the country and have a fantastic getaway. Instead, she'd gone all in.

She had nothing to show for it though.

All the anger that fueled her during the game had faded, and she simply felt weary, and lonely, too, as she flashed back to the pained look on his face, to the tortured gaze in his eyes, to the way he'd reacted when she'd pleaded.

Then she cast her mind further back to the night before when he'd tried so hard to find his way into her heart. Her chest tightened at the memory, and she longed so deeply to let him in the way he wanted, and the way she wanted too.

The very least she could do was say she was sorry. She grabbed her phone from her nightstand and began tapping out a message to the man she missed more than she had ever expected.

CHAPTER THREE

As he stepped off the red-eye from Los Angeles to New York the next morning, his email burst with a flurry of messages.

First, a note from Flynn about the Pinkertons, and how the deal was coming together for their next film. Then one from his friend Michele, reminding him that they had tickets to the theater in a week. Damn, he'd nearly forgotten they were going to see an adaptation of *The Usual Suspects* for the stage. Next, a quick update from an actor client, Liam, who was starring in that play and also opening a hip restaurant in Murray Hill. Clay had been advising him on the deal. Liam was a busy guy and Clay liked it that way. Then a note from Chris Mc-Cormick, the TV show host he'd met with in San Francisco after spending one more night with Julia.

One unforgettable night that had as much to do with her answering the door wearing only stockings and a shirt as it did with her finally starting to open up to him.

But that had all been a lie, he reminded himself, willing his heart to fossilize when it came to her. Telling himself not to linger on the memories of how she seemed to be sharing her fears, and inviting him into her life, because that was all up-ended when she lied about who he was to that thug on the street.

His fingers tightened on his phone, gripping it harder, as if he were channeling his frustration into the screen. He needed to get into Manhattan as soon as possible, make a pit stop at his boxing gym, and then get his ass to work. That was his plan of attack: the way to rid Julia from his mind. Head down, nose in work, client meetings—the recipe to numb him to the effect of that woman.

He scrolled through Chris's note, a quick summary of what he was most looking for in his next contract with the TV network that carried his show, and then he read Chris's previous contract that the host had handled on his own. *As you can probably surmise, negotiating on my own behalf is not my expertise. Happy to have you doing it for me going forward*, Chris had written.

He replied quickly to Chris, eager to prove his value to his new client. That the guy was marrying Julia's sister in a month didn't even factor into his decision. Because he wasn't thinking about Julia, not as he walked past security, responding to a note, not as he found his driver while answering another email, and certainly not as he slid into the backseat of a town car that would zip him into the city.

Then he saw a new email land in his inbox. From her. The subject line gave nothing away: *Hi.* But Pavlovian response kicked in, and he opened it before he could think. Because seeing her name still felt like a damn good thing, still held the promise of a sexy note, a naughty line, or a sweet nothing. But more than any of those options, it held the promise of *her*.

from: purplesnowglobe@gmail.com
to: cnichols@gmail.com
date: April 25, 4:08 AM
subject: Hi

Clay,

Hi. I'm lying awake in bed thinking of last night. How only 24 hours ago you were here with me. How much better it was to sleep with your arms around me, all safe and warm and snug. How much I would love to have you here again. But I know that won't happen. And I understand. I truly understand. If I were you, I would hate me too. If I were you, I'd be suspicious as hell. And I probably wouldn't trust me either. So I get 100 percent where you're coming from and I wish there were another way. I want you in my life so badly that I can feel this ache where you're supposed to be. But I know I can't have you, and I'm sorry I can't be open right now. You deserve more than this. More than me. All I will say is this sucks, and if I could turn back time and do certain things over there's a lot I would change.

But I wouldn't change a second with you.

Wow. I just re-read my note. I think that's the mushiest I've ever been with anyone. Damn, you did a number on me, and I've got it bad for you. I'm hitting send while I still have the guts in me to do so, even though I will probably regret it. Except this is all true.

Xoxo
Julia

He dropped his head in his hand, and cursed. A wave of frustration and longing rolled through him, and he knew he should turn the damn phone off and ignore her. But this woman, she was under his skin. He hated lies but he'd be lying to himself if he pretended he'd forgotten her in a day.

from: cnichols@gmail.com
to: purplesnowglobe@gmail.com
date: April 25, 7:12 AM
subject: Hi

I don't hate you. The farthest thing from it.

He hit send before the regret washed over him, as it eventually would, he was sure.

* * *

By the end of the day he wasn't feeling much. He was riding at the perfect levels of blankness. A day in the trenches had done wonders for him, and a night at the gym would drain him of any residual feelings that threatened to resurface.

The next day he did the same, burying himself in business, making sure every *T* was crossed and *I* dotted, that points were won, and clients weren't just making more money, they were being protected in their business deals. His job was a hell of a lot more than wringing more dollars from networks, studios and producers. It was checking out the fine print, making sure clients were looked out for when it came to two, three, four years down the road in a deal.

His days followed that pattern for the next week, and the regular routine of work, gym, business drinks or dinner, sleep, then rinse, lather, repeat the next day turned Julia into a hazy blur in the rearview mirror. Soon, she'd migrated to the back of his mind, and the fact that she'd been relocated there pleased him immensely. A few more days of supreme focus and she would be a distant blip on the horizon.

At seven-thirty on the dot on a Wednesday night, he left his office and headed for Times Square, threading his way through the crowds of tourists in their *I Love NY* sweat-shirts and *Property of NYFD* nylon jackets, with pretzels and hot dogs in hand, as they snapped photos of the neon signs and the famous intersection. He walked past the St. James Theater, tapping once on the poster for *Crash the Moon*, feeling a surge of pride for that show's quick success. His friend Davis had directed it, and it had become a smash hit in the first month alone, playing to packed houses every single night.

He crossed the street, dodging a cab stalled in traffic, as he made his way to the bright lights of the Shubert Theater where Liam was playing the Kevin Spacey character in *The Usual Suspects*. Michele waited outside the theater lobby, smiling when she spotted him, and Clay took some comfort in the reliability of a friend like her. She'd been here through the years, always available for a drink, always willing to chat, or to see a movie or show. She was a good one, steady, dependable, and patently honest. A warm feeling rushed over him with the reminder that there were people you could trust implicitly. She would never dance around the truth.

"Hey you," she said, waving her fingers, and then giving him a quick kiss on each cheek.

"Are we French now?"

"Of course," she said playfully. "We'll grab baguettes and sip espresso after the curtain call."

"That'd be nice," he said, as they walked into the theater and he handed two tickets to the usher who led them down the aisle to some of the best seats in the house.

Michele raised an eyebrow. "Impressive."

"Like this is a surprise? We always get the best seats. Your brother is a Tony-winning director," Clay said, gesturing for Michele to take her seat.

"I know. And I don't ever take that for granted. And you," she said, wrapping her hand around his arm, and leaning in close, "are the man behind the scenes who makes this stuff happen, too."

He waved off the compliment. He wasn't in the business for compliments. "Tell me about your day," he said, and listened as she shared the little details that she could, not breaking any client confidentiality but talking in general terms about her work listening to the woes of others as one of New York's finest shrinks. Her voice was calming and soothing, so he barely noticed that she'd kept her hand on his forearm the whole time.

When the curtain rose at the start of the play, she stayed like that, palm wrapped around him. A few minutes into the first act, he almost asked her to move her hand, but then it wasn't really bothering him, and they were old friends. Even if they'd kissed once back in college, it didn't matter that she was touching him, shifting closer. Her shoulder was brushing his by the time the cast took their bows. *She smelled nice*, he thought. Some flowery scent to her hair, maybe jasmine? He'd never noticed it before.

"Did you like the play?" he asked as the theater rang with cheers for the actors.

"Loved it."

"Never gets old, does it? Even when you know it's coming, the Keyser Soze reveal."

"It's a brilliant twist," she said, agreeing.

"I need to go see Liam." He gestured to the backstage entrance. "You gonna come along?"

"Of course."

Once backstage, Liam greeted him with a clap on the back and a hearty hug.

"Nice work. You were better than Spacey," Clay said.

Liam beamed and pointed his index finger at Clay. "Flattery will get you everywhere." Then he turned to Michele. "And who is the lovely lady on your arm tonight?"

Michele laughed nervously. "Oh, we're not together. Just friends," she said, extending a hand to shake.

Liam's green eyes twinkled. "All the better for me," he said, then ran a hand through his mass of dark hair. "Why don't you come along to The Vitale then for a nightcap? It's right next to the restaurant I'll be opening soon."

Clay wanted to roll his eyes. Could Liam be any more obvious? But Michele seemed to be enjoying it because she answered quickly. "I would love to."

"I would love to take you."

Liam was recognized a few times on the street, and again at the bar where he was amiable, and signed a cocktail napkin for a young woman who said she was a theater student at NYU and had always loved his work.

"That's so nice that she adores you so much," Michele said to Liam when the woman walked away.

"And I adore signing cocktail napkins," Liam said, with his trademark grin that made women swoon. "Signed a few in the Bahamas last weekend."

"How was your vacation there?" Clay asked. "Good times?"

"Amazing. Gorgeous blue skies, perfect weather . . . did some fishing. Oh, and listen to this. Some guy tried to get me to buy real estate there. A damn condo, of all things," Liam said, tossing his hands up in exasperation. "Do they think I was born yesterday? I know how those things work. It was probably for one of those deals where only one unit is done so they show you that. And then just pictures of the rest."

"And you want me to advise you on whether this is a good deal or not?" Clay said in a dry tone.

"Oh yeah. Exactly. Please tell me, because my poor little actor brain can't figure it out," he said, and the two men laughed.

"Actually," Michele chimed in, crossing her legs, and sitting up straighter in the bar stool as she kept her eyes locked on Liam. "I've heard that a lot of those scams try to prey on celebrities. Because so many celebrities can often make quick decisions with money."

"I can make quick decisions on other things," Liam said, waggling his eyebrows at Michele.

"Like what, Liam?" she asked in a soft, sexy voice Clay had rarely heard her use.

Damn, the flirting between the two was stirring up again. "And that's my cue to go," Clay said, slapping some money down on the bar. He patted Liam on the shoulder. "Poker tomorrow night?"

"Of course."

"See you then."

He started to leave, but Michele followed him to the doorway. "You're always just taking off," she said brusquely, crossing her arms.

"Didn't seem I was necessary around here. You two are hitting it off," he said with a shrug.

"Are you trying to pawn me off on him?"

"Pawn you off?" he asked as if she'd been speaking a foreign language. "You guys are getting along. I'm making myself scarce so you can keep getting along."

She heaved a sigh. "How was your trip to San Francisco last week?"

He could have done without the reminder. It took every ounce of will he had to strip his California girl from his brain. "It was fine."

"Did you ever hear from that woman you were crazy about?"

And his perfect hold on not thinking about Julia slipped through his fingers. One mention, one reminder of how he felt for her, and she came roaring back to the front of his mind. It was like a truck had slammed into his body, the weight and pressure of the memory of the woman he craved. "Michele, if you don't want to hang with Liam, I don't care. I'll tell him I need to take you home. Whatever you need. I'm not trying to pawn you off on him. I thought you were having a nice time with him and I wanted to get out of the way. If I read the signals wrong, I'm sorry."

"You do a lot of that, don't you?" she said, looking him fiercely in the eyes like they were locked in a battle to not blink first.

He squinted at her, as if that would help him understand what she was saying. "What do you mean?"

"Read the signals wrong, Clay. You read the signals wrong," she said, parking her hands on her hips.

"What signals am I reading wrong?"

"You really don't get it, do you?"

He shook his head in frustration. "Evidently I don't. And on that note, it was a pleasure spending the evening with you."

Once he returned to his home, he tossed his suit jacket on the couch, unbuttoned his shirt, and threw it in the laundry. He washed his face, brushed his teeth, shed the rest of his clothes, and then flopped down on his bed, surrounded by the sounds of silence.

He considered taking up meditation for a nanosecond. Then practicing a mantra. Hell, maybe he could even give yoga a shot. But in the end, none of those things suited him, so he did what his instincts told him to do. Reach out to Julia.

CHAPTER FOUR

from: cnichols@gmail.com
to: purplesnowglobe@gmail.com
date: May 2, 8:23 PM
subject: You

I keep thinking about what happened on your street. Can't stop worrying about you. Are you okay?

from: purplesnowglobe@gmail.com
to: cnichols@gmail.com
date: May 2, 11:24 PM
subject: Me

Mostly. How are you?

from: cnichols@gmail.com
to: purplesnowglobe@gmail.com
date: May 2, 8:25 PM
subject: Not my favorite day that's for sure

Been better . . .

from: purplesnowglobe@gmail.com
to: cnichols@gmail.com
date: May 2, 11:26 PM
subject: Wish I could change that

I hate the thought of you having a bad day. I want you to be happy.

from: cnichols@gmail.com
to: purplesnowglobe@gmail.com
date: May 2, 8:27 PM
subject: I'm not unhappy

I'm just worried about you. I feel like an ass. Like I just left you there on the street.

from: purplesnowglobe@gmail.com
to: cnichols@gmail.com
date: May 2, 11:29 PM
subject: You're not, but you have a nice ass :)

I'm a big girl. I made it home safely. But it's sweet you were worried.

from: cnichols@gmail.com
to: purplesnowglobe@gmail.com
date: May 2, 8:31 PM
subject: Sweet? Me?

I still am worried. Is Stevie bugging you?

from: purplesnowglobe@gmail.com
to: cnichols@gmail.com
date: May 2, 11:32 PM
subject: Soooo sweet . . . strong, confident, sexy too

He's fine. It will all be fine soon enough. Let's talk about something else. I came up with a new cocktail tonight.

from: cnichols@gmail.com
to: purplesnowglobe@gmail.com
date: May 2, 8:33 PM
subject: Mixing it up

Tell me about it.

from: purplesnowglobe@gmail.com
to: cnichols@gmail.com
date: May 2, 11:34 PM
subject: Delish on your lips . . .

It's lemonade, vodka and champagne.

from: cnichols@gmail.com
to: purplesnowglobe@gmail.com
date: May 2, 8:35 PM
subject: That describes you . . .

Sounds like something I'd never touch but that will be beloved by your bar goers.

from: purplesnowglobe@gmail.com
to: cnichols@gmail.com
date: May 2, 11:36 PM
subject: Love your innuendo

It is already. The gal I run the bar with served a ton tonight. Said it was a big hit. Everyone was happy-buzzed too.

from: cnichols@gmail.com
to: purplesnowglobe@gmail.com
date: May 2, 8:37 PM
subject: Double entendres too

Sounds like a perfect state of existence. Can I have one of those too? The happy-buzz, that is.

from: purplesnowglobe@gmail.com
to: cnichols@gmail.com
date: May 2, 11:37 PM
subject: Named it for you

I call it The Heist. What did you do tonight? If you were on a date, please just tell me you played with kittens at a rescue shelter or something instead.

from: cnichols@gmail.com
to: purplesnowglobe@gmail.com
date: May 2, 8:39 PM
subject: No pussy tonight

I saw a play. My favorite kind of storyline. (And thank you for the name. Maybe I will taste it sometime)

from: purplesnowglobe@gmail.com
to: cnichols@gmail.com
date: May 2, 11:41 PM
subject: Keep it that way!

The kind with a plot twist?

from: cnichols@gmail.com
to: purplesnowglobe@gmail.com
date: May 2, 8:42 PM
subject: Good memory

Yes. Call me impressed.

from: purplesnowglobe@gmail.com
to: cnichols@gmail.com
date: May 2, 11:44 PM
subject: You are on my mind

I remember everything about you . . . So . . . is today getting better for you?

from: cnichols@gmail.com
to: purplesnowglobe@gmail.com
date: May 2, 8:46 PM
subject: Yes. Since 20 minutes ago

Now it is.

from: purplesnowglobe@gmail.com
to: cnichols@gmail.com
date: May 2, 11:48 PM
subject: What was your favorite day ever?

Tell me a favorite memory from when you were younger. Pumpkin patch visit as a boy in Vegas? Lettering in varsity football? Prom? I bet you were prom king.

from: cnichols@gmail.com
to: purplesnowglobe@gmail.com
date: May 2, 8:49 PM
subject: I was not . . .

But I looked good in a blue ruffly tux.

from: purplesnowglobe@gmail.com
to: cnichols@gmail.com
date: May 2, 11:50 PM
subject: Pictures please

Dying to see THAT.

from: cnichols@gmail.com
to: purplesnowglobe@gmail.com
date: May 2, 8:51 PM
subject: Lawyers don't send pictures

I know better than to send self-incriminating evidence.

from: purplesnowglobe@gmail.com
to: cnichols@gmail.com
date: May 2, 11:53 PM
subject: Damn that lawyer photo clause

I will just have to imagine you in your tux, and even though you were probably an insanely hot teenage boy, I suppose I really should be perving on you as a man. An insanely hot man. And you probably look insanely hot in a tux.

from: cnichols@gmail.com
to: purplesnowglobe@gmail.com
date: May 2, 8:55 PM
subject: Tux fetish?

I suspect any tux I wore would look best with your hands on the buttons.

from: purplesnowglobe@gmail.com
to: cnichols@gmail.com
date: May 2, 11:56 PM
subject: You fetish

Unbuttoning them.

from: cnichols@gmail.com
to: purplesnowglobe@gmail.com
date: May 2, 9:02 PM
subject: Dangerous ground

We shouldn't be doing this . . .

from: purplesnowglobe@gmail.com
to: cnichols@gmail.com
date: May 3, 12:04 AM
subject: Say the word

Do you want me to stop?

from: cnichols@gmail.com
to: purplesnowglobe@gmail.com
date: May 2, 9:05 PM
subject: Don't stop

No . . .

He told himself he was safe from her web of lies and brand of hurt by the three thousand miles that separated them. As long as he stayed a continent away, he'd be okay. So when her name flashed across the screen with the enticing words—incoming call—he answered immediately.

"Hello."

"Hi," she said in a sleep-sexy purr.

"Are you in bed?"

"Only place I like to be when I'm talking to you," she said, and he loved knowing what she looked like all stretched out on her bed. Like an invitation. A beautiful fucking invitation for him with those long, strong legs, her curvy hips, her beautiful breasts, and that gorgeous red hair spread out on the covers.

"I bet you're wearing something sexy. Some little lingerie or bra-and-panty set," he said, keeping the talk to sexiness because he couldn't handle anything more right now.

"Do you want to know?"

"I want you to paint the image in my eye."

"I have on my bare legs."

A bolt of heat shot through his body, as he pictured her. "I like it when you wear those."

"And I hope you're not disappointed, but I don't have on a bra."

An appreciative growl escaped his throat. "Mmm. That is an excellent look on you. You do bra-lessness well. And now I'm picturing those naked shoulders of yours, kissing you all over, nibbling on your collarbone."

"Biting down," she said, continuing their imaginary travels.

"You taste so good, Julia. So sweet. Your skin is so damn sweet all over," he said, and the memory of her taste rushed back to him, blasting into him like a collision of senses in his memory. Her collarbone, the fruity smell of her hair from whatever shampoo she used, so much more enticing than any other woman's, the smell of her legs when she'd stepped out of the bath. And most of all, the scent of her arousal. The way he could tell just from inhaling her how he'd turned her on.

"Don't you want to know what else I'm wearing?" she offered, her voice as naughty as could be.

He stretched out on his own bed, and parked his free hand behind his head. He was so hard right now from picturing her, but he had to restrain himself because he knew he couldn't have her. But maybe this kind of teasing would be enough to get her out of his system. He knew this was trouble, he'd been there before, but this woman allured him like no other. She was a sexy drug and he wanted another hit.

"I do want to know," he said, his voice a low rumble.

"Hold on a sec," she said, and he heard a scatter of movement on her end. Then her voice again. "Go see."

Those two words shot straight to his groin, and he was fighting a losing battle with resistance when he scrolled to his screen, and thumbed open his text message to find a picture. A flash of white lace, a glimpse of her hipbone, and then her hand just barely dipped into the waistband of her panties. Suggesting what she was about to do if things continued.

Did he want them to?

No. And yes. And no. And yes. But as he tried to retain the reasons for hanging up, they all fell to dust when she whispered, "I'm touching myself and I'm thinking of you."

He groaned, unbidden. Everything in him craved her. Needed her. "Tell me what you're thinking."

She didn't answer right away, only breathed once, a low, sexy moan. In the span of those seconds, images flashed before him —her tied up to his bed, her bent over his desk, handcuffed to his balcony. Him pleasuring her, owning her body.

"Kissing you," she whispered, and his blood stilled because he'd been expecting something dirtier from her sexy mouth.

"Yeah? You like that?"

"I wouldn't like any of the other things if I didn't like kissing you first," she said, a gasp escaping her.

"What do you like about the way I kiss you?"

"Everything. Every single thing. Your lips are soft, and your stubble is rough, and you know exactly how to kiss me and make me melt for you," she said, and something about her voice was different this time; needier, hungrier.

"I love it when you melt into my arms," he said. "When I first see you and first kiss you."

"And it's like lightning or electricity or something," she said, and her breathing intensified.

"Like we can't get enough of each other, and can't stop kissing," he said, and a shudder wracked his body. "Tell me where your hand is now."

"Between my legs. Moving faster," she said, and let out a sexy cry that sent heat waves throughout his bones and blood.

"Are you writhing there on your bed?"

"Yes."

"With your legs wide open?"

"Yes," she said, her voice rising higher, and he could tell she was getting closer. "Are you touching yourself, Clay?"

"No," he said, though he was sure he'd need to handcuff his wrists any second to keep from grabbing his erection.

"Please," she said, her voice a delicious beg. That beg unwound him. It reached deep into his dirty mind and made him want to do everything with her, for her, to her.

"Please what?"

"Please touch yourself," she moaned, and he pictured her rocking her hips into her hand. With that image burned in front of his eyes, her voice in his ear, he knew it wouldn't take long. A few quick strokes, and he'd be there.

"Why do you want me to?"

"I like picturing you touching yourself. I like the image of your big, strong hand wrapped around your cock. Stroking yourself. Thinking of me."

"Yeah? That gets you hot?" His hands were trembling. He wanted so badly to give in to this moment with her.

"So hot. Anything you do turns me on. Don't you get that?"

"I think you just want to break me down. And make me think of you."

"But you already are, aren't you?"

"I already am," he admitted.

"Then come with me."

"What makes you think I'm going to come?"

"Because I know you. You will when you hear me in about thirty seconds," she said, and words fell away. She'd been reduced to moans and cries and pants, and there was no fucking way he could resist. It was either a cold shower for the rest of the whole night, or taking matters into his own hands. So he did, and it didn't take long for him to join her, pleasure rippling through every single vein as she cried out his name and he came hard and fast.

A minute later, after he'd washed his hands and returned to the dark of the bedroom, she spoke. "I wish I were there wearing your clothes right now."

He laughed. "That's what you want to be doing? Because I'd like to be fucking you if you were here."

"Well, that too. But then I'd put on your shirt."

"You like that, don't you?"

"I know you do too," she said.

"I do. Seeing you in my shirt and your heels is my kryptonite."

"Oh, is that it? That's your kryptonite?"

"Or maybe it's just that you are," he whispered, admitting more than he wanted to.

"I think the same could be said here."

There was a pause, and though they were three thousand miles apart, the silence was heady. He was in a drugged-out state tonight. This woman was his pill, and closeness with her was what he craved most even as he feared she would destroy his heart. Smash it to a million tiny pieces and eat it for lunch. But he had a built-in barrier in distance, and with no trips to San Francisco on his immediate calendar he saw nothing wrong with this temporary moment of relief from the pressure inside of him from wanting her. They couldn't be together in any meaningful way, and he couldn't get hurt if he didn't actually see her. Right? *Right*, he answered for himself.

"What are we doing, Julia?" he asked, and he was sure she could hear the longing in his tone, but he didn't care. There was no need to hide it after they'd just broken down and pleasured themselves together.

"I wish I knew," she said, her voice wistful and full of yearning. "I really wish I knew."

He heaved a sigh, trying to sort out his thoughts, but his brain was a mixed-up mess and he didn't know how to untangle all the threads. Or if he wanted to remain tangled up with her instead.

"What are you going to do when we hang up?" he asked, changing direction.

"Read a book."

"What are you reading these days?"

"A crazy story about a guy who treks across Antarctica."

"That does sound crazy."

"Yeah. He's kind of hallucinating and talking to penguins right now," she said with a small laugh.

"Can you blame him? I have to imagine if you're stuck in the polar ice cap that talking to penguins might be a rare source of comfort."

"As long as he doesn't eat the penguins I'll keep reading it."

"Here's to no penguin meals in the books we read."

"What will you do?"

"I suspect I will fall fast asleep and dream of a beautiful red-head on the other side of the country."

"She would like that dream very much," she said in a sweet voice, the kind that worked its way beneath all the hard edges in him, and settled deep in his heart. "Will I talk to you again soon?"

He took a fueling breath, and put his armor back on, steeling himself. "I don't know the answer to that."

CHAPTER FIVE

The next month passed in a paradoxical fashion. The days were long, but the weeks sped by as Julia won and lost for Charlie. She took the fall he asked for, but mostly she won, clearing another few thousand off her debt. The rest of the time, Julia mixed drinks at Cubic Z where she listened to Kim discuss whether to decorate the baby's nursery with horse or teddy bear wallpaper.

"Craig wants teddy bears. He says horses are too scary for little kids," Kim said, referring to her husband who helped out around the bar now and then as he looked for a regular bartending gig.

"Can I vote for otters instead?" Julia offered. "Have you ever seen an otter that's not utterly adorable?"

Kim laughed. "Can't say I've ever technically *seen* an otter at all. But I will hunt out otter wall-art now."

Julia held up her arms in the victory sign. "Ladies and gentleman, my greatest accomplishment may indeed lie in convincing my friend Kim to go for the otters."

She also helped her sister with final wedding prep, which included last-minute visits to boutiques and stores as McKenna chose gifts for the guests. No gifts for herself, though; McKenna and Chris had specifically asked for none, with the invitation saying, *Your presence is our gift. In lieu of presents, please consider a donation to your local animal shelter.*

Tonight, she popped into the bar to bring Julia a sample of cake. "I changed my mind at the last minute. I think I want to get this cake. Try it," she said, thrusting the carton across the bar.

Julia reached for a fork and took a bite, and her eyes rolled in pleasure when the sweet cake hit her tongue. "This is amazing."

McKenna clapped. "Oh good! Wedding cake is usually awful. But I want to have an amazing cake."

"Speaking of amazing things, try my newest concoction." She whipped up a Heist and slid it across the bar. "I named it for Clay," she said in an offhand way.

McKenna's eyebrows rose. "Wait! Are you back together with him?"

She shook her head. "No. We talk on the phone sometimes though," she said, adding an olive to the martini she'd just made for another customer.

"What do you talk about?" McKenna asked, her voice dripping with curiosity.

Julia shrugged playfully, remembering the late-night conversations with him, the way his voice went low and husky when he asked her what she was wearing, then when he proceeded to tell her exactly what he wanted to do to her when he'd removed every last shred of her clothing. "This and that." She handed the drink to the customer and returned to her sister.

"Are you having phone sex with him?" McKenna whispered, her eyes wide and eager for a yes.

She nodded. "And we talk too. About whatever. Our days. Movies. Books. Life. That sort of thing."

"Wow," McKenna said and her jaw was hanging open. "So are you going to see him again?"

"I think he likes the barrier. I think he probably figures it's for the best."

"Why?" McKenna asked, holding up a hand as if to say *what gives*. "I don't get it. You like him. He likes you. You have great phone sex. What is stopping the two of you from getting together?"

Instinctively, Julia's eyes flashed to the door, checking for Charlie or Skunk. Neither was there, but they might show up any day. That was the real thing keeping her and Clay apart. Keeping her distant from everyone, come to think of it.

"Who knows," she said evasively as a gray-haired and sharp-dressed man in a suit and tie raised a finger to grab her attention. "I need to go tend to some other customers. Can't wait for more cake this weekend."

She headed to the other end of the bar, slapped down a napkin, and flashed a smile at the older gentleman. "What can I get for you tonight?"

"A friend of mine tells me you make the most amazing cocktail ever," the man said, speaking in a most proper voice. He didn't have an accent per se; he simply had an air of sophistication about him, from the well-tailored suit to the classy speech. "A Purple Snow Globe, I believe?"

"Indeed. One Purple Snow Globe coming right up."

She mixed the drink and deposited it in front of him. When she returned five minutes later to check in, his eyes were sparkling and he was licking his lips. "That is a divine creation," he told her, then extended a hand. "I'm Glen Mills. I'm sure you'll be hearing from me soon."

"Why will I be hearing from you soon, Glen? You gonna offer me a job at some swank new bar you're opening?" she asked playfully.

"Not exactly," he said, with a twinkle in his eye, then he pushed off from the stool, and walked away.

She shook her head in amusement. The things men said in bars never surprised her, nor did she ever put any faith in them. Something about his name felt familiar though. *Glen Mills*. The named nagged at her brain for a spell, and she turned it over several times, like a strange object she could decipher if she looked at it from another angle, but she couldn't recall where she'd heard it before, so she let it go.

* * *

She could picture him perfectly when he told her he was crashed out on his couch, his shoulders sore in the way he liked from a hard workout tonight. She imagined him freshly showered, in shorts and a T-shirt, a combo she rarely saw her sharp-dressed man in, but a fantastic look nonetheless.

"Tell me why you like boxing," Julie said, as she closed the door to the tiny office at Cubic Z, slipping away for a short break while Kim handled the bar during a quiet time. She was spending her rare free minutes her favorite way. Talking to Clay. It wasn't the same as being in the room with him, but he was a far better phone date than any in-person date she'd ever had with another man. Though, he didn't call these stolen chats *dates*. He didn't call them anything. Maybe because the two of them were so undefined right now. They took what they could get from each other, but didn't push too far.

"Because I have to use my mind and my body," he said.

"Mmm. Two of the things I like about you." She sank down into the office chair, leaning back against it, letting his voice warm her. "And how do you use your mind when you're hitting a bag?"

"You have to focus with boxing. You have to know exactly where to land a punch, and then deliver on it."

"How did you get into boxing in the first place?"

"In high school."

"I thought you played football in high school?"

"I did. But I had no choice about boxing. Brent did it."

"And that meant you had to?"

"Can't let my little brother beat me. I had to keep up with him. Wouldn't let him have the chance to win. So I took it up too."

"I can beat McKenna if I have to," Julia joked.

"Girl fight. Don't get me excited," he said playfully.

"But I like getting you excited."

"And you're very good at it. You excel at that," he said, then paused and she heard the slightest rustling sound.

"You stretching out on the couch?"

"I'm making myself more comfortable."

"Do your shoulders still hurt?"

"A little."

She sighed wistfully, her eyes fluttering closed as she imagined being there with him, soothing out the soreness from the punches he'd thrown. "If I were there I'd rub your shoulders for you. You could lean back into me and I'd make you feel better."

"Mmm…I bet you would."

"You can rest your head between my legs while I massage you."

He laughed. "If I'm between your legs, there's no massaging going on. Unless it's of you and with my tongue."

She smiled and rolled her eyes. "Always able to make things dirty, aren't you, Clay?"

"If you're going to start talking about being between your legs, I'm going to start telling you what I'd be doing if I were there, and it wouldn't be lying still."

"What would it be?" She asked, unable to resist drawing out his naughty mouth.

"Wait. I *would* be lying still, now that I think about it," he said, quickly correcting himself.

"Oh really?"

"Yes, really. Because I'm tired, but I'm never to tired to eat you. I'd just need you to ride my face," he said. Hot tingles roared down her body at the memory of the ways he'd buried his face between her legs. On the chaise lounge in her bar after closing time the night they met, in the town car when she'd arrived in New York for their weekend together, and tied up on his bed, her ass in the air. Heat flooded her center, and she was going to need to change her panties before she went back out to work if this kept up.

"But maybe I want to do things to you," she said, taking the reins, so she didn't turn into a puddle of molten heat.

"All right. Have at me. What do you want to do to me?"

Her ears tuned into the noises from beyond the door. It sounded like more customers had just come in. She'd need to get back out there soon.

"Besides rub your shoulders and run my fingers through your hair?"

"Yes. Besides that."

"My favorite thing," she said in a sexy whisper, closing her eyes and picturing exactly what she wanted to do to him.

"What's your favorite thing, Julia? Tell me. I want to hear you say it."

"Tasting you."

He groaned, and she was sure his hand was already on his cock.

"Taking you in my mouth. Doing all sorts of things to you with my lips and tongue."

"What sort of things?"

"Taking you deep the way you like. Licking you all over. Using my hands everywhere on you."

"Everywhere?" he asked, and she could practically see him arching an eyebrow.

"Everywhere you'd want me to," she said, and soon his breathing intensified. "Are you touching yourself?"

"You leave me no choice when you talk about sucking me. I love those sexy lips of yours wrapped around my dick."

"And you love using your hands on me too while you're in my mouth. Grabbing my hair, pushing your fingers through it, pulling me closer to you."

"Making sure you take me hard," he growled.

"Of course. I want to make sure I rock your world with my mouth."

He drew a sharp breath, and she could tell he was getting close. "You do, Julia. You do."

"I can almost taste you right now," she said in a hot whisper, wanting to bring him there.

"You should be able to any second now," he said, breathing out hard, and groaning loudly.

She grinned widely, thrilled that she'd gotten him off like this. "You taste so fucking good," she said.

He sighed deeply, the sound of a contented man. She loved that she'd found a way to satisfy him even from this kind of distance. "Your turn," he said in that deep, sexy voice that sent sparks through her.

She shook her head even though he couldn't see her. "I need to get back to work. It's getting busy."

"Next time then. Because I want to hear you let go," he said, and a hot wave rolled through her as she pictured their nights on the phone, and how he drew out her cries of pleasure. "I love how you let go when you touch yourself."

"Why would I do anything else?"

"I want you to let go with me."

"I do, Clay. I've never held back."

"I don't mean sex. I mean other ways. I want you to be as free with me in other ways as you are when you're naked."

"I want that too. I swear I do," she said, and she was sure her neediness was coming through loud and clear. But she *needed* him to know. "I miss you."

"Yeah?" he asked, sounding doubtful.

"So much. I wish you were here with me."

He sighed heavily. "I wish I could be," he said, but it didn't sound as if he were wishing he could be there right now so he could touch her. More like he was wishing he would allow himself to be close to her again. Because in spite of all their late-night chats, and all the things they shared, there was a distance between them more palpable than the miles. She'd been getting to know him better, and yet, she had never felt farther away from him than she did now. "I have to go," he said, and now it *was* possible to feel even more distant.

When their call ended, she knew it couldn't go on much longer like this; this in-between state was wonderful and thoroughly unsatisfying at the same time.

CHAPTER SIX

Before the wedding she played another poker game. She was on some kind of streak the last few weeks, and she won most nights. "I only have $10,000 left," she said to Charlie at the end of the cash out. She couldn't hide the smile that curved her lips.

"You can count. But I also gave you a deadline and you have two more weeks to clear it."

"May isn't over yet," she said through gritted teeth.

"You could always ask your sister. I did a little research on her business. Seems she sold it for a pretty penny. Or perhaps you could just transfer your debt to the peppy Fashion Hound," he said, narrowing his eyes as he crisply punctuated the name of McKenna's fashion blog, making it clear he knew everything about the people she cared about. "I could find all sorts of ways for her to work for me. She has a nice dog, too."

Julia snapped, lunging for Charlie's throat in the restaurant. "Leave my sister and her dog out of this."

He cackled, grabbing her hands and flicking them off his skin. "I won't have to involve anyone if you do your job, Red."

She was tempted to ask McKenna for a loan, but she'd gotten this far on her own. She'd managed to keep her sister and Kim and everyone she loved out of Charlie's crosshairs. You

don't run the first twenty-five miles of a marathon to send rein-
forcements in to finish the last mile. Even if that last mile feels
like five hundred.

"I will do my job if it's the last damn thing I do," she said,
and some days it felt like it would be. Like she'd be under his
thumb until the day she died.

* * *

"Perfect."

Gayle rested her hands on Julia's shoulders, admiring her
work in the mirror. "Want to see the back?"

"Hell yeah," Julia said, and Gayle swiveled her around and
held up a silver hand mirror for her to use to see the French
twist.

"I love it," she said, carefully touching the tendrils that fell
on her neck.

"You do?"

"Of course! I love everything you do."

"Don't mess it up on the drive to the Presidio," Gayle said,
wagging a finger playfully in admonishment, though she surely
meant the directive too. Hairstyles were to be taken seriously.

"It's fifteen minutes away! What do you think I'm going to
do? Hang my head out the limo window like a dog?"

"If you do that please make sure everyone knows I was not
responsible for the mess. I only want credit for the good hair
days," Gayle said.

"Thank you for coming in early for me on a Saturday to do
this, when you're not even working," Julia said, gesturing to the
empty salon. The front door was locked.

"Anything for you. Now I'll walk you out. And by the way, I
want an update on your guy."

Her guy. Was Clay her guy? She didn't know what he was, except a sexy voice on the end of the phone. She'd gotten to
know more about him in this last month from their easy chat-

ter and conversations, and everything she learned made her long for him more. They never talked about a relationship. Never brought up seeing each other. Actual contact was off the table; they were only phone buddies.

But she didn't have time to fashion an answer to Gayle's question because when she opened the door to Fillmore Street, Skunk was pacing on the sidewalk like a big bored lion, walking back and forth in a zoo.

The hair on the back of her neck prickled in worry. Of all the days for Charlie to harass her. The bastard. A sister's wedding day should be a sacred one. A day even Charlie could respect.

Gayle didn't notice him at first while she locked up. Then she turned around, and Skunk spoke to the hairdresser.

"I was hoping I could get a haircut," he said gesturing to the salon with its pretty feminine windows decorated with silhouettes of women. This was clearly a salon catering mostly to the fairer sex, though Julia had seen a few men inside from time to time. They didn't look like Skunk, though. They weren't big beefy men with faces like slabs of meat, and ankle holsters holding guns. The men who walked through these doors were metrosexuals. Her eyes darted to his feet, and she saw the barest outline of his weapon. He never left home without it.

"We're closed now. Open again in an hour," Gayle said. "Someone will be here then to cut your hair."

"I'd really like one now," he said, then scrunched up his nose, squeezed shut his eyes, and covered his face with a hand as he sneezed so loudly it sounded like a honk. His forehead was sweaty, and he looked pale.

"I'm sure you do, sweetie, and ordinarily I'd open right up for you," she said in her best calm voice as she dipped a hand into her purse. She quickly found a tissue, and gave it to Skunk. He took it and muttered a *thanks*. "But I need to get some coffee in me, and if I don't my hands might be unsteady.

So why don't you come back and someone else can take care of you then?"

He blew his nose, then rubbed the tissue across it. His eyes looked red and watery. "Or, maybe go home, take a hot bath and have some tea and come back tomorrow? You might be getting a nasty cold, honey."

"I think I have the flu," he said.

"Here." She reached in her pocket for a slip of paper and handed that to him. "A twenty percent off coupon, just for you. For when you're feeling better. You go get in bed and take care of that flu."

Skunk relented, nodding. "Thank you. I'll be back."

He lumbered away, and Julia had a sinking feel that *I'll be back* referred to something other than where he'd be an hour from now.

They were circling her, trying to trip her up however they could.

Charlie had sent this message—his sick way of letting her know he'd uncovered another soft spot of hers in her friendship with her stylist. His subtle, or not-so-subtle way of reminding her that he had no mercy. He was willing to do whatever it took to get his money by his deadline.

The deadline was looming ever closer.

* * *

Julia pet her sister's dog over and over, as if the animal might have a calming effect. Dogs sometimes did that, right? Settled nerves and made people happier. She needed some of that right now, so she sat on the edge of the antique white couch stroking Ms. Pac-Man's soft fur, hoping it would turn these jitters inside her belly into a thing of the past.

She wasn't even the one walking down the aisle. She was the damn maid-of-honor and she was supposed to reassure the bride. But McKenna was ready, eager, and not a wink nervous, while all Julia could think about was the ticking clock. She'd texted Gayle a few times, ostensibly about her hair, but really to make sure her stylist was fine. Gayle was getting ready for an Arcade Fire concert, she'd said, so all was well.

Still, Julia couldn't help feeling as if someone was watching her. Waiting for her. Poised to take her down.

Focus on the bride.

Decked out in a vintage-style tea-length dress, McKenna applied her lip gloss then twirled once in front of the antique, gilded mirror in her suite at the swank Golden Gate Club in the Presidio, a coveted venue for weddings with its view of the San Francisco Bay and the Golden Gate Bridge.

"You look so beautiful, and this dress is so completely you," Julia said, even though she'd seen it many times. But that was her job—to shower the bride with extravagant compliments on her wedding day. It would also force her mind off the heightened state of panic inside her body.

"You're next, Jules," she said, and Julia scoffed.

She didn't even know how to respond. The notion of her being married was so foreign, her sister might as well be talking about orbiting Saturn right now. "Let's get you down the aisle," she said.

Julia washed her hands one final time. Yes, Ms. Pac-Man had had a pre-wedding bath, but even so she didn't want scent of a pooch on her as she held a bouquet. She grabbed her daisies, the perfect flowers for McKenna's sunny disposition, and held open the door for the other bridesmaids: McKenna's good friends Hayden and Erin, and Chris's sister, Jill, who had flown out from New York for the weekend, taking two days off from her starring role in the musical *Crash the Moon*.

They headed to the expansive grounds, across the rolling green hills, to the bluff overlooking the water. The waves lolled peacefully against the shore in the distance, and the afternoon sun warmed them. The weather gods were on their side today

—the sky was a crystal blue, and there was no wind. A rare blessing in this windiest of cities, and Julia was grateful.

White chairs were spread across the lawn, and their friends and family were there. Julia spotted Davis in the second row, and instantly her thoughts flicked to Clay. The two men were best friends, and she found herself wondering if her name had ever come up in their conversations.

The music began and the other bridesmaids walked down the white runner spread out on the lawn. Julia turned to McKenna and whispered in her ear. "I love you. I'm so happy for you," she said, then she squeezed her hand.

"I love you too," McKenna said, and her voice threatened to break. Julia reached out, and gently wiped the start of a happy tear from her sister's eye. "Don't ruin your mascara."

"I won't."

Julia took her turn down the runner, thrilled to finally see this day arrive. Though it hadn't been a lengthy engagement—in fact it had been markedly short, clocking in at two mere months—this was a day that she'd longed to see. Nearly two years ago, the man McKenna had been involved with dumped her via voicemail twenty-four hours before their wedding, leaving her with a houseful of mixers, pasta makers and place settings she'd never use. Her sister had been devastated. Chris wasn't like that, not in the least, but Julia had asked a few days ago if she'd had any lingering worries.

"You nervous at all now that it's so close?"

"Nope. I've never been more sure of anything in my life," McKenna had said.

She looked it, too, radiant in her joy today.

When Julia reached the raised stage, her throat hitched, and a tear slipped down her cheek as she turned to watch McKenna walk down the aisle. She delighted at the song that filled the air. McKenna hadn't picked Pachelbel's Canon or the wedding march. She'd chosen hers and Chris's song—*Can't Help Falling in Love.*

That was the best kind of love, wasn't it? The kind where the love was its own entity, a living, breathing presence between two people, demanding to be felt. A life force of its own. That's what her sister and Chris had, and her heart soared with happiness that McKenna had found *the one*.

Chris couldn't take his eyes off his bride as he waited at the edge of the bluff, watching her every step as she walked closer. The last words of the Elvis song faded out as she stepped next to him. *Take my hand, take my whole life too*. He whispered something to her, and she whispered back, and Julia was no longer jam-packed with worries over Charlie and Skunk. It had all been replaced by this torrent of happiness she felt for the two of them.

As the justice of the peace cleared his throat, Julia quickly peeked at the crowd, spotting familiar faces–Chris's family, McKenna's videographer, her dog trainer, her friends from the fashion world, along with Chris's brother who stood next to him, some of his surfing buddies in the seats, and people he worked with on his TV show. Then her eyes landed on the profile of a handsome man in the back row who was taking a seat. A latecomer, he'd just arrived. The man raised his face and Julia's heart stopped with a quick shudder.

Then it started again when, somehow, across the crowd of people, the sea of suited men and elegantly-dressed women, of family and friends and new faces, he made eye contact with her, locking his gaze on hers. The sounds of the ceremony, of the vows being exchanged turned to white noise, and all she could see, hear, and feel was *him*. No longer separated by a continent. No longer connected only by the tether of email. He was one hundred feet away, and he never once stopped looking at her.

Her skin was hot, and her heart was beating loudly, and as soon as the groom kissed the bride and walked back down the aisle, she was damn near ready to launch herself into his arms.

CHAPTER SEVEN

Sometime in the last few weeks he'd decided several things.

That she might be lying. That she might be trouble. That he might be about to become the poster child for *fool me twice, shame on me.*

But most of all, he'd decided that his gut told him she'd meant what she said. Even though she hadn't given him the details of why there'd been a man with a gun demanding her presence, he'd made the choice to believe her.

Blind trust, maybe. Or possibly blind something else. Either way, his instincts said she was telling the truth. His gut had served him throughout his career, so he'd decided to listen to it.

Now that he was here with her, he wasn't thinking with his gut. He wasn't thinking at all. He was feeling.

His whole body was humming, vibrating at a frequency only she could sense. His skin sizzled, and blood rushed hot through his veins. Nearness to her was an aphrodisiac.

"I like your suit," she said, going first.

"I like your dress."

"You're here," she said with wonder in her voice as she eyed him up and down. He didn't think he'd ever tire of the way she looked at him with hunger, need, and passion.

"I'm here," he said, quirking up his lips. They stood gazing at each other, but they hadn't touched yet. They were inches apart, and there was something almost fragile about this moment. As if they might break if one of them moved. He didn't know who would make the first move, but he hoped it would be her since he'd made the effort to show up.

"How?" she asked, still breathless.

"Your sister and her husband."

"They invited you?" she asked, her lips curving into a wide, gorgeous smile.

"Invited. Or insisted. Take your pick."

"Really?" she asked, and a breeze blew by, making the soft little tendrils of her hair flutter against her neck. He wanted to bend his head to her neck, layer her skin in kisses that made her shiver in his arms and melt into him, that turned her so hot inside her knees went weak and she nearly buckled with desire. He'd catch her, hold her, make sure she didn't fall, except into him.

He did none of that. His hands were stuffed in his pockets, or else he'd be touching her, wrapping his arms around her, running his fingertips along her hipbone, covered in the fabric of her black dress.

"Yes. Really. Chris invited me a week ago, and said he needed his lawyer here. Which was about the worst case of acting I'd ever heard, since no one needs his entertainment lawyer at his wedding, so McKenna grabbed the phone, reprimanding him, and then laid it out."

"What did she say?"

"She said she thought it would make you happy if I were here, and that you being happy was the greatest gift she could have on her wedding day. Well, besides marrying Chris," he said with a happy shrug. "Far be it from me to deny the bride of my newest client her greatest wish."

He watched Julia process his words. She swallowed, drew in a sharp breath, and clasped her hand over her mouth, covering a sob. A tear slipped down her cheek.

Instantly, he reached for her, swiping the tear away and leaning in close. "You okay?"

She nodded. "I just love my sister so much," she said in a broken voice. "But she's wrong."

Clay stiffened. No. Not now. Not after he'd taken this big chance. This big leap. Not after all their emails and calls. "Why is she wrong?"

Julia shook her head. "Because I'm not just happy. I'm *unbelievably* happy that you're here."

The darkness lifted, and his entire body felt light and full of hope. She wrapped her arms around his neck, threading her fingers in his hair, and tilting her chin up to him. He ached all over just being near to her. She licked her lips, kept her eyes on him, and he'd never seen a more beautiful woman, nor had he ever wanted to kiss someone as much as he wanted to this very second.

He ran the backs of his fingers softly against her cheek, watching as she leaned into him, her eyes floating closed for a brief second as she whispered, "You may kiss the maid-of-honor."

"Now that makes me unbelievably happy," he said, gathering her in his arms, tugging her beautiful body close to his, and brushing his lips gently across hers. She gasped lightly when he made contact, that involuntary sound the most perfect reminder of why he'd listened to Chris and McKenna, snapped up a ticket, and flew across the country. Why he took the chance once again with Julia. He could pretend he was doing this for a client, simply responding properly to an invitation for a social occasion. He knew better than to lie to himself. He was doing this because he'd made the choice to trust her. The alternative—being without her—was too much to bear.

But he was also choosing to let go of the past. He wasn't going to blame Julia for Sabrina's problems, nor punish himself either by reassigning them to her. The month apart from her—all talk and no contact—had reset his head in some unexpected way, reassuring him that he could try again.

By God, how he wanted to try again as she melted into him, her body so tantalizingly close as they kissed under the sun, surrounded by wedding guests who surely didn't care what two random people were doing because they weren't the bride and the groom. They were the maid-of-honor and the man who *had* to have her, no matter the cost. He kissed her tenderly at first, light and soft as the moment called for, here on the bluff, San Francisco Bay waves rolling on by. But as she inched closer to him, pressing the full length of her gorgeous frame against his, the gentleness fell away. A groan worked its way up his chest. He pulled her harder, needing her as close as could be, needing her mouth. She whimpered and parted her lips, inviting him to taste more. He explored her with his tongue, kissing her the kind of way two lovers kiss when they haven't seen each other in a month.

What a long, hard month it had been. She wriggled her hips subtly against his cock, which was straining now against the zipper of his pants. The barest of contact with his erection sent his body spinning. "Julia," he whispered harshly, her name a warning.

Her mouth fell away from his, and she brushed her lips along his jaw, up to his ear. "I want you," she said, in a hot murmur. "I want you now."

Nothing else mattered but grabbing her hand, and finding the nearest coat closet so he could slam the door and take her.

But the second he laced his fingers through hers, someone tapped on her shoulder.

"Picture time!"

The bride was beaming, and her smile could light up a midnight skyline, he reckoned. But then, that's how it should be on your wedding day.

Julia brushed her hand once over the front of her dress, as if she were smoothing it out, then McKenna caught Clay's eye.

"You made it," she shrieked, then threw her arms around his neck. He angled himself so she couldn't feel his hard-on. The last thing he needed was the bride thinking he was a pervert, or telling the groom that his new lawyer had been sporting wood.

"Congratulations, McKenna. I'm so happy for you and Chris," he said, and when she pulled away he continued. "And I donated to the New York City ASPCA in your honor."

"Oh, you didn't have to," she said, then patted the outside of her leg, and a blond Lab-Hound-Husky arrived at her side, parking herself perfectly in a sit. "But Ms. Pac-Man thanks you."

"She's even cuter in person," Clay said, gesturing to the dog, before he extended a hand to the groom, congratulating him as well on the nuptials.

Soon, McKenna scurried her sister, her husband and her dog away for photos. Julia leaned in to give him a quick peck on the cheek before they headed to the bluff for a round of pictures.

Clay took a deep breath, and hoped the photographer made quick work behind the lens.

"Fancy meeting you here."

Clay turned to see his buddy Davis. "Hey man," he said, clapping his friend on the back, though Davis was joking— Clay had told him the other night that he'd be at the wedding. Davis was here with Jill, the groom's sister.

"Guess we're the odd men out," Davis said, tipping his forehead to the wedding party that included the women both of them were involved with.

Wait. Was he involved with Julia again? Or was it crazy to think that, given the track record they both had of running? He didn't know what they were, or what they would be.

"Yep. Looks like we are," Clay said. "Think this'll be you anytime soon?"

Davis nodded, a sneaky glint in his eyes. "As a matter of fact, I believe I will be popping the question at the Tony Awards next month."

Clay smiled widely, then hugged his friend. "Congrats, man. That's fantastic. You two are great together."

"I think so too."

As he chatted with Davis, neither of them did a very good job of looking anywhere but at the wedding party, Davis's eyes on Jill, Clay's on Julia. There was something both peaceful and right about this moment, this wedding, these people he barely knew who'd invited him into their most important day. It felt fitting to be here, and soon the gorgeous redhead would be back by his side where she belonged.

* * *

There was no time for a quickie. The moment the photographer had finished shooting the wedding party, the cocktail hour started, as waiters passed out flutes of bubbly champagne. The festivities had moved inside to a gorgeous reception room with a baby grand piano and floor-to-ceiling glass windows overlooking the water. The decor reflected the bride's and groom's passion for games and animals with the name cards at place settings stamped with Mr. Monopoly, and the centerpiece flowers boasting a wooden cutout of a hound dog.

Chris tapped a fork against a glass, cleared his throat and stood next to his new wife by the head table. "First of all, thank you so much for coming. I'm pretty sure I'm the luckiest guy in the world simply because I have this woman as my wife. To also see so many friends and family here makes the occasion all the better, even though I'd have married her anywhere—in a box, on a boat, in the rain, on a train," he said, then paused to look at McKenna. She rolled her eyes playfully. "What? It's true," he said to her, but loud enough for everyone to hear. He faced the guests again. "Anyway, I'm going to keep this short and sweet, and turn the microphone over to the best man and the maid-of-honor. And since I'm a ladies first kind of a guy, we'll start with Julia. Take it away."

Julia crossed the few feet to Chris and took the microphone, then turned to the crowd. "It's truly an honor to be here and to be able to say a few words about my favorite person in the world and *her* favorite person in the world," she said, stopping to gesture at Chris.

"Hey! You're still a favorite," McKenna called out.

Julia waved her off playfully. "I'm still a little surprised though as to why Chaucer isn't here to give a toast. Do you all know Chaucer?" she asked the crowd. Most of them shook their heads. "Let me tell you a story. Chaucer is our friend's Siamese cat, and he was something of a matchmaker for Chris and McKenna. He's one of those dastardly Siamese cats who likes to make his mark in the world. But, lest everyone think cat pee is a bad thing all the time, there are the rare cases where cat pee brings two people together. Because when Chaucer peed on McKenna's camera many months ago, she brought it to the electronics store to find a replacement. And who would she happen to meet there but this man," Julia said patting Chris on the shoulder. "And Chris, being an industrious and resourceful fellow, and naturally, being completely smitten with McKenna from the second he saw her, gamely offered to repair her camera," she said, a smile breaking across her face as she told the story. From across the crowd of glittering lights and gorgeously arrayed tables, she spotted Clay, his eyes fixed on her. Suddenly she felt as if the whole room had disappeared and she was talking only to him. Sharing a love story with her man. "Of course, it wasn't always easy, and McKenna had a bit of a stubborn side about some things."

"I'll say," Chris chimed in, as he draped an arm around his wife and planted a sweet kiss on her cheek, earning a collective *aww* from the guests.

"But here we are, despite the stubbornness from my big sis, because she realized what a good thing she had in front of her, and that giving up her stubborn ways was worth it." She locked eyes with Clay once more, and the lightness of the speech drained away, replaced instead by the deeper possibility of whether she could give up the things she held too tightly. She'd never truly considered it until that moment, but was there a chance she was being stubborn, too, by clutching her secrets and her shame in her hands? She'd always considered her troubles to be completely solo problems, but they were growing far less solitary given Charlie's encroachment on her personal territory lately, from his heated asides about McKenna to sending his heavy with the runny nose to her salon that morning.

But she didn't want to think about Skunk or any of them right now. She wouldn't let them mar this day.

With a quick swallow, she soldiered on. "And, as anyone can see, they are perfect for each other, from their shared love of karaoke, to their steadfast belief that California is the *only* suitable place to live, to their affection for games, from Candyland all the way to Halo and Qbert. Because ultimately, isn't that part and parcel of what makes a love last through the years? Common interests and passion, whether it's for adventure," she said, and now she was talking *only* to the man across the room, "or a good crime flick. Or even just the same, how shall we say, *preferences*," she said, taking a beat to enjoy the way he fought back a naughty grin. "I like to think those little things are also big things. And Chris and McKenna have all of that. So, here's to the bride and groom." She held up her champagne glass.

As Chris's brother began his toast seconds later, she threaded her way through the guests and clinked glasses with Clay. "Cheers."

"That was a beautiful speech," he said, his deep brown eyes searching hers.

"I meant every word."

"Every word?" He raised an eyebrow as he took a drink.

"Every single one."

* * *

After the first dance, McKenna tugged her friends to the floor when Jill belted out a karaoke version of Matchbox Twenty's "Overjoyed." Julia felt the soprano's voice literally vibrate through the reception hall, her Broadway belt glittering with energy and strength as she wowed the crowd. "She's totally going to win a Tony for Best Actress in a Musical, isn't she?" Julia said to Clay, with chills on her arms as a result of Jill's talent.

"Honestly, I don't see how she can't. She brings down the house every single night in *Crash the Moon*."

Once Jill stepped off the stage, the music shifted back to the sound system and Billie Holiday's jazzy voice warbled through the speakers. "My sister loves the old standards. Sinatra, Holiday, the King," she said by way of explanation.

"As do I," he said, taking her hand and leading her to the dance floor as "All or Nothing At All" piped overhead.

Clay's hands found their way to her hips, settling in comfortably as she roped her arms around his neck, her fingertips brushing against his soft, thick hair. The song played as other couples danced, and they swayed past Jill and Davis, and Chris and McKenna. Julia kept her gaze on Clay, loving the intensity in his eyes. "I'm glad you're here," she said, because it felt so much better to be patently honest with him than to deny what she felt. She'd flopped back and forth between shooing her feelings out the door and acting upon them. She didn't want the back and forth anymore.

"So am I."

They twirled in lazy circles, as the words and music filled the room.

"All or nothing at all. Half a love never appealed to me. If your heart never could yield to me then I'd rather have nothing at all."

The words pulsed around Julia like living, breathing creatures, then slipped into all the crevices of her hardened heart. They reminded her that halfway was the worst way. She'd tried so desperately to pack herself in ice, to feel *nothing* at all those nights at Charlie's games, but instead she'd felt everything. She felt the shame of Dillon's betrayal, the anger at being Charlie's pawn, and the cruel distance she had kept with the man she was falling for. She'd always thought she was protecting her family and friends by keeping her own secrets, but the events of this morning outside the salon were a cold reminder that blindfolding them to her problems might not work forever. Whether she liked it or not, she might very well need help. Clay had offered to listen, to sort through things. She knew he couldn't snap a finger and make her debt magically disappear, but maybe he could at least be there for her as she raced to meet Charlie's moving target of a deadline.

"Clay," she began nervously, and already she could hear the potholes in her own voice. She'd have an easier time speaking with marbles in her mouth than saying *this*.

"Yes?" he asked, tugging her closer, warming her skin with his body.

All or nothing at all. If it's love there is no in-between.

Billie Holiday whispered in her ear, urging her on, reminding her to be strong. "You know when you asked me that night at my apartment what was going on?"

"Yes," he said, like a gentle invitation for her to keep speaking. She could do this. She could tell him. After all, he'd flown all the way across the country. He'd opened his heart to her, taking chances left and right that she'd barely earned. He wanted her honesty more than anything else, and though she might scare him all the way back to New York when she told him, she also knew he wasn't a man who trafficked in fear. This man could take on anyone.

"I'm ready to tell you," she said, the words tumbling on top of each other, jostling to break free.

"Tell me," he said, gripping her hips harder as his eyes widened. He stopped dancing, grasped her hand, and guided her outside of the reception hall.

Once outside, she shivered. The evening had settled in, bringing with it the California chill from the bay. He took off his suit jacket, and slipped it over her shoulders. The gesture emboldened her.

"You remember that guy who came up to me outside my apartment?" Her stomach nosedived as she began. "When I lied about who you were?"

"Yes. Of course."

She inhaled sharply, letting the cool air fill her chest, hoping it would settle her flip-flopping insides. "I lied because I was scared. Because I was trying to protect you. Which I know sounds silly, because you're this big, strong man," she said, reaching out to touch his arm lightly. "But I don't want him or anyone going after you because I care about you."

"Why would he or anyone go after me?"

This was the hardest part. When she told him *why.* The words threatened to lodge in her chest, refusing to come out, but she shucked off the red-hot shame. "My ex? The one who's gone—I told you about him that night in your bath?"

His features tightened, and his brow furrowed. "Yeah. Where is he?"

"I still don't know. The IRS is looking for him, and I haven't a clue. He left the country, and he left with $100,000 stolen from the mob. He claimed the money was a loan for me to expand my bar, so when he took off, the mob boss came to collect. With me."

Clay's mouth hung open.

She never thought this polished, confident man would be speechless, but that's what she'd done to him because he'd gone mute from the shock. Seconds ticked by, then a full minute, it seemed. He scrubbed a hand across his jaw as if he were thinking, trying to process what she'd said.

"I know it's probably not something you hear too often. *Hi, sweetie. I'm wanted by the mob.*"

"No," he said, managing a brief, dry laugh. "Don't hear that very often at all."

"So when Stevie came by he needed me to go to a game."

"Game?"

"I play poker for this guy, Charlie. Stevie is his enforcer. I'm Charlie's ringer. He makes me play in rigged poker games to win back the money Dillon stole."

Clay stepped away, looking unsteady on his feet and ashen. "Are you serious?"

She nodded. "Completely. I'm really amazingly good at poker. Always have been. And I win most of the time. And now I hate playing because I'm forced to play for him to pay off a debt that isn't even mine."

"That's a fucking mess, Julia," he said, his voice a raw scrape. And it scared her.

He was going to run now, wasn't he? Nobody wanted this kind of mess in their lives. He probably didn't believe her, either. Probably thought she was lying to him like Sabrina had done, and figured she was going to ask him for money too. Crap. She had to fix this.

She moved closer. "Did I scare you off?"

"No. I'm just . . . I just . . . I didn't think that was the issue."

"What did you think it was?"

"I honestly don't know. But that's some crazy stuff, Julia," he said, and she detected a note of skepticism.

She cycled through things to do or say to prove herself. "I want you to trust me and I know you have every reason not to trust me. You also have to know I'm not asking you for money. I've never asked anyone for money. If I were going to I would ask my sister, but I have kept her and everyone I love out of this because it's my problem. I want you to believe me. Do you believe me?"

His lips parted and he paused briefly then said yes. But she needed him to believe it with every ounce of his being.

"No. I want you to believe me with the same certainty that you want to fuck me," she said, pushing hard on his chest now. Flames of anger licked her chest. She'd opened her deepest, darkest secret and she didn't want a shred of doubt.

He held up his hands as if he were backing off from her. "Fine. I believe you."

"The expression in your eyes tells me otherwise. You asked me to open up to you. I'm baring my fucking heart to you. Charlie gave me a deadline, and he's threatening my bar and my co-worker, and he showed up this morning at my hair salon, and he's circling me," she said, holding her hands out wide. She flashed onto something he'd told her once about a friend of his. "I am mad and I am terrified. I'm not asking you for money. I'm asking you to believe me, and you need to believe me completely. So call your friend."

He crinkled his nose as if her words didn't compute. "My friend?"

"The lawyer who runs people down for you? You said he tracked down intel on people you weren't sure about."

"Yeah, my friend Cam. He can get the goods on anyone."

Julia dug into her small satin clutch purse and grabbed her phone. She thrust it at him. "Call him. The guy is Charlie Stravinski, he owns Mr. Pong's restaurant in China Town," she said, rattling off the address. "He also owns Charlie's Limos. I'm sure your friend can verify who he is. That's the guy who owns me."

"Julia," he said softly, his voice strained, and that sound was terribly familiar. It felt lethal. It was the sound of his voice when he ran. It was the way he'd spoken to her on the street. She tensed all over, and she wished she could unwind the last fifteen minutes of honesty, zip them up and toss them in a body bag into the ocean. She should have continued leaving him in the blissfully ignorant state that made him jet out to San Francisco to see her. He'd been falling for her; she could see it, feel it, sense it. Now she'd shattered what they could have had. Whoever said honesty was the best policy didn't have the mob on her tail.

He breathed out hard, pressed his lips together, and seemed to be debating. "Julia," he said again, his expression softer. "You don't have to prove it. I came out here because I trust you, and if we're going to be together the way we want, the way I want, the way you want, I'm not going to ask you to prove who some guy is."

But she needed him to know she wasn't making up Charlie. "It's important to me that you know this for certain and not just because I said so. I need to have proven myself to you. Call your friend, give him the info, and you'll know I'm not lying. I have a price tag on my head."

CHAPTER EIGHT

It was almost too crazy to believe, but the truth was messy. Lies were ironclad. They added up too neatly. Lies were padded so thick they became airtight and couldn't breathe. The truth was frayed, like the tattered end of a rope. The truth was full of holes that were evidence of its veracity. Still, he could tell proof was vitally important to her, so he pulled his own phone from his pocket and dialed Cam.

"Hey man, can you run a quick check on someone for me?"

"Abso-fucking-lutely for you," his friend said in his gregarious voice.

Clay gave him the basic details. "Just let me know what kind of business he's running. Doable?"

"This is easy. I'm in front of my laptop right now, and will run a few quick searches. That is, if my lady friend doesn't come back and try to distract me."

Clay smiled briefly. "Have fun with Tess. But take care of me too."

"You bastard, you owe me so much. I love it when you owe me. I love running down shit for you because it gives me one more thing to add to my totals. There's only one other person I do this for free for," Cam said, his voice stretching across the country like a big old Texas-style hug.

"Who's that?"

"I'm not saying but she's a lot prettier than you."

"I should hope so."

He hung up, and returned to Julia. She looked different than she had before. She'd always been tough, strong, a woman of the world. Now she looked empty, as if she'd shed all her emotions and replaced them with cool blankness. He reached for her, gripping her arms gently but firmly as he kept his eyes fixed on her. "That story is crazy, and I hate what he did to you and I hate that anyone wants to hurt you, and here's the thing —I won't let them now. You know that, right? You're with me, and that means I'm here to help you. You tried to protect me and that was the most adorable, sweetest, sexiest thing anyone has ever done, but you don't have to because that's my job. Got that?"

She said nothing, just stared hard at him. She was shutting down, and he was having none of that. Not after she'd finally opened up. "I'm not running," he said firmly, refusing to let her look away. "I'm here for you. I'm here with you, and I want to help you. That's what I do. That's what I want to do for you."

"Why?" She crossed her arms over her chest.

"Why?" he said, his voice louder. He was going to have to make this abundantly clear. "Because I flew here to see you. Because you are under my skin. Because this fucking bastard left you with a shit ton of problems and if I ever find him I will make sure he pays. And because you have the mafia after you."

"That doesn't scare you? Make you want to run?" She shot him a challenging stare, almost as if she were daring him to walk away.

"No," he said crisply.

There wasn't a chance in hell that was happening. He straightened his spine, planted his feet wide, making it clear in every way that he was staying. "It makes me want to stay."

"Why do you want to help me?"

He shook his head in frustration, but deep down he understood why she was behaving like this. She'd admitted something terribly private, and self-preservation was familiar ground for her.

"May I remind you of your toast in there?" He tipped his chin to the reception. Through the glass, the guests were still spinning on the dance floor, the twinkling lights illuminating their steps. Waiters moved nimbly about, passing out appetizers. "Common interests and passion? Ring a bell?" he said, waiting for her to acknowledge what she'd said a mere hour ago. She nodded once. "I feel the same."

She didn't answer him, so he reached for her hands, unpeeled them from her chest, and drew them behind her back.

"Now, don't go cold on me. If you do, I will have to tie your hands the next time I fuck you," he said, fixing her with an intensely serious look.

Her lips quirked up, as if she were trying hard to hold in a smile. "That's a promise, gorgeous," he added.

"But that's a promise I like," she whispered, and her words were a straight shot to his groin. They had to have set some kind of record for most hours being near each other without tearing off clothes. He pressed his hips against hers, holding her in place, watching her eyes go hazy as she felt him.

"Now listen. I made the phone call you asked me to make. I don't care right now about what Cam is doing, or finding out, or anything. I care about you, woman. And I haven't fucked you in a month, so if I were you I'd be thinking about how you're going to spend the rest of the reception without any underwear on because it's about to come off."

"Is that a promise too?" she asked, and the playfulness he knew and longed for had returned to her voice.

"Yes. Now I'm going to deliver on it." He grabbed her hand and linked his fingers through hers, guiding her across the lawn, past the reception hall, and to a back door that led down a carpeted hallway. This was the kind of place that had swank bathrooms, and that was what he needed right now. He walked quickly, scanning the area for an opening. When he spotted a bathroom, he knocked once, opened the elegant white door, and locked it quickly behind them.

The bathroom was small with marble floors and a sink that had just enough room for Julia to perch on. He lifted her up onto the edge of the vanity.

She was trembling.

Concern sliced through him. He lifted her chin gently. "You okay?"

She nodded, but didn't speak.

"Julia, what is it?"

She shook her head, and seemed to swallow back a tear. "I'm sorry, I'm just super emotional today."

He leaned into her, resting his forehead against hers. "It's okay to be emotional. Your sister got married, and you shared something intense with me."

She reached her arms around his waist, her hands gripping the back of his white shirt. She still wore his suit coat and looked unbelievably hot in it. "And I want you to make love to me right now," she said in a breathless voice, her cheek pressed against his.

"Then I will make love to you," he said, bringing his hands to her face. He cupped her cheeks, and raised her chin so she met his eyes. "You're so fucking beautiful," he said, the words spilling out without control. He had to say it, had to tell her over and over.

"So are you," she said, and ran her hands down the buttons on his shirt, her fingers reaching his waistband. She unhooked his belt, then in seconds she was unzipping him, reaching a hand into his briefs.

His head fell back when she touched his cock for the first time in a month. He groaned as her soft, nimble fingers gripped him. She stroked him up and down, and he could almost stay like this because the feel of her hand on him was like a quick dive into a zone of white-hot pleasure. He rocked into her hand, and she gripped him tighter, making a fist that felt so fucking good wrapped around him.

Far too good.

Somehow, the part of his brain that wasn't drugged out on her sent a message to his hand, and he wrapped it around hers, making her stop. He shook his head, narrowing his eyes at her. "Now, Julia. You're not playing fair, and when you don't play fair, it means I'm going to have to take matters into my hands."

"What do you mean?"

"It means," he said, sliding off his belt, watching her eyes widen with lust as he dangled it in front of her, "that you're wearing this."

A wicked grin played across her lips and she wriggled closer. "Where?" she said breathily and he loved how she went with it. She didn't freak out. She *wanted* this kind of play. With his free hand he traced a line down her cheek, savoring her reaction as she shivered, leaning her face into his touch.

"Your hands," he said, reaching for them and placing a kiss on the inside of each of her wrists before he ran the leather along the outside, wrapping it around once, twice, and carefully pulling the end through the buckle. He gave it a good tug to make sure it was secure, but not so tight that the leather would dig into her skin.

"Now what?" she asked, holding out her bound hands in front of her.

"Now this," he said, gently pushing up the fabric of her dress, inch by inch, revealing more of her delicious skin. When he reached the apex of her thighs, he breathed in deep as a bolt of lust slammed into his body. "Keep your hands in your lap, Julia. Don't move them," he said, and kneeled down in front of her. "Do you understand?"

"Yes."

"Don't move your hands at all."

"I won't," she said, and her soft voice was a promise.

"Open your legs for me."

She parted her legs wider, spreading open for him as she sat perched on the sink, her immobile hands against her belly. He pushed the skirt to her waist, and ran his nose along the outside of her underwear, inhaling her, and letting her flood his senses completely. She gasped sharply. The sound of her pleasure tore through him like electricity.

He looked up at her to see her eyes floating shut. "Watch me," he commanded, gripping her thighs in his hands. "Watch me as I make you come with your panties on."

"What are you going to do to me?" she asked breathily.

"I just said what I'm going to do to you. Did you think I was joking?"

She shook her head, and he flicked his tongue across the panel of her panties, wet already with her heat. "I can taste you even with your underwear on," he murmured, his mouth against her. "I can make you shudder and writhe without even touching your pussy."

She moaned, a desperately needy whimper of desire. "You can. Yes, you can."

"You are so hot for me right now, aren't you?" he said, flicking his tongue against the swollen outline of her clit. She cried out a *yes,* and tried grabbing at his hair with her tied-up hands, managing to brush a few strands. He looked up at her. "Let me," he growled. "Let me control your pleasure."

He returned his mouth to her legs, tasting her once more through the cotton. She was so wet her panties were soaked through. The scent of her arousal washed over him, desire coursing thickly through his veins. He pressed his hands on the inside of her thighs, spreading her wider, lavishing fast, quick flicks against her wet center. It was as if the scrap of fabric was no longer there. He could taste her juices on his tongue, her desire so intense that she cried out loudly with every touch. Panting hard, she tried to grab at his hair again. He gently swatted her hands away. "Let go," he said roughly. "Let go so I can bring you there."

"Bring me there, Clay," she groaned as she wriggled her hips into his face, trying to get closer to the source of her pleasure. "Please bring me there."

"I will, gorgeous. I always will," he said, his lips returning to her wet pussy that tasted so delicious even with her underwear still on. He reached his hands underneath her ass, holding onto her cheeks as he pressed his tongue harder against her clit, licking, kissing, tasting until she bucked against his mouth.

She cried out, her mouth falling open, her eyes squeezed shut, her body writhing into him.

Once her movements slowed, he rose and pulled off her panties, and brought them to his nose. "You smell so fucking good," he said, then stuffed them into his pocket. "These truly are useless now."

Her lips rose in a sweet smile. "What if you turn me on again? And I walk around the reception hot and dripping between my legs?"

He buzzed his lips against the column of her neck, traveling up to her ear. "Then tell me and I will slide my hand up your legs, coat my fingers in your wetness and suck it off."

She breathed out hard, her reaction telling him she liked his idea.

"Now, I believe you wanted me to make love to you?"

She nodded, biting gently down on her lip. "So badly."

"I'm going to," he said, stroking her cheek, then running his fingers along the smooth skin of her collarbone. "And I want you to know that all this time I've been fucking you and making love to you. But this time, I'm only making love to you."

"That's what I want right now from you. That's all I want," she said, her voice layered with honesty and need as she leaned her face into his hand. Then held up her wrists in front of him. "But what about this?"

* * *

"Put your hands around my neck," he instructed.

She shot him a quizzical look as she raised her bound hands. He offered his head, letting her slide her hands behind his neck. "Like that?"

"Yes. Now you can't let go of me as I make love to you," he told her as he reached inside his briefs, and freed his erection once more.

"But I don't want to let go of you," she said, and she felt like a new woman being able to say these things to him, speaking so freely, even if it was about sex. Saying all those other things, as hard and as harrowing as it had been, had lifted a terrible weight from her shoulders, and now she experienced a freedom she hadn't known in a long time. She could say what she felt and not be afraid. And she could tell from the look in his eyes, so tender and hungry too, that he loved this side of her.

"Good. That's how I want you to feel," he said as he gripped his cock, and rubbed the head against her wet folds. She cried out again in pleasure.

"I want you so badly, Clay. *Please.*"

"I know you do," he said, dragging his hard length along her. She wanted him to know how much she trusted him with everything. In this moment she was trusting him with her pleasure, so she opened her legs more.

"I'm yours," she whispered, holding his gaze. "Take me how you want me."

He breathed out hard, her words of submission clearly sending him soaring. "You are mine," he said, his voice rough, but his touch so tender, as he slowly pushed inside her.

"Oh God," she whimpered. "You feel so good."

"It's been too long," he said, but still he took his time entering her, and she savored it, the feeling of being filled inch by delicious inch. He was so hard and so thick, and she could feel him stretching her once more.

"I don't want to go without you again," she whispered.

"Don't go without me." He buried himself in her, holding on hard to her hips as he sank deeper. She couldn't move. She was under his control, from him holding her hips, to her hands locked around his head, but he took care of her, thrusting in that deliciously tantalizing way he had, rolling his hips, taking his time.

He rocked into her, and she moved with him, hitting an exquisite synch. He groaned against her neck, pushing the strap of her dress down her arm. "I love it like this," he said, brushing his lips along her naked shoulder.

"Why do you like me tied up sometimes?"

"Because." He cupped the back of her head in a strong hand. "Because the way I feel for you is so out of control that this is one way for me to feel in control again," he said, his voice a low rasp in her ear.

She shuddered from his words. "Then control me," she whispered, arching her back, showing him that she could give in to this need he had. "Because," she began, echoing his word as hot molten sparks shot through her body, "I love everything you do to me."

"And do you love this?" he said, holding on tight, driving into her so she could feel him deep and hard inside her. "You like when I make love to you like this? Because that's what I'm doing right now."

"I know," she said breathlessly, and after a night of revealing her secrets, she could no longer keep the truth hidden. "You are, and I love it because I feel everything. I feel everything for you," she said, coming as close to saying those three words as she could.

He hitched in a breath. "God, Julia. I feel everything for you. Every single thing. And I want your pleasure again. I want to feel you come on me. Show me that I can do this to you over and over, and make you feel everything."

Pleasure spun through her body on a wild ride, racing through every corner, touching down in her belly, in her breasts, along her thighs. Even in her toes. "You can do anything to me," she cried out, as she felt herself reaching the brink. She tightened her arms around him trying to tug him as close as he could be. He held onto her, his cock buried inside of her, his lovemaking touching her so deep with its intensity that she was in another world, another realm, where she was bathed solely in the never-ending bliss of a climax that promised to rocket through her body.

Her head leaning back, her mouth falling open, she tried desperately to keep her noises to a minimum but it was futile as waves of pleasure slammed into her, and she came hard on him. He followed her there, his body shuddering, his chest heaving, as he thrust one final time. She felt as if she could never be close enough to him.

Never.

"I'm going to help you," he said, his voice strong as he promised her something she knew would be tough to give. "This is a promise. I'm going to find a way to help you out of this, and then I'm going to find your ex."

She didn't know that he could do either, but the fact that he wanted to was one more reason to fall into him.

CHAPTER NINE

The bride sat on the groom's lap, and his arms were wrapped around her waist. Julia held a glass of champagne and laughed at something Chris said. Jill reached across to punch Chris on the shoulder, and he rubbed the spot where she swatted him, clearly pretending it hurt. Then they all laughed, and Clay made up the words they were saying in his head.

He stood outside, watching the reception unfold through the windows. His phone was pressed to his ear.

"So what did you learn?"

"That Charlie Stravinski loves greenbacks more than anything in the world," Cam said.

"How so?" Clay turned away from the scene, and walked down the hill.

"He's got his fingers in all sorts of pies. He runs this limo company, right? Charlie's Limos. Totally legit, but it's his Bada Bing," Cam said.

"The strip club in *The Sopranos*."

"Yep. It's a clean business, and everything flows under that. He's got the market locked up in San Fran on sports betting. That's his big cash cow. He does concert tickets too—steals them and resells them at scalper prices. His growth market, though, is in poker. He runs a lot of big executive games in the

Valley. He just started running some games in New York too," Cam said, and Clay stopped at a tree, setting his palm against the trunk.

"He's working out of the Big Apple now?"

"Seems he is. And he's a big-ass loan shark too."

"Oh well, of course," Clay said sarcastically, because Charlie was growing more conniving with every new detail. "Did you get the story behind Mr. Pong's?"

"You bet your ass I did. Used to belong to good old Mr. Pong himself. But Mr. Pong needed money to pay off an investment that went belly up, so Charlie loaned him the dough, putting up his restaurant as collateral."

"Let me guess. He never came up with the money."

"Bingo," he said enunciating every syllable. "Charlie took over, and word on the street is Mr. Pong is living on the street."

"He's homeless?" Clay said, his voice thick with shock.

"That's what I hear. His restaurant was all he had, and it's all Stravinski's now. Tons of VCs in the city eat there. Charlie runs his games above the restaurant and he has lunch there every day at twelve-thirty. Those fuckers love their routines, don't they?"

He steeled himself for the next question. "What about drugs?"

"Nope. He's as squeaky clean as they come in that regard. But . . ." Cam said, his voice trailing off into a territory that Clay wasn't so sure he wanted to go. But he had to.

"But what?" he asked wearily, as a cold gust of wind snapped. The night cooled off quickly by the bay.

"My sources say he might be making a move into the world's oldest profession, so there's that."

Clay clenched a fist, his fingers digging hard into his palm. He could slam it against the tree, bang it hard and unleash this coiled ball of anger eating up his chest, but that wouldn't do him a lick of good. He gritted his teeth, and turned away from his temptation.

"'Course, if it were up to me, I'd advise him to stay out of that racket," Cam continued.

"Thanks for looking into all that, man," he said. Then he stopped in his tracks. "Wait. There's someone else I need you to look into."

"Who's that?"

But Clay didn't know Dillon's last name. "I need to get more info. Let me get back to you on that."

"You know where to find me. And I'll see you Saturday for our game?"

Clay nodded. "I'll be there," he said, and as soon as the words were spoken, something started to click.

He ended the call, but he didn't head back inside. Instead, he watched from a distance, rubbing a hand across his jaw as he began to hatch a plan.

* * *

A few glasses of champagne later, Julia was feeling like the drink herself—bubbly and effervescent. Though that might simply be due to the gorgeous man with his arm draped possessively around her. He'd been by her side since he returned from making his phone call, and she loved that he found ways to touch her all night, whether he brushed her fingertips *accidentally* when he took her glass to refill, or when he absently traced a soft line along her hipbone as the cake was being served.

Having him here with her almost made her forget about the troubles that awaited her. He had that effect, as if he were a magic elixir that erased all the bad. Or maybe that was the magic of falling, the way it was the ideal blend of intoxication, and could blot out all but the tingling in her shoulders, the flip in her belly, the thump of her heart when he looked at her. His gaze was filled with intensity and passion, with desire and tenderness. That was how his eyes roamed her as he held open the door to a taxi after they'd said goodbye to the few remaining guests, the bride and groom having been sent on their way already.

The second the door closed, she leaned into him and sighed happily as she grazed her fingers along his collar. "You're coming home with me," she said.

"That I am, gorgeous. That I am," he said, and removed her hand from his shirt. She shot him a curious look as he knotted his fingers through hers. The cab sped out of the parking lot and down the twisty, hilly roads. He grasped her hand harder as if he were about to make a point. "I have a plan."

"Already?" she said, arching an eyebrow.

He brushed a finger against that taunting eyebrow, sending it back into place. "Yes, already. What do you think clients pay me the big bucks for? To sit on my ass and not think quickly?"

She laughed. "Fine. You got me there. But let me make one thing clear, Mr. Big Bucks, you are not paying it off for me."

He held up his hands as if in surrender.

"You were going to try to, weren't you?"

"Actually no," he said firmly.

"Because there's no way I'm taking it. I haven't asked anyone for money. I meant what I said—if I were going to ask for help, McKenna would be the first person I'd turn to, and I haven't breathed a word to her, so don't even think about it."

"You considering letting me get a word in edgewise?" he asked as the cab slowed to a stop at a light.

"Maybe. But if you even think about offering, I will do this," she said, putting her hands over her ears and singing, "La la la, I am not listening."

He pulled her hands off her ears. "You think I don't know you? You think I don't listen? That I can't figure out already from knowing you the way I do that you'd never ever take money from me or another man?"

She narrowed her eyes at him playfully. The fizzy effect of the champagne was still rolling through her bloodstream.

"I know you, woman," he continued. "You are independent and stubborn and fiery. Give me some goddamn credit. I would not make you an offer I know you'd walk away from."

"Ooh, you're going to make me an offer," she said, tap dancing her fingertips along his arm. "I. Can't. Wait."

He rolled his eyes. "You are red-hot trouble."

"Tell me about it," she fired back. "And now you know exactly how much trouble you have gotten yourself into," she said and laughed, the kind that vibrated through her whole body and made her clutch her belly. It felt so damn good, because she hadn't laughed about her situation in ages. Never, come to think about it. Now she could because she was no longer in it alone.

"And yet, I'm not walking away, am I?" He grabbed hold of her arms and pulled her close for a hard, fierce kiss that made her feel giddy and wanted at the same time. She was no longer living with armor on. She'd shucked off the heavy metal layers, making herself vulnerable, but lighter too. Something that felt disturbingly like joy raced through her veins as they kissed, and though their kisses had always rattled and hummed like a rock concert, this one was poetry too. It was bliss and beauty as the world shined bright in her heart.

She wasn't finished with Charlie; but for the first time, she could see a way through because she had a teammate.

She broke the kiss as the cab turned a corner into her neighborhood, and still she was smiling. She wanted to know Clay's plan, but she was also enjoying this newfound freedom from releasing all her own secrets she'd clutched tightly to her chest. "No, you're not walking away. You're driving away with me. Like we're in a getaway car. Or cab, really," she said, gesturing to the driver.

He shook his head, clapped his hand down on her thigh. "Let's focus now, Julia. You know how you said Charlie took the fun out of playing? How he perverted your love of the game?"

She nodded. "Yep. He sure did."

"I know how to get it back," he said, as the cab swerved around a bus onto her street. She jerked sideways, her shoulder bumping hard against his.

"Ouch," she said, rubbing her shoulder.

"You okay?"

She nodded. "You just have a really hard shoulder."

The car pulled up to the curb. "Hard shoulders are good things," he said, and reached for his wallet. "I got this."

"Thank you," she said, and opened the door and stepped out of the cab. She lifted her face to the night sky, breathing in the cool air and the starlight until she heard a voice.

"Hey."

She swiveled around and saw Max stalking towards her from the front stoop of her apartment. Tension roared back into her body in a heartbeat as Skunk's goon-in-training with the baby face and the barrel body stared coldly at her. She glanced over at the cab where Clay was busy handing the driver a credit card.

"Charlie sent me to find you."

"It's Saturday. I'm not playing tonight."

"Yeah, but he wants you to know you're going to New York next weekend for a game. He has some new blood in the city from the startups there, and he wants you to hustle them."

She straightened her spine, liquid courage coursing through her. "What if I don't want to?"

His eyes widened with anger, and in seconds his hand was on the back of her neck. "You think you can talk to me that way?"

He grappled at her skin, digging in. She swatted at his arm, trying to knock him away, but he was more than double her size. "Let go of me," she spat out.

"Let go of her," Clay said in a cool, cold voice.

Max shifted his focus to Clay, who was now by her side. "Who the fuck are you?"

"I'm the guy who's going to make you let go of her," he said, and before Julia could process what was happening his elbow came down hard on Max's arm, freeing her from his grip. Then Clay's fist connected with Max's jawline with a loud crunch. Julia cringed, the sharp snap echoing down the street.

Max grunted, his eyes nearly popping out from surprise. His gaze darted down at his ankle, and fear flashed hard and fast before her eyes. Oh God, did he have a gun?

"No!" she screamed, but the sound was cut short when Clay slammed a fist into Max's belly, and the man unleashed a loud grunt as he doubled over. He was fast for his size though, and quickly straightened up. Clay cocked his fist to swing again, but this time Max was faster, landing a punishing jab on Clay's cheekbone, his hairy knuckles cracking hard against his temple. She swore she could hear bones crunching as Clay stumbled, the back of his head smacking hard against the brick wall of her apartment building. He grunted loudly from the pain, and all her instincts told her to run to him and comfort him.

"Stop! Please stop," she shouted, and she wasn't sure if she was talking to Clay or Max, or just praying to the universe for an end to this fistfight. But when she looked around, the street was empty, and she knew this was going to be between the two of them.

Clay lunged forward quickly, brushing off the double-blow like it was nothing, but Max went after him again, raising his fist and swinging hard. Clay dodged that blow, then Max threw another, landing one on Clay's shoulder that barely seemed to bother him. Especially since he grabbed Max's hand, twisted it around his back and yanked hard.

"Don't ever touch her again," he seethed, jerking the arm higher. Then he let go and reacquainted his fist once more with Max's jaw, sending the big man stumbling backward and landing flat on his ass on the sidewalk. Max was helpless, huffing in a heavy pile, staring up with wide-open eyes at the man who'd landed the final blow. With fists clenched at his sides and anger radiating off him in hot waves, Clay bent over him. "Now I'm giving you five seconds to get up and run the hell away."

Max nodded once, scurried to his feet, and took off down the street. When Clay turned to Julia, he was breathing hard and blood streaked from his temple down his cheek.

CHAPTER TEN

He flinched as she dabbed at the cut with a wet washcloth.

"It's okay," she said softly.

"I know," he muttered, rubbing the back of his head where he'd hit the building.

Kneeling between his legs, she gently cleaned the blood as he sat in her bathroom. "Does it hurt?"

"No."

She shot him a doubtful look. "Not even a little?"

"Not even a little," he said, but the expression on his face told her otherwise when she wiped off the last drop of blood. She reached for the Neosporin, applied some to the cut, and then opened a Band-Aid, pressing it gently along his temple.

"There," she said. "You look totally rugged now."

He managed a small laugh as she rose, dusting his other cheek with a kiss. Handing him two Advil and a glass of water, she said, "For your head."

He swallowed the pills and gave her the cup. She set it down on the sink. "Now let's get you out of your clothes and you can rest."

"I'm not resting," he said, rolling his eyes at her.

"You need your rest."

"It's only a cut. I've been cut worse at my gym," he said, and she knew he was trying hard to be the big, tough man. She was having none of that. He'd gone to the mats for her, and she was going to take care of him until he was no longer bloodied and bruised, and even then some.

"I don't care," she said, parking her hands on her hips and giving him a sharp stare. Then she bent forward and began unbuttoning his shirt.

"You're not taking off my shirt to go make me lie down in bed," he said roughly, trying to swat her hand away. She grabbed at his hands and stilled his moves.

"Oh yes I am," she said sternly. "Watch me."

She worked her way down his shirt, unbuttoning the fabric, spreading it open and gently taking it off, trailing her fingertips along his chest as she did. He moaned low and husky as she touched him. "Don't get any funny ideas, Mister."

"It wasn't a funny idea. More like a dirty one," he said with a sly grin.

She reached for his hand. "Come on. Bed. Now."

"Bed for other things," he said, but he let her lead him out of the bathroom and into her bedroom. She unbuttoned and unzipped his pants, then he stepped out of them. After laying the clothes neatly on a chair, she turned around to find him already in her bed, briefs on the floor.

"You're fast."

"Zero to undressed in no time," he said in a tired voice.

"We'll add that to your skill set."

"Come here," he whispered, resting on his side under the sheets. "Let me unzip your dress."

She moved to him, perching on the edge of the bed. He reached his hands up the back of her dress, those same hands that had defended her and protected her, and gently lowered the zipper on her dress, his knuckles softly grazing her spine as the dress fell to her waist. She shifted her body, so she could watch him. He smiled faintly as he unhooked her strapless bra.

She stood and turned to face him, sensing he needed to show he could take care of her, even when he was the one hurting. She placed his hands on her hips, guiding them to slide the dress down her legs. Off came the shoes, then she curled up next to him in bed.

"Thank you," she said, gently tracing his other cheek with her finger. "For doing that."

"Julia," he said, pulling her in close. "I can't believe that's what you've been dealing with."

She sighed. "Yeah. That's my life."

"This needs to stop. You're not safe," he said, concern thick in his voice.

"He's not even usually the one assigned to me. My regular has the flu or something," she said, flashing back to Skunk's pale face and peaked look earlier that day.

"You can't keep doing this," he said firmly as the shadows from the moonlight streamed across the bed, casting the room in a blue midnight light. "So this is what I didn't get to say in the car. I play every week. With actors, clients, colleagues and some of my friends. It's not a rigged game. It's a real game with real stakes and real money. Come to New York this weekend, and join us. Play for real. Play in a game that's not a set-up where you're not hustling. And take us down. Win on your own terms," he said, and the idea took hold instantly, planting roots inside her. She craved that feeling—w*in on your own terms.*

His offer was so alluring, like a faint scent of something delicious trailing through the air. But then, did she still know how to win on her own terms?

She scoffed out of self-preservation. "What if I lose?"

He scooped her hair off her neck, nuzzling her. "Where is my badass woman?"

"Huh?"

"*What if you lose*? I thought you were a poker shark? Don't lose. Come to New York. Play your ass off. You're a card player.

You don't come to lose. You play to win. So play, and win fair and square," he said, and there was something immensely appealing about his offer.

She quirked her lips in consideration. "It does sound like fun," she admitted.

"And if you lose—which you won't—let me pay him off," he said, his eyes locked on her the whole time. The look in them was intense, and true—he wanted this. He wanted to help her. She had always known he had this side, but now she was seeing it in action, and the gesture was slinking its way around her heart, loosening yet another layer of her stubborn woman-against-the-world attitude.

"Clay," she chided softly, lightly running her fingers along his strong chest. "I don't want you paying my debt."

"All the more reason for you to play hard."

She stared sharply at him, determination in her eyes. "I always play hard."

"I know you do."

"If I do this, you can't make it a rigged game. Don't make it fake."

"I would never do that."

"I want to win for real. Because I'm good."

"You're going to kick unholy ass. And if for any reason the game ends, and you're not in the black, I will take care of the debt. Deal?"

"I really don't want you paying it off," she said, grabbing his wrists for emphasis. "Promise me it's a real game, and we go to the end of the night. We play until everyone else folds."

"I promise you."

"I don't want to have to take your money. I want to prove that I can do this."

"And you will. I offer it as insurance. That's all. And that's why you'll win. Because you want to do this on your terms. Because the thought of anyone paying your way makes you dig your heels in like a batter at the plate swinging for the fences.

Come to the plate. And hit it out of the park," he said, as if he were making a motivational speech.

A damn powerful one.

She wanted to say no, to insist on doing it her way. But he'd taken a hit for her. And he was offering her a way to fall in love with poker again and to win on her terms. He was offering to be there with her, for her, not to own her, but to help her. With every move he made, she was falling harder and harder, and she was sure there'd be no turning back from this man. She'd been so closed-off from the start about letting someone into her world. Now, he was all the way in, and the only thing she was afraid of was him not being part of her world.

So she did the thing she'd never have imagined doing a mere month ago. Hell, a week ago. "Then we have a deal."

"Good," he said with a happy, woozy smile as he lay flat on his back, pulling her on top of him, angling up his hips. He was growing hard against her. "Now I'm tired and I'm wounded and I could use a little — "

She cut him off. "There's only one true cure for a wounded man," she said, and went under the sheets. She stroked him to a full erection, then dropped her mouth onto him.

He groaned as she wrapped her lips tightly around his cock. He pushed back the sheets so he could watch her. She looked up at him, wanting him to see the desire in her eyes. His went dark and hazy as he stared at her mouth moving lovingly along his shaft. She tucked her knees up under her, getting into the perfect position for giving him the blow job he deserved.

She let him fall from her lips for a moment, but kept her hand wrapped around him. "Enjoy this. Enjoy everything I'm going to do to you, my gorgeous, sexy, wounded man who rescued me," she whispered, pushing her other palm on his flat abs, feeling his washboard belly as she returned her mouth to him. She took him in deep, the way he liked, and used her hands too, touching his stomach, squeezing a small, dark nipple, causing him to jerk his hips up hard into her mouth.

She moved her hands lower, down his body, stroking his muscular thighs, settling deeper into the space between his legs. He parted them, giving her room to get cozy, and she thrilled inside at how he gave his body to her, trusting her with his pleasure just as she had with him. She drew him into her warm mouth as far as he could go. She sucked hard and passionately, wanting him to feel flooded with sensations that blotted out any of the lingering pain from the fight. Cupping his balls in one hand, she slipped another hand under his ass, squeezing a cheek hard in her palm.

He groaned loudly in response, and the sound sent heat flowing through her body.

"I'll take another hit to my head for this," he murmured, his voice both weary and thoroughly needy. He reached for her head, threading his hands tightly in her hair.

She let go momentarily. "Pull my hair if you need to," she said.

He gripped hard as she returned to him, tugging her hair over to the side, yanking her head so he could stare hungrily at her face as she licked and sucked the full length of his fantastic cock.

"So fucking gorgeous," he said, outlining her lips with a finger, tracing the edge of her mouth as she held him tight and deep, swirling her tongue along his shaft the way he loved.

She was sure he groaned louder than he ever had as she worked him over with her hands and her mouth, touching him in all the ways that drove him crazy. His body was a playground for her fingers, and she ran them along his thighs, over his ass, and in that spot just under his balls that drove a man wild. He gave himself over to her, rocking his hips into her mouth as she traveled to his favorite places. A pinch there, a touch here, a squeeze of those sexy cheeks: she was showing him that she knew how to control all his pleasure too. Then, as she gripped his firm ass in her hands, she fucked his cock with her mouth until she felt the shudders roll through his body.

He grappled at her hair, his breathing turning wildly erratic as he gripped her head, thrusting and calling out her name as the taste of his release slid down her throat.

Minutes later, she nestled herself in next to him. With his arm wrapped around her, she kissed his neck, his stubbled jaw, his tender cheek. "You like it when I let you control me, and I like it when you lose control for me," she whispered.

"Mmmm," he murmured. "We are a good combo."

"The best," she said as she closed her eyes, feeling like they were partners in everything at last.

* * *

Another pair of Advil did wonders to mute the throbbing in his skull, but the dull ache was a useful reminder of what he was up against as he pushed open the door to Mr. Pong's shortly after noon the next day. The smell of fried pork and noodles filled his nostrils. Waiters bustled around delivering plates of pepper steak and lo mein to the lunch crowd.

It was your standard order Chinese restaurant with thick menus and illustrated pictures of the twelve signs of the Chinese New Year— such as horses, snakes and rats, along with an illustrated dragon image presiding over them all.

Fitting, he reasoned, as a hurried waiter rushed over to him.

"One for lunch?"

"No. I'm joining someone. You can tell Mr. Stravinski that I'm here."

The waiter looked confused. "Sorry. Who should I tell him is here?"

"Tell him the guy he's expecting to see."

"Okay," the waiter said, narrowing his eyebrows briefly at the request before turning on his heels to find the man in charge.

Moments later, a tall man in a sharp suit strode over to him. He had thick, dark hair and muddy-brown eyes and some of the worst teeth Clay had ever seen. He wasn't thin, he wasn't fat; he was simply the sturdy type.

He extended a hand to shake.

"Clay Nichols," he said.

"Charlie Stravinksi. I had a feeling I'd be seeing you. Come," he said, gesturing grandly to the restaurant as if he were quite proud of the joint he'd taken over on a debt that went belly-up. "There is a table for us near the kitchen."

"Fantastic," Clay said coolly, as if this were just another lunchtime business meeting.

After they sat, a waiter handed Clay a menu. "Thank you."

Charlie tapped the menu. "Everything here is delicious. But may I personally recommend the kung pao chicken," he said, bringing his fingertips to his mouth and kissing them as a chef does.

"Consider it done," Clay said, pushing the menu to the side. He had every intention of not only talking to Charlie, but breaking bread with the man. If there was one thing he'd learned in his years as a lawyer, it was that the more you knew about the opposing side, the better off you were. And the less fear you showed, the more likely you'd win the points you wanted. Besides, he had a hunch Charlie was the type of man who would act supremely gentlemanly to a worthy adversary.

Clay planned to be just that.

"So, you messed up the nose of my new guy," Charlie began, leaning back in his chair and crossing his arms.

"It got in the way of my fist."

Charlie scratched his neck, as if he were a dog itching fleas. "He shouldn't have been there. He's too hot-headed to be on the street."

"Yeah?"

Charlie shook his head, and blew out a long stream of air. A man frustrated, he placed his elbows on the table and steepled his fingers. "Stevie was supposed to give her the message, but he came down with the flu, he claimed," Charlie said with a scoff.

"I'm guessing that's the last time he'll duck out of work for a sick day," Clay said dryly.

Charlie laughed, throwing back his head and letting loose several deep chuckles. Then he took a deep breath, and the laughing silenced. "What are you here for?"

"Seems we have something in common, don't we?" Clay said, establishing first their mutual interests.

"Red."

"That's what you call Julia?"

"Yes."

"Here's the thing, Charlie," Clay began, keeping his voice completely even and controlled as he knew how to do. "Can I call you Charlie? Or do you prefer Mr. Stravinski?"

"Charlie is fine."

"So here's the thing," he repeated, leaning back in his chair, mirroring Charlie's moves. "You're going to need to go through me now."

Charlie arched an eyebrow. "I am?"

"You are."

"And why would I do that?"

"I'm her lawyer and I'm handling you. And that's how it's going to work. You want your money, I presume?"

"I would like it," Charlie said. "I am fond of money."

"I had a feeling you were, so I brought some extra to settle some matters," Clay said, then dipped into his pocket for his wallet. Taking his time he opened it up, wet a finger, and counted some crisp bills. He laid $500 on the table. "This is for your guy. It's a way of saying I'm not sorry his nose ran into my fist, but I do aim to take responsibility for my actions."

Charlie eyed the money approvingly. "Go on."

He peeled off another five $100 bills, adding them to the stack. "This is for you to leave her alone this week."

A laugh fell from Charlie's lips. "It's going to cost more than that."

Clay added $500 to the pile, then raised an eyebrow in question. Charlie nodded. "That'll do."

"And this," he continued, adding five more to the pile, "Is a promise that we will have the $10,000 remaining on the debt to you by next weekend."

"Or?"

"There's no *or*," Clay said firmly, never wavering as his eyes remained locked on the man across from him. "It will be paid. And you will be done with her. Is that clear?"

"Why should it be clear?"

"Because that's how deals are done, Charlie. When the final $10,000 is paid, she's free and clear and I never want you to talk to her, be in touch with her, or send your men after her again," he said, his eyes locked on the man he despised, never wavering.

"Are you going to ask me to sign something? A legal contract, perhaps?" Charlie said in a mocking tone.

He shook his head. "They don't make contracts for this kind of deal. That's why I paid you the extra just now in good faith. Those are the terms of our contract. Good faith."

Charlie paused, and cocked his head to the side. Looked Clay up and down. Then his lips curled up. "I can live with those terms."

"And you can live with the other ones? When this is done, it's over and out?"

"If she has the money for me, I will not ever need to see her again," he said through gritted teeth.

"I told you. We will have the money. But she's not playing in your games anymore."

"Really?" Charlie said, doubt dripping from his mouth. "What is she going to do? Play the slot machines in Vegas to get my ten grand?"

Clay laughed and shook his head. "No. But does it matter? Do you care where your money comes from, or just that it arrives in a neat, green package?"

"Green is good. But I will be in New York next weekend. I'm moving a game there."

"What a coincidence. I happen to live in New York," he said.

"You will pay me there. By Sunday morning I want it. One week," he said, holding up his index finger in emphasis. "We will meet at eleven at my favorite restaurant in the Village. I will get you the name."

"Consider it done."

"And we will do business like men. We will shake on it when the deal is done."

"I'll be there."

The waiter arrived then with two orders of chicken and two sets of chopsticks.

"Dig in," Charlie said.

Clay took a bite and nodded in approval. "That's some damn fine kung pao chicken."

"As you can see, it would have broken my heart to drive this place to the ground like I could have. I kept it open for the chicken. It's rated best kung pao chicken in San Francisco. Nothing makes me prouder."

"It's the little things in life, isn't it?" Clay said, holding up a piece of chicken between his chopsticks as if in a toast to the dish.

"Indeed it is," Charlie said, a smile spreading across his face. "I like you. You have balls. You should work for me. I can always use a good lawyer."

"Thank you. But I'm going to have to pass on that. I have a pretty full client list at the moment."

They spent the rest of the hour talking about sports and eating chicken, and discussing whether San Francisco or New York had better restaurants. Though he didn't enjoy the time, and in fact, he spent the vast majority of it in a coiled state of restraint so he wouldn't strangle the man with his bare fists, at least he left understanding the enemy.

And that always counted for something.

CHAPTER ELEVEN

"How much do I bring to the game?"

Clay glanced up from the check, shooting Michele a quizzical look. "The game?"

"Yes," she said emphatically, holding her hands out wide. They'd just finished lunch at McCoy's on Madison, in between their respective offices. He tossed his credit card on the table.

"Saturday night. Your game," she added.

"You don't usually come to poker," he said as the waiter scurried by with plates for another table.

"Am I not invited?" She crossed her arms.

"Of course you're invited, Michele," he said, trying to settle her. He didn't want her to be irritated, but she seemed in a seesawing mood. "I was just surprised."

"Liam invited me," she said, drumming her fingernails against the table as if she were trying to get his attention. But he was paying attention already.

"Oh yeah? You guys are a thing now?" he said, though he knew the answer because Liam had called him a couple of weeks ago to make sure it was all right to ask Michele on a date. Clay had said yes in a heartbeat, and then had barely thought about it afterwards. He had a two-track mind these days—work and Julia.

"Sort of," she said with a shrug, as the waiter rushed over to the table.

"He's a good guy. He'll treat you right," Clay said, handing the waiter the check and the credit card. "Thank you," he said to the waiter.

"He is a good guy, so when he asked me to the game I said yes," Michele said, tapping the table once more. Then she took a deep breath, and spoke quickly, the words tumbling out. "And your lady friend is going to be there, right?"

"Yes, she'll be there. My lady *friend*," he said, sketching air quotes. "Her name's Julia."

Michele only knew that Julia was coming to the game. She didn't know about Julia's financial troubles. None of his friends did, because it was no one's business.

"Julia," Michele repeated, saying the name as if it had ten syllables and they all tasted bitter on her tongue. "So I can approve of her then," she said, changing her tone, seeming suddenly light.

"Sure," he said, going with it. Because, women? Who knew how to read them sometimes? And every now and then, Michele was impossible to figure out. "I'm sure you'll approve."

"I need to make sure the men I care about choose the right women for them. I worried about Davis. I worry about you," she said, reaching across the table to rest her hand on top of his.

Ah, he got it now. He understood what was going on with her. "You don't have to worry about me, Michele."

"But I do," she said, lowering her eyes.

"I know," he said, softly. She worried about a lot of things. It was her nature. She hated to see the people she loved get hurt. She'd been like that since her parents died, and Clay had wondered from time to time if she was trying to somehow prevent more hurt in the world. Odd for a shrink, but then he wasn't one to try to psychoanalyze anyone. "I know you worry. But I'm okay. You'll like Julia. I know you will."

"You think so?"

He nodded. "I do."

Something sad flashed in her eyes. "Do you ever think what would have happened if . . .?"

"If what?"

"If we'd . . ." she said, her voice trailing off as she gestured from him to her.

He raised an eyebrow. She couldn't possibly be referring to that kiss in college, could she? Nah. She must just be in one of those melancholy moods.

"If we'd have become something," she added.

"But we are something. We're friends," he said, reminding her of what she meant to him. "I can't imagine us not being friends."

"Right," she said, with a sharp nod as the waiter returned with Clay's credit card. "I can't either," she added, and she sounded resolute.

Or, as if she were trying to seem resolute.

After he said goodbye to her and walked up Madison, he mulled over her question. Why would she possibly want to know what could have been between them? The two of them being more than friends was the strangest notion to him. It was as if she'd suggested he start walking on his hands. It simply didn't make any sense.

But he had no more time to contemplate because when he returned to the office, Flynn was there with the Pinkertons to review the details of their next film. He rolled up his sleeves and settled in for the afternoon, his focus only on his clients, giving them his absolute best because in another few hours, Julia would be in his house.

* * *

As the plane began its descent, Julia flashed back on the last five days. They'd consisted of otters, poker prep, and packing for New York.

Kim had waltzed into work on Wednesday announcing she'd gone with otters for the baby's nursery, and minutes later she'd left early when she thought she was having contractions.

Turned out she'd just had heartburn, but Julia didn't mind shouldering the extra load at Cubic Z because the week had been blissfully uneventful. After Clay's talk with Charlie that past Sunday, Julia had operated in a sort of protective cocoon. No one, neither Charlie, nor Skunk, nor that asshole Max had bothered her, and they hadn't gone near Gayle or Kim either.

She'd played online poker in her free time, fiddling around too with some poker apps on her phone just to keep her skills sharp for Saturday's big game. She knew a few extra hours on a screen weren't going to make the difference. Luck would be a deciding factor, but she also had to be sharper than the rest of the players at Clay's game—the actor Liam Connor, who was about to open a new restaurant; the cable TV show producer Jay Klausman, whose show on drug dealers, *Powder*, was a huge hit; and Clay's friend, Cam. She'd researched Klausman and Connor and found bits and pieces of intel on their card-playing skills. The actor was a Leonardo diCaprio style player, someone who bet big and played for fun, but Jay, a shrewd producer, was the bigger threat. The wild card, though, was Cam. Julia had a hunch he'd be the one to beat. A man like that, used to taking chances, and possessing some kind of magical touch—he was going to be trouble for her.

This was the kind of trouble she thrived on though, and she was ready, reviewing her strategy once more as she walked through the terminal.

Clay had a last-minute meeting with a client, so she hailed a cab into Manhattan. He'd left keys for her with the guy who owned the coffee shop next door to his building, and she was secretly grateful that she wouldn't have to see him the second she arrived. She wanted to, oh how she wanted to, but sometimes, a woman wanted to be fresh and clean when she saw her man, and there was nothing quite like washing off a six-hour plane ride. When she reached his apartment, she opened the door, locked it behind her, and soaked in the silence and the oddly welcoming feel of his place. The last time she'd been here she bolted. Now, she felt like she belonged. He hadn't left a welcome basket on the dining room table, but the simple fact that he'd left the key said all she needed to know about him—*trust*. It was given, and it was shared, and there were no questions asked.

He trusted her. She trusted him.

She dropped her suitcase on the bedroom floor, and patted the side, touching the outline of the gift she'd picked out for him that was safely tucked inside. She shed her clothes and stepped under a hot shower.

As she wrapped a towel around herself ten minutes later, she didn't feel any pull to sift through his drawers or paw through the medicine cabinet. She wasn't a snooper, and there was nothing she needed to hunt out in his place. Besides, he was the definition of an open book, and there was something so reassuring about knowing that intrinsically. With Dillon, there were moments when he'd seemed a little shifty, from a joke here about not needing to report all the income he made from Charlie, to a little moment there when he'd told a story about stealing a milkshake glass from a diner in college. Fine, those were college hijinks, but as she looked back with 20/20 vision she could see hints of who he was.

Clay was the opposite—he didn't hide. He put himself out there for her from the start. No bullshit, and hell, she could use that in her life.

She hung up the towel, rubbed lotion on her legs, and went straight for his closet. Not to snoop, but to choose an outfit. She didn't need to rifle through her suitcase for jeans and a camisole when she knew what he wanted her in.

One of his shirts. She slipped one on, buttoned it to her breasts, and considered herself fully dressed.

She heard the door open, and her heart tripped over itself. Excitement tore through her body because he was here, and she damn near wanted to race down the two flights of stairs. But she knew this man, and knew what he wanted. He didn't need her running into his arms. He'd want to discover her. She padded down the steps quietly, turning the corner at the second floor just as he was leaving his phone and keys on the kitchen table.

She leaned against the top of the railing, her hip resting against the iron, her fingers toying with the top button. Waiting. Waiting for him.

When he looked up, his eyes locked on her face. He stroked his chin, and shook his head in appreciation.

"I could get used to this," he said, his deep, gravelly voice turning her to liquid as he stalked over to her, up the six steps, then cupped her cheeks in his big strong hands. "*You.* In my house. In my clothes. Here for me."

She melted as sparks raced over her skin. "All for you."

Neither one of them said another word as he looked at her as if he were inhaling her, as if the very sight of her was oxygen in his lungs. Electricity charged through her under his gaze. She wanted him to eat her up, to taste her, to touch her all over. Everywhere—this man needed to be everywhere on her body, in her body, in her heart, in her mind.

She reached for the collar on his shirt, gripping it hard. At some point they were going to kiss, they were going to crash into each other, but now the moment was heady with silence, drenched in anticipation of them coming together.

She stepped backwards, clutching his shirt. He followed, matching her until the back of her knees hit his couch.

Then it happened. Like fireworks, an explosion at the end of the Fourth of July, loud and powerful, that rang in your ears and lit up the sky. Everything became a frenzy of heat and vibrant color as he touched her. Before she knew it, the buttons on her shirt—*his* shirt—had scattered to the hardwood floor as he tore it off her. His shirt was gone next, pants unbuttoned, yanked down to his knees, then off. Like a leopard, he sprang fast, heated and fevered too, and before she knew it she was naked on her back on his couch, her legs up on his shoulders as he held her down hard with his big body. His arms, like steel, held her thighs in place as he entered her in one mind-blowing thrust. She was pinned, deliciously pinned, by this position. She couldn't move her legs, but her hands were free to touch his beautiful face, and she reveled in the chance to stroke his five o'clock shadow, to map his features with her fingers, to draw her thumbprint over his jaw that she loved.

Loved.

He moved in her, fucking her the way he kissed her, deep and consuming, in a claiming of her body. He was owning her, marking her, his fingers digging hard into her shoulders, clutching her tightly, as if he couldn't bear to let go. He took her hard and he took her slow at the same time. She felt him in her bones, on her skin, down to her very cells. He was inside her, he was outside her, he surrounded her. A symphony of sensations flooded every vein, and soon it became impossible to tell where one note ended and the next began. She could no longer distinguish between her body and her heart; they were one and the same, swallowed whole with longing for *him.* She and Clay had smashed into each other, atoms and particles colliding, combusting into this never-ending bliss.

"Do you think this will ever stop?" she whispered in between breaths.

"Wanting you like this?"

"Yes," she said, inhaling sharply as she held his face, never taking her eyes off his.

"No," he said, his voice ragged. "Because of how I feel."

"How do you feel?"

"I am obsessed," he said, raw and heated, his words touching down in her soul. "Utterly obsessed."

"The same," she whispered, barely able to form complete sentences, but not needing to. He took possession of her mouth, his lips devouring hers as he rocked deeper into her. He kept her restrained with his body, his arms, his cock, his lips, his tongue, his power, his control that he desperately needed to balance his obsession. She felt it all too, every ounce of him, of his desire and his need for her. Giving herself to him, she let him take her how he *had* to, because when he did, he brought them both over the edge.

She grasped his neck harder, holding on tight as pleasure ricocheted through her body, and the world spun so far into ecstasy that she never wanted to return.

Eventually she came back to earth, and he reached for her, nuzzling her neck, kissing her cheek, unable to keep his lips off of her. A kiss on her shoulder, another at the hollow of her throat. He stopped kissing her to trace her arm, holding her gaze as he did. "I want that every day. I want you every day," he said, his voice rumbling over her skin, drugging her with its sexy warmth.

"Me too. So much," she said, still high on him, them, the moments that had stitched together into bliss. Maybe that's why she felt bold enough to say the next thing. "It was different this time, Clay," she murmured.

"How?"

"I don't know. Maybe more connected. This is going to sound crazy, and you know I don't talk this way. But it felt deeper. Like we were the same," she said, a flush creeping over her cheeks as she opened her heart to him more and more every time. But she wanted him in now. She didn't want an arm's-length Clay anymore. "Does that make sense?"

"Yes. Do you know why it felt deeper?"

"Why?" she whispered, and the moment felt suspended, like they were on a bridge, holding hands, about to jump into the water below.

"Because there aren't secrets anymore between us," he said, brushing the backs of his fingers against her cheek, softly, oh so softly that she melted into his touch. "Because we're in this together."

"That's all I want. To be together with you," she said, the warm rush of falling blotting out everything else in the universe. Surely, nothing existed beyond these four walls. The city had disappeared and they were all that was left.

"No more lies. No more secrets. Only the truth," he said, his voice strong and steady.

"Only the truth," she repeated, and nothing had ever felt more true than this moment. "Like this. How I feel for you is like nothing I've ever had before."

"Me neither. I can't get close enough to you, Julia," he said, linking his fingers through hers, and that gesture, so tender and loving, was like stripping off a final layer. "I can't have enough of you. I want more of you. All the time."

"You can have all of me," she said, watching the reaction in his eyes. As if she'd given him all he ever needed with those words.

"You're all I want," he said, and it felt like a promise of what they might have together.

"What will you do with me after tomorrow night, once I have all this free time?" she asked, shifting from the intensity of their admissions to something a touch more playful, like they'd always been together. They'd had that from the start, from their very first night. She loved that they had so many sides.

"I figured you'd have your fill of poker, and be ready to move onto bridge. Strip bridge," he added, raising an eyebrow.

"We could try canasta, even. Or if you really want to go wild," she said, punctuating her words with a quick trip of her finger down his strong arm, "we could do Go Fish."

He pretended to fan out several cards in his hands. "Julia, do you happen to have any sevens?" he teased, as if they were playing the kids' game.

She mimed handing over a pair. "I'll miss my lucky sevens," she said with a pout.

"We'll make new luck. Because I know what we're going to do with all your free nights."

"What's that?"

"I'm going to take you to Vegas. Play for fun. We'll play blackjack."

"I'd love to go to Vegas with you."

"You can meet my brother. We'll go to Brent's comedy club, then I'm going to take you to one of those late-night clubs in the Bellagio, where it's dark and smoky and the music is low, and you'll dance with me."

"You dance?"

"Gorgeous, with you and me, dancing would be foreplay. I'd have you grinding against me on the dance floor," he said, flipping her around so her back aligned with his chest.

She wiggled her rear against him in demonstration. "Like that?"

"Yeah, keep practicing that," he said, low and husky in her ear.

"We'd play the slots, too," she added, keeping up their Vegas dreams.

"We'd lose money and not care," he said, brushing her hair off her shoulder. Planting a kiss on the back of her neck. Making her shiver.

"See a show."

"Fuck in a limo on the strip," he said, tracing her hipbone with his strong fingers.

"Fuck in the elevator," she said, sliding her leg through his, wanting to be wrapped up in him.

"Leave work behind. Leave the past behind."

"Not look at my phone. Not think about my phone."

"No one could reach us," he whispered. "We'd get drunk on each other."

She turned back around, needing to look at him, to see him. She ran a thumb over his lips, watching his eyes float closed as he hitched in his breath. "I'm already drunk on you, Clay."

"Stay that way," he said. "I need you to stay that way."

"I will."

CHAPTER TWELVE

He didn't want the time with her to end. He didn't want anything with her to end.

As he stepped into the elevator after dinner at an Italian restaurant that evening, he was painfully aware of the ticking clock marching towards tomorrow's game, then Sunday morning when they'd meet Charlie at eleven, then Sunday afternoon when he'd put her on a plane and let her crisscross the country. As they reached his floor, the thought of sending her home again was like a cut inside the mouth, an annoying reminder that couldn't be ignored. Because he wanted so much more with her. He wanted these moments to unfold every damn day.

But all he could do was make the most of this moment.

"I have a gift for you," he said when they were inside his home.

A smile teased at her gorgeous lips. "A gift? I love gifts. However did you know?"

"Of course you love gifts," he said, with the confidence of knowing her.

"Why do you say 'of course?'" She leaned against the doorframe in his kitchen, tilting her head to the side in curiosity.

"Because," he said, running his fingers across the top of her skirt. "Because you know how to enjoy things. Because you don't deny yourself. Because you let yourself feel pleasure and want. And that's the kind of person who likes gifts. The kind of person who knows how to enjoy life." He lowered his head to her neck, unable to resist brushing his lips against her soft skin. She shivered, and grabbed onto his shirt, tugging him close. "My point exactly," he added.

She broke the embrace and made grabby hands. "Gimme, gimme, gimme."

Stretching his arm around her, he scooped up the pink box that he'd left on the counter that morning. He handed her the gift, and tried his best to record every frame of her reaction. The way her eyes lit up as she ran a palm across the box, then as she untied the satiny white bow, letting it fall onto the counter. She lifted the top and peered inside.

"Ooh," she said appreciatively, then took the black thigh-high stockings from the box, and laid the box on the counter. "Your favorite thing."

He nodded.

"You want me to put these on now?"

"No. Save them. I need you to wear them tomorrow night."

She narrowed her eyes at him. "Why?"

"It's my poker handicap."

"What is that supposed to mean?"

"I don't want to win tomorrow. If you're wearing those, I won't, because it's all I'll think about," he said, brushing his fingertips from her knees up her thighs.

Her lips parted as he neared the apex of her legs, but she pressed a hand against his chest, holding him back. "I want to win fair and square. I told you that. You promised."

"I know you do. But you don't need to prove to me you can beat me, Julia. I'm on your team," he said, grabbing her hand and linking his fingers through hers. "And I need you to wear those tomorrow night for me. Say you will."

He watched her. Her shoulders rose and fell, and she didn't speak for a moment, as if she were considering it. "Why do you have to be so damn convincing?"

"It's my job to make a good argument."

"You're too good at what you do. But I'd wear them for you anyway. And since it's evidently Christmas early at your house, I suppose it's as good a time as any to let you know I have something for you."

"I love Christmas," he said as she took his hand and guided him upstairs. When she reached her suitcase, she unzipped it and dipped a hand into the inside pocket.

"This is a surprise, so close your eyes."

He did as she said. "I love surprises too. Did you know that?"

"No. But that suits you as much as you said my loving gifts suits me."

"Why do you say that?"

"Because of the time you surprised me at my apartment. And then at McKenna's wedding," she said, as her heels clicked across the floor, and he felt her near him.

"Hold out your hands," she told him, her sexy, sultry voice turning him on.

He opened his palms. "Put this on me," she said, and he felt soft fabric fall into his hands.

When he opened his eyes and looked down at his hands, he breath caught. A silk scarf was in his palms, and she was stripping off her clothes. "Blindfold me," she said.

He flashed back to their night in San Francisco last month. She'd told him it was the only thing she didn't want to do. "*The thought of it makes me feel a bit too vulnerable, and for a woman with trust issues, well, I'm not sure it's the best kind of kink for me.*"

"But you said," he began, but his words were swallowed dry as he watched her clothes fall in a heap on the floor, and she wore only her lace panties and heels.

"I know what I said." She ran her hand down his chest, her touch sending tremors through his body. "But things changed, and I want to do this for you. This isn't the same as you helping me out of my troubles, but even so, I want to give you what you want. Let me do this for you."

He shook his head. "Don't do this to say thank you."

"I'm not doing it to say thank you," she said firmly. "I'm doing it because I want to give you everything you want."

"You don't have to," he said, his voice hoarse, as he fought back the desire burning inside of him for *this*.

"I would never do something with you that I felt I *had* to. Everything I do with you I want to. I have so much want for you I don't know what to do with it all, but to give you more of it. So sit down," she said, and began to press her hand against him. She stopped. "Wait." Her lips curved into a wicked grin. "I don't think your fantasy is me telling you to sit down. You tell me what to do."

Oh, fuck. He was done for. His body was dangerously close to overheating, and she hadn't even touched herself. But this wasn't his fantasy for nothing. He knew how he wanted her—al fresco. "I want you on my balcony."

"As you wish," she said, her eyes catching his, a spark in them as she glanced back at him and headed down the steps, giving him a perfect view of her gorgeous ass as she walked. His cock twitched hard against his jeans as he pictured all the things he wanted to do to her ass. When she reached the sliding glass door and tugged it open, she cast her gaze to the outdoors, then crooked a finger, beckoning him.

"On the lounge chair," he told her, and she crawled across the cushions. He kept his eyes on her the entire time, savoring every move of her body as cars and cabs raced by five flights below. If he peered over the brick railing he could watch the Manhattan night roll along, the people walking down the cobblestoned street in the Village. But he wasn't looking anywhere except at her. She shifted to her back, her red hair fanning out over a pillow, her long, luxurious body stretched across the wooden lounge chair. A warm breeze floated through the dark night, blowing wisps of hair across her cheek.

He straddled her, running the end of the silk blindfold over her belly, her breasts, then her throat, so the fabric teased her skin. Gently, he pressed the material over her eyes. She lifted her head so he could tie it behind her. As he tightened the knot, she wriggled her hips against his pelvis, and he felt the heat from her against the fabric of his jeans. "You want this," he rasped out. "I can feel it. I can feel how fucking hot you are."

"I do want this," she whispered.

He lowered his head to her neck, buzzing a trail up to her ear. "I know you can't see anything now, but you can feel everything. That's why I want this. I want to watch you *feel* every single thing," he said huskily, licking the shell of her ear.

She looped her hands around his neck. "It's very dark where I am, and I need to know you're here the whole time. You can't look away from me."

"I promise I will have my eyes on you the entire time," he said, as he inched down her body. "You'll feel me."

"How?"

"Trust me, Julia," he said, as he settled in at the end of the lounge chair, giving him a perfect view of her body, a straight shot of her long, luscious legs. "I'm going to sit and watch you, and I'll tell you when I'm ready, and until then keep your hands at your sides."

She nodded, and he drank in the sight of her, from her beautiful breasts, so round and gorgeous, to her rosy nipples, hard and practically demanding to be sucked on, to her soft, flat belly. Then the thong panties between her legs, beckoning to him. His fingers ached to touch her there; his mouth craved her taste. She arched her hips ever so slightly as he stared at her legs, and it was as if she knew, without being able to see him, that he was looking at her with such longing and heat.

"You can feel me looking at you, can't you?"

She pressed her teeth into her bottom lip, and murmured, "Yes. I can feel your eyes on me."

"Good. Spread your legs," he said, and heat flared across his skin as she parted her legs, opening them wide for him.

He bit back a moan as he caught sight of the small scrap of fabric and the wetness on the cotton panel. This woman was so responsive, so aroused by him that it was almost a crime not to bury his face between her legs right now, send her hips shooting up into his mouth, and fuck her with his tongue.

"This is also how you'll feel me," he said, circling her ankles with each hand, then gripping them, and holding them down, her feet bound by him.

"Oh," she said, arching her hips and rocking into the cushion before she'd even touched herself.

"Now tell me how much you want to be touching yourself right now."

"I'm so turned on," she said, and her voice was hot and whispery.

"Are you aching to be touched right now, Julia?"

"Yes," she moaned, her mouth falling open as she licked her lips. "Can I?"

"Do it," he said. "Leave your panties on and slide those fingers between your legs."

She dropped her hand into the waistband, then lower, then lower still, and she drew a sharp breath when she made contact. God, it was a beautiful sight, her lips falling open as her fingers reached her pussy. He wanted those fingers to be his, he wanted his mouth on her, his cock inside her, but he wanted this torture more. He craved watching her, knowing how she looked when she was all alone. He wanted to witness how her body reacted to her own touch.

"Tell me how it feels," he said, as he gripped her ankles, her legs unbearably sexy in those heels.

"So good," she moaned. "So wet. My fingers are sliding all over, and I'm imagining it's your tongue."

Sharp agony rang in his body, and every instinct told him to tear off her panties and fuck her hard. But that wasn't the point. He needed the torment of seeing her naked body writhing in pleasure. He was hungry for the waiting, for the tension that gripped him as he forced himself to hold out until she'd already come from her own hand.

"And how does my tongue feel right now, Julia?" he asked as he stared greedily at her hand, moving quickly beneath the lace. "How does my tongue feel on your sweet little clit as I suck it between my lips and make you writhe into my mouth?"

She arched her hips into her hand, and moaned loudly, digging her heels firmly into the cushion. "Your tongue is so fucking good on me. I'm picturing riding your face right now," she said in a smoky voice that betrayed all her lust, all her want, and made him ache deep in his bones to touch her.

"Take off your panties. I need to see all of your pussy if you're getting this worked up so quickly," he told her.

She grabbed at the waistband, and pulled them down quickly to her knees. He tugged them off the rest of the way, taking them in one hand. "I need to smell you while you do this," he said, and brought her panties to his nose, inhaling her. The scent of her was a direct line to his cock, painfully hard beneath the denim of his jeans, begging to be freed.

"How do I smell?" she asked as she dipped her hand back down between her legs.

"So. Fucking. Aroused."

"I am," she said in broken breaths as she stroked faster.

"Let your legs fall wide open, Julia," he told her. "I want to see everything you do to yourself."

She spread her legs further, so beautiful, so vulnerable, so open on his balcony. A black scrap of silk over her eyes, heels on her feet, and her body that he desired every single damn hour of the day, here for him. He could take her now; he could yank down his jeans and thrust inside of her, sliding into the warm, wet home of her pussy. But he wasn't going to. Not yet.

"Are you touching yourself, Clay?" she asked as her fingers flew across herself.

"Do you want me to be? You can't see me."

"I know. But I can picture it. I want to know that your cock is fucking your fist right now," she said as she rocked her hips into her hand.

"You dirty girl with a dirty mouth," he said, with utter appreciation for the way she talked.

"I am, and you love it," she said, and the moment shifted from her submissiveness to her taking over somehow. He hadn't expected this, but then, she had a way of surprising him. "You love every filthy word from my mouth. You love watching me fuck myself, don't you?"

"God, I fucking love it so much," he said, hitching in a breath, and pleasure ripped through his bloodstream at the sights and sounds. "I can't think of anything that can get me off more than the woman I want fucking herself in front of me," he said, as he unbuttoned his jeans, slid down the zipper and let them fall to the ground. "I've been dying to know what you look like when you're getting yourself off to me. Now I'm going to find out," he said, rubbing his cock through his briefs. He wanted to close his eyes and give in to the pleasure, but there was no way he was missing this moment as her fingers raced across her swollen lips. "Show me. Show me now," he said, as he pushed down his boxer briefs and took his cock into his hand.

And there it was. A loud cry of pleasure. An exquisite moan as her back bowed and her hips shot up into her hand, her fingers flying fast and furiously. "This," she said, breathing hard, and erratic. "This is me picturing you licking me, eating me, fucking me, taking me. Any way you want. That's what I'm imagining now, Clay. Oh God, I want you so badly to fuck me now." She gasped, and her words were drowned out by her cries of pleasure as she rocked into her own hand, coming hard and beautifully for him.

In seconds, he was over her, untying the blindfold, watching her eyelids flutter open. Her pretty green eyes were hazy with lust. Never had he seen more heat in her gaze than in that moment. She'd loved every second as much as he had. He locked eyes with her as he reached for her hand, bringing it to his mouth and sucking on her index finger first, then her middle finger, licking her from her fingertips down to her knuckles so he could taste every drop of her.

"Perfect. You're so fucking perfect," he said, as he savored the taste of her desire in his mouth.

"Do you like?" she asked, all breathy, awash in the afterglow of her orgasm.

He shook his head, moving closer to her. "I *love*," he whispered, pressing the word softly against her lips. He kissed her eyelids, his way of telling her thank you for trusting him. Then he kissed her cheek, her neck, and her ear. "You're beautiful all the time, and so beautiful when you come with me."

"So was it everything you hoped it would be? Your fantasy?"

"Gorgeous, you are my fantasy come true," he said as he grasped her hand and wrapped it around his erection. Immediately, she stroked him, her soft fingers providing some kind of relief. He drew a deep breath, fueled by the electricity that shot through him from her touch. "I want to see those lips wrapped around me."

She let go, grabbed his hips, and pulled him down to her, lifting her mouth to him. The moment she made contact, he grabbed the top of the lounge chair. He had to hold back because all he wanted now was to fuck her mouth hard, and come in her throat. His bones were humming, his blood was rushing thick and hot, and he wanted the same release she'd had.

"No," he said, stopping her a few seconds later.

"Why?"

"Because I want it like this," he said and pulled her up to her knees, then pushed her down on all fours. "Because I need to touch you at the same time."

He guided his cock back to her lips, and she opened wide, taking him all the way in, her warmth surrounding him. He gripped the back of her head with his hand, her hair spilling over his fingers as he moved in her mouth. He slid his other hand along her back, enjoying the soft, smooth skin, then down to her ass, spreading his hand over one perfect cheek, and squeezing.

She caught her breath from that motion, even with her mouth full. He dropped his hand lower, slipping it between her legs. "Think you can handle being touched again right after you came?"

She nodded.

"Good. Because I was so jealous of your fingers the whole time I was watching you, and now I want my hand on your sweet pussy," he said, sliding his fingers over her lips, from her clit down through her wet folds, rubbing her in circles. She began to respond by rocking against his hand, moving her ass against him all while sucking him hard and as deep as he liked. Soon, he started to feel the build in the base of his spine, the threat of orgasm within his reach. All he had to do was thrust into her inviting mouth, let her take him as she wanted to. Every instinct in him said to keep fucking her mouth, especially given how she pushed back against his fingers, rocking into his touch. But that pussy, that delicious, beautiful pussy, was where he wanted to be right now. He gently reached for her, cupping her cheeks and pulled her off of him.

"You have no idea how much I want to come in your mouth," he whispered, holding her tight in his hands.

"So do it. I want to taste you. You know how much I love tasting you."

He shook his head, breathing hard, his chest rising and falling. "I want to look at you when I come. I want to watch your face when I make you come again. I want to be inside you."

She drew in a breath, and sighed sexily. "That sounds pretty damn nice too."

He sank down on the end of the chaise lounge, and shifted her on top of him. He reached for the blindfold behind him, and dangled it between her breasts. "I like my gift so much, and there's one more way I want to use it."

She somehow sensed his need before he told her, because she moved her arms behind her back, aligning her wrists along her spine. "Is this how you want me?"

"Yes," he growled. "This is one of the fifty million ways I want you."

"Are you going to tell me all the other 49,999,999 ways?" she asked playfully as he looped his arms around her.

He smiled as he tied her wrists together, and bound her forearms, until they were neatly restrained along her back. "How is it possible that you can do this to me?"

"I think you're doing things to me," she said, her lips curving in a grin.

He ran a finger along her lips, tapping her lightly. "No, funny woman. How is it that you can make me laugh as I tie you up?"

"One of my many talents with my mouth," she said, pouting sexily.

"Your sexy mouth is one of my favorite playgrounds," he said, grasping her hips, raising her up, and then lowering her gorgeous body onto his cock. She inhaled sharply as he filled her.

"The blindfold is the gift that keeps on giving," he said, and she smiled in return, then laughed deeply as he thrust into her, and he was sure it was her laughter that did him in. That melted his heart, absolutely and completely for this woman. He was there already, feeling everything for her, but for her to laugh like that during lovemaking, a joyous sound, sealed everything for him. He was a done deal when it came to her. She was the only woman he'd ever felt so much for, and he wanted her. Always.

* * *

She rode him up and down, but not a fast and furious kind of rhythm. More lingering and sensuous, taking her time, because they had time. There were no clocks, there were no deadlines; there was nothing but the two of them, entwined with each other.

He gripped her hips, guiding her moves at times, at others letting her set the pace. He kissed her breasts, burying his face against her chest, sucking one nipple, then the other. She desperately wanted to grab the back of his head and hold him tight against her, but her arms were shackled by the silk, and truth be told, she didn't mind one bit. She didn't mind being tied up by him, or tied down. Everything he did to her was designed to make her feel amazing—he fucked her like she was unbreakable, and he kissed her tenderly like her heart was the most fragile thing he'd ever touched, the thing he'd never want to break.

"I missed you this week," he said as he blazed a trail of kisses up her chest to her throat. "I missed you so much."

"I missed you too," she said, breathing hard as he filled her.

"I need to see you more, Julia," he said, and his voice was bare and emotional, stripped down to the simplest of needs.

"I need that too."

He looped his arms around her waist, then up her back, tilting his face to look at her as they made love. "Do you have any idea how much I want you?"

"Tell me," she said, locking eyes with him. "Tell me how much."

"I want you in every way possible."

"I thought it was fifty million ways," she said, teasing him, and he thrust hard in response. "Tell me some of them."

He gripped her wrists in one hand. "You know what I want? I want to fuck you in every way I can."

Her eyes widened with those words, with the possessiveness of his tone. "How?"

He dropped a palm to her ass, gripping her tight. "I want to fuck your pussy as I'm doing now." He drove deeper into her and she arched her back, letting him know she liked it. "I want to fuck your mouth, again and again," he said, running his finger across her lips, then sliding it into her mouth. She sucked long and hard. He dropped his hand to her chest, tracing a line between her breasts. "I want to fuck you between your breasts," he said. Then, in a flash, his hand had returned to her backside and he slipped a finger between the tops of her buttocks, causing her to draw a sharp breath. Inching his finger lower, she both tensed and thrilled as she sensed where he was going. He slid his hand between her legs, coating his fingers in her wetness, then began slowly traveling back up. "I want to fuck your hand, and I want to fuck your pretty little ass," he said, stopping to rub a finger against her rear.

"Oh God," she said, her eyes falling closed.

"Do you think you'd ever let me?" he asked, his voice all hot and husky against her throat as he pressed the tip of his finger further. He was barely inside her ass, but the twin sensations were so intense, tearing through her with a pulsing kind of tightness.

"I don't know," she admitted truthfully, in between breaths.

"Can I do this though?" he said, pushing deeper, and a bolt of pure, white heat lit up her body.

She could barely speak; words had become impossible to form. How could anyone put syllables together when he was inside her like *this*? When her entire body was trembling from pleasure, and from the unexpected intensity of both his cock and his finger penetrating her?

"Is that a yes?" he whispered, his voice low but firm. He needed an answer. He needed to know how far he could go, and there was a part of her that felt utterly helpless. She was tied up in his lap, with bound hands and spread legs. And yet, there was nothing he'd ever done to her that wasn't short of spectacular. He was a drug, and he delivered hits of pure pleasure through her heart, mind and body.

"Yes, you can do that," she said, swallowing thickly as he thrust his finger deeper. She'd never experienced this before, this double dose of intensity, but there it was, her entire body spiraling into a new land of ecstasy as he did what he'd said he wanted to do. He fucked her everywhere. He fucked her all over. He owned her and consumed her, and turned her world into blinding hot rapture as she rode him. He rolled his hips up into her, his cock driving deeper, his finger sending waves of pleasure through her. She was nearing the brink, racing to the precipice, and she needed to be closer to him.

"Untie me," she said desperately, through heavy pants.

Immediately, he undid the knot around her wrists, letting her hands fall free. She wrapped her arms around his shoulders, tugging him near, needing contact, needing to hold him as her orgasm vibrated wildly through her body. She gripped him tight, ecstasy carving its way through her in the most beautiful plundering, as he stole her body, her heart, and her very soul. She clutched him as his shoulders wracked with shudders too, joining her, his own grunts and moans piercing the night.

"I need you all the time too, Clay. All the time," she said into his neck, slick with sweat.

"I feel the same," he murmured stroking her back with his strong hands, and soon after she'd come down he carried her upstairs, turned on the hot shower, and bathed her, soaping her up and rinsing her off, then drying her, and taking her to bed, nestled and warm in his arms.

"We have to find a way to see each other more," he said, running his fingers through her hair as he faced her in bed, the dark of the night cloaking them, only a sliver of moonlight revealing his face. "It's not negotiable."

She arched an eyebrow. "Oh really, counselor? Is that how you play ball?"

"Certain terms are not up for negotiation. This is one of them."

"How do you propose you win this point in your client's favor? The client, I presume, is you?"

"You know what they say about representing yourself."

"That you have a fool for a client?"

He nodded, and smiled at her, his lips curving in that sexy grin. Then his expression changed. Shifted. Turned more serious. "Julia, when I first came to San Francisco, I had no idea *this* would happen."

"What's *this*?" she asked, nerves fluttering through her. She was terrified to attach definitions to what she was feeling. Better that he go first. He was always the braver one.

"You and me," he said, and the words made her heady. They'd both come so close to voicing the most dangerous one of all. "I didn't come to San Francisco that first night looking for this. I wasn't looking for anything."

"What did you come for? What did you want?"

"I didn't want anything," he said, staring deeply into her eyes. She felt as if he were looking far inside her, beyond her skin, beyond her cells, to know the heart of her. And that it belonged to him.

"And now?" She asked, her throat dry with hope.

His deep brown eyes searched hers, holding her gaze, holding her tight. "Now I want everything."

CHAPTER THIRTEEN

Her instincts had been one hundred percent right. Klausman, the show producer with the completely shaven dome and ever-present frown, had been tough as steel. He was hard to read and calculating, but she'd managed to separate him from about $1,000 by sticking to her guns, studying her cards, and quickly analyzing what had been played and what hadn't. Klausman was a fierce opponent; the guy showed no emotion, and he reminded her of how she played in Charlie's fake games.

Except tonight, she didn't play like that. She played loose and carefree on the outside, laughing and joking, and mixing a drink here or there at the restaurant Liam was slated to open in two weeks.

Speakeasy, he was calling it, and the place was gorgeous. There were booths in fine brown leather, and gorgeous oak tables, as well as a long, polished wooden bar. She loved that he hadn't gone with the overly slick look of so many bars and restaurants these days that draped themselves in chrome and steel. This restaurant was classy and warm, with rich red-framed abstract prints on the walls, and burgundy stools at the bar.

Liam finished dealing to Cam, then slapped down the last card for Klausman. He picked up his cards and considered them, his cold blue eyes on the hand in front of him. He'd never be the type invited into Charlie's games; he wasn't an easy target. Julia held her own cards, not too tight, not too loose, as Clay rested a hand absently on her thigh. His white button-down shirtsleeves were rolled up, showing off his fabulous forearms. He wore his purple tie, knotted loosely. His lucky tie, he'd called it. He puffed on a cigar, looking sexy and oh-so-masculine doing so.

But she wasn't focused on him right now. Her real focus was on Klausman, and she tried to study him, to gage his next move.

"Well, this is just a shit hand," Cam said out of nowhere, slapping his cards down with a loud smack, and shaking his head. "I'm so out I'm beyond out. They're going to need a new word for how out I am in this round." He brought the cigar he was smoking back to his mouth.

Julia smiled faintly at Clay's lawyer friend. He was exactly as Clay had described: big personality, big voice, lit up the room. He even smoked grandly, puckering his lips around his cigar and taking deep inhales.

"So, Miss Julia," he said, "what is your favorite drink to make? Absolute favorite in the entire universe of spirits?"

"How about you let the woman play?" Clay said, as Klausman pushed a black chip to the center of the table, muttering that he was in.

Cam's eyebrows rose at Clay's question. "What? Your woman can't talk and play cards at the same time?"

Julia raised her eyes. " Champagne for happiness. Whiskey for loneliness. And vodka for anything else," she answered as she slid a chip into the pile.

Cam blew out a long stream of smoke, making rings with his big mouth. "Well, look at that. She's a poet. That was fucking beautiful. Was that not a beautiful ode to drinking?" Cam glanced around the table, at Liam, at Michele, at Klausman and at Clay, waiting for them to respond to his question

"It was lyrical," Liam said, glancing up from his cards to flash one of his charmer smiles. It was so clear he was an actor, because he had that *it* factor, the charisma that made him shine on stage. "Like a gorgeous soliloquy." Tossing a chip into the mix, he turned to Michele who stayed in the round yet again, even though she hadn't once won. Julia had to give her credit. The woman wasn't backing down, even though she'd had nothing decent all night, and could barely play. But she had iron nerves, and kept on ticking. Even Liam, who couldn't keep his hands off her, hadn't distracted her from her cards. Not when he nuzzled her neck, ran his fingers through her hair, or flirted like a movie star with her.

"I'm gonna drink to your ode to drinking," Cam said, holding up a glass in a toast across the table.

Julia raised an imaginary glass. "Cheers," she said, and soon it was time for hands to be revealed.

Clay went first, laying down his cards: only a ten high.

"Oh, you bluffing bastard!" Cam shouted. "Did you actually think you were going to win with that?"

He simply shrugged, and the corner of his lips quirked up. His secret? He was protecting her secret. "Man's gotta try," Clay said dryly, leaning back in his chair. He ran a finger over Julia's thigh as she placed her cards on the table, showing her pair of sevens.

"Lucky sevens," she said proudly, then she noticed Michele looking at her. Or rather, at her leg. At the exact spot where Clay's hand was, as he ran his finger across the fabric of her stocking. Maybe it was coincidence, or maybe there was something more to the stare.

Meanwhile, Klausman laid down his cards, and he had a pair of fives.

A phone rang, and Liam reached into his pocket. Glancing at the screen, he said, "My film agent. Let me go take this." He rose.

"Wait. Liam, what do you have?" Michele asked.

He waved off his hand. "I got jack shit. That's what I got. You show them my hand," he said, bending down to kiss Michele on the forehead. She tilted her face up and let out a small murmur. Maybe she did like him.

After he left, she shrugged and said, "I guess it's my turn. And I think I might have won my first hand," she said, showing two kings.

Julia's chest tightened and annoyance threaded its way through her body. *Damn.* The last person she'd expected to win was Michele. But then she told herself to let go of the annoyance. This was poker, and you didn't win every hand. Besides, she was having fun *not* playing with Skunk watching over her. Not having to show her cleavage to take down a VC. She had her eye on the prize, and she planned to snag the brass ring of victory, and then march into the breakfast meeting with Charlie tomorrow, shove the greenbacks in his face, and tell him to kiss the fuck off.

Klausman pushed back from the table. "Since there's a break in the action, I'll take a break."

Julia turned to Cam, who was finishing his scotch. "Want another?"

"I would love one," he said.

Michele waggled her empty glass. "I could use another. I'll join you."

"Sure. We'll make it a ladies night behind the bar."

* * *

She was beautiful. She could hold her liquor. And she'd known him for years.

"Here's your scotch," Julia said, sliding the glass to Michele, who brought it to her lips and took a swallow.

Julia knew she shouldn't be jealous, not after what she and Clay had shared, but this woman was *here*. In New York City. She could see her man anytime she wanted to. Julia studied her as she drank, that pretty brown hair, those gorgeous brown eyes, and her body. But she fought back the sliver of envy that snaked through her. She'd never been the jealous type. Had never been the insecure type either, and she certainly wasn't going to start down that road tonight. Women didn't need to battle each other or be bitchy.

"You two seem pretty happy," Michele offered once they were out of earshot of the men.

"I suppose you could say that," Julia said with a grin. "And what about you and Liam? He's rather fond of you."

"Oh. He's great," Michele said quickly. Too quickly.

"When did you start seeing him?"

"A few weeks ago."

"He's very sweet. And quite a charmer."

"You and Clay haven't been together for very long either, have you?" Michele asked. She clearly had no interest in discussing Liam.

"Two months."

"That's really not much, is it?"

"I don't know. Is it? Isn't it? Sometimes I think it takes all the time in the world, and sometimes it takes no time," she said.

"You're crazy about him, aren't you?" Michele said, and her voice sounded sad.

Julia rested her elbows on the bar. "I am. Absolutely. In every way."

"I can tell," she said, casting her eyes down at her glass.

"I'm glad it's obvious. Are you okay, though? You look . . ." Her voice trailed off as her bartender instincts to listen to patrons' woes kicked in.

Michele raised her eyes, and fixed them on Julia. "I want him to be happy," she said firmly. "My brother and I care deeply for him. We've been friends ever since college." Then she added, "Clay and I."

"He mentioned you went to school together."

"He was there for me when I was having a hard time with my parents' death."

"I'm so sorry to hear that."

"It was a while ago. But I had a hard time with it in college, and he was there for me," she said, and it was the second time she'd voiced that word – *college*. She glanced over at Clay as he chatted with Cam, blowing streams of smoke. Clay reached for his phone, flicking his thumb across the screen casually. *Strange for him to be on his phone,* Julia thought; he rarely was. But then he put it away quickly.

"I'm glad he was there for you," she said, and Michele simply nodded, barely listening as she looked at Clay. That's when it hit her—it hadn't been a mere coincidence when Michele had watched his hand on her thigh earlier in the game. It wasn't a coincidence at all. It was a sign of longing, and now Julia knew something about Michele that Clay didn't know. Something that Michele had been hiding for years.

Or maybe he did know that she longed for him. Maybe he simply hadn't told Julia yet.

That possibility pissed her off, but somehow she'd have to use it to fuel the game.

CHAPTER FOURTEEN

Two hours later, she'd pushed thoughts of Michele aside. Clay was with her and only her. Julia might be possessive, but she was not a jealous woman. How could she be jealous when she was closer to her goal? She was almost halfway to the prize, and Liam was making bigger and bigger bets. God bless an actor like him. He was simply flush with cash and didn't seem to mind parting ways with it.

She revealed her two aces, and Liam laughed, shaking his head. "Got me again," he said, shoving all the chips to Julia since everyone else was out for this hand.

Another step closer. She felt buoyant, bubbles rising to the surface. She could do this. She could win on her terms. Be free of her debt. The way she wanted to, by clawing her way out of her troubles. The prospect of not having to rely on Clay's bailout sent a surge of adrenaline through her. She didn't want a safety net. Her blood pumped faster, turbocharged with anticipation. She could taste freedom on her tongue, like sweet sugary crystals, and that drove her as they played another round, then another, and each time, she added to her totals.

Clay leaned in to nuzzle her neck. "You're winning, gorgeous. I knew you would."

"Don't jinx me," she said softly.

"No jinxes. Just complete confidence in you."

A blast of pride raced through her. He was proud of her because she was good, because she'd earned it. Clay was the opposite of her ex. Dillon had taken her for a ride and fooled her. Clay was upfront about everything, and he believed in her. He'd never try to hoodwink her. "I'm glad you feel that way about me," she said as he knocked back a scotch. "Want me to freshen that up for you?"

"No, bring me a Purple Snow Globe or a Heist. The drink you named for me. Or wait. I have a better idea. Make me a new drink and call it the Long Distance Lover," he said, wiggling his eyebrows.

She laughed. "You want me to whip up an impromptu cocktail? You don't even like mixed drinks."

"I might if you made me one, but I'd probably just want to lick it off of you," he said, his dark eyes raking over her.

"You're drunk."

"I assure you, I would lick it off you sober, drunk, bone-tired, or sick as a dog," he whispered in her ear, flicking the tip of his tongue over her earlobe.

"I'm changing your name to Captain PDA."

"What can I say? I have my woman here with me, and I'm out with my good friends. All is well in the world," he said, then pulled back to catch Liam's attention across the table.

"Liam, we have a bartender in the house. Let her show you how much you wish you had her drinks on your menu here at Speakeasy."

Julia rolled her eyes, and pushed his shoulder. He grabbed her and kissed her on the lips.

"Man, do I need to book you a room at the Plaza?" Cam said, slamming his hand on the table.

"Yeah, 'cause we know you have connections everywhere," Clay said.

"Hey, I told you I got out of that racket."

"Well, you two boys just keep up the chest thumping, and

I'll go a-mixing," Julia said, heading to the bar. She perused the offerings, considering gin, vodka and rum, then decided to start with a tequila as the base, adding in some fruity mixers, a little lemon soda and then something special—a secret ingredient. She held up a glass when she was done. "Who wants to be my guinea pig for the Long Distance Lover?"

Liam raised a hand, waving broadly. "My place. I go first." He trotted over to the bar, brought the glass to his lips, and tasted. "Mmm, this is superb," he said, smacking his lips. "You're like a mad scientist of the liquorian variety."

"Call me a chemist. I'm all about new flavors," she said with a big smile.

"You need to text me the recipe."

She shook her head. "A good bartender doesn't give up her recipes for free."

"Then give me your number and we'll make a deal for it."

She pointed her finger at him playfully. "Now you're talking," she said, and rattled off her number.

Liam spun around and used his big stage voice to call out to the table. "Everyone needs one of these."

After whipping up more cocktails, she returned to the table and served drinks to the rest of the players.

"Mmm, I love it," Clay said to her after he tasted the drink. He was pretty carefree and happy. Maybe it was the alcohol loosening him up. Or maybe it was because she was winning. He pulled her into his lap.

"Since when do you like mixed drinks?"

Julia looked up to see Michele asking Clay the pointed question.

"Every now and then I like to break out of my habits," he said.

"You're always a scotch drinker," the brunette added pointedly, and there was something protective in Michele's voice. Almost like a lover, or an ex. An ex who knew things about someone. "You were never like that in college."

"I was never a lot of things in college."

College. Julia's ears pricked at that word. Why on earth did Michele keep hearkening back to college with Clay?

"You were some things," Michele said.

"C'mon, enough about drinks and college. Time to deal," Klausman said gruffly, and started doling out the cards.

Julia slid off Clay's lap and back to her own chair. *Focus*, she told herself. She was almost there. She had to keep riding this wave of luck and skill to the tune of another few thousand dollars and she'd be free and clear.

She appraised her cards, and soon the betting began. Then the strangest thing happened. Michele won the next hand. And the next. And the next. With each successive win, Julia grew more tense, and she noticed Clay's light-and-easy mood slip away. He was no longer leaning casually in his chair. He was more focused on the game, his eyes shifting back and forth, and he kept looking at his watch too. The ticking clock, winding down to Charlie.

Michele cleaned up once more with a full house that made Clay sit up straight in his chair and reach into his back pocket. Maybe for his phone. But then he stopped, resting his hands on the table, and checking out Julia's dwindling stack of chips.

By the time the woman who'd known him since college had sliced Julia's winnings in half, she was ready to lunge at her and it had nothing to do with her staring at Clay, but everything to do with how jealous Julia was of Michele's hands all over the money she needed.

She probably didn't even need it. She'd probably use it for a goddamn spa weekend, not to pay off a mob boss.

"I swear it's beginner's luck," Michele said with the kind of laugh that sparkled. A pure laugh, a happy laugh, but it grated on her to no end because Julia wanted those chips to herself. "I have no clue how to play."

"What are you going to use your money for, baby?" Liam said, leaning over to kiss her on the cheek. "Take me out someplace nice, will ya? I want to go to the Bahamas again."

"Yes, and have your picture taken by someone trying to sell you real estate."

Julia latched onto one word—*Bahamas*. And it nagged at her brain. "My ex is probably in the Bahamas," she muttered.

Clay's eyes snapped up. "Dillon?"

She shrugged. "He always said he wanted to go there," she said in a low voice.

"He did?" Clay whispered.

"Yeah, but everyone wants to go there. He could be anywhere," she said, and something inside of Julia coiled tightly, like a viper rising through her chest. Maybe it was her mention of Dillon. Maybe it was Michele's carefree way with money. Or maybe it was the simple fact that when Liam kissed Michele's neck, her eyes didn't flutter closed. She didn't part her lips to sigh. And she didn't slide her body closer to his.

Instead, Michele peered out of the corner of her eye at Clay. And the look in her brown eyes was one of such deep longing, and something more. Something much more. In a blinding moment of clarity, Julia no longer sensed that Clay hadn't been truthful about their relationship. She *knew*. There was something more to them, and she didn't care about the game, or the money, or Charlie. She cared about whether she'd been played again.

She pushed back from the table. "Excuse me," she said, and she tapped his shoulder and cleared her throat. "I need to step outside for a second, and get some fresh air."

"I'll join you," he said, rising and resting his hand on her lower back as she walked to the door, pushed hard on it, and then felt the rush of warm night air on her face. It was close to midnight, and the city was still lively, cars and cabs and people racing by.

"What happened in college between you and Michele?" She crossed her arms.

"What?" he said, blinking his eyes.

"Were you involved with her?"

"No."

"Did anything happen with her?" she asked once more, and this time she felt like the lawyer, turning over the question again and again until the witness answered.

"What do you mean?"

"Do I need to spell it out?"

"Yeah. You do," he said firmly.

She pretended to mime sign language as she spoke. "Were you involved with her? Because I'm getting a serious vibe from her that she's tripping down memory lane from the days of old," she said, now holding her hands out wide. "*College this. College that.* Clay in college. It's like she's holding on to something in college with you."

"We kissed once. We weren't involved."

He said it so matter-of-factly, but it slammed into her, and she nearly stumbled backwards. He reached for her, but she held him off. She was fine. She didn't need him.

"Ohhhhh," she said, long and exaggerated. "Right. Of course. A kiss. That's not involved what-so-fucking-ever."

"What the hell, Julia? I was never involved with her. She's a friend. Not an ex-girlfriend."

"You kissed her," she said, jutting her chin out at him. "That makes her kind of an ex, wouldn't you say?"

"I don't think that constitutes an ex." The low-key way he answered her pissed her off, because he truly seemed to believe his own line of bullshit.

"Okay, let's get technical and legal about it then, if you're going to be like that. So I'll walk you through what constitutes being involved. When you've kissed someone, and I ask 'Were you involved with her?' that's the moment when you say 'Yes, I kissed her once, Julia, and it meant nothing to me, and we've been great friends ever since then, and I have drinks with her every Thursday night and talk about you, but don't worry that I had my tongue down her throat because we're just friends.'

It's not at the fucking poker game I'm losing that you tell me," she said, practically spitting out the words through her anger.

"Are you pissed because you're losing, or are you pissed that I kissed her?" he asked her through narrowed eyes.

Anger flared deep inside her. Anger over that woman. Over Charlie. Over the three thousand miles between her and Clay. Anger, annoyance and frustration all fused into a cocktail of heat and rage as she grabbed his shirt collar. "Thanks for pointing that out, because it's kind of both. I have a shitstorm of trouble waiting for me back home if I don't win," she said.

"That's not true. I told you I'd help you," he said, and his hand moved briefly towards his pocket, but then he stopped.

"Why do you keep reaching for your phone? That's not your style."

"Flynn is out with the Pinkertons. Just wanted to make sure it's all going well," he said, then shifted quickly back to the matter at hand. "But I wish you'd stop worrying about the game. You're going to be fine."

"I don't want you to help me, though. I want to win on my own," she said, and she was damn near close to digging her heels into the sidewalk. Didn't he *get* it? Didn't he understand how important this was to her? But everything had collided right now. The game; Michele; the possibility of truth and lies.

"And you will."

She pushed her hands through her hair. "I just wish you'd told me when I asked you in San Francisco if you'd been involved with her. I asked you if Michele was your ex and you said she was just a friend, and always had been. But now it turns out you kissed her," Julia said, but she knew deep down it wasn't the kiss that bothered her. That wasn't why she was upset about Michele.

"It just wasn't important, but it's not as if you've been totally honest with me."

"I didn't lie, though. I told you there were things I couldn't tell you."

"I feel like we're parsing words here. I don't understand why it matters that I kissed her. Hope this doesn't come as a shock to you, but I've kissed other women before."

"I know," she hissed.

"So why does it matter so much that I kissed Michele once? I don't even think about her like that."

"Because. Because she is here, all the time. Because she sees you. Because I don't get to."

"We can change that," he said, his voice suddenly soft, all the harshness banished from his tone.

"How? I live far away and she lives a block away," she said, dropping her face in her hands, hating the sound of her own voice. "Ugh. Look what you've done to me. I've become this whiny woman pining away, and she's lovely and smart and funny, and it pisses me off that she can see you any time she wants."

He gently peeled her hands away from her face, tucking his finger under her chin and lifting her gaze to his. "I don't feel a thing for her. I didn't tell you when you asked if she was an ex because I don't even think about her like that. I don't think of her as an ex. It was one kiss, one time, one drunken night. Nothing more. I don't think about her because you're all I think about. To the point that I'm sure no man has ever felt this way for a woman. You shouldn't be jealous of her. She should be jealous of you."

She stared at him, narrowing her eyes. "Seriously, Clay? Cocky much?"

"It has nothing to do with me, and everything to do with how I feel for you," he said, moving his hands down to her arms, holding her tight. "Every woman should be jealous of *you* because of how I feel for you. Because no man has ever wanted a woman like I want you. No man has ever craved a woman as deeply as I crave you. And no man has ever fallen this hard and this fast for a woman."

Her heart stopped, then thundered furiously against her chest, wanting to leap into his hands. "I'm sorry," she murmured, all her anger draining away. "I'm a jealous witch. It's just hard for me to see her and know you're so friendly, and that she's so in love with you."

He froze like a statue. Then seconds later, though it felt like a minute, he looked at her as if she'd just spoken Russian. "What are you talking about?"

"You don't know that?" she asked, shocked.

"No."

"It's patently obvious to anyone who spends ten minutes with her. She's madly in love with you, Clay."

He swallowed, and shook his head, as if he were shaking the strange notion away. "How can you tell?" he asked, the words coming out all choppy.

"Because of how she looks at you," she said, as if it were obvious, because to her it was.

"And that's enough for you to conclude she's in love with me?" For the first time ever she'd truly surprised him. She hadn't intended to drop a bomb, but he so clearly didn't see it at all.

"Yes."

"Why? How? How can you tell she looks at me like she's in love with me?"

She rolled her eyes. "Because I recognize the look."

The look on his face was no longer shock. It was hope, and the dawn of something so much more. "You do?"

Then she realized she'd practically said it. "Yes."

"How?"

"Because it's how I look at you," she said, the words falling from her lips in a tumble. Time slowed, and the moment became heady, rich with possibility. The air between them was charged, electric, like a storm. They were magnets, needing their opposite.

He reached for her, cupping her cheeks, brushing his thumb over her jaw then her bottom lip, watching her shiver. She looked up at him, and his eyes were fixed on her. Waiting for her. His lips parted, and she was wound tight with anticipation of what he'd say. "I love the way you look at me."

Tingles ran down her spine, spreading to her arms, her fingers, all the way to her toes. "You do?

"I do. I love the way you touch me," he said, taking her hand, and spreading her palm open on his chest. "I love the way you talk to me. I love everything about you. And I recognize the look in your eyes, too. Do you know why?"

She shook her head, and her entire body was trembling with want, with hope. "Why?"

"Because it's the same as in mine. Because I love you, Julia. I am completely in love with you, and I love you, and I want you to love me," he said, never breaking his gaze from hers, his beautiful brown eyes flooded with love.

"I do. I do. I do," she said quickly, the tension in her chest disappearing, and relief washing over her in waves. "Clay, I love you so much."

He ran his hands through her hair, burying his fingers deep. She felt him trembling. He returned a hand to her face, brushed the backs of his fingers against her cheek, and she leaned into him, savoring the gentleness of his touch. Feeling the reverence that he treated her with, like she was precious to him. He ran his hand down her neck to her throat. "*Julia,*" he said, his voice low but so intense as he spoke. "I have never fallen in love like this."

His words bathed her in some kind of bliss, as if her veins flowed with liquid gold. "How have you fallen?" she asked, overwhelmed with all she felt for him, with the way her body seemed to reach for him, to need him.

"With everything I have. There is no part of me that isn't in love with you. There is no part of me that holds back," he said, his voice steady, certain.

Allness. That's what it was for her, too. An utter *allness.* A love so deep and consuming it filled her organs, it rode roughshod over her skin. It was a mark on the timeline of her life. Before. After. She raised her hand, and touched his face, stroking his jawline, watching with wonder as she made him gasp after a simple touch. He grasped her hand, linked his fingers through hers, and brought her palm to his mouth, kissing her there. "I love you." He bent his head to her neck, brushing his lips ever so softly against her skin, then up to her ear. "I am so in love with you," he said, as if he couldn't stop telling her. "I love you so much."

"I am so in love with *you.*" She stretched her neck so he could kiss her freely as he wanted to as she ran her hand through his hair. "So in love."

He stopped kissing her, pulling back to look her in the eyes once more. His gaze melted her from the inside out. "I can't wait to take you home with me tonight. To spread you out on the bed. To make love to you all night long."

"I want that. I want that again and again. And over and over."

"Now go back in there," he said, gesturing to the restaurant. "Even though you look like you've just had sex."

Her cheeks felt rosy. She was sure there was a glow in her eyes. "I feel like I've just had sex. Sex with the man I love," she said, playing with his hair, not wanting to let go of him, but needing to.

"You will have that. I will give you everything, Julia."

* * *

He'd join her shortly. He would. He just needed to take care of this matter. The text on his phone was loud and clear. Business came first right now, and later, he'd find a way to explain.

CHAPTER FIFTEEN

Julia skipped down the sidewalk at two in the morning. Every move she made brought a smile to his face, and touched down with happiness in his heart.

She'd done it. She'd won big. After precariously losing to Michele for a while there, she'd made a few big bets on a few big hands, and had pulled out ahead. She'd wrapped her arms around the chips, and tugged them in tight. She sure looked like she wanted to kiss them, to bring each and every one to her lips, and then shake them at the sky victoriously. Instead, she'd stacked them, handed them to Liam since he'd acted as the bank, and watched with wide eyes as those chips turned into cash.

She threw her head back, twirling on the street, as if she were a kid catching snowflakes on her tongue.

"And here's your money, sir," she sang, pretending to hand it over to Charlie. "Now, go fuck off forever."

She was jubilant, ready to lead a victory march. Clay grabbed her arm and pulled her in for a kiss, bending her back and kissing her like they were on a postcard. Let the whole damn city be jealous. Let the world want what he had. He claimed her mouth with his own, kissing her hard and passionately, like he planned to always. He'd never tire of the way her lips tasted, of her sweetness, of how she responded to him. She wrapped her arms around his neck, and held on tight.

"Take me home, now," she said. "I want to know what it feels like to have you as a free woman."

He tensed briefly as she said that. But that was ridiculous. She *was* free. Completely free. He hailed a cab, and ten minutes later he had her in his home, stripping her clothes off as they somehow made their way up the stairs, tangled up in each other. He was still buzzed on the night, on the things he'd said, on the way she'd won, on her sheer and utter happiness, and on telling her he loved her.

It didn't matter that one of those things was a lie.

There would be time in the morning to tell the truth. When day broke, and the sun rose, that's when he'd let her know. The night was for *more*.

"Did I ever tell you I have a thing for mirrors?" he said as he left his clothes in a heap on the floor.

She raised an eyebrow, as she stepped out of her skirt. "Then join me in the bathroom, handsome," she said, taking his hand and guiding him to the spacious room. She hopped up on the sink with the mirror behind them, roped her arms around his neck, and pulled him in close. Resting her forehead against his, she ran her hands down his naked chest, making him shiver with desire. "Thank you, Clay," she whispered. "Thank you for doing that for me. I can't tell you how much it means to be free of Charlie, and free of Dillon on my own terms. And I loved it. I loved playing for real. Playing in a game that wasn't fake. Where I had to rely on chance and skill and myself," she said, and her words were like a tight knot in his gut. But he let her continue. "It means so much to me. *You* mean so much to me. I am so glad you walked into my bar, and into my life, and into my heart."

He kissed her softly, brushing his lips against hers. At least this part was true. This contact. This touch. "That's the only place I want to be. In your heart," he said, then took a beat. "Though I like being in your pants, too."

She laughed. "Then get in my pants. Except I'm not wearing any," she said, gesturing to her naked body, covered only in the stockings he'd bought for her. "So this ought to be really easy."

He shoved everything else aside, clearing his mind. He wanted to be with her completely. "Nothing worth having is easy," he said, lifting her off the counter and setting her down on the tiled floor. He shifted her around so she faced the mirror above the vanity, then spoke low in her ear. "I want to watch us. I want you to watch us."

She gasped a yes as he dipped a hand between her legs, running his other hand up her belly. He entered her slowly, rolling his hips, savoring the delicious wetness, the tightness. Her eyes floated closed as he rocked into her. "Look in the mirror," he told her, and she opened her eyes, meeting his dark eyes in the reflection. There was so much want in her gaze, so much openness. "*Watch.*"

"I am," she said, breathing in, breathing out. "I am watching."

"What do we look like to you?"

Her eyes were hazy, her lips falling open.

"Like two people in love," she answered.

He nodded against her neck. "Exactly. That's what we are. And I'm going to take you there, Julia. I'm going to take you over the edge. Because I love fucking you, and I fucking love you," he said, tugging her tighter, holding her closer as he thrust into her. She stretched out her neck, leaning against his shoulder, her body becoming a canvas for his hands as he touched her breasts, her belly, her neck, and her throat. He wrapped one hand around her throat, not so tight that it hurt, but tight enough to let her know she was his. He was possessing her. "Tell me you're close."

"So close."

"Tell me who's fucking you right now."

"The man I love," she said in between broken breaths, her lips open, her green eyes watching him in the mirror.

"That's right. The man you love is fucking you. The man you love is making you come," he said, watching her face contort in pleasure, feeling her body tighten on him, feeling her heat all over him as the sound of her ecstasy rang in his ears and he followed her there, chasing her to the other side.

He breathed out hard, and so did she as he wrapped his arms around her when they were done.

"Julia," he started, and he should have been nervous or scared, but he wasn't. Not one bit. He knew what he wanted. "I hate the thought of you going home tomorrow afternoon."

"Me too, but I have to."

"I know, but what if you come back, and this bathroom becomes our bathroom? And the bedroom becomes our bedroom? And this home becomes our home? I can't stand being without you. I want you here in New York."

He searched her features, but her expression gave nothing away. Her mouth was set in a line; her eyes were stoic. He tried to read her, to understand what was going through her mind, but he came up empty. And that's when the real fear shot off inside him. Had he scared her away? Asked for too much from a woman who needed to live life on her terms? He opened his mouth to backpedal, to say he'd take what he could get, because a little of her was better than losing her.

But then she turned around, face to face. "I could give you some long answer about how that's too hard or too complicated, and how I don't know how to pull it off or make it work, and how I have a job and a family and a business in San Francisco, and that's all true . . ." she said, then stopped talking, and in that silence his heart thumped hard against his chest, and he swore she could hear every heartbeat of his fear, could tell that each persistent pound was the soundtrack of his misery, of her leaving him.

"And?" he asked, his throat dry.

"And," she answered, the corner of her lips curving up, "and if you're willing to work with me and help me figure all that out, then I can't give you a single reason why this shouldn't be my bathroom, because I love your tub," she said pointing at the tub, and a smile broke across his face. She leaned back and tapped the mirror. "And I love this mirror." She gestured to the bedroom. "And your bed."

"Our bed," he said, correcting her.

"*Our bed*. I love our bed. Now, take me to bed, handsome. Because I want to sleep in my home. Tomorrow we can figure out all the details."

Yes, tomorrow. There were so many details for tomorrow.

CHAPTER SIXTEEN

They're freaking out about the film. CALL ME.

The message blared at him, his phone vibrating on the nightstand, his eyes bleary from little sleep. But this was the third time his phone had rattled on the wood. He read it one more time, an emergency text from Flynn. *Shit.*

Grabbing his phone, he scrambled out of bed and down the stairs so as not to wake Julia.

"What's going on?" he asked, stepping out onto the balcony, greeted by the early morning June sun rising in the sky. The hot and muggy days of late spring were coasting into New York. Heat vibrated in the air.

"They're worried that we can't handle the studio. That we're not big enough," Flynn said, his voice shaky.

"That's crazy. I've dealt with that studio many, many times. So have you."

"I know," Flynn said, exasperated. "And they were fine with it from the start. But now I think they're getting nervous. I'm worried they're going to back out. I have a breakfast meeting with them in thirty minutes on the Upper West Side."

Clay didn't stop to consider the sleeping woman in his bed, or whether she'd be annoyed that he had to take off. All he could focus on was making sure this film deal went through.

Flynn had busted his ass to land the Pinkertons, and if they needed to have egos smoothed or cold feet made toasty, it was his job to do so. The bottom line rested with him.

"I'll be there. Text me the location."

"Thanks man, I need you," Flynn said, relief loud and clear across the phone line.

He headed inside, walked quietly past a sleeping Julia, curled up on her side with her red, flaming hair spread across the white pillowcase, looking like a goddess. His goddess. And he was going to have to tell her what he'd done before they met Charlie.

He showered and dressed quickly, and she snoozed the entire time, barely moving. He imagined she was in the most peaceful land of dreams, finally sleeping easily now that the price tag was off her head.

At least he'd been able to do that for her.

He bent down to softly kiss her cheek. She sighed lightly, but didn't wake. Gently, he shook her shoulder. He was greeted with an inhale, and an exhale. "Julia," he whispered.

Her eyelids fluttered. "Hi," she said, opening them briefly.

"I need to go. I have to meet Flynn and the Pinkertons," he said, glancing at his watch. "Should last an hour. Two, tops. I'll meet you at ten thirty and then we'll see Charlie together."

She nodded sleepily. "Call me at ten, so I can shower?"

"Of course. Don't go without me."

"Do I look stupid?"

"Sassy from the moment she wakes up," he said, shaking his head in amusement.

"Back to sleepy time for me," she said, roping her arms around his neck. "But first. *This*."

She pressed a sweet kiss to his lips. "I love you," she murmured, and his heart thumped painfully against his chest, lurching toward her. He desperately wanted to stay, to sit her down, and to explain. She'd forgive him. Of course she would, right? But he also had made a promise to Flynn and to himself that he'd take care of business. He had time for both. He could manage both. He'd tell her before they met Charlie. "Can we go shopping later for new towels?"

"You don't like my towels?"

She shook her head. "I like big, fluffy ones."

"Then let's get you some big, fluffy towels."

"And I kind of think you could use a more comfortable bench on your balcony. Those wooden slats are hard."

"Considering what I will do to you on that, let's get it today."

She smiled again. "My flight's at three."

"Then we will shop or we won't shop, but whatever we do I will love every second of it because I'll be with you, and I love you so much," he said. "And if I could blow this off and spend the morning inside you, I would. Believe me."

Believe me. His words echoed. He needed her to believe him.

"It's okay. Soon, we'll have plenty of Sunday mornings to be lazy and naughty together."

"Lazy and naughty. Gorgeous, that is a promise."

He'd keep that promise. He would absolutely keep that promise.

* * *

Coffee. She needed coffee, stat. Her brain was fuzzy and her muscles were sluggish, and the late-night poker and even later-night sex had worn her out. After a quick shower, she grabbed her clutch purse and her phone, and headed downstairs. She didn't bother hunting out coffee in the kitchen. She was a coffee-shop kind of woman, and besides, she really should get to know the cafes in this neighborhood. It was going to be *her* neighborhood soon, and that prospect brought a grin to her face as she pressed the down button in the elevator.

Her elevator.

Her lobby.

She couldn't believe she'd said yes so quickly, so easily to his question. She should be terrified of packing up and moving across the country. She should hem and haw, and think and consider. But as she pushed open the door of *their* building, stepping out into the bright morning sun on *their* block, she knew.

There was no question about it.

She and Clay were more than solid. They had a future, a bright and beautiful, smart and seductive future. He was her match; he was the one she hadn't been looking for, but who had found his way to her regardless. He was the one she couldn't imagine being without. To think they'd started as a one-night stand, and now they'd become . . . well, they'd become indispensable to each other.

As she ordered her coffee—black with room for cream—she considered that it might be a risk moving here with him. She could get hurt. She could be left. Worst of all, she could be played like a fool.

And yet, this was Clay, and he wasn't that kind of a man. He'd be more likely to travel to Pluto than to play her. Maybe love made you take chances, or maybe real love made you take the right chances.

She poured cream in the coffee, knowing he was the right chance.

She left the cafe and ran a finger over her right breast. Not because she had a hankering for self-booby love, but to double-triple check that the money for Charlie was still tucked safely in her bra and ready to turn over. Safe and sound, and nestled against her.

Her phone buzzed, and she pulled it from her purse.

On my way. Be there in ten minutes. Love you.

She couldn't help but smile because he couldn't stop saying *I love you.*

Her stomach rumbled, a reminder she hadn't had much dinner last night. The restaurant where they were meeting Charlie was one block away, but she wasn't going to show up early to eat and risk running into Charlie alone just because her tummy was growling. She was a big girl and could withstand hunger. Besides, once they were through with the mobster she was planning on ordering French toast with butter and syrup, and enjoying every single bite. She texted back, letting Clay know she was parked outside the cafe at a tiny little sidewalk table.

She sank down in a metal chair, took a drink of her coffee and scanned the block that would soon become second nature to her. With her sunglasses on, she watched the world of the West Village go by on a Sunday morning, checking out hip families with young children racing ahead of them, surveying couples draped over each other, guys and guys, girls and girls, girls and guys, then an inked young man heading to a tattoo shop across the street called No Regrets. *Great name for a tattoo parlor*, she thought, as he entered, probably to add to his markings.

Her phone rang, and it was a 917 number she didn't recognize, so she answered in case Clay was borrowing Flynn's phone. Maybe his cell had died.

"Hello?"

"Hey, Julia! It's Liam. I hope I didn't catch you at a bad time."

She leaned back and smiled. "Nope. Just enjoying this gorgeous June morning in Manhattan."

"That was a fun game last night. You play fierce."

"Why, thank you. I rather enjoyed taking your money from you. Perhaps we'll be able to play more. Seems I might be moving to Manhattan," she said, and if she could bottle this feeling —happiness, hope, possibility—and sell it, she'd be rich. Because everyone should want to feel this way. Effervescent.

"You are shitting me," he said.

She laughed. "Why would I joke about that?"

"Because I was going to ask you if there's any way you'd consider being my bartender at Speakeasy. That drink you made last night was amazing."

"Well, you're easy, then, if I sold you on one drink," she said, figuring he was joking.

"I'm serious, Julia. Your drink was to-die for, and you also have the right attitude that I want behind the bar. Tough, but friendly. Playful, but not flirty. Smart, but inviting."

Pride bloomed in her chest. Her luck was changing. She was coming out ahead based on skills, not looks. She was landing options in life, rather than having them taken away from her. Her future was unfurling before her like a smooth open road, the top thrown down and the radio blasting. "Tell me more about the job," she said, and Liam shared details on the pay, the timing, and his plans.

"Sounds interesting," she said, playing it cool. "But I do already own a successful bar in San Francisco. I'm a little beyond the just-a-bartender level. I'm not that interested in working for someone when I can work for myself."

"I could even offer you an ownership stake if you'd like," he said.

"Let me think about it and get back to you. I'll have to see what my lawyer thinks," she said playfully.

"We have the same one. Let's hope he has the same interests."

"In any case, I am honored you asked. I'll get back to you soon."

She hung up and shook her head, amazed at how this treasure map was revealing itself. And there, in the middle of it all, inside the chest weren't gems or rubies, but the most precious gift of all—a real love. She was a lucky woman, and this could be her life, here in the Village in New York.

She returned to her people watching. A pretty woman in a little black dress and high heels yawned as she passed Julia, likely wearing last night's clothes. She wondered how many of these people were neighbors, and if she'd soon get to know the gentleman who owned the cafe, or the guy across the street walking a pug, or this fellow in the black suit coming into view.

But when she looked up to see the face of the man strolling past her, her heart plummeted six feet underground. Then burrowed even farther when the man stopped, his muddy brown eyes on her, his dark hair freshly combed, his suit neatly pressed.

"Red. Fancy meeting you here."

The voice was an icicle on her skin.

She swallowed back her fear. Nothing to be afraid of. She had his money. That's all he wanted, anyway. Even if Clay wasn't here to protect her. He'd be here any minute, and besides, she could handle *this*.

Charlie crooked his arm at a right angle and looked at his watch. "I am early for our pointless meeting, but I will join you anyway," he said, pulling out the chair next to her.

"Pointless?"

"So pointless," he said with a bored sigh. "Except for the handshake part."

She kept her face stony and impassive, but her mind was whirring. She had no clue what he was hinting at. She didn't plan on letting on, though. One more time with the poker face for Charlie, because he didn't deserve her emotions.

She reached into her bra, and took out the bills. "I have what you wanted, and I believe this means we are through."

He gave her a look as if she were an idiot child, and waved her off. "We are all good," he said, raising his hand dismissively.

Her eyebrows shot up. Forget hiding her reaction now. "What do you mean?" she asked, as a cab screeched to a stop. "You suddenly decided to forgive my debt?"

He scoffed at her. "That is funny. But I am not a forgiving man. He paid me. Your lawyer. Good man. Better than that ex-boyfriend of yours," Charlie said, stopping to scratch behind his ear. Julia's jaw dropped. She was sure she was hearing things. He couldn't possibly have said just that. "Dillon Whittaker always seemed a little shifty to me. I hear he's peddling island real estate."

But the words about Dillon didn't register, because she was still reeling from the blow. It was as if she'd been punched out of nowhere. A jab to the right. A hit to the left. Her head was spinning, and she was seeing stars.

Then she was seeing Clay. Standing next to her, fists clenched at his sides, staring at Charlie. "We weren't supposed to meet until eleven," he said to Charlie through gritted teeth.

"I was out for a stroll since this is such a lovely neighborhood, and look who I ran into," he said, gesturing to Julia. "Lucky me. I got to spend to spend a few minutes with her. She even tried to pay me. But I had to tell her the matter was already settled between men."

It was as if a truck had slammed into her, smashing everything in her body.

Clay looked at Julia, and she saw it in his eyes. Guilt. He was cloaked in it. He reeked of it.

"Clay," she began slowly, but her brain was quickly lining up the pieces, and she had a sickening feeling that she knew what he'd done. "Charlie says— "

He cut her off. "I can explain," he said, sitting next to her, reaching for both her hands and clasping them in his.

"What do you have to explain? The fact that you paid him already?" she said heavily, the words like tar in her mouth. She hoped she'd heard wrong. She prayed that Charlie was lying. He was a liar, right? That was a more likely explanation than that her man had lied to her.

He closed his eyes briefly, and the shame washed over his features. It was evident in his mouth, in his eyes, in his jaw. "It was all a fake? The game was rigged?"

Clay shook his head adamantly. "No, the game wasn't rigged. It was all real. I swear."

"Then why doesn't he need the money I won? Is it true you paid him already?" Her heart, so full of hope and joy, was turning black, like it had been painted over with a brush, becoming dark and cold in seconds.

"I paid him yesterday," he said, grasping her hand tighter. But she shook him off, tears threatening to spill down her face as that word—*yesterday*—rang in her ears. The only thing that stopped the waterworks was the presence of Charlie. She bit her tongue so she wouldn't cry in front of that man. "I did it because I love you. Because I needed you safe."

"When? When yesterday did you pay him?"

His jaw tensed. "Last night."

"But when last night?"

"During the game."

"When?" she asked once more time. Biting out the word. "It. Matters. When?"

"He called earlier in the day, and said he needed it by midnight," Clay said. Julia was used to Charlie's capriciousness, to the way he changed up times and dates and deadlines to suit himself. This was Charlie's M.O. "And you were losing, and I didn't know if you were going to pull it off," he said, and his words cut her to the quick. "So I wired him the money."

"Answer the question, Clay. When exactly did you wire him the money?"

Clay looked as if stones were in his mouth. "Around eleven-thirty."

"After I told you I loved you?"

He nodded.

"After our conversation about Michele?"

Another nod, followed by a heavy sigh.

"After you told me you were texting Flynn about the Pinkertons?"

"Yes."

"Were you texting Flynn or Charlie?"

He looked down, and in his silence she knew his answer, and it ripped through her body like a painful tear, like invisible hands were shredding her to pieces.

A loud scraping sound met her ears. Charlie had pushed back his chair. "As fascinating as it is to witness a lover's quarrel, I have business matters to attend to. Mr. Nichols, I thank you very kindly for securing the transaction last night so that I could get on my flight to Miami. I have business to attend to there. I believe the final term of our deal was a handshake," he said offering his hand to Clay. The two men shook and Julia wanted to bite both of their fingers, leaving teeth marks, and making them both yelp. Charlie patted Julia on the shoulder. "And that means, Red, you are free and clear. It has been a pleasure working with you. You made it entertaining for me, and I will miss my top ringer. But I will surely find someone else who owes me soon. Enjoy Cubic Z. I will not be drinking there again," he said. That was what she wanted, what she'd been fighting for, and she somehow knew Charlie meant every word. There was honor among thieves. His word was good on this matter.

He walked off, leaving Julia alone with the man who'd played her. "I don't understand. You think this is okay because you did it for love?"

"No. Yes," he said, his voice wobbly as he shoved his hand through his hair. "*Yes*. Julia, I didn't want anything to happen to you, so I got him the money."

She softened for a moment, because she understood some part of his actions. Deeply and truly. "I get that. I honestly do. I understand you wanted to protect me, and I don't fault you for that. Because I'd have done the same for you, and I'm okay with that," she said, dropping her hand on top of his. Relief flooded his eyes when she made contact. But it was short-lived because she took her hand away, placing them both in her lap. Her anger stole all the softness, replacing it with only the sharp, cruel betrayal she felt. "But I don't understand why the hell you didn't tell me. It's been twelve hours since you sent him the money. You had so many chances to tell me that the rules of the game had changed."

She watched him swallow hard, a terribly pained look in his eyes. "I wanted to tell you."

"But you didn't. You let me play the end of the game thinking it mattered. I was losing, and you told me to go back in there and kick ass, knowing it didn't matter how I played. You sent me back to play a game that was, for all intents and purposes, rigged. Because it didn't matter what I did," she said, her voice threatening to break. "That's the moment, Clay. Then. There. On the street. After you told me you loved me. That's when you needed to tell me about Charlie's new deadline. I'd have understood completely if you pulled me aside and said, 'Hey gorgeous, bad news,'" she said, dropping her voice to imitate a man's deeper tones, "'Charlie called and we need to get him the money now.' That's *all* you had to say. That's it."

"I know. I should have. But you were happy and determined, and I wanted you . . ." He let his voice trail off.

"You wanted me to believe I could do it," she supplied.

"Yes," he said with a heavy sigh.

"You wanted me to think I'd pulled it off myself. But I only wanted one thing. To not be played. And you took that away from me. You, of all people, should know better. You hate lies and you hate liars, and you lied to me by *not* telling me. You patted me on the ass and sent me into a game that didn't matter, but you led me to believe it did. Then I won and I practically danced down the street afterwards, and you kissed me and told me you were proud of me. I thanked you for making it possible for me to win on my own terms. And that was another moment that you could have told me."

She stopped to grab him by the arm, trying to make her point. "Instead, you let me believe I'd won my freedom," she said, and now the lump in her throat was so painful that it felt like a swollen ache. She brought her hand to her mouth, as if she could keep the crying at bay. But one rebel tear streaked down her cheek as she whispered, "Then you made love to me in your house, in front of the mirror, and asked me to move in with you. And you *knew* then. All you had to do was tell me. I would have still said yes."

"I wanted you to be happy. And I didn't know how to say it," he said, trying to reach for her, to tug her back in for an embrace, but she held him off.

"You're a goddamn lawyer. You talk to people for a living. Your whole world is semantics and details," she said, the words breaking on her tongue like salty waves. She took a deep breath, trying to somehow settle the tears that threatened to wrack her body. "You could have found a way to tell me. Instead, you spent the whole night telling me you loved me, and asking me to move in, when you should have been telling me the truth. FIRST. Because the truth is fine. The truth isn't what hurts. It's the time you had when you chose to not tell me the truth. And that makes me feel like I gave you my heart and you played me like a fool."

"I only did it to protect you."

"I did something once to protect you. I lied about who you were to protect you," she said, reminding him of that morning on the street in San Francisco when Stevie showed up. Clay winced as she mentioned it. "And what happened? You walked away."

"You've got to understand. I was trying to help you last night, Julia," he said, his words slick with desperation.

"I know your intentions were good, but this isn't about your intentions. It's about your actions, because those matter more to me. I have been deceived so badly over money by men." She grabbed his shirt collar, her eyes locking with his. "I need you, the man I love, to never deceive me. I want to be on your team, but you've got to play fair. I'm fine with what you did, but I am not fine with *how* you did it. I am *not* fine with those twelve hours that you had to tell me the truth. If you had time to ask me to move in with you, you certainly had the time to tell me about Charlie's demands," she said, as she stood up quickly, pushing away from the table.

"Please don't go."

"We are making a scene, and when patrons at my bar make a scene I ask them to leave, and that is what I'm doing," she said as she walked down the street.

He kept pace alongside her. "I am sorry. That is all I can say. I fucked up, and I'm so sorry."

She stopped outside his building, parking her hands on her hips. "Do you know how I feel right now? Do you?"

"Terrible?" he offered up weakly.

"*Stupid.* Like I'm the biggest idiot in the world," she said, erecting a wall inside her to keep the tears locked up. She had to say this. He had to know. "And it makes me feel as if everything that happened between us last night was a lie."

"The way I feel for you is not a lie, Julia," he pleaded, and she could hear every note of his pain. But she hurt too. "It's the truest thing in the world."

"Then you ought to act like that," she said, staring sharply at him as she grabbed the handle of the door.

"So what happens next?"

"I'm leaving New York. And I'm going to go home to my house, and that's as far as I know right now."

"Please. Give me a chance to make this up to you," he said, practically begging.

Once inside the elevator, she placed her hand on his chest. "I understand you want to. But I have to leave for the airport in two hours, I need to pack, and I'm hungry as hell."

"At least let me feed you. Let me get you something to eat."

"If only this were as simple as French fries," she said as they stepped out onto his floor. "But you can help me pack."

"Then I will gladly help you pack," he said, and together they went upstairs, both like beaten-down ragdolls, listless when they should have been joyful. They didn't speak as she gathered her lotion, shampoo and makeup from the bathroom, dropping them into a plastic bag, and layering that on top of her clothes. Maybe there was nothing more to say. The time for words had passed. This wasn't about arguments, or trying to convince someone you were right or wrong. This was about whether she'd listen to her heart or her head, and what both had to tell her.

"So what happens, Julia?" he asked as he zipped her bag. "Are you coming back?"

She met his eyes, the sadness in hers reflected back. "I want to, but I really need to think about everything now. I need a solid week apart. No contact. To make sure I'm not making a mistake. It's easy for you if this doesn't work out. You're not giving up anything. I'm changing everything."

"And I would never take that or you for granted. I promise, I will cherish you, as I already do. Will you let me buy you a ticket to return?"

"You are free to do whatever you want, but I need to be certain that this is right for me. So I can't promise you I'm going to use it. This has been a crazy weekend, from the game, to things ending with Charlie, to you and me. You hurt me, and I need to go home and take some time alone to make sure I'm not being foolish again, Clay."

"You're not," he said, reaching for her hand, clasping it in his. Oh, how she wanted to fall into his arms. Those strong sturdy arms that had protected her, fought for her, held her. But this wasn't about him. It was about her, and whether she could let herself turn so much of her life, and her heart, and her home, over to someone else again. "I swear."

"You asked me to move my life across the country for you and I said yes in a heartbeat. Because I love you. And the whole time you were hiding something from me. And that something makes me feel like a fool," she said, whispering the last words like a eulogy.

To her, it was the worst name in the world she could call herself. Because she'd been there. Oh, had she been there.

* * *

A little while later, she walked to the door, down the stairs, and to the waiting town car that would whisk her to the airport. He'd offered to ride with her but she'd declined, saying it would be too tempting, and she needed not to be tempted in that way.

He held onto that sentiment like a fragile glass globe of hope, clutching it for several minutes on the way downstairs. But then, he knew better. They'd always been good together physically. What was happening between them now was no longer about chemistry. It was about trust, and she needed to know he was a man of his word in all matters. There was no room for anything less. He had to keep all his promises to her, the big ones and the small ones. Life was rarely about the big things; it was usually about the impact—the potentially damaging impact—of the little things.

After the driver stowed her bags in the trunk, Clay reached for her, pulling her in close. She tucked her face in the crook of his neck, her breasts pressed against his chest. He could feel her heart beating against him and he could have stayed there all day. As she broke the embrace, she cupped his cheek with one hand, a soft fingertip tracing his jaw, sending tremors like quicksilver through his body. He would miss her touch; he would miss all of her.

She stood on tiptoes, brushing her soft lips against his, lingering slowly on his mouth. The kind of kiss that stays with you for days. The kind of kiss you never forget.

Because of how it tastes.

Like goodbye.

CHAPTER SEVENTEEN

He clicked on the flight tracker, and watched the black arrow snake across the Midwest. He dropped his head in his hand, and looked back up minutes later, as if the computer would tell him something. As if she'd appear on some futuristic TV screen from the plane, waving, saying he was forgiven.

"It's okay. I know you were just so caught up in loving me that you forgot to tell me," she'd say with a twinkle in her green eyes, then a pretty wink. She'd press her soft lips against the screen and blow him a kiss. "I'll be back," she'd say and the screen would crackle out, like static, fading to black, but everything would be okay and she'd return to him.

Instead, his life was up in the air. Because he'd been an ass. He'd been scared, wanting to secure his future before he faced his present. He, of all people, should have known better. You don't ask someone to sign until you give them all the facts, and spell out the terms. He'd gone about it the wrong way, thinking that by asking her to move in first, he'd be able to keep her without reservation. But you don't get the girl until you've gotten the girl. And even then you have to put in the effort every single day to keep her. You don't win before you've won. You keep playing, and fighting for love every day.

He reached for the screen, running his index finger across the cartoonish line of her airplane, scurrying her back to San Francisco. Was she sleeping on the plane? Watching a movie? Having a drink? Vodka on the rocks, probably.

Wait.

If she was drinking, it was whiskey.

Whiskey for loneliness.

But then, maybe she wasn't lonely, he figured as he shut his laptop and made his way to the kitchen, opening the cabinet. Maybe she was happy, and toasting with champagne to better days without him. Chatting it up with the random stranger next to her in seat 2B. Sharing her story. Telling the stranger about what an ass Clay had been. They would laugh at him, and he deserved it. Maybe he didn't deserve anything but to have lost her this way.

This foolish way.

He should have taken the chance, and told her when it happened with Charlie's change-up, rather than waiting. Waiting never did anyone any good. When you waited, the world passed you by. Life passed you by. And the love of your life flew in the dark of night over the country, stretching the distance between you to so much more than three thousand miles.

He left the kitchen and opened the door to his balcony, walked to the railing, and stared at the city as he finished his glass, the liquor burning his throat as he wanted it to.

They should have spent those precious last few hours tangled up together. Or having lunch together. Or shopping together. He wasn't even fond of shopping, but he'd have happily taken her anywhere, letting her pick out the towels she wanted, the new bench for the balcony. Hell, she could redecorate the whole house from stem to stern, any way she wanted. They've have shopped, and then wandered through the neighborhood, his arm around her, discovering the places in the Village that would become theirs: a cafe here, a store there. He'd have gotten her worked up at lunch, touching her legs under the table, slipping his fingers under her skirt, driving her so wild he'd have had to pull her into the restroom at a cafe and fuck her against the wall, her legs wrapped around him, certain that she'd be returning to live with him.

Instead, he was left with this loneliness that could have been avoided with a few simple words spoken hours before.

Avoided with the truth.

He held up his glass, cocked his arm, and considered chucking it five stories down to the street below. Cabs and cars streaked by on a Sunday night, and soft jazz music floated up from a few floors below him. Some kind of melancholy John Coltrane song that might as well have been ordered up for him by the gods of regret.

Maybe that's what whiskey was good for. Maybe whiskey was best for regret, because that was all Clay could taste tonight.

He lowered his arm, the glass still in his hand. He wasn't going to make a mess for someone else. He'd somehow have to find a way to clean up the mess he'd made of this love.

He left the balcony, closing the door behind him as if he could seal shut the memories of all they'd done there. But he couldn't. She was everywhere in his home. She was naked on his couch. She was undressing on his stairs. She was laughing joyfully over a gift in his kitchen. She was dancing in his bedroom. She was sleeping peacefully on his bed. She was giving him her most vulnerable *yes* in the bathroom, telling him she'd leave her life in San Francisco for him.

Like a ghost shadowing him, she was everywhere and nowhere.

He returned to the kitchen, dropping the glass into the sink. Turning around, he reached for the whiskey bottle, and tucked it back into the cabinet. But the bottle rattled. He steadied it quickly, then peered in the cupboard to see what had knocked it off-kilter.

An envelope.

He took the envelope, fat and stuffed. His name was on the front, and his stomach dropped when he read the words: "*This belongs to you. Thank you for the loan. I always pay back my debts.*"

But there was no *xoxo*. No secret message to decode that would reassure him she'd be coming back. There was only money, all ten thousand dollars that she'd won, and he'd lost.

* * *

The next day he wasn't any wiser as to whether she'd be returning. He hadn't heard from her: no emails, no calls, only a text to say she'd landed safely. He took some small solace in the safety update, but it truly wasn't enough for him. He wanted all of her. He needed all of her. And he had virtually none.

He'd zombied his way through the day, grateful that the Pinkertons had signed on the dotted line after the emergency soothe session the day before. Warding off that near-fiasco had given him the mental space to manage the bare minimum he needed to get through the contracts and phone calls on his agenda.

He emailed her the ticket back to New York. He'd booked it for two weeks from now, hoping that was fair—a week apart, a week to plan. She replied with a *thank you*.

He checked countless times for messages from her. Each time he'd come up empty.

He scrolled through his emails on the subway home just to make sure he hadn't missed one from her.

After a workout at his boxing gym that left his shoulders sore and his body tired, he still was no closer to knowing whether she was going to need those fluffy towels or not.

The time without her was like a black hole, a vacuum that gnawed away at him. He'd subtract a few years from his life simply for a note that gave him some sense of which way she was leaning. Something, anything to hold onto, to give him purchase. How had it only been twenty-four hours when it felt like a fucking year?

But that was what love does. It changes your perception of everything, of your own capacity for pain, for hope, and most of all—your perception of time. Because now, time was measured by her, by her presence, by her absence, and his relentless desire for her *yes*.

He checked his phone once more on the way home from the gym, like an addict. He was going to wear a hole through the screen with his thumbprint from all the times he'd swiped it. He needed company; he needed someone. He showered and headed uptown, reasoning that if he wasn't going to find an answer from her, he could at least ask questions of someone else.

When he arrived at the building off Park Avenue with the green awning, the doorman buzzed her apartment. "You have a visitor. Clay Nichols is here to see you," the man said, then paused. "Very well."

He hung up.

"She said to come on up," the doorman said, gesturing to the elevator.

Clay hadn't been here in a long time. He hadn't needed to. Now, he did.

When Michele opened the door, she was wearing a tank top and slim jeans, her hair pulled into a high ponytail, showing off her neck.

A neck that he'd once kissed.

He didn't mince words, or bother with preambles.

"Are you in love with me?" he asked as he walked inside.

"I have been for years," she said, as the door closed behind them.

CHAPTER EIGHTEEN

"I've been thinking of new names for cocktails. Well, Craig and I have," Kim offered during a lull in the crowds on Monday night.

"Yeah? Do tell."

"We came up with a whole list of great names while you were out of town."

"Your hubs is usurping my spot as a partner-in-crime?" Julia asked, resting a hip along the bar as she wiped down glasses.

"Ha. Hardly. But he does like to name drinks. Here's what we've got. A shot called the Long, Hard Night. A stiff drink called the One Night Stand. And a variation on the lemon drop martini that we called Lemon Drop Your Panties," Kim said, and the edges of Julia's lips lifted in a smile.

"Great names," she said, then looked away from Kim because all of them—every single one—reminded her of Clay. He'd been her One Night Stand, her Long, Hard Night, and she'd dropped her panties countless times for him. Every time, he'd risen—no pun intended—to the challenge, stripping her down to the bare essentials of pleasure and desire, and somehow all that desire had morphed into so much more. Into a mad and passionate love. The kind of love that thundered down the road with wild hoofbeats after midnight. Desperate, reckless, and headfirst.

That was the problem. She needed to pull back and analyze. To think. To consider. "Hey, can I ask you a question?"

"Fire away."

"Has Craig ever lied to you about something because he thought it was for the best?"

Kim shot her a quizzical look. "Well, how would I know?"

"I mean something he eventually 'fessed up to," she added.

"Ah, gotcha," Kim said, scrunching up her forehead as she considered the question. Then she thrust her finger in the air. "Yes! He used to tell me he loved my pot roast when we were first dating, and it turned out he really thought it was dry and stringy."

Julia laughed. "Tell the truth, Kim. Is your pot roast dry and stringy?"

Kim threw back her head and chuckled. "Evidently, I make *the* worst pot roast in the entire universe. It's that bad. But you know what?"

"What?"

"Now if he ever bugs me by leaving his dirty socks on the floor, or failing to put the toilet seat down, I just threaten him with my pot roast. Keeps that man in line," she said, straightening her spine like a drill sergeant issuing orders.

A pair of young men in suits sidled up to the bar and Kim turned her attention to them. Julia's mind stayed put on Kim's story and how it had a happy ending. Wasn't that what everyone wanted? A happy ending? But was a pot-roast fib the same as an omission of the truth?

She didn't know, and wasn't sure how to arrive at an answer. Her brain had grown cloudier in the last twenty-four hours, fuzzier with the distance. Had she overreacted? Been too quick to anger? She was a hot-tempered woman. She knew that about herself. But she valued independence more than anything. Even more than love. If she were to give up her independence, her job, her bar, her home, her sister, even her hairdresser, she had to know with the same clarity she had about how to make a kick-ass cocktail that uprooting her whole damn life—like she were picking up a carpet and shaking everything off it, come what may—was as right as right could be.

Come what may.

That was the real risk, wasn't it? Charging headfirst into the great unknown. Throwing away the self-protective armor she'd built since Dillon's betrayal, and shedding all her fiery independence for a chance that could flame out and fade away. Living in close quarters could turn the two of them—two strong-willed, stubborn, controlling people—into a collision course for disaster.

Or they could become better together, come what may.

"Hey Kim," Julia called out as her co-worker deposited the drinks to the customers. "I just thought of another name for a drink. Come What May."

"What's in it?"

"Something risky. Something that makes you want to take a chance. What do you think?"

"I think we need to break out our beakers and start mixing," Kim said, bumping her hip against Julia's.

"Ouch, I think you whacked me with your gigantic belly."

"It's a weapon of mass destruction. Beware," Kim said, rubbing her hands over her beach ball-sized stomach as she reached for spirits to test. "Let's start with— "

But Kim's suggestion was cut short by the clearing of a throat. Julia swiveled around to the bar and spotted a familiar face. She couldn't connect a name to the man, or why she knew him, but the older, dapper gentleman was giving her a serious case of déjà vu, and she hoped he'd alleviate it soon.

"Good evening. I was hoping to find Julia Bell," he said, and that didn't help her one bit. In fact, all her instincts told her that he was working for Charlie, or looking for Dillon, or somehow that she was going to be in a heap of trouble again. A fleet of nerves launched inside her, and she could feel the inklings of flight or fight kick in.

"That's me," she answered, calling on her best tough-chick-behind-the-saloon-bar persona.

"We met briefly before," he began, and something about his classy voice tickled her memory. He wasn't one of Charlie's men after all. Charlie's men were rougher around the edges. This man was proper and finished, like a gentlemanly professor. "And you made me the most fantastic drink I've ever had."

Her lips curved up, a smile threatening to break across her face. "Was it my Purple Snow Globe?"

"Indeed it was." He extended a hand to shake. "I'm Glen Mills, and my magazine has been running a search for the best cocktail ever."

Julia took his hand. "And I trust you found that cocktail here at Cubic Z?"

* * *

Clay sank down onto Michele's couch. "Why didn't you ever tell me?"

She flashed a small, sad smile. "Why didn't you ever notice?"

He held out his hands, showing they were empty. "I don't know."

"Did you? Notice, finally?" she asked, and her voice rose, touching some kind of hopeful note as she sat down across from him in a dove gray chair in her apartment.

He shook his head. "No. But then, lately, I haven't been so astute at connecting the dots, in the right time or the right fashion."

"Then how did you figure it out?" she asked, cocking her head curiously.

"I didn't. Julia did. She mentioned it when we went outside during the game."

Michele winced, then dropped her head in her hands. "She must hate me," she muttered.

"No," he said quickly, needing to reassure her. "She doesn't hate you at all. She's not like that. She thinks you are lovely, and smart, and funny," he said, repeating Julia's words from Saturday. "And I happen to agree with her."

Michele raised her face, and rolled her eyes in self-deprecation. "Some good that did."

"Michele," he said gently.

She shook her head several times. "I feel like an idiot."

"Please don't. You're the farthest thing from that. If anyone's the idiot, it's me. I didn't have a clue."

She managed a small laugh. "I wish I could say that's because I was so good at hiding how I felt, but seeing as Julia noticed it instantly and you didn't have an inkling for ten years, I'm going to have to go with you being completely blind to what's in front of you sometimes. I just have to wonder, though, Clay, how could you not tell?"

He raised both shoulders, shrugging. "I've been trying to figure out how I missed it and all I can conclude is this—I care about you so deeply as a friend, and you're Davis's sister, and I feel like the three of us are kind of in the trenches together. Like we've risen up together in our jobs, and we're this great threesome of friends somehow. I guess I only ever saw you that way."

"Let me ask you a question then," she said, taking a deep breath, the look in her eyes one of fierce determination. "If you'd have known how I felt, would it have made a difference anyway?"

He locked eyes with the woman he'd been friends with for so long. With his best friend's sister. With the gal he had drinks with every Thursday night. The person he'd turned to for advice on the woman who had confused him. She was his friend, always had been, and that's how he wanted to keep her. He shook his head, and sighed. "No," he admitted. "I'm sorry."

She held up a hand. "Please," she said firmly. "No pity for me."

"It's not pity."

"I mean it, Clay," she said. "I'm going to be fine. I've been in love with you for ten fucking years, and have managed it. Now it's time I get out of love with you."

He sank deeper into the couch, and breathed out hard. "Why didn't you say something, if you felt that way?"

She closed her eyes briefly, then opened them. Her mouth was set in a firm line. Then she spoke. "I think, deep down, I knew it was unrequited. That even if I told you, I knew that it wouldn't change a thing. That whatever that kiss was about in college was all it was ever going to be, but it did a number on me."

He tilted his head, stared at her as if she were a science project he was in the middle of constructing. "Why? From one kiss?"

"It was the kiss, but most of all, it was you. I thought you were the most handsome man I'd ever met, and smart, and funny, and most of all, you had your act together. You have no idea what my days are like," she said, with a light laugh. "I love my job. But I spend my days with a lot of messed-up people. And you're the least fucked-up person I've ever known. You don't have issues. You don't have baggage. What you see is what you get. For someone who spends all day fixing people, I suppose I really have been longing for someone I didn't have to fix."

"I take it Liam isn't doing it for you?"

"See, that's not fair. How can you be so observant about my feelings for Liam, but so clueless about how I felt for you?"

"Pretty amazing how I can have blinders on about certain things, isn't it?"

"I do like him . . ." she said, then let her voice trail off.

"But?"

"But, it's hard to like someone when you've been focused on someone else."

"I can understand that," he said, since Julia was his whole world.

"You're madly in love with Julia, aren't you?"

"Madly doesn't even begin to cover it. But we really don't have to talk about her," he said softly.

"I'm a big girl. I can handle it. Talk to me."

"I mean it, Michele. I don't want you to be uncomfortable. You need to tell me if it upsets you if I talk about her."

"I survived six hours of poker with you having your hands all over her, and watching that dopey look of love in your eyes the whole time," she said, both teasing and being truthful. "I can handle talking about her. And if I can't, I'll let you know."

He patted the couch. "Sit next to me."

"I don't know if that's such a good idea."

"What, are you going to throw yourself at me? I'm strong. I'll fight you off."

"Oh, gee. Thanks."

"C'mon. We're friends, and hell if I'm letting you go over this."

She moved off the chair and sat next to him on the couch, tentative in the way she folded her legs up under her, keeping a bit of distance. He took her hand, clasped it in his. "I need plenty of fixing. Trust me on that."

"Okay," she said playfully. "You need Dr. Milo again?"

"I always need Dr. Milo, but I also need you to know I think you're an amazing, beautiful person, and you are going to make some man the happiest man on the planet, and you probably won't need to fix him either."

She squeezed his hand, and it felt good, comforting. Like something he didn't want to lose. "But now you need me to fix something, don't you?" she asked, raising an eyebrow.

"You just said you're tired of fixing people all day. I'll be okay."

"I said I don't *want* to fix the man I'm going to be involved with. But I think we've established that we're friends. And besides, I have a feeling—call me crazy—that you might really need my help. You screwed things up with Julia, didn't you?"

He nodded, guilt written all over his face.

"Tell me everything," she said.

He didn't tell her everything. He'd promised Julia to keep her secrets about her debt. But he told Michele enough about what he'd done. "So what do I do? Just wait for her to decide if she'll move to New York for me?"

Michele nodded. "I'm afraid in this situation, patience is going to be a virtue. But I also think you need to find a way to show her that you can fix things. That when a mistake has been made, you can do more than apologize. Show her through your actions, not just your words. Show her you can fix the things that matter to her."

And with blinding clarity, he knew what to do.

CHAPTER NINETEEN

Julia's jaw dropped at the mention of all the zeroes. "That's the size of the prize?"

Glen Mills nodded and said yes, again and again and again.

"I won a contest I didn't even know I was in AND you want to just give me that much money? No strings attached?"

Glen chuckled, and even his laugh sounded proper. "Well, the string attached is we would very much like to offer you a contract to manufacture the drink in conjunction with Farrell Spirits," he said, mentioning the name of one of the world's largest premium drink makers that was home to many top-flight rums, vodkas, gins and whiskeys bottled around the world.

"Oh my God, like those cosmo and mojito mixes you see in grocery stores," Kim said with a shriek.

Julia turned to Kim, and it was like looking in a mirror and seeing a grin as wide as the sea, eyes twinkling, surprise and shock etched across her face. She returned her gaze to the gray-haired gentleman, who'd become something of a Santa Claus. Dropping in unexpectedly, bringing only presents, and a *ho, ho, ho*. But Santa wasn't real, and there had to be some loophole he'd spring on her. The devil lived in the details, and bathed himself in fine print. She rearranged her features, fixing a more serious look on her face. "There has to be some kind of catch? Do I have to give up my bar, or my firstborn, or an arm, maybe?"

Glen laughed, and shook his head. "No, Ms. Bell. We simply want to be in business with you. Farrell Spirits contracted my magazine to embark on a nationwide hunt for the best cocktail and the string attached is that the company would very much like to make it and turn it into a mass-market available product."

Chills raced over her skin, goose bumps of sheer possibility. She didn't know what to do or say. But this must be what it felt like to win the lottery: disbelief of the highest order. "So you want the recipe, of course?"

"We are going to need the recipe if we agree to the terms, but I assure you it will not be printed in the magazine. It would become a trade secret of course, and Cubic Z can remain the only bar where the drink can be made or ordered fresh."

Julia grabbed Kim's arm in excitement. "Do you have any idea what that would do for our business? It'd go through the roof," she said, now shrieking. "And that'll be so good for you and Craig and the baby."

"I know," Kim said, her face glowing.

"There is one small item though," Glen said, interrupting, and Julia's shoulders fell. This was the moment when the devil revealed himself. There was no such thing as a free lunch. Her life was not *X-Factor with Cocktails*. There would be a catch; there always was.

"Yes?" she asked through a strangled gulp.

"Even if you don't accept the Farrell offer, I will still be writing about this drink in our magazine because it is divine," he said. "And there are no strings attached to that recognition. I would simply be shirking my journalistic duties to do anything less."

Julia's smile returned. "Far be it from me to turn you into a shirker of duties," she said, and extended a hand to shake.

Later that night, when she returned to her home, she couldn't wipe the damn grin off her face if she'd tried. Because for the first time in a long time, she'd won something based on her skills. Sheer talent alone had made this happen. She wasn't saving the world, and she certainly wasn't curing cancer, but she could mix a damn fine drink, and build a damn fine bar, and no man could ever take that away from her.

Funny that she hadn't even known she was a contender, but that made this victory all the sweeter. It was her victory, her prize, and her success. Based on something intrinsic to her that no one, no mobster, no douche of an ex-boyfriend, could ever twist or manipulate.

As she unlocked the door to her home, she was filled with a sense of pride over a job well done.

The only trouble was there was someone she desperately wanted to share this moment with.

She settled for her sister instead. McKenna had just returned from her honeymoon, so Julia called her to tell her the news.

* * *

Three days later, McCoy's was bustling with the usual lunch crowd. This was Midtown Meeting Central, and everyone must have gotten the memo to wear a suit today because the restaurant was packed with sharp-dressed men and women, angling for deals, pitching their wares, hoping to get the person across the table to sign on the dotted line. Clay recognized that hard and hungry look in many of their eyes; he had it himself. Only this time he was hunting out information, and the best purveyor of intel in all of Manhattan was digging into his steak right now.

"Someday I'm gonna charge you, but for now, let me say this is delish, and I will happily take my payment in the form of a meal," Cam said, as he stuffed a forkful into his mouth.

"Like I wasn't going to pick up the tab. And you know I'd pay you in a heartbeat for your services," Clay said as he worked through his pasta dish. "But are you ever planning on telling me what you found out?"

"No. I'm going to eat this steak and run," Cam joked, with his mouth full. He chewed, and then took a long swallow of his dry martini. He subscribed to the notion that steak was meant to be enjoyed properly with spirits, the time of day be damned. It was one of the very many reasons Clay called this man a friend. He was steady, reliable, amusing as hell, and loved to share his special talent of finding anyone or anything with friends, asking only for the cost of a meal.

Picking up the tab was nothing if he could deliver what Clay needed.

Cam wiped his mouth with the cloth napkin, then set down his fork and knife for a break from the food. "I'll put you out of your misery. My guys found him. All those stories Liam was telling about real estate in the Bahamas? You were onto something."

Clay's eyes lit up, and a spark of anticipation ran through him. Could it be this simple? That he'd been found, coincidentally, in the very place where Liam had randomly been asked to buy a condo? "He's in the Bahamas?"

Cam scoffed, and waved a big hand. "No. That'd be too easy. What world do you live in? The land of coincidence? He's not in the Bahamas, but you were right to put all those clues together from what this fucker did. He's taking pictures of homes."

"Exactly what he was doing when he was in San Francisco," Clay added, raising an eyebrow in question.

Clay had supplied Cam with the clues, tracking down every last one Julia had ever told him about her ex. He'd shot homes for realtors. His niche behind the camera was making rooms look much bigger, and Dillon had told Julia on their first date that someday he'd be sipping a drink in the Bahamas. Clay had added up those details, alongside Liam's unexpected recon work, and Charlie's brief comment at the cafe on Sunday, and went with a hunch that Dillon might be in the islands snapping shots for scams.

Cam tapped his nose with his index finger. "Bingo. Because here's the thing about men like that who run scams. They tend to fall back on old habits. They do what works. Whether it's taking pictures, or conning money. And he seems to have gotten in good with some of the scam artists on a certain island, trying to hustle money selling time-share condos that don't really exist. His job is to take the pictures of the one good condo, make them look majestic, and the other guys peddle the properties that don't really exist."

"But where is he?" Clay asked, because that was all that mattered, and he damn near wanted to cross his fingers with hope, but he wasn't a finger crosser. He was a man who knew the law, and knew that when you ran afoul of it there were certain islands where it was better or worse for you to be.

He hoped to hell that Dillon was in one of those countries that would be worse for Dillon.

"Can you say Montego Bay? Because if you can, I've got the address for where Dillon Whittaker is living now," Cam said, and slapped a piece of paper on the table.

Clay grinned, a pure, wicked grin broke across his face as he picked up paper. "God bless Jamaica and its fine extradition laws with the United States of America. Looks like someone is going to need to pay the taxman."

Taxes were a bitch.

* * *

"So what's your verdict?"

"Uncross your legs," Gayle said.

"I hardly think uncrossing my legs is the answer to all my romantic woes," Julia said after telling her stylist most of the details of her situation.

Gayle winked at her in the mirror as Julia followed orders. "I don't know, sweetie. Kinda sounds like uncrossing your legs has been working pretty well for you with this guy."

Julia laughed. "Fine, you got me on that."

"Champion race horse in the sack, right?"

She covered her mouth with her hand daintily, pretending to be shocked. "Did I say that?"

"No. But it sure as hell sounds like it, from the stories you've told me about his prowess."

"Prowess doesn't even begin to cover it. But that's not what we're talking about. I need to know what you think I should do next. A woman can't make this kind of decision without consulting her stylist."

"Don't consult me," Gayle said, brandishing her silver scissors playfully in the mirror.

"Consult the scissors?"

Gayle shook her head. "Ask the ink," she said, and tapped her bare arm with the silver scissors, pointing to the cursive letters on her arm spelling out *I want to be adored.* Julia had always admired the tattoo, even more so because Gayle's wish for love had come true. Julia leaned in close to the tattoo and whispered, as if offering a plaintive plea to an oracle. "Ink, what should I do?"

"Allow me to translate for the ink," Gayle said as she resumed snipping hair. "Do you love him?"

"Yes."

"Can you forgive him?"

When phrased like that, the answer seemed patently obvious. "Yes," she admitted in a small voice.

"And most of all, does he adore you?"

Julia tried to suppress a smile, as if she could hold in all that she felt by not admitting the pure and honest truth. But she blurted it out anyway. "So much."

Gayle gave her an approving nod. "One more question. Do you have any idea how devastated I will be to no longer do your hair if you move to New York? Fortunately, I still go there every few months to cut Jane Black's hair," she said, mentioning the Grammy-winning rock singer.

"Name-dropper."

"I'll see if I can squeeze you in after Ms. Black."

"Watch it. I'm going to be famous now, too. You'll have to start calling me Ms. Purple Snow Globe."

"You do know that sounds like the name of a vibrator, right?"

"Which makes it an even better name for a drink. Because when you drink one, it makes you feel like a vibrator does," Julia said, and cracked herself up, along with her stylist.

"That should be the marketing slogan. But you don't need a vibrator with your champion racehorse."

"*If* I take him back," Julia added, emphasizing that one word. *If.* Because she had promised herself a week to make this decision.

Gayle rolled her eyes. "A woman's stylist always knows."

* * *

All night Julia was tempted to text Clay. To let him know what happened with Farrell Spirits. To tell him which way she was leaning. But she also knew she needed to give this a week. The time apart was less about him, and more about her. It was about what she wanted in life, but more so, what she needed. As the days had passed with necessary silence, her heart had become clearer. She trusted him. She'd become sure of that. The question remained, though—did she trust herself? Did she have enough faith in her own gut to make the right choice when it came to men? When it came to love?

As she settled into bed, she glanced at the clock on her nightstand. It blared one-thirty in garish red. Tomorrow would be Saturday, and her self-imposed Clay exile was nearing an end. Only twenty-four more hours until she gave him her answer.

She reached for her phone so she could reply to McKenna. She and her sister had been texting earlier in the day about getting together for a Saturday girls' lunch. She hadn't seen her sister since the wedding, and she missed her something fierce.

"See you at noon, and get ready for a tackle-hug, because that's what I'll be giving you," she typed.

Her sister replied seconds later. "You better get ready to receive one too."

That left Julia with a big, fat smile. Then she clicked over to her email for one final check before bed, and her heart stopped when she saw his name. The email had been sent a few hours earlier in the evening, and she was only seeing it now. Part of her wanted to berate him, to tell him to give her the space she'd asked for. But mostly, she felt giddy. She missed that man, and the happiness over simply seeing his name in her email was a potent reminder, like someone had underlined it with yellow highlighter, of what she should do.

from: cnichols@gmail.com
to: purplesnowglobe@gmail.com
date: June 7, 10:48 PM
subject: For You

Julia,

I've seen enough movies to know that when it comes to romance, the man usually screws up and then makes some sort of big gesture for the woman. The boom box in the rain, the trip to the top of the Empire State Building, or sometimes just flowers, candy, or a note. But you're not that kind of a woman—the kind who needs or wants flowers, candy, or a note. Though I'll gladly give you all of that if you let me. But I want to make good on a promise I made to you at your sister's wedding. I spend my days helping my clients to make more money and to protect their interests. But I can protect you too. And I can give you something I know matters more to you than flowers, candy, or a note. Because I know you, Julia. I know you so well. And what I can do is this—I can right a wrong for you. Please click on the link and you'll see.

She hovered over the blue link, without a clue what she would find. She tapped it, bringing up a small blog called *Death and Taxes*. Julia eyed it curiously at first, then the possibility slammed into her of what he'd done. Some kind of wild hope bloomed in her chest as she scrolled through the short, succinct blog posts, each one detailing a tax-evading citizen who'd been caught. Then she found the one that had her name written all over it.

California resident Dillon Whittaker has been served with an extradition order from Jamaica back to the United States where he is currently under investigation for failing to pay taxes on $100,000 in income from the previous year. The IRS said it learned of Mr. Whittaker's non-compliance with the tax code under its Whistleblower Law that encourages tipsters to turn in tax cheats by bringing forth evidence on potential tax evasion to the IRS. If the information is substantive enough, the individual may receive a portion of the back taxes paid by the tax *evader. We will continue to report on the outcome of the investigation into Dillon Whittaker. Sources tell us jail time is coming soon.*

Julia leapt out of bed and shouted victoriously, pumping a fist in the air. She brought her phone to her lips, kissing the screen over and over. She was sure she'd soon take flight, and rocket around the city on this crazy glee she felt. "Take that, fucker."

She'd never realized how sweet revenge would taste, but it tasted fucking spectacular, especially when she clicked back to her email and read the last line from Clay. *I had my friend track him down in Jamaica, and I called the IRS to turn him in.*

The only thing that tasted better was the next note from Clay. A separate email, also sent a few hours ago. She only noticed it after she stopped dancing on her bed. She dropped back down to the mattress and read more of his words.

from: cnichols@gmail.com
to: purplesnowglobe@gmail.com
date: June 7, 10:52 PM
subject: You

Just remember this, for what it's worth. I adore you. Absolutely, completely, with everything I have. I will give you everything, all my heart, all my love, anything you want. You mean more to me than I ever imagined. Being without you is hell.

Without thinking, she clicked over to her texts to call up his number and ring him, but the reflection of the red numbers in the mirror stopped her. It was after one in the morning here, so it was the middle of night in New York. He'd be sound asleep. But someone else she knew and loved was wide awake. Someone who knew a little something about big gestures herself.

She called McKenna, who answered immediately. "It's late. Are you okay?"

"Everything is perfect. Or it's going to be after I see you. I'm on my way over."

CHAPTER TWENTY

Her back was smashed against the Qbert machine, and her hands were raised in front of her face. McKenna had landed another punch to the ribs, then one to her shoulder. And now, it was coming: the noogie. Her sister grabbed her hair, and dug her knuckles into Julia's head.

"Don't ever, ever, ever do that again!"

"Okay, okay, okay," Julia said, relenting for the twentieth time.

McKenna backed off, huffing. "I would have helped you," she said, her eyes on fire with frustration. "I would have given you the freaking money like that." She snapped her fingers in emphasis. "That's why you deserve to be beaten up. You're supposed to let your big sister help you."

"I know, McKenna. Trust me, I know," she said, placing her hand on her heart. "But I had to keep you safe. Don't you get it? I love you and I love Chris, and I'd do anything to protect your happiness."

"Including not telling me a frigging mobster had a price tag on your head and was waving guns in your face?"

Julia lifted her shoulders casually. "Technically, the gun was never waved at me."

McKenna pushed her hands roughly through her blond hair. "I'm soooo mad at you. I love you so much, and if anything had happened to you and I could have solved the problem, I would have died. Do you know that? Died! Like this," McKenna said, then flopped down on the floor, and played dead for effect. Ms. Pac-Man trotted over and licked McKenna's face.

She craned her neck up at Julia. "See? Do you feel bad now? I would have been dead without you, and my dog would be sad."

Julia kneeled down and offered a hand, pulling McKenna to a sitting position. McKenna flung her arms around Julia's neck. She'd always been prone to theatrics. "Promise me," her sister said, "that if you ever get in a pickle with the mob again you will come to me right away, and I will pay whatever you need."

Julia laughed, but nodded into her sister's hair. "Promise."

"Pinky swear?"

"Pinky swear," she said as they twisted their little fingers together. "But, um, that's not actually why I came here."

McKenna rolled her eyes. "I know. You need my special touch, and I know just how to pull this off. But I'm paying for it, and there are no ifs, ands, or buts about it."

"Fine. But only because you want to."

"And we're going to need Chris's help."

"Somebody call my name?" Chris said, walking bleary-eyed down the hall, wearing only his lounge pants.

"Did you actually wake up when I said your name?" McKenna asked.

"No," he said, rubbing his hand against his eyes. "I'm pretty sure it was the '*Don't ever do that again*' screeching that rousted me at three in the morning."

"We need your help."

"Is this another crazy scheme of yours, McKenna?" he asked arching an eyebrow.

"Yes, but it's in the name of love, and isn't love worth every-thing?"

He looped his arms around his wife and planted a kiss on her cheek. She leaned into it, and smiled. Julia didn't feel jealous. Not one bit. She had that in her life. Waiting for her on the other side of the country. "Of course," he said.

* * *

"I'm going to miss you so much," Julia said.

"I'm going to miss you too. But we'll see each other."

"We will."

"And don't worry about a thing. I'll take care of everything. Every-single-thing. Now go."

Julia wrapped her sister in one final hug, and then said goodbye as the sun rose over San Francisco.

from: purplesnowglobe@gmail.com
to: cnichols@gmail.com
date: June 8, 9:45 AM
subject: You too

I would have called you last night when I read your note, but it was one-thirty in the morning my time, and I didn't want to wake you up. But I was over the moon! I literally danced on my bed, and screamed with happiness. Does that make me an awful witch for celebrating a man's potential in-carceration? I hope not. And I can't think of a better present. Well, I can think of a better present . . .

from: cnichols@gmail.com
to: purplesnowglobe@gmail.com
date: June 8, 6:47 AM
subject: Late-night calls

Did I somehow give you the impression I would be unrecep-
tive to a middle of the night call from you? I'd answer anytime. Be ready anytime. I am always ready.

from: purplesnowglobe@gmail.com
to: cnichols@gmail.com
date: June 8, 10:12 AM
subject: Ready or not?

I didn't want to be rude and wake you up. But what you did
is amazing. I can't believe you found him. Wait. I can believe
it. You are some kind of master fixer.

from: cnichols@gmail.com
to: purplesnowglobe@gmail.com
date: June 8, 7:27 AM
subject: Call me Mr. Fix-It

I can fix things around the house too. I am very good with
my hands.

from: purplesnowglobe@gmail.com
to: cnichols@gmail.com
date: June 8, 10:52 AM
subject: Yes. You are.

I believe I am well acquainted with your manual dexterity.

from: cnichols@gmail.com
to: purplesnowglobe@gmail.com
date: June 8, 8:01 AM
subject: Come again

You should get reacquainted with it.

from: purplesnowglobe@gmail.com
to: cnichols@gmail.com
date: June 8, 11:20 AM
subject: Your note from last night . . .

So . . . this whole adoration thing . . . are we talking pedestal, shrine or just overall worship level?

from: cnichols@gmail.com
to: purplesnowglobe@gmail.com
date: June 8, 8:31 AM
subject: More than worship

You are adored on every level. I can't even joke about it because it's all too true.

from: purplesnowglobe@gmail.com
to: cnichols@gmail.com
date: June 8, 11:48 AM
subject: Exciting news!

I won a contest for my Purple Snow Globe!

from: cnichols@gmail.com
to: purplesnowglobe@gmail.com
date: June 8, 9:07 AM
subject: As you predicted the night I met you

Tell me more.

from: purplesnowglobe@gmail.com
to: cnichols@gmail.com
date: June 8, 12:32 PM
subject: Be my attorney

Big drink company offered me a contract. I might need a lawyer to look at the fine print.

from: cnichols@gmail.com
to: purplesnowglobe@gmail.com
date: June 8, 9:48 AM
subject: Waiving my fee

I'll do it for you. You can pay me in blow jobs.

from: purplesnowglobe@gmail.com
to: cnichols@gmail.com
date: June 8, 1:05 PM
subject: My kind of payday

I'd give you those for free.

from: cnichols@gmail.com
to: purplesnowglobe@gmail.com
date: June 8, 10:23 AM
subject: Mine too

I want more.

from: purplesnowglobe@gmail.com
to: cnichols@gmail.com
date: June 8, 1:33 PM
subject: Restrained

I'd give you more anyway. Maybe you can tie me up, tie me down, or tie me all around.

from: cnichols@gmail.com
to: purplesnowglobe@gmail.com
date: June 8, 10:52 AM
subject: Bound and Tied

Don't tease me. You know I love the way you look in my ties.

from: purplesnowglobe@gmail.com
to: cnichols@gmail.com
date: June 8, 2:16 PM
subject: Yes to both

I'm not teasing.

from: cnichols@gmail.com
to: purplesnowglobe@gmail.com
date: June 8, 11:28 AM
subject: Yes you are

You've never been a tease. Except when you tease.

from: purplesnowglobe@gmail.com
to: cnichols@gmail.com
date: June 8, 2:44 PM
subject: This is not teasing.

I miss you like crazy.

from: cnichols@gmail.com
to: purplesnowglobe@gmail.com
date: June 8, 3:07 PM
subject: Fix for that

I have a pill you can take that cures that. It's called *come live with me.*

from: purplesnowglobe@gmail.com
to: cnichols@gmail.com
date: June 8, 3:49 PM
subject: Question

How much do you adore me?

from: cnichols@gmail.com
to: purplesnowglobe@gmail.com
date: June 8, 4:02 PM
subject: Answer

So much I can't measure it.

from: purplesnowglobe@gmail.com
to: cnichols@gmail.com
date: June 8, 4:11 PM
subject: And another

How much do you love me?

from: cnichols@gmail.com
to: purplesnowglobe@gmail.com
date: June 8, 4:18 PM
subject: Hit me with another

More than I know what to do with.

from: purplesnowglobe@gmail.com
to: cnichols@gmail.com
date: June 8, 4:20 PM
subject: One more

How happy would you be if I said yes to your offer?

from: cnichols@gmail.com
to: purplesnowglobe@gmail.com
date: June 8, 4:25 PM
subject: One word

Immeasurably.

Iron. He'd cloaked himself in iron. He'd resisted. He hadn't asked for an answer. He hadn't pressured her. He'd simply kept up the volley, letting her lead as she seemed to need at the moment. He held tight to his phone, keeping it on his lap as he worked through the latest set of papers for the Pinkertons from home.

He'd hoped to catch a movie with Davis, since his friend was back in town after working in London for the last few months. But Chris had called him that morning, telling him he was sending a bottle of vintage scotch over as a thank you for his new contract.

"The delivery guys said they'll be there between four and five, so I guess you can just have the doorman sign for it if you're out?"

"I don't have a doorman, but it's not a problem. I've got things I can take care of at the house, so I'll sign for it myself."

"Thanks, man," Chris had said. "It's the least I can do. You rocked the hell out of my new deal."

"If you're pleased, I'm pleased."

But it was four-thirty and the scotch hadn't arrived yet. He was looking forward to it, but not as much as he was looking forward to another note from Julia. The clock was ticking, lurching towards midnight. If he were a betting man, he'd put money on Julia using up every second of her week of thinking, and giving him the verdict when the clock struck twelve. That would be fine by him. She was worth waiting for.

He scanned the page in front of him when the message light dinged on his phone.

from: purplesnowglobe@gmail.com
to: cnichols@gmail.com
date: June 8, 4:32 PM
subject: One question

Do you still love surprises?

Before he could reply, his phone buzzed with a text message. *Balcony.*

He closed his eyes briefly, a spark racing through him with the possibility. Was she reminiscing about the things they'd done on the balcony or was there more to it? He stood up, walked to the door and slid it open. With his heart in his throat and hope winding its way through his bones, he crossed the distance to the railing, and looked down.

His heart stopped, and then started again, thumping hard against his chest with desire, happiness, and mad love.

She was the most beautiful sight in the world. But it wasn't the stockings and the heels, the skirt or the little tank top. It wasn't even her hair falling in waves along her shoulders. It was the two humongous suitcases, one on each side of her. She waved at him as his phone rang.

"My driver left me here on the sidewalk with all my things. Don't suppose you know a big strong man who could help me carry them upstairs to my new home?"

He grinned like a crazy man. "As a matter of fact, I do."

Within seconds—okay, maybe a minute—he was downstairs, looking both ways, and sprinting across the street to her. He gathered her in his arms, and it was like coming home. Her body melted into his as she roped her arms around his neck, and they kissed, and they kissed, and they kissed.

Finally, they pulled apart, but neither one let go. He needed to hold her. To feel her. To know she was real. He ran his hands along her bare arms. The feel of her skin was some kind of magic. He bent his head to her neck, inhaling her scent, the delicious, intoxicating smell of the woman he craved in every way. He lifted a hand to her hair, threading his fingers around her gorgeous flames. The sound of her sweet happy sigh was a shot of pure joy to his heart. She was here. She'd said yes.

"I made sure my flight had Wi-Fi so I could surprise you. Did you think I was in San Francisco the whole day? The time on my laptop was set to Pacific until I landed."

He nodded. "I did, and I take it there's no vintage scotch arriving between four and five?"

"I'm the vintage scotch. I hope you like your surprise."

"You taste better than any scotch, than anything I've ever had to eat or drink. So you're here to stay?" he asked, needing to hear it from her.

She nodded. "I'm here to stay."

"No more running."

"No more running," she repeated.

"We're together."

"Absolutely."

"Which reminds me . . . it's been a week."

She wiggled her eyebrows. "Why do you think I wore a skirt?"

A bolt of pure lust slammed through his body. "Fuck me now," he said, pushing a hand through his hair.

"That's sort of the plan," she said, tipping her forehead to the door to his building. *Their* building.

"Get inside," he growled, lifting a heavy suitcase in each hand. She grinned seductively and strutted across the street, glancing behind to watch him watching her. So perfect, so sexy, so beautiful for him. Once inside the elevator, he pressed the button for the fifth floor.

She reached past him, and hit the stop button. "We're not getting off 'til we get off."

He shook his head appreciatively. "You are my woman. You always have been. You always will be," he said, then reached under her skirt, pulled her panties down and slid his fingers across her. She was ready, oh so ready.

She was eager too, judging from how quickly her nimble little fingers had unzipped his jeans. "You did miss me," he said playfully.

"So fucking much," she said as she guided him between her legs.

He lifted her thigh, hitching her leg around his hip, and sliding home. "Oh God." She gasped, dropping her head back, and rolling her eyes in pleasure.

"Don't ever forget, Julia. I can always do this to you," he said, in a hot whisper in her ear as he thrust into her.

"I know. I want it always."

"We have all of Manhattan for fucking. We have restaurants and bars, and theaters and museums, and I'm going to want to take you everywhere."

"No pun intended," she said, in between sexy little moans and pants.

"Take you *and* take you," he added. "Fuck you and make love to you. I'm not going to hold back. I'm going to seduce you all over this city, and make you come every single day and night."

"Please do," she said, her voice rising higher, her breath coming faster.

"All the time," he said, gripping her thigh harder, driving deeper. She responded by running her hands up his spine, and digging her fingernails deep into his skin.

"Leave marks on me," he told her, and she dug in harder. "I want scratch marks from you."

"You feel so fucking good, you're going to get them, Clay. Oh God, you're going to get them," she said, holding on tight

420 · LAUREN BLAKELY

and hard, dragging her nails along his muscles as she cried out, rocking her hips against his as she came, and soon, he chased her there with his own orgasm.

He wrapped his arms around her, needing to hold her, even in the stalled elevator. He layered kisses on her neck, already hot and sweaty. "Julia, I won't always take you hard like that, but sometimes I'm going to have to," he whispered.

"You better take me hard, and you better take me slow, and you better make love to me all night long," she said, pulling back to look him in the eyes. Hers were both fierce, and full of love.

"That's a promise, and I keep my promises to you," he said, running his thumb along her cheek.

"I know you do. That's why I'm here to stay."

That's where he always wanted her.

EPILOGUE
Two Months Later

"What can I get for you?"

The pair of young women in slouchy tops revealing bare shoulders had parked themselves in the burgundy bar stools at Speakeasy, where Julia was now a part-owner. They perused the cocktail menu, and then the blonde one lifted her face to Julia, the look in her eyes full of excitement. "Can you make the Purple Snow Globe? We heard this is the only bar where we can get it made fresh," she said, emphasizing that last word like it was made of sweet sugar. "I served some at a party last week from the store and everyone loved it, but we wanted to try the real thing."

"And I will be delighted to make it for you. But I should let you know, this isn't the only bar. There's a little place in San Francisco called Cubic Z that also makes a Purple Snow Globe, so if you ever find yourself out west, you know where to go," she said, and started mixing.

"Our friends are going to be so jealous. Everyone is loving this drink," the woman said.

"I'm thrilled to hear that."

After she set down the drinks, she headed to the back of the bar to retrieve more napkins. Along the way, her phone buzzed in her pocket, so she grabbed it. There was a text from Kim.

How's business? Booming as always, like it is here?

Julia tapped out an answer. *Always.* She dropped her phone back into her pocket, glad that Craig had taken over behind the bar for her. She still owned a stake in Cubic Z, but Craig had needed a job, and her move had given him the perfect chance to help his wife while she was busy with the newborn. Charlie hadn't been heard from, and while Julia and Clay had toyed with spreading a nasty rumor on Yelp about Charlie's chicken, they'd decided not to. Charlie was a man not to be messed with, so they'd chosen to leave him and his chicken in the past. But Julia couldn't deny she was pleased when her sister forwarded along a few new online reviews for Mr. Pong's that all noted the restaurant was less popular at lunch these days. Seemed that Charlie had lost a good portion of his venture capital patrons at the restaurant. Hunter with the laughing tell might have been kicked out of the poker circuit, but had managed the last word after all, telling his friends to find a new haunt for their kung pao chicken hankerings, hitting Charlie where it hurt him most.

As for her apartment, McKenna had packed up everything for her, deciding what needed to stay and what needed to go. She trusted her sister completely with that choice, especially when the boxes had arrived with only her favorite items in them. She didn't need her fluffy towels, though. Because she and Clay had bought new ones, with some of the $10,000 she'd won at the poker game, along with a bench, some softer pillows, and a new set of scarves. They'd considered ropes but they'd always been more DIY when it came to restraints, opting for belts, ties, panties and whatever was on hand, and that was likely to continue.

She pictured returning home tonight after her shift behind the bar. She'd find him naked in bed, sound asleep on his stomach, his strong back on display with the sheets low around his hips. The lights would be dim, the only sound the faint rhythm of his sleeping breath. She'd strip down to nothing, and run her hands along his skin. He'd groan lightly, roll over and pull her on top of him, and they'd have slow, sleepy, middle-of-the-night sex.

That image was burned in her brain as she returned to the bar to serve a new customer. A man in a suit had just sat down. Then she realized that man was her man. Her man in a suit, and by God, did he ever look sexy as hell in it. Maybe it was the little bit of cuff showing, or the cufflinks, or the purple tie he wore.

She rested her elbows on the bar, and flashed him a smile. "What can I get for you there, wearing your lucky tie?"

He ran his fingers down the fabric, and raised an eyebrow. "You noticed my lucky tie."

"I always notice what you're wearing," she said in a whisper, her words just for him. "Are you thinking you're getting lucky tonight?"

"I'm a lucky man every night because I have you."

"Flattery will get you everywhere. But you still must pay for your drink," she said and poured him his standard scotch, placing it in front of him. He took a long swallow, then reached for her hand, threading her fingers through his.

"Hey, gorgeous," he said softly.

"Hey, handsome."

"What would you think about going to Vegas this weekend?"

"So we can see your brother's show, then play a little blackjack?"

"For starters," he said, and there was a twinkle in his brown eyes.

A ribbon of possibility unfurled in her. "Are you going to propose to me in Vegas?"

He laughed. "Wouldn't you like to know?"

"I would like to know," she said, as the corners of her lips curved up.

"But I love surprises, Julia. So I guess you'll have to wait and see if I propose, or if maybe I take you there to elope."

She clasped his hand tighter, her way of saying she liked that idea. Either one. Both. "So I won't know till you take me to Vegas?"

He shrugged playfully. "Maybe I'll do neither. But I'll tell you this much. We will have an excellent time, and I fully intend on marrying you someday. Someday soon."

"Oh you do, do you?"

"I do."

"You practicing saying those words?" she said, teasing him like she'd always loved to.

"Maybe I am. Do you like hearing them from me?" he said, and every day she found new ways to fall in love with him. This was today's.

"I do, Clay. I do."

THE END

While Clay and Julia have a happy ending here, their story isn't done. Based on requests from readers, I have written another installment in their love story. ONE MORE NIGHT is the third book starring Julia and Clay and it releases July 8. For more details, see the coming soon section next.

RELEASING JULY 8 on Amazon, iBooks, B&N and other retailers!

ONE MORE NIGHT
Book #3 in the Seductive Nights Series

"I want it hard, rough, and against the wall."

Sure, everyone wants that, but happy endings don't come easily. They're hard-won and Clay Nichols is going to have to keep earning his...

Now living together in New York with her debt safely paid off, sexy bartender Julia Bell and hot-as-hell entertainment lawyer Clay thought their future was clear sailing.

But life doesn't work that way and these two red-hot lovers run into a new slew of challenges as Clay tries to put a ring on it. Trouble looms in every corner – trouble from clients, trouble with timing, and most of all trouble from her past returns on their trip to Vegas. A dangerous man who knows much more about Julia than he should surfaces in Sin City where they're supposed to be enjoying a weekend getaway. Following her in the casino, watching her every move at the pool, targeting her as she plays blackjack.

Too bad Clay is called away repeatedly, leaving Julia alone in a sprawling hotel full of dark corners, back rooms, and unsavory characters.

Can Clay save her from danger one more time, and then finally get down on one knee? Or will he be too late for the woman he adores?

Stay tuned for ONE MORE NIGHT, a novel in the Seductive Nights series packed with more sex, more dirty talk and more danger.

Check out my contemporary romance novels!

Caught Up In Us, a New York Times and
USA Today Bestseller! (Kat and Bryan's romance!)

Pretending He's Mine, a Barnes & Noble and
iBooks Bestseller! (Reeve & Sutton's romance)

Trophy Husband, a New York Times and
USA Today Bestseller! (Chris & McKenna's romance!)

Playing With Her Heart, a
USA Today Bestseller! (Davis and Jill's romance)

Far Too Tempting, an Amazon romance
bestseller! (Matthew and Jane's romance)

And my USA Today Bestselling
No Regrets series that includes

The Thrill of It
(Meet Harley and Trey)

and its sequel

Every Second With You!

and

Burn For Me, a new release from Entangled's
Brazen line starring a sexy fireman and his woman!
(Smith and Jamie's romance!)

Stay tuned for NIGHTS WITH HIM, a standalone novel in the erotic romance Seductive Nights series, starring Michele Millo and her lover, slated for a fall 2014 release...

Jack Sullivan is a Sex Toy Mogul.

An extremely eligible bachelor in New York, he's the full package, right down to his full package. Hell, this man could be the model for one of the toys his company, Joy Delivered, peddles. Instead, he's the powerful and successful CEO and he's got commitment issues a mile-long after the tragic way his relationship with his fiancée ended.

He's looking for a way to erase the pain and that arrives in the form of Michelle Milo. From her pencil skirts to her high heels, she's his perfect fantasy, especially since she has no idea who he is the night they meet at a hotel bar. He doesn't have a clue either that she's the brilliant psychologist his sister has arranged for him to see to help him get over his past. She's simply the stunning woman he takes to bed that night and delivers many Os of joy too.

His touch helps her forget that other man.

When he shows up at her office door the next day, there's no way in hell she's going to treat him after they've slept together. Jack isn't willing to let go of the first woman he's felt anything for in years so he proposes a deal – share her nights with him for thirty days. At the end of one month of exquisite pleasure, they walk away, having helped each other move on from their haunted pasts.

But soon, all those nights threaten to turn into days as the lines between lust and matters of the heart start to blur. Can two people so terribly afraid of love truly fall head over heels?

CONTACT

I love hearing from readers! You can find me on Twitter at LaurenBlakely3, or Facebook at LaurenBlakelyBooks, or online at LaurenBlakely.com. You can also email me at laurenblakely books@gmail.com.